The Enemy Inside

The Enemy Inside

A Paul Madriani Novel

Steve Martini

An Imprint of HarperCollins*Publishers*

HarperCollins books may be purchased for educational, business, or sales promotional use. For information please e-mail the Special Markets Department at SPsales@harpercollins.com.

FIRST HARPERLUXE EDITION

HarperLuxe™ is a trademark of HarperCollins Publishers

ISBN: 978-0-06-239286-2

15 ID/RRD 10 9 8 7 6 5 4 3 2 1

To Marianne and Keaw, without whose devotion, love, and assistance, none of this would be possible

The Enemy Inside

One

"I saw it in the paper this morning," says Harry. "Sounds like a barbecue without the tailgate. Driver flambéed behind the wheel in her car. If you like, I'll take it off your hands, but why would we want the case?" To Harry it sounds like a dog.

I ignore him. "The cops are still trying to identify the victim," I tell him.

Harry Hinds is my partner of more than twenty years, Madriani & Hinds, Attorneys at Law, Coronado near San Diego. Business has been thin of late. For almost two years we had been on the run, hiding out from a Mexican killer named Liquida who was trying to punch holes in us with a stiletto. This is apparently what passes for business in the world of narco-fueled revenge. And the man wasn't even a client.

For a while, after it ended and Liquida was dead, the papers were full of it. Harry and I, along with Herman Diggs, our investigator, became local celebrities.

Everything was fine until the FBI stepped in. They announced publicly that they were giving us a citizen's award for cooperation with law enforcement. For a firm of criminal defense lawyers, this was the kiss of death, Satan giving Gabriel a gold star.

Referrals on cases dried up like an Egyptian mummy. Everywhere we went, other lawyers who knew us stopped shaking our hands and began giving us hugs, frisking us to see which of us was wearing the wire. Harry and I are no longer welcome at defense bar luncheons unless we go naked.

"You look like hell," says Harry.

"Thanks."

"Just to let you know, a beard does not become you."

I have not shaved since yesterday morning. "I was up at four this morning meeting with our client at the county lockup in the hospital."

"You or him?" he asks.

"What?"

"Which one of you was being treated?" says Harry.

"I look that bad?"

He nods.

"Alex Ives, twenty-six, arrested for DUI. A few bruises. No broken bones," I tell him.

"That still doesn't answer my question. Why are we taking the case? Is there a fee involved?"

"He's a friend of Sarah's," I tell him.

"Ahh . . ." He nods slowly as if to say, "We are now reduced to this."

Sarah is my daughter. She is mid-twenties going on forty and has a mother complex for troubled souls. She seems to have been born with a divining rod for knowing the naturally correct thing to do in any situation. Not just social etiquette, but what is right. Sarah lacks the gene that afflicts so many of the young with poor judgment. You might call her old-fashioned. I choose to call her wise. For this, I am blessed. For the same reason, when she asks a favor, I would very likely come to question my own judgment if I said no.

"The kid didn't call me," I tell Harry. "He called Sarah. Apparently they've known each other since high school."

"So what did he have to say?" says Harry. "This client of ours?"

"Says he's sorry, and he's scared."

"That's it?"

"The sorry part. The rest hung over him like a vapor. You'd think he'd never seen concrete walls before." Alex Ives seemed to be dying of sleep deprivation, and still the fear was dripping off him like an icicle. "Said he'd never been arrested before."

"What else?"

"Apart from that, he can't remember a thing."

"Well, at least he remembered that part. Hope he told the cops the same story." Harry looks at me over the top of his glasses, cheaters that he wears mostly for reading. "You believe him? Or do you think maybe he was just that juiced? If he's telling the truth, with that kind of memory loss he probably blew a zero-point-three on the Breathalyzer."

"He was unconscious at the scene. We won't get the blood alcohol report until this afternoon. Cops said they smelled alcohol on him."

"And, of course, while they were treating him and he was unconscious, they sank their fangs into his neck and drew blood," says Harry.

"A passing motorist pulled him from his car and away from the flames. Otherwise we wouldn't even have him. Everything inside both cars was toast."

"Thank God for small favors." Sarcasm is Harry's middle name.

"It looks like Ives T-boned the other vehicle at an intersection, a dirt road and a two-lane highway east of town out in the desert. Way the hell out, according to the cops. McCain Valley Road."

"He lives out there?"

"No. He lives in town. A condo in the Gas Lamp District."

"What was he doing way out there? That's fifty miles as the crow flies," says Harry.

I shake my head. "Says he doesn't know. The last thing he remembers is being at a party up north near Del Mar, about seven thirty last evening, and then nothing."

"Was he drinking at this party?" says Harry.

"Says he had one drink."

"How big was the glass? Anybody with him? I mean, to vouch for this one-drink theory."

I shake my head. "He says he was alone."

"Let's see if I've got this . . . unconscious at the scene, smells of alcohol and the other driver is dead. And now he can't remember anything, except for the fact that he had only one drink. I'd say we got the wrong client. Why couldn't Sarah know the cinder in the other car? Her blood kin at least will have a good civil case." What Harry means is damages against our guy. "Tell me he has insurance and a valid license." Harry doesn't want to be stuck fending off a wrongful death case with no coverage while jousting with a prosecutor over hard time for vehicular manslaughter.

I nod. "He has insurance and a license that hasn't been revoked as far as I know. They ran a rap sheet and found no priors. So he doesn't look to be a habitual drunk."

"That could mean that he's just been lucky up to now." Harry is the essential cynic.

"He could be lying about what he remembers. Like I say, he's scared."

"He should be," says Harry. "He could be facing anywhere from four to six years in the pen."

In a death case, prosecutors will invariably push for the upper end. MADD, Mothers Against Drunk Drivers, has sensitized district attorneys and judges who have to stand for election to the realities of politics. By the same token, the other party is dead and you can bet the prosecutor who tries the case will be reminding the jury and the judge of this fact at every opportunity.

"Anything by way of an accident report?" says Harry.

"Not out yet," I tell him.

"What does our client remember about this party he went to?"

"According to Ives, he was invited to the gig by some girl he met at work. The scene was a big house, swimming pool, lots of people, music, an open bar, but he can't remember the address."

"Of course not," says Harry.

"He said he'd recognize the place if he saw it again. The street address was on a note that he had in his wallet. Along with the girl's name and phone number."

"So he'd never met this girl before?"

"No. And he can't remember her name."

"She must have made a deep impression," says Harry. "Still, her name will be on the note in the wallet. The cops have it, I assume?" says Harry.

"No. As a matter of fact, they don't. I checked. They got his watch, some cash he had in his pocket, and a graduation ring from college."

"That's it?"

"They figure the wallet must have been lost on the seat of the car, or else he dropped it somewhere. . . ."

"So, assuming this note existed, it probably got torched in the fire." Harry finishes the thought for me. "You can bet the cops will be looking for it. If our boy was falling-down drunk when he left the party, there will be lots of people who saw him, witnesses," says Harry, "but not for our side. Without the wallet, how did the cops ID him if, as you say, he was unconscious?"

"Fingerprints. Ives had a temp job with a defense contractor a few years ago, a software company under contract to the navy. His prints were on file."

"And the girl who invited him, did he see her at the party?"

"He says she never showed, or at least he doesn't remember," I tell him.

"Convenient." Harry is thinking that there was no party, that Ives got drunk somewhere else, maybe a bar, and doesn't want to fess up because he knows there were witnesses who can testify as to his lack of sobriety. Harry goes silent for a moment as he thinks. Then the ultimate question: "How are we getting paid for this? Does our client have anything that passes for money?"

"No." I watch his arched eyebrows collapse before I add: "But his parents do. They own a large aviation servicing company at the airport. Quite well off, from what I understand. And they love their son. I met them at the hospital. Lovely people. You'll like them."

"I already do." Harry smiles, a broad affable grin. "Thank Sarah for the referral," he says.

Two

Here is the mystery. Alex Ives's blood alcohol report showed up at our office this morning. And surprise, Ives was not over the legal limit. In fact, he wasn't even close. In California, the threshold is set at a 0.08 percent blood alcohol level. Ives barely tilted the meter at 0.01. You would probably show a higher blood alcohol level hosing out your mouth with some mouthwash. There is no question concerning the accuracy of the test. They drew blood. It is beginning to look as if Ives's story of having only one drink is true. He may not have even finished it.

In the world of simple citations for a DUI, driving under the influence, that would probably be the end of the case. The prosecutor would dump it or charge Ives with a lesser-included offense, speeding or weaving in the lane if they saw him driving. But the charge of vehicular manslaughter has them looking deeper. The cops are now back, burning Bunsens in their lab looking for drugs. The chemical tests for these take a lot longer. So we wait.

Harry and I have delivered the good news and the bad news to Ives in one of the small conference rooms at the county lockup.

"You sure you weren't on any medications?" I ask him.

"Nothing," says Ives.

We are trying to prep for a bail hearing tomorrow morning, looking for anything that might stand in the way of springing him from the county's concrete abode.

Ives looks at us from across the table. Sandy haired, big bright blue eyes, well over six feet, a tall wiry rail of a kid, and scared. Jimmy Stewart in his youth unburdening his soul to two hapless angels.

"If there is anything in the blood they will find it," says Harry.

"I don't do drugs," says Ives.

"Good boy," says Harry.

"What do we have on the other driver?" I look at my partner. Harry hasn't had time to read all the reports. They have been coming in in bits and pieces over a couple of days now. "Any alcohol in her body? Could be *she* was drinking."

"If she was, it went up in the flames," says Harry. He is master of documents this afternoon, a growing file spread out on the metal table in front of him. "According to the accident report, the victim's name was Serna, first name Olinda. Forty-seven years old. Out-of-state license, driving a rental car. . . ."

"What did you say her name was?" says Ives.

Harry glances at him, then looks down at the page again. "Serna, Olinda Serna. I guess that's how you'd pronounce it."

"Can't be," says Ives.

"What are you talking about?" I ask.

"Can't be her," says Ives.

"Can't be who?"

"Serna," he says.

I glance at Harry who has the same stagestruck expression as I do.

"Are you telling us you knew her?" says Harry.

"No, no. It must be somebody else. Maybe the same name," says Ives.

Harry gives me a look as if to say, "How many Olindas do you know?"

"Assuming it's her, I didn't really know her. Never met her. I just know the name. It's a story we've been working on at the *Gravesite*. My job," says Ives.

Harry is now sitting bolt upright in the chair. "Explain!"

"We've been working on this story close to a year now. Major investigation," he says. "And I recognize the name. Assuming it's the same person."

"Where was this person from?" asks Harry. "This person in your story. Where did she live? What city?"

"It would be somewhere around Washington, D.C., if it's her."

Harry is looking at the report, flips one page, looks up and says: "Is Silver Spring, Maryland, close enough?"

"The cops never told you who the victim was?" I ask Ives.

"No, I didn't know until just now. No idea," he says.

"Do you know what this other woman, the one in your story, did for a living?" Harry looks at him.

"She was a lawyer," says Alex.

"Mandella, Harbet, Cain, and Jenson?" says Harry.

Ives's face is all big round eyes at this moment, his Adam's apple bobbing.

"Well, I guess if you have to kill a lawyer, you may as well kill a big corporate one," says Harry.

According to the police report, the cops found business cards in the victim's purse, what was left of it. They ID'ed her from those and the VIN number on the burned-out car that was traced back to the rental agency.

Mandella is one of the largest law firms in the country. It has offices in a dozen cities in the Americas, Europe, and Asia. The minute the ashes cool from the Arab Spring, you can bet they will be back there as well. They practice law the same way the US military fights its battles, with overwhelming force, cutting-edge weapons, and surprise flanking power plays. If their clients can't win on the law, they will go to Congress and change it.

The multinational businesses that are not on their client list are said not to be worth having. One of their long-dead managing partners, it is rumored, got the feuding Arab clans to put down their guns long enough to set up OPEC, the world oil cartel, at which point the Arabs stopped robbing camel caravans and started plundering the industrialized West. If you believe Mandella's PR, lawyers from the firm secured the foreign flag rights for Noah's ark. They would glaze the words "Super Lawyers" on the glass doors to their offices, but who needs it when the brass plaques next to it show a list of partners including four retired members of the US Senate and one over-the-hill Supreme Court Justice. The finger of God is said to be painted on the ceiling of their conference rooms, franchise rights for which they acquired when Jehovah evicted their client, Adam, from the Garden of Eden.

"Listen, you have to believe me," says Ives. "I had no idea. I don't remember anything about the accident or anything about that night. Nothing. I don't remember the other car. I don't remember hitting it. I don't remember getting in my car to drive. The last thing I remember is going to the party, having a drink, and then nothing." He looks at us for a moment, to Harry and then back to me. "I mean . . . I know it looks bad. The fact I even knew who she was. But I never met her."

"It appears that you ran into her at one point," says Harry. Bad joke. "You have to admit, it's one hell of a coincidence. Let's hope the cops don't know."

Harry and I are thinking the same thing. The police may change their theory of the case if they find out there was any connection between Ives and the victim before the accident.

"Tell us what this story is about," says Harry. "The one involving Serna."

"Oh, I can't do that," says Ives.

"What?" says Harry.

"Not without an OK from my editor."

"An OK from your editor?" says Harry. "Do you understand what you're facing here? If the cops get wind of any involvement between you and the victim, they are going to start turning over rocks looking for evidence of intentional homicide. Depending on what they find, you won't be looking at manslaughter any longer but murder. Was there any bad blood between you and her?"

"Not on my part. It was just a story. Nothing personal," says Ives.

"What is this story about?"

"You don't really think I killed her on purpose?"

"For my part, I don't. But I can't vouch for the D.A.," says Harry. "So why don't you fill us in."

"It's big. It's a very big story. At this point there are a lot of leads. What we need is confirmation."

"Confirmation of what?" Harry is getting hot.

"That's what I can't tell you," says Ives. "It's not my story. I don't have any personal stake in it. That's what I'm saying. I didn't have any reason to harm Serna. I never met her. She was a name. That's all."

"But she was involved?" I ask.

"Her name kept popping up during the investigation," says Ives.

Alex is what passes for an investigative reporter in the age of digital news. The changing tech world has dislocated everything from journalism to jukeboxes. It has untethered us from the world we thought we knew and left us to swim in a sea of uncertainty. Like primitive natives, we are constantly dazzled by shiny new stuff, smartphones that respond to voice commands and mobile hot spots the size of a thimble that connect us to the universe. But like the native jungles of the New World, the industries in which we work may disappear tomorrow, victims of the shiny new stuff, the treasures that have seduced us. Where newspapers once existed, now there are blog sites. More nimble, faster, some of them blunt-edged partisan weapons for dismantling a republic. Alex works for one of these, a blog site headquartered in Washington. He is their West Coast correspondent.

"I'm not sure how much I can tell you. We've been working on it for about a year now. Mostly in D.C., but also out here on the coast. It's the reason I know her name."

"If you want us to represent you," says Harry, "you're going to have to trust us."

"I do. But you have to understand the story is not mine, it belongs to the *Gravesite*." Ives is talking about the *Washington Gravesite*, the digitized scandal sheet owned by Tory Graves, Ives's boss and the purveyor of the hottest political dirt since the days of Drew Pearson and Jack Anderson. What TMZ is to celebrity news and entertainment gossip, the *Washington Gravesite* is to those who work in politics. It parcels out breaking news to the various cable stations, which feed upon it depending on their particular partisan political bias. It is unclear how Graves makes his money, whether he gets paid for exclusive stories or is funded by various interest groups with an ax to grind. Either way he seems to be surviving in what is by any measure a political snake pit of Olympian proportions.

"Did you ever talk to Serna, interview her, have any direct contact with her at all?" asks Harry.

Ives is shaking his head.

"Did you communicate with her in any way?" I ask.

"No. And I can't tell you anything beyond that, not until I talk to my editor."

Harry and I look at each other. I give Ives a big sigh, shrug my shoulders, and slowly shake my head. "We're just trying to help you."

"I know you are and I appreciate it," says Ives. "But I can't talk about my work. That's confidential. It's off-limits."

"Let's hope the court agrees," says Harry. "But I can tell you it won't."

"Let's leave it for the moment," I tell him. "I assume your parents are good for the bail bond?"

"I think so. How much do you think it'll be?"

"No way to be certain until we get in front of the judge. It's a bailable offense, at least at the moment. But the D.A. will probably try to up the ante. Make it expensive. Have you done any recent international travel?"

"For work," he says.

"How long ago and how often?"

"Europe, twice in the last year."

"Where?" says Harry.

"I went to Switzerland with my boss, Tory Graves."

"We can assume Serna wasn't into chocolates," says Harry. "Watches? Rolexes?" He looks at Ives. "Banking!"

The kid's face flushes. He looks up at Harry.

"Bingo. Well, we can't put him on the stand," says Harry. "They won't need a lie detector to test his veracity. Just measure the movement of his Adam's apple. I hope you don't play poker, son. If you ever take it up, try to sit under the table."

"You can be sure they will want your passport until this is over," I tell him. "As for bail, you have a job and contacts in the community. That's a plus. Superior Court bail schedule says a hundred-thousand-dollar bond for a death case involving DUI. That means you or your parents have to put up ten percent, ten grand."

Ives shakes his head, looks down at the table. "I suspect my parents can raise it. But I'll want to pay them back."

"Of course."

"And your fees," he says.

"Let's not worry about that right now." Harry gives me a dirty look.

"What about the girl, the one you say you met who invited you to the party? What can you tell us about her?"

"Not much," he says. "Only met her the one time."

"How did you meet her?" says Harry.

"Let me think. I guess it was about noon. I was out in the plaza in front of my office trying to figure where to go to grab a bite. This girl came up to me, real cute, you know, and she asked me for directions."

"To where?"

"I don't remember exactly."

"Go on," I tell him.

"It must have been somewhere close. I mean, she didn't come out of a car at the curb or anything. Not that I saw anyway. So I assume she was on foot."

"Was she alone?" I ask.

"As far as I could tell, she was."

"But you don't know where she was going?" says Harry.

Alex shakes his head.

"And then what?" I ask.

"We got to talking. She had a great smile. Said there was a party at some rich guy's house that night. She said she was gonna be there. It might be fun. Said she was allowed to invite some friends. Would I like to go? What could I say? Beautiful girl. I had nothing going on that night. I said sure. She gave me the information . . ."

"How?" I ask. "How did she give you the information?"

"A note," he says. "It had the address and a phone number. The address was the location of the party. She said the number was her cell phone in case I got lost. It wouldn't have mattered. I went to call her when she didn't show and my phone was dead."

That means we can't subpoena the cell carrier to try and triangulate the location of the house where the party took place.

"All I can remember is it was someplace up near Del Mar. Big house in a ritzy neighborhood. I remember it had a big pool, great big oval thing. I might recognize it if I saw it again. The problem is, you use this high-tech stuff, GPS, you tend to rely on it and you don't remember anything because you don't have to."

Alex is right. How many of us can remember telephone numbers for friends or family? We push a button and it replaces our brains.

"I loaded the address into the GPS in the car and I didn't pay any attention. I just followed the verbal directions. It took me right to the front door," he says.

And of course Alex's car, which he borrowed from his parents' company, was charred in the accident. Its GPS is toast. I make a note to check and see if we can access the information from its provider, OnStar or NavSat or one of the others.

"Oh, there was one more thing," says Alex. "She gave me a name. Some guy. She said that if anyone stopped me at the door, I was to tell them I was to be seated at this guy's table."

"What was the name?" says Harry.

Ives looks at us, first to Harry and then to me. Shakes his head. "I can't remember," he says. "Bender or Billings, something like that. I think it started with a *B*."

"This note, with the address on it. Did she write it down or did you?" I ask.

He thought about it for a moment. "Come to think," he says, "neither one of us did. She already had it written out. She just handed it to me."

"Didn't you think that was a little strange?" says Harry. "A girl you just met handing out invitations to a party to strangers on the street?"

"She looked like the kind of girl who would have rich friends," says Ives. "When I got to the party, I realized I wasn't exactly dressed for it," he says.

"What do you mean?" says Harry.

"I mean, there were guys there wearing tuxes, women in expensive dresses and a lot of jewels. And they were all older. Gray hair everywhere I looked. I felt out of place, like maybe she should have warned me. I went looking for her. My first thought was maybe there was a younger crowd somewhere in the back. It was a big place, a lot of ground in the yard. Chinese lanterns lighting everything up. She was right about one thing. Whoever owned the place was part of the one percent," he says. "A lot of money.

"When I didn't see her or anyone our age, I decided to leave. That's when he came by."

"Who?" says Harry.

"The waiter with a tray of drinks. They didn't have any beer, but they had champagne. I took one glass, and that's it. That's all I can remember until I woke up in the hospital."

"Do you remember what he looked like, the waiter?"

"Not a clue. Didn't even look. It was crowded. There were people everywhere. I grabbed the glass and that was it."

"Do you remember what the girl looked like?" I ask him.

"Yeah. You couldn't forget her. Asian. Beautiful face. Great smile. Long straight black hair down to the middle of her back. Dark eyes. Bronze skin. About this tall." Ives puts his hand flat on edge as if drawing a line across his upper body about nipple high.

"What are you saying, about five five, five six?" I ask.

"Yeah, I'd say that's about right."

"Was she slender, heavy? How was she built?"

"Yeah." Ives gives me a kind of quick sheepish grin, the college jock. "I'd say she was pretty well built. You know what I mean?"

"Tell us." Commander Lust, Harry wants all the details.

"Well, you know . . . showing some good cleavage. It was a nice sunny day. Summertime. A lot of the women, secretaries, come out of the buildings into the plaza showing a lotta thigh, short skirts. Hers was right up there. You couldn't miss it," he says. "As I remember, she was wearing a blue print dress of some kind, tight, a lot of curves, all in the right places, and . . . oh, yeah, she had a tattoo."

"Yes?" I look at him.

"It looked like the tail of a dragon, blue and red; it was a colorful thing. It was on the inside of her left thigh. Fairly high up. By the way she was dressed I could only see the bottom part of it. But you could bet I wanted to see more."

"Looks to me like she was waiting for you," says Harry. "Everything but a pole with a lure on it."

"With that kind of a lure, she didn't need the pole," I tell him.

This thought is not lost on Ives. "I've wondered about that."

"Do you think you could have been drugged at the party?" I ask.

"I've thought about that, too," he says. "I guess I'm pretty stupid. But they didn't rob me. They didn't take any money, my watch, my phone, nothing."

"Any idea how you got way out to the accident site?" says Harry.

"I'm not entirely certain where that was," he says.

"Try sixty miles out of town," I say. "East, out in the desert."

He shakes his head. "It doesn't make any sense. You think I could have driven all the way out there, gotten into an accident, totaled two cars, killed somebody, and not remember anything?"

"I don't know," I tell him. "The only connection from what you're telling us is your job, this story you were working on."

"She was part of it," says Ives. He's talking about Serna.

I sit there looking at him, waiting for him to fill the nervous void. "Just give me some clue," I tell him.

"In general terms?" he says. "What it's always about when it comes to politics and business. What do they say? Follow the money. What the Swiss bankers call Ben and Bin."

"What does that mean? Ben and Bin?" says Harry.

"In international financial circles, Ben is a hundred-dollar bill. Bin is a five-hundred-euro note," says Ives. "Follow the money. It's always about the money." Then he suddenly gives us a distant stare as if he's looking right through the cement wall in the cubicle. "That's it!"

"What?" says Harry.

"Her name. The girl. The one who invited me to the party. Now I remember. Her name was Ben."

Three

Cletus Proffit, the managing partner of the Mandella law firm, looks a lot like one of the characters from an old Hitchcock movie. It was the cadaverous assassin in a tux, brandishing a pistol at the Albert Hall in *The Man Who Knew Too Much*. The title, if you put it in the present tense, would have made a fitting moniker for Proffit's business card. Though at the moment he was more worried about what he didn't know.

"Clete," as his associates call him, was an up-from-the-bootstraps lawyer, a graduate of Harvard Law, originally out of the Midwest, a man who kept climbing his entire life and never looked back. His father had been a store clerk in a small town in Iowa, a fact that Proffit spent most of his life trying to forget. You could mark the significant waypoints in his career by the scandals he had sidestepped and the bodies he had climbed over along the way.

He had spent a few years in government, but never as a civil servant. Clete always believed in starting near the top; undersecretary of defense in the waning days of one administration and special assistant to the president in another. He was rumored to be on a short list for a Cabinet spot, perhaps attorney general, as soon as his party was back in power. Poster boy for the revolving door but always, in the end, back to the firm. It was the chair that was always there whenever the music stopped.

Quiet, in the same way a leopard is before he jumps you, Proffit was always the last to speak on any controversy at a meeting. Not because he was shy but because he was searching for qualities of leadership in others. Leading from behind was the best way to identify competitors so you could sink your canines into the back of their neck while they were still moving forward.

The firm's headquarters were located in Los Angeles, though Proffit spent much of his time skipping like a stone off the stratosphere between there and Washington, D.C. He had spent too much of his life getting his hand on the spigot of power to let go now. Increasingly, that elixir and the people who were under its delirious effects resided in Washington, as did the mounting threat to Proffit's future and his continued leadership of the firm: Olinda Serna.

"She's gone now. You can relax," said Fischer.

"There's everything to worry about." Proffit froze Fischer with an icy glance. "You don't kill a vampire in a car crash. That requires a silver bullet or a wooden stake. Take your pick. And even then you can't be sure she hasn't left toxic entrails behind." He was curious as to details of how she died. According to the sparse reports, the accident happened on a deserted road some miles from San Diego. What was she doing there? He had already told his secretary back in L.A. to get a copy of the accident report as soon as it was prepared.

Proffit hated Serna in a way that left its mark on the core of his very being. They both prayed at the altar of progressive politics, and in a public fashion that no one could miss. Proffit did his time on the board of the ACLU and took his share of high-profile pro bono cases for the poor, minorities, the oppressed, and every other needy group.

Serna wrapped herself in the body armor of women's rights as protection against the male lawyers who dominated the firm. She served on the board of directors of several women's organizations and carried the banner of liberation like a cattle prod. She poked Proffit in the ass with it enough times to remind him that electricity could hurt. The last thing you ever wanted was an injured woman coming out of the woodwork screaming sexual harassment when your name was on the short list for power player of the week in a rising administration. To those in the glass bowl of power it was all a matter of perspective. If your heart was in the right place and your behind was on the correct side of the political divide, such claims would wither in a desert of disregard. But woe unto those in the wrong party, or worse, who had made enemies in the activist camp. For them the ninth circle of hell would provide a refreshing interlude from the pounding they would take before Senate committees in confirmation hearings. Tales of pubic hairs on cans of cola were mild compared to the nuclear crap that would rain down on you from the cloud and the Internet, which had a habit of breeding other victims and cloning new complaints. All of this could be yours if you fell into the cross hairs of the wrong activist group, something that Olinda Serna could guarantee if you got on her wrong side.

"You worry too much," said Fischer.

"Is that right? Tell me," said Proffit, "how much do we really know about what she was involved in, here at the firm, I mean? Do you know?"

Fischer stood there, his lower jaw beginning to quiver with disclaimers. "I just meant . . ."

"I know what you meant. She was running her own secret empire within the firm. You know it and I know it. What we don't know are the details of what she was into."

"As I recall, you didn't want to know," said Fischer.

"That was when she was alive," said Proffit.

Cyril Fischer was Proffit's number two, managing-partner-in-waiting at the firm, and a man who Proffit knew would never get there. He lacked the instincts for survival as well as the searing coals in the belly that fired ambition. This was the reason Proffit kept him around. He was useful as a pair of eyes and ears, but he was no threat. Fischer ran the Washington office, at least on paper.

"If she had people on the cuff in Congress that she was paying off, you're damn right I didn't want to know. If you mean poisoned e-mails from Olinda to keep me in the loop, you're correct. I had no desire to be on that mailing list."

It was the kind of stuff a wily lawyer and pillar of the community like Proffit generally didn't want to know about. He had imagination enough to fill in the blanks. And if Serna got in trouble, Proffit would pro-tect himself like a mobster with at least three or four layers of subordinates to insulate him from accountability. But now that Serna was dead he had no choice. If there were damaging documents lurking in her files, he had to protect the firm, and by extension, himself. They would have to find some lawyerly way to inoculate themselves and disinfect the office.

Serna was the firm's "juice lady," specializing in political law and lobbying—"mother's milk," political money, action committees, and donor lists—the dark side of democracy. She had no personal life, no family, and seemingly no existence outside of the steaming swamp that was Washington and in which she seemed to thrive. For some time now, from what Proffit could see, her ambition had gotten the better of her. She had turned her job into a launching pad in an increasingly obvious campaign to unseat him at the head of the table within the firm.

"I've got two trusted associates and three secretaries auditing her files and checking her e-mails as we speak," said Fischer. "If there's anything there, I'm sure we've got it contained."

This is what Proffit expected. They were looking in all the wrong places. "What I'm worried about you won't find in her files." Proffit knew that anything in her office files, short of hostage notes or blackmail letters, the firm could probably throw a blanket over under attorney-client privilege or lawyer work product and probably make it stick. "That's not the problem."

"What then?" said Fischer.

"Sit down for a minute and let me think."

Fischer wandered toward one of the client chairs across from Proffit's enormous mahogany desk, slumped into the deep cushions, and stared at his boss across the shimmering plate-glass surface.

What troubled Proffit was that Serna was a loner. If she had shot a dozen people in a shopping mall they would have said she fit the profile. Usually in a hurry, irritable, always on her own mission, a cipher you couldn't read if they gave you the code. She was dedicated to her work in the way a zealot is to his ideology. She had her fingers in almost everything the firm handled if it had to do with the gods of politics. She blanketed Congress, the regulatory agencies, and the White House and did it all by herself. At times Proffit was left to wonder if she had cloned herself. If she had posted a sixty-hour day on her billings no one who knew her would have accused her of padding the bill. Her work ethic wasn't the problem. The fact that she had an ambition to match it was.

More to the point, Serna had her own power base outside the firm, mostly friends on Capitol Hill and in the bowels of the administration. She was a registered lobbyist, one of only three in the firm. She either directly or indirectly ladled campaign money on members of the House and Senate from well-heeled clients, many of them large well-organized trade associations and corporate business groups. It wasn't her money, but as far as the recipients were concerned, it didn't matter. She was on the giving end. Otherwise, it would have been an easy task for Proffit and his supporters in the firm to outflank her, undercut her, and send her packing. The problem was, if they did that, they couldn't be sure of the political or economic fallout.

If deals were made on critical legislation with Serna in the middle and her friends in Congress on the doing end, high-paying clients of the firm might feel more comfortable with her than with Mandella. Especially if they started receiving phone calls or e-mails from Serna's friends in the Capitol. She had come from congressional staff when they hired her, consultant to the Senate Banking Committee. She had a lot of friends there. It was a delicate problem, not one that was easily or quickly dealt with.

"Where did she live?" Proffit looked off into the distance to the side away from Fischer as he asked the question.

"Somewhere in Silver Spring. We have the address in our records."

"Has anybody been over there since the accident? Anybody with a key?" Proffit turned and burned two holes through Fischer with his gaze. He didn't have to wait for an answer. The expression on Fischer's face said it. Fischer hadn't thought about this.

"She wasn't married, had no lovers that we know of. Lived alone, right?"

Fischer nodded. "As far as I know."

"She didn't or I would have known about it," said Proffit.

Fischer didn't ask how. Clete always had his sources.

"If there is anything we should worry about, it's not going to be in her files here at the firm. It's going to be in one of two places," said Proffit. "She may have stashed documents at her house. That includes her home computer, any thumb drives or other portable storage devices, and paper records. Perhaps a safe-deposit box. Did she have one?"

"I don't know."

"The weight of what you don't know could sink us," said Proffit.

"What is it exactly that you're worried about?" asked Fischer. "If you could give me some specifics it might help."

"I'm worried about whatever it is that I don't know," said Proffit. If Serna had been one of their corporate

lawyers, even one of their stables of criminal trial lawyers, Proffit wouldn't have been so concerned. It was
the nature of her work that scared him, and her ambition. She was in a position to do real damage both to
himself and the firm. They were one and the same as
far as Proffit was concerned. From what he could see,
she was already in the process of doing that damage
when she died.

"Who is her next of kin?" he asked.

Fischer shook his head, shrugged a shoulder.

"Well, goddamn it, find out! See if she had a company life insurance policy. If so, there should be a named
beneficiary. That may be it. Did she have any other
property besides the place in Georgetown? A vacation
hideaway where she may have stored documents?"

Again Fischer didn't know. But by now he was taking
notes on Post-it slips from the little square holder on
Proffit's desk.

"Did she own or rent the place in Georgetown?"

"Owned. I think."

"Well, find out!" said Proffit. "We don't want some
nosy landlord traipsing through the place looking
at things until we've had a chance to do it ourselves.
Did she have anybody else in the firm she trusted, any
associates?"

"She wanted to hire an assistant. You said no."

"I know what I said. Was there anybody in the office she confided in?"

"I didn't follow her into the ladies' room, if that's what you mean. Vicki Preebles was her secretary. I assume if she trusted anybody it would have been her."

"Was Preebles upset by the news? Serna's death, I mean?"

"Sure. Wouldn't you be? She wanted to stay and help out, but I told her to take a couple days off. I felt it was the thing to do," said Fischer. "We can wait a respectful period and then debrief her. See what Serna may have told her. If anybody knows anything, I suspect it's her."

"Hmmm."

"And I changed the locks on Serna's office just like you said."

"Good." Proffit thought to himself that if Cyril Fischer ever got disbarred, perhaps he could make a living as a locksmith.

Four

Her principal value rested not in her ability to kill her victims, though she was proficient in this. Her usefulness flowed from her knowledge of forensic science and, in particular, trace evidence, hair and fibers, minute particles of dirt, pollen, and other microscopic bits of information that could compromise a job. Sometimes she worked alone and sometimes with others to make sure they made no mistakes and left no telltale signs behind.

You could call her a hired mercenary, but of a special kind. She seldom, if ever, worked in a war zone; almost always in developed countries, Western Europe, the first world nations of Asia, the Middle East, and the Americas.

Governments and large corporations hired her because they knew her skills and could afford the price of her services. She spoke several languages, Spanish, Portuguese, French, a smattering of German along with some Russian. Her English, though fluent, if you listened closely, carried a hint of what sounded like a Spanish trill, so that you might mistake her background as Latin American if you didn't know better.

Ana Agirre was Basque, born in the Pyrenees Mountains between France and Spain. Her great-grandfather died in the bombing of Guernica by the Germans in 1937 during the Spanish Civil War, a travesty made famous by Picasso's painting of the same name. Both her father and her mother worked in the Basque underground before the end of the Franco regime and then afterward, part of the ETA, the Basque separatist movement. Her mother died smuggling explosives during an ETA mission in Barcelona. Her father was taken prisoner. She never saw him again. At the time Ana was eight.

Raised by her maternal grandmother, she excelled in school, particularly in science. She graduated from secondary school a year ahead of her classmates. Given her family background and the fear of retaliation by the Spanish government, Ana was sent to college in Paris. She could have taken courses preparing her for medical school or any of the research fields. Instead, she chose criminalistics and later took a job in the crime lab of the

Police Nationale, successor to the fabled Sûreté. The French didn't seem to care about her family's background. In fact, some voiced sympathy for the Basque people and their repression under Franco. There she learned and refined her forensic skills.

One would have thought she was on a mission to rehabilitate her family so earnestly did she study, absorbing everything she saw and learned with the zeal of a monk. What she masked was anger, anger at the world for having taken from her the one person in her life who she loved more than life itself, her mother. It was a painful loss, one she could never get over. It came to her in her nightmares, the brilliant flash of fire, the sensation of heat and the shattering sound of the explosion that ripped her mother to pieces. Though she had not witnessed it, she had now seen enough to know what it would have been like, the aftermath of a blast from nearly two kilos, four pounds, of RDX, what the American military called C-4 and the British termed PE-4.

Since she was ten, when she had overheard the whispered conversations of her aunts and uncles in the parlor of her grandmother's house, Ana had known that her mother's coffin, buried in the graveyard of the small church in their village, was empty. There was no body inside. After the blast, police and firefighters had found nothing except bits of charred fabric from her mother's clothing, none of them larger than a few centimeters in size. They determined the source of the explosion from chemical tests at the site.

C-4 was stable. It smelled like motor oil and had the pliable texture of children's clay. But when subjected to heat or the shock produced by a detonator, it would explode with a fiery ear-shattering blast that could level half a city block.

Ana concluded that the bomb must have already been armed with a detonator when whoever made it handed it to her mother. It went off on a quiet street in a Barcelona suburb. The only victims were her mother and Ana, who was left to fend for herself.

She remained with the Paris crime lab for six years before moving on to a private laboratory that contracted its services to the French military. There she came in contact with representatives for corporate mercenaries who ultimately hired her as an independent contractor. Ana set up her own business. For large fees, sometimes seven figures, she asked no questions and did whatever was asked of her.

Want to burn down a building? Ana would provide you with an incendiary device that would completely consume itself in the flames. Investigators might find the precise location where the fire originated, and if they had sufficient equipment they might sniff out the chemical accelerants. But as to any other evidence, there would be none.

With the money she earned, she purchased a small estate in the hills above the Côte d'Azur in the South of France. There she moved in her grandmother and one of her aging aunts.

While they quietly plied the garden and cooked, Ana traveled the world rendering advice to her corporate and government black-bag clients on how best to sanitize crime scenes, the proper clothing to wear to avoid leaving trace evidence, as well as ways and means to commit undetectable "accidents," almost all of them fatal.

Drug overdoses were often the death of choice if for no other reason than that most people, including the authorities, believed that those who possessed power and wealth might also be possessed by powerful demons. If there was any hint of past drug use, police seldom looked too far in the direction of criminal homicide unless there was some reason to do so. Ana's job was to make sure there was none. This was the kind of subtle refinement that the terrorist community was edging toward as a means of avoiding state-led military retribution whenever possible. If authorities could not prove an intentional killing, it was politically difficult to strike back. Yet the result was the same: an enemy was dead. There was a growing demand for Ana's services, acts that seldom made bold headlines in newspapers and were a blip on the radar of networks and cable news stations.

At times she would render personal service, hands-on expertise, but that always required a substantially higher fee because of the risks involved.

As you might assume, one did not find a listing for Ana Agirre in any phone book or on the World Wide Web. To those who used her services, she was known as "L'architecte de la mort," "the Architect of Death." Jobs were always on a referral basis, from those she trusted and who had used her services previously. One always kept a low profile in her business.

She was lean and strong, five foot nine, a little taller than average, a face you would not notice in a crowd, neither ugly nor fetching, a passing figure no one would ever remember. Ana the Architect did nothing to alter this appearance. She wore no makeup, never donned high heels, and wore no jewelry. Her uniform of choice was a dark sweater-jersey, dark slacks, and black flat rubber-soled deck shoes. Nothing expensive or unique with intricate sole patterns. Her hair was cut short in the fashion of early photographs taken of Audrey Hepburn, something that a victim would have difficulty getting a grip on in a frenzied attempt to fight her off—that is, if they ever saw her coming in the first place. Usually she was so quick and agile that all they would catch was a glimpse through glazed eyes of her back as she walked away. It would likely be the last thing they would ever see.

This morning she was busy reading the online version of the *San Diego Union-Tribune* about an accident near San Diego, California. She sipped her coffee while sitting at one of the outdoor tables at Le Sancerre on the rue des Abbesses in Paris. It was close to the apartment she maintained in the city. She read the scant details on her e-tablet using the portable hot spot in her purse.

"A single fatality, an unidentified woman. The other driver was arrested, believed to have been under the influence of alcohol. The survivor, a man in his twenties, suffered only minor injuries and was taken to a local area hospital for treatment. No identification of the dead driver has been made pending notification of next of kin."

Ana did not know the dead woman's name, but she knew she had been murdered. The French mercenaries, a group of high-tech engineers who had constructed the equipment that caused the accident, had told her to watch the news in this part of California, the area around San Diego.

She had seen only digital pictures of the items, including the large rolling case that was highly unique. It was too big to carry on board an airplane, so it had to be checked. They had marked the case with holograms, making it easily identifiable at baggage claim so that no one would carry it off by mistake. You could just grab it and go. They also sent the specs for the equipment.

This was composed of a computer, its software, and a portable satellite antenna dish capable of overriding most of the electronics and computer-driven safety and other features built into late-model passenger cars.

Ana made a down payment on the equipment because she needed it for a job in Europe. It was a highly lucrative contract involving the untimely accidental death of an executive, the managing partner of a large multinational corporation. If the schedule on the contract for the executive was to be maintained, the gentleman was slated to be dead in two weeks. After that, bad things would happen to the people who hired her.

Ana was anxious to get her hands on the equipment and get the job done. However, the French technicians who built the system insisted on "field-testing" it first before they delivered it to her. They said nothing about a field test at the time she ordered the equipment. Now the stuff was off in California somewhere. According to the French makers, if all went well there would be two dead targets, separate motorists in separate vehicles on a two-lane highway in a rural area east of San Diego. The Frenchmen gave her the date and told her to watch the news. They seemed giddy with excitement.

The news story gave the sorry details. They had not banked on the intervention of a passing motorist. By then it was too late. The surviving victim had been pulled from the burning wreckage. What should have been two clean fatalities and a closed accident file suddenly turned into vehicular manslaughter with dangling threads and probing lawyers who, if they persisted, might find their way back to her. She wanted her software and her equipment back, or better yet destroyed so that no part of it could end up in a crime lab.

She had visions of Lockerbie, where a massive Pan Am passenger jet was brought down by a small explosive device. Two years later scientists in a crime lab managed to identify a single electronic component from the bomb's detonator, a piece of plastic smaller than a baby's fingernail. They traced it back to its point of sale, and from there to two Libyan nationals, who were delivered up by Libyan dictator Muammar Gaddafi.

Ana worried that the same could happen with the equipment she had commissioned if it fell into the hands of the authorities. They would trace it back to its French builders, and from them to her, even though she had never used it. She could end up dressed in an orange jumpsuit in the place the Americans called Gitmo.

The whole thing, the field test, had an air of the unprofessional about it. It had the scent of the American CIA, whose budget was being slashed and whose better operatives were being turned out to pasture in the post–Iraq War world, with other unaligned terrorist groups rampaging through the ruins. She couldn't be sure who the French makers of the equipment were dealing with.

It was true what they said about the Americans. No one could rely on them any longer. They had reached their zenith and were now on the way down, a toothless lion dying in its den. Not only did their government lack the political resolve to defend itself or its allies, it was now missing the basic proficiency to carry out politically sensitive covert operations. To silence those who needed silencing.

A US military clerk with low or no security clearance had taken highly classified government cables, copied them to thumb drives, and delivered them to Internet bloggers for transmission to the public over the World Wide Web. The embarrassment that followed compromised US diplomats removed from their posts, the State Department held up to ridicule, and the National

Security Agency exposed for eavesdropping on US allied leaders. Another clerk had stolen top secrets and absconded first to China and then Russia, leaving a trail of confidential American secrets like bread crumbs in his wake. No one knew yet the full extent of the damage, certainly not the American public. Their government was powerless to do anything about it other than downplay it and look for political cover.

At the same time, Washington was awash in amateurish domestic scandals and clumsy cover-ups. To listen to them, every computer the government owned had crashed on cue, coincidentally destroying evidence of government-committed crimes in the process. No one believed the obvious lies—"the spin," as they called it from the White House—but those in power didn't care. They couldn't be prosecuted because they controlled the machinery of enforcement, and to them, that was all that mattered. They had lost all sense of the art, always to provide one's prince with the refuge of credible deniability, what the British called a scintilla of truth.

Ana made a mental note. These people, whoever they were, were incompetent and, for that reason, dangerous. She would do whatever was possible to learn who they were so that she could avoid doing any business with them in the future. But first she had to recover the laptop, the software, and the small dish antenna that the French mercenaries who built the device had given them to field test.

She finished her coffee, paid the waiter, and grabbed her purse. A minute later she was racing down the street astride the blue Piaggio BV500, helmet on her head, cruising toward the train station and her trip south back to her estate in order to pack for her trip to L.A.

Five

This morning we huddle in the conference room at our office, behind Miguel's Concina and the Brigantine Restaurant on Orange Avenue in Coronado.

Pages and files are spread out all over the table as I sit with Harry and our investigator, Herman Diggs, trying to gain a handle on the latest blizzard of paper affecting Alex Ives.

Alex is staying with his mother and father at their home following the bail hearing. This was an exercise that proved to be easier than we thought and is still a mystery to me as to why. There was good news and good news. The first being the apparent lack of knowledge on the part of the cops regarding Ives's connection to Olinda Serna. They seem to be blissfully ignorant of the fact that Ives and his employer were working on a hot news flash in which Serna presumably had a talking role. We don't know the details because Ives still isn't telling us, and his boss has, to date, been unavailable, at least to me. I have left three phone messages for Tory Graves at the *Washington Gravesite*, the digital dirt sheet for which Ives works. None of these have been returned. We assume that if the cops knew about the connection between Ives and Serna, the prosecutor would probably have dumped it on us during the bail hearing, evidence of possible intent in an effort to deny bail. Though this is not a certainty. Using this information in a surprise package at trial could do wonders for a conviction, even if they made no effort to enhance the charges. Letting the jury know that Ives knew Serna and was pursuing her when he passed out behind the wheel and killed her is one of those "wow" factors certain to light up the jury box.

The other happy news was the cost of bail, a mere twenty-five-thousand-dollar bond imposed by the judge, well below the local bail schedule. How this happened is a mystery, though it appeared not to be the doing of the prosecutor as much as the man seated behind him. Beyond the bar rail in the first row of spectator seats was another man, suited up for combat and packing a slick patent-leather briefcase. We found out later this was one of the premium-priced lawyers, a criminal practitioner from Serna's law firm up in L.A.

Apparently they thought enough of her to send somebody down to watch. He conferred with the deputy D.A. over the railing and, after they talked, the prosecutor asked for only twenty-five thousand dollars bail. Even the judge was surprised.

The D.A. then went on to explain that Ives had a job and family contacts in the community. He even gestured toward Alex's mom and dad sitting behind us, as if the state had produced them, shining character witnesses for the defendant. He told the judge it was a first offense, only marginal evidence of alcohol in the defendant's system. He never even mentioned the French-fried cadaver in the other car, so that by the time he was finished, there was nothing left for me to talk about. I sat there with my thumb in my mouth. If you can't say anything on behalf of your client that is more helpful than what the D.A. has to say, it is best not to say anything at all.

When the judge demanded that Ives surrender his passport and agree not to leave the state pending trial, I looked at the prosecutor wondering if he might object. It was almost as if somebody wanted Ives to skip town and jump bail.

His parents posted the bond out of pocket change. I had a come-to-Jesus moment with the kid outside the courtroom and told him in no uncertain terms not to wander too far. Even if his boss demanded that he travel back east on business, he was not to go. He promised me that he would not, smiled, and they left. Stranger things have happened to me in courtrooms, but not recently. It left me to wonder.

"According to the accident report, neither driver appears to have applied their brakes prior to impact," says Harry. He has the document prepared by the California Highway Patrol in front of him on the table. "No skid marks on the pavement, though the intersecting road traveled by Ives was dirt until it reached the county highway where they impacted. Still nothing on the pavement to indicate any braking. Serna's rented car was moving at a relatively slow rate of speed, estimated between thirty and forty miles an hour at the point of impact," says Harry.

We are in the process of trying to find out if the navigation satellite system and its proprietors will be able to supply us with any information as to the car Alex was driving and the location of the party that night.

"Let's start with the time of the accident."

"According to the report, the estimate of time is about eleven P.M." says Harry. "The witness who pulled Ives from the burning wreck called it in at eleven-oh-six. He said he tried to get to Serna, but the flames were too hot. That slowed him down on the call."

"What was the speed limit?" I ask him.

Harry flips back one page. "Fifty-five," he tells me.

"So why was Serna going so slow?" I ask.

"Maybe she was looking for something," says Herman. Herman Diggs is a big man, African-American to the soul, former athlete who blew out a knee in college and lost out on a career in football. He has been with us for ten years now, long enough and on such intimate terms that he is now part of the family.

"Not much out there to look for," says Harry. He turns the file toward Herman, who looks at the printout, a satellite photo, probably from Google Maps, showing an overhead shot of desolate desert, a narrow strip of concrete like a gray ribbon running across it with a red marker at the fatal intersection.

"There is the other road," says Herman. He means the dirt strip traveled by Ives. "Maybe she was looking for that."

"You think they were meeting up out there?" I ask him.

Herman shrugs a shoulder. "What did the kid tell you?"

"Nothing. Says he can't remember," I say.

"If they were getting ready to meet, we can be relatively certain that Ives wasn't sitting around waiting for her," says Harry. "According to the report, the estimated speed of Ives's car, a late-model luxury sedan, was approaching eighty miles per hour and accelerating as it entered the highway and impacted the other car. Caved in the entire driver's-side door on Serna's car. Bent it like a pretzel."

"Sounds like a missile," says Herman. "Where'd a kid that age get a ride like that? Must be six figures fully dressed out with all the gadgets and gizmos."

"It was owned by his parents' aviation servicing company," I tell him. "They let him use it from time to time."

"Bet they don't do that again," says Herman.

"According to the accident report, this kind of high speed and acceleration prior to impact is consistent with a driver who has fallen asleep or gone unconscious behind the wheel." Harry is still on point, trekking through the report.

"Still, she makes no effort to evade him. She must have seen him coming," I say.

"On a dirt road doing eighty. That would likely send up a dust trail a blind Indian could follow," says Herman.

"Let me see that photo again," I tell Harry. He passes it over to me. It is difficult to tell from the air, but there doesn't appear to be any elevation, rises that might obscure Serna's vision of the approaching vehicle. No trees or other obstructions.

"She could have been looking at something in her car," says Harry. "A map. Maybe her cell phone. That would explain why she was traveling so slow."

"Maybe." I pass the report back to him.

"More interesting," says Harry, "is the fact that the preliminary toxicology report shows the absence of any drugs in Ives's system."

This was the big surprise of the day. We are all smiles around the table with the news. While it may not cut our client loose entirely, it offers a big headache to the prosecution, who now must explain to the jury how the defendant became unconscious behind the wheel.

The cops are now batting zero for two. No alcohol, at least nothing approaching the presumptive level of intoxication, and no drugs. So that means we have an unconscious client under the influence of nothing.

"Any kind of medical condition," asks Herman, "might account for his problem?"

"Not that we know of," says Harry.

"I asked Ives on the phone this morning and he says no," I tell them. "He's never passed out, never fainted. Had a physical two months ago and passed it with flying colors."

"So what caused it?" says Herman.

"Could have been drugs," I tell him.

"But they didn't find any," says Harry.

"Some of the more complex drugs take a while. Could be weeks before they have a final report. And then there are some they don't even look for in the routine screenings unless there's a reason."

"You mean roofies?" says Herman. "The date rape drug?"

"There's that one and there's others. It is a possibility," I say. "Police don't usually order them up in the normal toxicology screening."

These are known as predator drugs, used by some perpetrators either to engage in sexual assault on the unconscious victim or to rob them. Either way the victim usually remembers nothing when it's over.

They work like conscious sedation and in some countries are used as an anesthetic. Those under their effect lose motor coordination. Their eyes may be open but nothing is being registered in the brain. They result in near total loss of memory during the period that the victim is under the influence.

"Fits the profile of what Ives described as his symptoms," says Harry. "They're absorbed into the system quickly. All trace gone within at most seventy-two hours. They show up in urine tests. Here they drew only blood." Harry's skimming through the report. "Here it is, 'Benzodiazepine.' They didn't check the box, didn't ask for it."

"It's too late now," says Herman.

"I asked Alex about the possibility the last time we talked to him, you and I at the jail," I tell them. "The question whether somebody might have slipped something to him. It wasn't lost on him. The thought had crossed his mind before I mentioned it. He wondered about the girl, the one who invited him to the party, and whether it was a setup. The single glass of champagne. The fact she never showed at the party. It weighed on his mind."

"I know what you're saying," says Herman. "There's no way Ives coulda driven like hell and gone out into the desert if somebody slipped him a roofie. What that means, somebody delivered him out there. Accident was staged. Is that what you're sayin'? That whoever did it, killed Serna? So there was no mishap involved."

I nod.

"Here we go again," says Harry. "Why can't we just keep this simple? Straightforward DUI with the cops showing no evidence. We push hard enough and they'll kick him loose. Case over. We can move on."

"They nearly did that at the bail hearing," I tell him. "The question is why? Think about it. What do we know?"

"Not much," says Harry.

"On the contrary. We know that Ives was shadowing Serna, not in a physical way, but he had her in the journalistic cross hairs over something. According to Alex, it's big, but for the moment off the record. Somebody drugs him and takes him out into the desert. They smash two cars together, one of them at high speed carrying Alex, the other one with Serna inside. Was she conscious at the time?" I ask.

"What, you think they drugged her too?" says Harry. "Why not just drown her and dump her on some beach somewhere?"

"Because then there would be evidence. Somebody would have to walk in the sand to dump the body. She might struggle. You'd get bruising, maybe something under her fingernails. This way there is nothing. Major collision and fire. The bodies are burned. If it had worked out the way they planned it, both of them would be dead and we wouldn't be involved to ask any questions."

"You think they were out to get the boy as well?" says Herman.

"Be my guess. Given the reckless nature of the collision. There was certainly no assurance Ives would survive the impact, let alone the fire. The only reason Alex is alive is because a passing motorist pulled him from the wreck. If I had to guess, I would say that our

Good Samaritan wasn't part of their opera. Something they failed to plan for."

"You know you're getting paranoid," says Harry. "Soon you'll be seeing black helicopters."

"Give me another theory that explains the events," I tell him.

"OK, tell me one thing," he says. "Both cars were moving. If both Serna and Ives were unconscious, how did they do that?"

I think for a moment, shake my head. "I don't know."

"There you go," says Harry. "Problem with your theory is it doesn't work."

Harry goes back to the accident report, looking for something. He finds the pages and starts to read, running his finger over the paper.

"Have you talked to the kid about this?" says Herman. "The fact that somebody may have tried to kill him?"

"Not in so many words."

"Don't you think you should? Assuming you're right, if they tried once, what's to stop 'em from trying again?"

"Nothing, I suppose."

"He can't run," says Herman. "Can't hide. Bail conditions see to that."

"Yeah. It's all pretty convenient, isn't it?" I tell him.

Herman arches an eyebrow. "So what do we do? Where do we go from here?" He flips open his little notebook ready to jot down whatever little tidbits I can give him.

"Two unknowns," I tell him. "First the mystery girl. We have only a partial name and a description. Asian, very good looking, long dark hair about the middle of her back, about five foot five or five six. First name or nickname, Ben. She has a tattoo on the inside of her left thigh, red and blue, probably a dragon or the tail of a dragon."

Herman is still scribbling on the notepad.

"I would start with the local tattoo parlors."

"Hell, there must be seven thousand of them," says Herman, "and that's only on one block downtown."

"Got your work cut out," I tell him. "Harry and I need to go to work on Alex, to loosen his tongue regarding this hot news tip he's got involving Serna. Makes sense that if that's the only connection between the two of them, and if the accident was staged to trap them both, that the story he was working on is probably the reason."

"OK, tell me this," says Harry. He finally looks up from the report. "Says here there is no evidence of mechanical malfunction in the steering or brake systems of either car. And catch this, no evidence of any malfunction or tampering with the accelerator, cruise control, or other speed maintenance systems in either vehicle."

"They can tell all that from the burned-out remains?" says Herman.

"Steel doesn't burn," says Harry. "So, if he was unconscious, on roofies, unable to coordinate his arms or his legs and there was no alteration to the steering, the accelerator, or the cruise control, how did they do eighty miles an hour and steer one car into another in the space of a small intersection? And don't tell me they did it remotely because if they did, there would be evidence of hardware left behind no matter how small it was. The cops would have found it." Harry looks at me across the table, tapping the page of the accident report with his finger.

It is a good question, and one for which I have no answer.

Six

The phone on her desk buzzed. Maya Grimes reached for the receiver.

"Senator, you have a call. The man refuses to identify himself but says you know him."

She thought for a moment. "OK, put him through. And hold my other calls and appointments." She put the receiver down and a few seconds later it buzzed again. Grimes picked it up. "Hello."

"Sorry to bother you at your office."

"I told you never to call me here. You're not calling from a cell phone, are you?"

"I'm at a pay phone. It was unavoidable. We've got a problem. We have to talk."

"Not here," said Grimes. She glanced at her watch and thought for a moment. "The bench on the north side by the reflecting pool. You know the one."

"Where we met last time?"

"Give me fifteen minutes." Grimes hung up the phone.

Early spring, and the Mall outside the Capitol was already bustling with early tourists and busloads of children on school field trips. Senator Maya Grimes walked quickly, trying to melt into the crowd, as unobtrusive as possible. Still, her face was recognizable to some of the passersby who stared at her and others who stole second glances as she clicked along quickly in her high heels down the path.

Usually, if she had a private meeting, she would do it at some offbeat restaurant in the suburbs, take a car from the congressional fleet with darkened windows and a driver to deliver her to the door. But she wanted no record of this meeting popping up in the computer in the motor pool.

Grimes had been twenty-two years in the US Senate, chairperson of the Committee on Banking, vice chair of Senate Finance, and a senior member of several subcommittees on financial affairs. She came from California, where the cost of an election to the Senate was approaching thirty million dollars. This, coupled with her political gravitas around the Capitol, gave her more hours on television than most seasoned pilots have in the cockpit. Hers was one of those faces that people tended to recognize. She lost count of the number of times some idiot had stopped her on the street wondering what film it was they had seen her in. Usually she didn't mind, but today she had a terminal case of bad temper. She nearly ran down a couple of third graders who aimlessly bolted into her path in a misguided game of tag.

A grandmother and seasoned politician, Grimes could usually turn on the charm for kids. Today she gave them a look from the Wicked Witch and kept moving quickly toward a small clump of trees along the north side of the reflecting pool. The walkway curved a little to the right. As she made the turn she saw him sitting there alone on the bench.

Grimes slowed down and looked around to make sure no one was watching, there were no idle picture-takers with their backs to the pool glancing at the bench and the bushes behind it. Of course they could be a mile away with powerful optics listening through an electronic bug the size of an aspirin glued to a man's chest.

She walked slowly toward the bench, passed him by, and stopped. She stood there for a couple of seconds with her back to him, a few feet away. There was no one in earshot. "What do you want?"

"You want to walk and talk?" he asked.

"No!"

"Suit yourself. I'm just trying to help. You wanted to be kept informed. That's what I'm doing."

"So what is it?"

"She's dead."

"I know that!" It had been in the early-morning paper, identification of the woman killed in a car crash in Southern California. The *Washington Post* had played it up, page three with a two-column headline. Serna was a local political player, a lobbyist who was in and out of the Capitol on a regular basis. She had friends, lots of them, most of them women. Some of them were powerful. Grimes was no doubt at or near the top of that food chain.

"But there is still a problem," he said.

"What do you mean?"

"Loose ends," he said. "It wasn't done cleanly—"

"I don't want to know the details!" She cut him off quickly through clenched teeth. "I don't know what happened and I don't want to know. I am not part of it!"

"Of course not." He smiled, looking at her from behind. For a woman in her early sixties, she still had a pretty good body. There were times when he wondered what she might be like in the sack; whether all that intensity would translate into sexual energy once you got her there. "Why don't you come over and sit down." He gently patted the slatted wood on the bench next to him.

He was lean, about six feet, gray-haired, tan complexion, blue eyes with just enough wrinkles in the forehead and the bags above his cheeks to look distinguished. It was a face that had seen some wear. His three-piece pinstriped navy suit might just as well have been a uniform around the government buildings and monuments in Washington. So ubiquitous were his looks that he was nearly invisible. This was well practiced and honed over the long course of his career. He had lived in many countries and could disappear like a ghost in almost any of them. He carried a walking cane, though he seldom used it. This was insurance against a trick knee that at times could go out on him without notice, the result of an injury sustained in his youth. The cane sported the sharp-beaked head of an eagle cast in silver. It was the work of a Mexican silversmith. The bird's slitted eyes, tarnished a little from wear, mimicked its owner's. Ever vigilant, they peered out at the world in cold judgment.

"Loosen up. Relax. You seem troubled." He studied her body language, tense, wary. "There is no one here but the two of us."

"How can I be sure?" she said.

"If we wanted to expose you, you would already be sitting in a federal penitentiary. Oh, one of the country clubs, to be sure," he said. "They would never subject you to, what is it they call it, the general population." He smiled, though with her back to him she couldn't see it. "There's supposed to be a very nice one, I think they call it Pleasanton, out in your neck of the woods in California. I am told it is not a bad place. At least it's close to your family."

Whenever he met up with her he always stoked the coals, feeding the fires of anxiety that burned within. Keeping her on edge was part of the practiced technique, honed over generations by its practitioners.

Still, his words today made the women's correctional facility at Pleasanton sound almost idyllic. There were nights when she lay awake, unable to sleep, wishing that they would pull this cord, put her out of her misery. At least the worrying would be over. That was the worst part, wondering if and when the world would cave in on her. They would remind her first of how far she had to fall, and in the next breath tell her she had nothing to worry about. She often thought this must be how they lived in the old Soviet Union, constantly in fear, wondering when they might come for you.

"Please. Sit down. You will worry yourself into an early grave," he said. "In time you will learn to trust us."

"That'll be the day," she told him.

"Believe me, we have absolutely no interest in doing you any harm whatsoever. Why would we? Think about it. We are invested in you, long term," he told her. "We are like partners in a business enterprise. Simple as that."

"If that's true, I'll be happy to sell you my interest cheap," she said.

"Sounds like you'd like to retire?"

"I've thought about it."

"Sorry, but it's not that easy," said the man.

Dealing with the devil never is, she thought.

"We gave money to your last campaign. A lot of it. I'll bet you didn't even know that."

"I didn't," she said.

"The donations were not in our own name, of course. The media, to say nothing of the federal election commission, would have made a big stink over that. But it was support nonetheless. Come, sit down."

"Save the pleasantries. Can we keep this short? What is it you want? I don't have a lot of time."

"Make time." he said. "After all, I'm not one of your fawning constituents looking for a photographed handshake to put on my mantel."

She took a deep breath, released some of the muscles in her back, dropped her shoulder, and slowly turned around to face him.

"That's better. I came here to warn you."

"Warn me about what?"

"It's possible that the press, some of the media types, might be contacting you now that Serna is no longer with us," he said.

This caused a spike in the adrenaline already running through Grimes's body. He saw the startled look in her eyes.

"Why would they be calling me?"

"The two of you ran in the same circles. She plied the Capitol, came in contact with you regularly. It's only natural."

"She came in contact with a lot of people," said Grimes.

"Yes, but she managed money for two of your campaigns before she registered as a lobbyist."

"I thought you said that'd been taken care of? That the records were purged."

"We thought they were," he said. "Seems we were mistaken. Some old tapes containing FEC reports on campaign funding apparently got out. There's nothing to worry about. Nothing illegal about any of it. She just shows up as the campaign finance chair on two of your early reports, that's all. That's it."

Grimes put a finger to her lips, as if to seal them as she thought and looked away from him off into the distance. Those records placed them in the same universe, the circle of hell that led Serna to Maya Grimes's life of sin. If she found it, so could others.

"It's not important," he told her.

"That means they know we had financial dealings," said Grimes. "If they start poking around and somebody finds out we had a falling-out, they'll want to know why. One thing leads to another."

"Relax! We're confident they don't know anything."

"Where did these tapes go?" she asked.

"Purchased by some Internet news group."

"Which one?"

"I don't know," he lied. "It happened more than a year ago. I'm sure it's nothing. For all we know, they have probably thrown them out by now."

"You're telling me everything, right?"

He raised two fingers. "Honest injun," he said.

"I'm not sure I believe you," said Grimes.

He looked at her, arching an eyebrow as if to say, "What else is new?"

"I'm just trying to give you a heads-up. I'm not saying they will call. Just that they might, ask you a few questions."

"And what do I say if they do?"

"Don't deny it, the fact that she worked on your early campaigns, that's all. Just tell them that you and Serna were friends way back in the early part of your career. Ancient history," he told her. "She helped you run a couple of your campaigns and that's it. But don't bring it up unless they do. If they are doing an obituary on her, it's only natural that they might contact you. I didn't want you to panic if they should mention the campaign stuff. That's all."

"Still, I don't understand why they would call me," she said. "There are plenty of others who were closer to her. It's not like we were friends. What if they know we had a fight?"

"They won't."

"What if they know about Ginger and Spice?"

"They don't. Trust me, how could they know?"

"You found out." Grimes almost spit the words at him.

"Yes, but we had the means."

"So did Serna."

"That was your fault," he said. "You were careless. Now stop worrying. They know absolutely nothing. Of that we are certain."

"How can you be sure?"

"If they contact you, just give them a few happy remembrances, how much she'll be missed, what a great person she was, and hang up. That's all you have to do. It shouldn't be difficult. Just a little white lie. Think of it as campaigning," he said.

"You said there was still a problem. Some loose ends. Plural," said Grimes.

"Yes, well, leave that to me. Forget I mentioned it." He didn't want to load her up with too many worries at one time. There was no purpose in telling her they had failed to bag Alex Ives, or that Ives and his boss were the ones digging for dirt, and that she might be hiding in the hole where they were shoveling.

The *Washington Gravesite* was stepped around gingerly like a poisonous serpent by any shrewd politician in the Capitol. It had a bite that was toxic and it seemed to be growing another rattle every year. Grimes didn't need to know about Ives or the story he was working on. If she had known, she would have panicked. That and the girl. Ives, no doubt, would by now have told his lawyers about the little Asian beauty. They definitely had some mopping up to do.

"How serious is it?" she asked.

"It's nothing for you to worry about. You just take care of the items on your agenda. You have two up this week. Make sure the votes go the right way."

A pained expression crossed Grimes's face.

"What is it? What's wrong?" he asked.

"There's a problem with the appropriation on the Siderail Software deal," she said.

"What kind of problem?"

"I need one more vote. I was counting on Mendez. Senator from Arizona."

"I know who Mendez is."

"He won't return my calls," she said. "He's avoiding me. His assistant says he has problems with the item, something about a manufacturer back in his state who wants a piece of the contract. Mendez won't vote for it unless he gets a guarantee."

"It's too late for that," said the man. "We need that bill."

"Without Mendez I can't get the item out of committee."

"Don't worry about Mendez. When the vote comes up he'll be on board. But you should have called me. I can't help you unless I know," he said.

"How are you going to do that?"

"Leave it to me."

Before he could say anything more, a man came into view walking quickly toward them. He was carrying a brown bag in one hand and a plastic bottle of Coke in the other. In his twenties, he had on a dark pair of slacks, a white shirt, and a tie. His collar was open. He had that hurried look, one of the sea of civil servants punching the clock for lunch. He plunked himself down on the other end of the bench and started opening the brown bag.

The man in the three-piece looked over at him and said, "Do you mind? This is a private conversation."

The younger man was good-sized. He appeared fit. And apparently this was not his day to take shit. "You want privacy, find an office!" he said.

"I'd prefer you find another bench." The man in the suit twisted the handle on his cane just enough to release the bayonet thread so that the razor-sharp blade slid a few inches out from the cane. He could have shown him the SIG Sauer nine-millimeter under his coat, but why go nuclear in a quiet park?

The man with the brown bag looked at the glint on the blade and swallowed. "No problem." He didn't even look up at Grimes. Instead he got up, grabbed his Coke, and walked quickly down the path away from them.

"Does that make you feel big?" she asked.

"I don't have a problem with it. Oh, I forgot. That's right, you don't like weapons. I apologize," he said. He gave her a sinister grin. "I forgot your crusade. That you authored all those bills to outlaw, what was it, assault rifles and large clips? And you worked behind the scenes so quietly to sell all that used US military brass to the Chinese, mountains of it, just so that crazy gun loaders in America couldn't get their hands on any of it. That was a stroke of genius," he said. "Must have really put the press on the gangbangers in South Chicago. Only being able to kill a hundred people or so a night now. All those years pushing the ATF button to push them in the face of the gun dealers. Put as many of them as possible out of business, along with the manufacturers. You're just up to your little honkers in good works, aren't you?"

He stopped for a moment and looked at her, the smile gone from his face. "But then, of course, you have a permit to carry, don't you?" He knew she did. He sometimes wondered if she might bring her pistol, a snub-nosed .38, to one of their meetings and try to put an end to it. But it wouldn't do her any good unless she turned it on herself. "Where exactly do you hide it?" he asked. He looked her up and down with a kind of lustful leer as if the next thing he might do was strip-search her.

A good number of the political class constantly railed against guns and gun owners and then used their influence to obtain permits so that they could carry concealed weapons themselves. This was done mostly when they were back in their districts. Firearms were frowned upon in the highly sanitized atmosphere of the Capitol, where security was now so tight that members of the public had to make appointments, sometimes weeks in advance, and get ten-printed just to do the public tour of the hallowed halls that for more than thirty years had been the scene of the collective crime.

"I got that permit years ago when I was being stalked!" She said it with a tone of defiance. The instant the words left her lips she knew it was a mistake.

"Oh, I hope he didn't hurt you," said the man.

She shook her head, said nothing. Why compound the error?

"Thank God for that!" He shook his head. "It's a sick world out there. You do have to wonder what's going on in some people's minds. That an honest, hardworking public servant such as yourself would be the victim of a stalker. You do have to wonder what could possess someone."

The way he said it and the fact that he seemed to be waiting for an answer made her feel like a bug pinned under his microscope.

"One who didn't know better might think you had done something wrong," he offered. "But then, of course, we know better. Like I say, it's a sick world."

She stood there, the quiet anger fixed in her eyes. He was right about one thing. She had no one to blame but herself. Back in the Senate Office Buildings or in the Capitol she was part of the aristocracy. Out here she belonged to him.

Under the dome she might be whisked into the private members' elevator between floors, and be able to jump aboard the little private underground choo-choo that chugged them beneath the sweltering streets of Washington so they wouldn't wear out shoe leather or have to mingle with the unwashed.

Here, faced with the reality that others knew her secret, she was forced to stand by silently and accept the humiliation. She hoped in time he would let her go. He assured her that they would at some point. Until then there was nothing she could do, nothing she could say. Serna had discovered Grimes's secret and had tried to extort favors and money from her only to discover that she was standing in line, that the people in front of her had a prior claim and that they held it with a death grip.

Seven

"M r. Madriani, call for you." Brenda Gomes, my secretary, looks over at me from her desk, her hand cupped over the tiny microphone on her headset.

I am out front looking for a file in one of the cabinets. "Who is it?" I mouth the words so as not to be heard at the other end of the line.

"Mr. Diggs," she whispers.

"I'll take it in my office." Seconds later I am behind my desk, the phone to my ear. "Herman. Paul here."

"Benjawan Tjahana," says Herman. "I'm not exactly sure how she spells it. But the man says that's how she pronounced it. He remembers because he was very interested. So interested he wrote it down. It seems your client didn't lose his entire memory. According to the guy at the tattoo shop, she's a real dish. A regular rare-earth man magnet," says Herman.

"Lucky for us she made an impression," I tell him. "Otherwise you might be looking forever."

"Makes sense," says Herman. "They needed something to attract Ives. What better bait?"

"Does he have an address for her? This man at the shop?"

"No."

"Damn!"

"But he got her cell number."

My eyes light up. "Good man!"

"And a good part of her life story," says Herman. "Seems that dragon on her leg is pretty good-sized, from just above her knee to the sweet spot on the inside of her thigh. The little dimple," says Herman.

"Sounds like you had a very detailed discussion with this man."

"And he got pictures." Herman allows this to settle in.

"Of her face?"

"Among other things," he says. "They had a long time to talk while she was on the table and he was doing his art. Says she's an Indonesian national. Came here on a student visa to study computer science at the local

C.C." Herman means the two-year community college. "That was eight years ago."

"She's overstayed her visa," I say.

"Unless they offer advanced degrees in digital rocket science," says Herman, "she's in the country illegally. Could give us some leverage."

"Or turn her into a rabbit," I tell him.

"According to what she told the man at the shop she was working at a private club out near the beach."

"What club?"

"He gave me the name and address, but he says you won't find it in the phone book or on the net. It's in a commercial building near the pier. From what he was saying, it sounded like one of those places wouldn't pass muster with the health department."

"Why is that?"

"Where the female help cleans the tables with their bare behinds after you eat. Businessman's lunch," says Herman.

"When's the last time he saw her?" I ask.

"He did the dragon in two sessions. Last one was three weeks ago. She may still be working there. I paid him a few bucks and he e-mailed two of the pictures he took. I'm sending them to you soon as I hang up. The guy got a couple of very good ones."

"I don't need any thigh shots," I tell him.

"How do you know until you look?" says Herman. He laughs. "A clear, crisp head-and-shoulder close-up, and one a little farther out. She's wearing a robe from the shop. Do me a favor and forward them on to your client. Give him a call and make sure it's her before we get too excited."

"Will do," I tell him.

"In the meantime, let me see if I can find this club, see if she's still working there. If we get lucky maybe vice hasn't closed it down yet."

"If you strike out there, try her cell phone records. See if they have a home address."

"That's always sketchy," says Herman. "The way young folk move around. She's had more than enough time to blow through a two-year contract with the carrier, and if she's nervous about anything . . ."

"You mean like being in the country illegally," I say.

"That and who knows what else," says Herman, "then there's a good chance she's probably prepaid. I long for the days of the old landline," he says, "when people were nailed to the ground if they wanted modern conveniences. This keeps up, pretty soon they'll be able to take a digital dump long distance online. Then you'll never be able to catch 'em at home."

"Send me those pictures," I tell him. "And call me as soon as you find this place. That is, if she's still working there. And do me a favor, Herman, don't talk to her, not yet. Just locate her and call me. I don't want to scare her off until we can nail her down."

"How you gonna do that?"

"I don't know. Let me think about it."

Eight

If there was any debriefing to be done with Serna's secretary, Proffit would do it himself. Serna's original secretary had been lured away by another firm at an obscenely high salary more than a year earlier. Proffit had secretly guaranteed the woman's increase in pay with the other firm for two years in order to get her to move on.

Vicki Preebles, her replacement, was hired by Serna, but from a short list of applicants, all of whom had been carefully selected and screened by Proffit beforehand. They were paid for their time and sworn to secrecy. They signed nondisclosure agreements in blood and were told that they would be legally drawn and quartered if they revealed anything told to them during the selection process.

Olinda Serna had been making a move on Proffit to replace him as managing partner for about eighteen months. She had been meeting privately with other partners in the firm, flying from office to office, lining up support for a palace coup. Proffit knew this from travel records and pieces of information he had gleaned from others in the firm, people who were loyal to him. He was taking no chances and no prisoners.

It was how he confirmed the details of the budding rebellion: pillow talk with Vicki Preebles. After she was hired by Serna, Proffit wasted no time setting Preebles up in an apartment, a place the secretary could never have afforded on her own salary, where, from time to time, he would visit her whenever he came to town, which was almost every week. He ordered in catered dinners, intimate evenings spent discussing office gossip, sometimes over champagne and, on more frisky occasions, shots of tequila.

Proffit was married. He had three grown children and two grandchildren. But he was not averse to mixing a little business with pleasure. Besides, it was a necessary arrangement. He could have just paid Vicki for the information, but that might not have purchased her loyalty. Emotional connections, though sometimes volatile, were invariably more trustworthy.

This afternoon the grieving secretary was still off work as he visited her.

"What will happen to me now that she's gone?" asked Preebles. "I don't want to seem cold or uncaring . . ."

"No one could accuse you of that," said Proffit. "And there's no need to explain. I understand. Don't worry. You have a solid future with the firm. A job as long as you want it." He smiled warmly as he lay bare chested in his boxers atop the thick feather comforter on her bed.

Preebles was under the covers, naked, lying on her side, one breast partially exposed, her nipple hard as a nail head and twice as large.

Proffit picked at the carefully arranged pieces of fresh fruit from a large platter that lay on the bed between them. It looked like a scene from one of DeMille's Roman orgies. The only things missing were the slaves with their feathered fans and the jingling belly dancers.

"Yes, but who will I work for?" she asked.

He knew she was going to be trouble. But there was time for that later. "We will find a job for you that you will love. I promise."

"Why couldn't I just work for you?"

He shot her a quick glance. When he found her studying his face he rapidly turned his eyes back to the fruit.

"You're almost always here in town. It's almost as if you live here. I know your office is in Los Angeles, but you could use someone in Washington. I mean, it would be very convenient for you, wouldn't it?"

He nibbled at a piece of pineapple and said nothing. "Well, it would, wouldn't it?"

When he finally looked up at her, she smiled. A sexual ether seemed to float across the hills and valleys of her body under the blankets like mustard gas on a battlefield. Her hand drifted toward him but the plate was in the way.

Proffit felt the urge. But thankfully at his age it took a while to recharge the batteries. Time for new tactics. "I meant to ask you, one of the lawyers handling Olinda's estate at the firm asked me if she kept a spare key to her house anywhere at the office."

"You mean her place in Georgetown?" said Vicki.

"Yeah. She didn't own any other property, did she?"

"No. She stayed in town almost every weekend, unless she was traveling on business. A key, let me think. . . ." Preebles put a finger to her lips, the long shapely nail against the red gloss of her lips a little smeared from their recent antics.

"We've looked but haven't found one," said Proffit. "They need to gain access in order to inventory the property at the house."

"Of course. I understand. If she had one, it would be in the big partner's desk. The oak antique against the wall in her office."

"We've looked there. We didn't find anything."

"You wouldn't," said Preebles. "There are hidden compartments all over that thing. It's like one of those Chinese puzzle boxes. You know, the kind with sliding wooden compartments and hidden drawers."

"Yeah," said Proffit. "I had one of those when I was a kid."

"Anything she didn't want you to find she put in that desk."

"Really?"

"Emm. You know you need a secretary," she said. "Why can't you just assign me to do that? After all, you are the boss," she said.

"You've seen these compartments?"

"I have."

"How many are there?"

"I didn't count them."

"How big are they?"

"Big enough for a key," she said.

"But not papers?"

"I thought you were looking for a key?"

He gave her a look as if to say, "Stop with the bullshit."

"I suppose it would depend," she said.

"On what?"

"On the form these papers were in."

He looked at her, a big question mark.

She chose not to read it. "Tell me you don't need your own personal secretary and I'll stop bugging you." She stirred under the blankets and rolled away from him as if she were about to get up.

"OK, I could probably use a secretary," said Proffit. "I admit it."

She stopped with one naked thigh already out from under the covers, settled back down, looked over and gave him the smile of victory. "If the papers were on a thumb drive they'd easily fit in one of the little hidey-holes in that desk."

"Did she use a thumb drive?"

Preebles nodded. "She wore it on a lanyard around her neck, hanging down her top where you couldn't see it. I saw her hide it in the desk on a few occasions when she was dressed in something where she couldn't conceal it in her clothing. But never overnight and never when she left the office."

"How do you know?"

"Because I checked," said Preebles. "That's why you hired me, wasn't it?"

He nodded.

"I noticed that she used it mostly after certain phone calls and never on the office line. Only her cell phone. She'd talk and then take it off from around her neck, plug it into her computer, save whatever it was she was typing to the thumb drive. Then she'd take the drive out of the machine and put it back around her neck. Mostly it was like columns of numbers. She never let the little drive out of her sight. I assume it probably went up in the flames with her out in California," said Preebles.

Proffit couldn't afford to make that assumption. "How is it that she allowed you to see all this?"

"She didn't know I was looking."

"What were you doing, hiding under her desk?"

"On the bookshelf behind her," said Preebles. "What they call a pinhole camera. It's wireless. They sell them at the spy shop here in Washington. It showed up in a little box in the upper right-hand corner of the monitor to my computer outside her office. It had pretty good resolution. If you expanded to the full screen you could read the monitor on her computer. But I didn't want anybody to catch me doing it."

"Good thought," said Proffit. She'd gone way beyond the call of duty.

"The camera toggled on and off with one key on my keyboard. Anybody came by I just turned it off and the little box on my screen disappeared. I removed the camera the minute I found out she was dead."

"Did this camera have a tape?"

"I couldn't afford it," said Preebles. "Those get really expensive."

"I can imagine. Let me ask you a question. Do you know how to get into all the little hidden places in that desk?"

She propped herself up on one arm. "I think I could remember. I know I could if I was your personal assistant in the Washington office. You need my eyes and ears. You know you do." She plucked one of the large strawberries from the platter and dragged it lasciviously across her nipple, breaking into a smile and then giggling a little as she did it.

He could have the desk dragged out to a medical office somewhere and have it x-rayed if he had to. And then take a chainsaw to it. He made a mental note to get a safe with double locks installed in his D.C. office and have it swept for bugs hourly before he allowed Preebles anywhere near the place.

Nine

Herman called me. He found the place. The gentlemen's club is in a building in a commercial area a few blocks in from the pier at Ocean Beach, what is left of the amusements from the old boardwalk era.

As I cruise slowly down the main drag, its denizens are T-shirt shops and souvenir stands. An antique cotton candy machine on wheels sits forlornly chained to the side of a building in front of a taffy shop. Late afternoon, middle of the week, most of the tourist haunts are closed.

The only place showing signs of life is a microbrewery doing a brisk business, people grabbing a cold one on the way home from work. All the storefront little businesses are neatly painted, mostly pastel colors, some of them with sparkling awnings out front. What you would think of as an upscale California beach community. I know the area. There are million-dollar homes just a few blocks away.

To the naked eye the gentlemen's club is invisible. According to what Herman told me on the phone it lurks in a back alley under a sign posing as DARKSTONE'S BAR AND GRILL with an arrow pointing up a flight of stairs.

I pull into one of the diagonal parking spaces out on the street. I'm driving my old Jeep, a 1980s vintage Wrangler that I've stored for years. I use it for work from time to time just to keep the engine alive. I've had it since before Sarah was born. I retain it for sentiment as much as anything else. A time machine for going back to the past whenever I'm behind the wheel, if only for a brief illusion.

Home is not the same anymore. Joselyn and I have been living together for more than a year. She has been away on a project in Europe for two months now, her job with the Gideon Quest Foundation. During a recent excursion up north, she suffered a traumatic incident; I nearly lost her. She fell under the influence of a man who was suffering from mental war wounds and who very nearly took her life. She is recovering, but we are still working to restore our relationship. It was difficult for me to see her go, but it was necessary to give her some space as part of the process of recovery. I'm looking forward to her getting back. Joss, like me, is also a lawyer, but one who left her practice to do good works—in this case as director of a foundation dedicated to the nonproliferation of weapons of mass destruction. After my being alone for years, my wife deceased, the Fates brought Joss and me together while the tensions of a world gone crazy seem to keep us apart. I am missing her and wishing she were here. We keep in touch on Skype.

Sarah is gone, no longer living near me, now on her own up in Los Angeles. She has a new job, a career, and friends. I see her only occasionally on weekends. She is busy with her own life, getting on, and getting away. She's had enough of my law practice and the problems that it caused in our lives. I can't say that I blame her. Growing up without a mother—Nikki died of cancer when Sarah was young—was only part of it. Having to hide out from a psychotic named Liquida, a killer hired by the Mexican cartels who crossed my path like a black cat, the result of my practice, was enough to send Sarah packing.

She has no interest in being a lawyer or anywhere near a courtroom. I have at least cured her of that. I have often wondered why it is that children, when they come of age, often shy away from what their parents do for a living. The tailor's son won't make clothes and the banker's boy wants to be a doctor.

A few of Sarah's friends have come to me asking for letters of support to law schools. Of course, when they've asked me about a career in law, I do what every other lawyer does. I lie. What others perceive as lucrative and glamorous, your own kid sees up close for what it is, rancorous, dispute-ridden, and sometimes dangerous. They should ask Sarah. Criminal law is largely long hours, seedy clients, uncertain pay, and short-tempered judges, the stuff of which ulcers are made. How do you tell that to some bright-eyed grad with sufficient grades to get into Stanford? You don't want to pop their balloon with the barbed stinger of cynicism. Listen, kid, the only reason the system tolerates you at all is that it grinds on and could not grind without you. Like the tango, human dispute is impossible without at least two to argue. The criminal defense lawyer's sole claim to existence.

Suddenly, a shadow from the other side of the car. Herman taps on the window. I reach over and unlock the door. He slips into the passenger seat and closes the door behind him.

"The place is upstairs." Herman points down the street toward a line of buildings on the other side. "It's hopping," he says. He's already checked it out. "Place is like an old speakeasy. You don't see or hear a thing 'til you get inside. Then they got a subwoofer give you a nosebleed," he says.

"Late on a weekday in the afternoon I can't imagine they'd be doing that much business."

"Guess again," says Herman. "Lotta pent-up libido in this town. Not what it used to be when the navy was young." Herman is right. San Diego used to be a military town, mostly navy and marines. At one time, I am told, the shore patrol combed the bars and clubs downtown like they owned them. But that was decades past. Whoever is running Darkstone's Bar and Grill is probably paying somebody to look the other way.

"Did you have any trouble getting in?" I ask.

Herman shook his head. "As long as you pay the cover, they open the door," he says. "Top of the stairs they got a steel door thick as a safe, speaker system, and a camera. You talk nice, they let you in. Inside's like an air lock. Once the door closes, they own you. They frisk you with a metal wand, check your ID, look you up and down and see if they smell a cop. If not, you pay and they let you in."

"How much?"

"That's the rub," says Herman. "A hundred bills."

I look at him in disbelief.

"They take a credit card," he says. "I guess they figure, you can pay, you must be a gentleman. You get two drinks and you can talk to the girls. Anything more, the sky's gonna be the limit," he says. "I'm only guessin', of course." He smiles at me as he says it.

"You're sure she works there?" I am talking about the girl we know as Ben, the one who invited Alex Ives to the party and the fiery crash afterward that he can't remember.

"Yeah. I talked to one of the girls who works there, showed her the picture I got from the tattoo shop owner, and the gal ID'ed her. Says her name is Crystal. Stage name, of course. None of them use their real names at work. Said Crystal works the evening shift, four to whenever things go slack. They try to catch the guys going home from work. Noon until two or three in the afternoon, and then four thirty until closing."

I look at my watch. It's twenty past four. "She should be there," I say.

"Give her a few more minutes," says Herman. "If the shift starts at four thirty, she's probably backstage getting ready. Don't wanna appear too anxious. I already rented a room at the hotel down the street." He points.

I see the blue neon sign.

"Room number seven." He hands me the key. "We need a quiet place to get her to talk."

I take his lead on this. Herman is streetwise. He certainly has more experience in this realm than I do. We sit in the car.

"We need to think this out. What we're going to do," I say. "Why don't *you* approach her, figure out how to get her to the room. Once she's inside we can both talk to her."

"She's more likely to go with you. Oversize black guy with a shiny shaved dome is more likely to put her on edge."

"Statistics show that most serial killers are middle-aged white guys."

"Be that as it may," says Herman. "You keep the key. We approach her inside the club, start talking about Ives and the accident, she's liable to wanna go to the ladies' room, powder her nose," says Herman, "and disappear. That's if things go well."

Herman gives me a briefing on what the place looks like inside, dark with a lot of mirrors, colored smoke, and laser lights. Cocktail tables and booths with a bar along the far wall. An elevated stage with a pole out front for dancing.

"I didn't see any muscle. Nothing at the door. But you can be sure there'll be some," he says. "Chances are if there are problems they won't be calling the cops."

"You're saying a frontal assault is not the height of prudence."

"I don't know about Prudence, whoever she is, but if the one we know as Ben makes a stink it could get damn ugly," says Herman. "We'll be up to our armpits in bulging bouncers, or worse, the business end of a sawed-off shotgun."

Herman is thinking we need to get her on neutral turf before we start to talk about the business at hand, and then we pay her for the information, her time and trouble. He's suggesting we go in separately so they don't know we're together. Sit at separate tables. That way we don't overwhelm her.

"Makes sense. One thing bothers me, though," I tell him. "We're assuming that the minute we tell the cops that we have a witness who can put him at the party and that she was paid to do it, they'll drop the charges on Ives."

"It's what we're hoping," says Herman. "Makes sense to me."

"Yeah, but you're not a prosecutor. If they find out we paid the girl for the information, and they will find out, they're going to say we paid her to lie. To give Alex an out. If they force us to trial on a reckless charge, vehicular manslaughter, I put her on the stand, the first thing the D.A.'s gonna ask is whether we gave her anything in return for her testimony. They'll impeach the hell out of her. That and the fact we found her working in a strip club and I offered to hire her for sex to get her to the hotel. They'll impeach both of us. Her testimony won't be worth a damn and I'll be wearing a scarlet letter branded across my forehead during closing argument."

"You're the lawyer," says Herman. "But what other alternative do we have?"

Herman has me there. The cops have no evidence of drugs in Ives's system, yet he can't remember anything and he was clearly unconscious at the scene and for some time after. If we put our own medical expert on the stand to tell the jury what we already know, there is only one set of drugs we know of that causes memory loss like this and disappears from the bloodstream that fast—the date rape drugs. How are these normally used in criminal cases? Dropped into one drink, what Ives said he had, without the drinker's knowledge. The police have no way to explain an accident that killed a prominent lawyer. We hand them the answer. It wasn't a DUI. Our client was drugged against his will. Used as cover for a murder. That bumps it all up. A much bigger case for them. "Her testimony works. I just don't like the idea that we're paying her."

"You can ask her to testify out of the goodness of her heart," he says, "but I doubt it's gonna work."

He's right. I look at my watch. "Let's do it."

Ten

"OK, what do we have?"

"Are you on a secure line?"

"No. So let's keep it cryptic."

"We have overlapping objects on the matrix. One of them in a vehicle outside. He was joined by someone else about six minutes ago. Right now the two of them are just sitting there. The girl is in the building."

"How close?"

"Less than eighty meters."

The man gripped the tarnished eagle and moved his hand slowly over the smooth oxidized surface of the cane's handle as he thought. "It could just be a coincidence," he said.

"Possible, but not likely."

The loose ends were multiplying. "Any idea who the other man is in the vehicle?"

"We're working on it. Nothing yet."

"How much time do we have?"

"We're not sure. Depends when she leaves and where she goes. Assuming her usual ride, her boyfriend, we are four by four. Positive nav system is breachable." In a word they were ready to go. "What do you want to do?"

The Tarnished Eagle thought for a moment. "We sit tight and wait. Don't do anything until you clear it here. If she exits the building, I want to know it. Understood?"

"Yes."

"If either of them make any effort at contact, call me at this number. Do we have a cage over the twitter, hers and his?"

"Affirmative."

This meant that if either of them tried to contact the other by cell phone, the call would be picked up and recorded. There was no reason to believe that either of them had the other's cell phone number, or that they had ever communicated or met. Still, how did they find her? It hit him like a bolt out of the blue. "If you have a cage up, you have his number?"

"Correct."

"Is he on the grid now?"

"Negative."

"Can you turn him on?"

"Just a moment." Several seconds passed. "Yes. We have him."

"Copy it. Everything. Even if it's not clear, copy it all!"

"Copying now."

"When you're done, stream it through. You know the drill. And give me a transcript."

The ability to turn on a cell phone without the owner's knowledge or consent was old technology. It had been used by the FBI to bring down members of the Genovese crime family more than a decade earlier. It was the reason heads of state do not carry cell phones and why they are often stripped from members of their entourage as well. It was a modern-day fact of life. If you carried a cell phone with a live battery, you were wired for sound, and anybody with the right hardware could listen in, not just to phone calls but to any face-to-face conversations as well. Anything within earshot of the phone could be recorded. Carrying a live cell phone was the electronic equivalent of wearing a bug.

The place is everything Herman described and more. I am seated at a table in the middle of the room up nearly to my waist in purple smoke. This comes from a machine that heats glycol mixed with water, producing a thick vapor. It is blown like a ground-hugging fog over the stage until it spills down and piles up on the floor like bilious clouds of melted purple marshmallow. This is occasionally pierced by laser lights that scatter in the fog like bullets, every color of the rainbow.

It is crowded. The pounding music vibrates off the walls, rattling the ice in my drink as I finger the tumbler on the table.

Men are piled up against the bar at the other side of the room trying to get more libation, many of them rowdy, half gassed and working toward a full tank.

So far I see no sign of the woman we know as Ben, Crystal to her friends here. Though with this mob it's hard to tell. Every once in a while I glance at Herman, who is seated at one of the booths higher up against the back wall where he can get a more panoramic view while he keeps one eye on my table. He scans the room and shakes his head. He doesn't see her either.

Across the room a bunch of young guys in an overly festive mood seem to be vying for top honors, most obnoxious group in the house. I am guessing it's an office party.

One of them pulls his tie up around his head and wears it like a sweatband. Suddenly this becomes the craze. It is cloned among his followers until everyone has their tie draped down over their right ear like some new fraternal order. Who says people aren't sheep?

They compete with each other, ordering drinks, making lewd gestures, shouting until it reaches a crescendo in the contest to see who can become Emperor Odious. You could float a boat on the drinks they spill. The place seems to have a flexible definition of the term *gentlemen*. They are shouting and screaming at the top of their lungs just to be heard over the sound system. By morning, if they keep it up, one of them will be naked and the others will be missing their voice boxes. It is what passes for a good time among the young and stupid.

I glance back at Herman. Still no sign.

A few of the more sober types wait in ambush as the young women filter out from behind a curtain at the other side of the room.

The sign above the curtain reads EMPLOYEES ONLY— out of bounds, sanctuary for the women if they fall into clutches and are able to make it that far.

New customers keep coming through the door. I am surprised by the number of people already here, and it's still early. A quarter to five and the place is two-thirds full. If things continue like this, by ten o'clock it will be a human press.

A few of the men sitting at tables by themselves appear to be wallflowers. Though I suspect they might say the same thing about me. Herman clearly has more confidence in me than I do. In this scene, I exhibit the same shy reluctance I did in high school. It's not my kind of place and I begin to wonder if I can pull it off, catch her interest long enough to get outside.

Others appear to be regulars who have already staked claims. The girls cuddle up to them in the booths. One of them takes a seat on a guy's lap, wearing a short tight skirt that leaves little to the imagination, and with no preliminaries, she starts to move to the gyrations of the music.

There is a loud recorded drum roll from the PA system and a husky male voice announces: "Give a warm welcome to Carlotta, let's hear it." A few stuttering claps and a wolf whistle later, a girl with dark hair and a costume that is mostly a mirage from the designer's memory enters the stage, leg first, through a slit in the curtain. She moves like a snake charmer, her feet and lower legs disappearing in the fog that spills from the stage. I wonder what the OSHA claim would look like if she sucks this crap into her lungs. Worse, I begin to wonder what my claim might be if I sit here much longer. That is when I see her.

She enters the room through the curtain on the other side of the raised stage. There is no missing her. Even in the dim light with the fog and the disorientation from the laser lights, Ben stands out. Slender, petite, and with all the feline curves that nature designed for a sexual lure, to any guy with good vision, her form alone would be enough to stun sound judgment and put his libido on steroids. Your average caveman would have her by the hair dragging her back to his den before you could say "beat my time." Two of the more rowdy guys from the party try to corral her. She sidesteps them and keeps going. Apparently she's not into head ties.

I stand up, wave my arms, and call the waiter over. He sees me but doesn't move. I hold up some green, two crisp twenties to get his attention, and he skates toward me through the fog like a star in the Ice Capades. "That girl over there. I think her name is Crystal. I'd like to buy her a drink."

"Oh, yes, sir. A lovely girl. Good choice." He says it like I'm ordering vintage wine as he snatches the twenties from my fingers.

Before he can move, I see some guy on the other side of the stage grab her by the arm and start to hustle her off to his table. The only thing slowing him down is his staggering gait. I wonder if he's with the wedding party. I look to the waiter. "It's worth a hundred to you if you can get her away from him and over here," I tell him.

"Yes, sir. Let me see what I can do, sir."

"And open a tab for me."

"I will do that immediately."

"After you get the girl," I tell him.

"Yes, sir. Of course, sir." He is gone in a servile flash.

I glance back at Herman. He gives me a shrug with one shoulder, then quickly nods toward the other side of the room. By the time I look back the waiter has arrived at her table. She is now seated as he whispers in her ear. Slowly she rises from her chair and looks my way. Before she can move, the drunk is up grabbing at her arm, haggling with the waiter. He reaches for his wallet. What started out as a well-laid plan is turning into a meat auction with the girl caught in the middle. The customer has hold of one of her arms, the waiter has the other, each of them pulling in a different direction as if she is a wishbone.

I swing around to look at Herman, who turns both palms up as if to say, "What can we do?"

The girl has a panicked look, embarrassed and at the same time scared. It's a stalemate. She appears stuck in limbo. The waiter puts his free hand up against the customer's chest and gently pushes until gravity takes hold. The drunk stumbles backward toward his chair, releasing her arm as he goes in order to protect himself as he falls. He lands in the chair. Before he can assemble his legs into a coherent force to rise once more, the waiter has his prey in tow and is headed back to my table. What a hundred bucks will do.

"Ms. Crystal, this gentleman would like to buy you a drink."

I'm on my feet. "Please, join me. My name is Paul. Have a seat." I pull the chair out for her and she settles gently onto it like a hummingbird on a perch. She is wearing a tight micro-mini dress that climbs precariously up her shapely thigh as she crosses one leg over the other.

I have one eye on the drunk, who finally manages to get up. He is looking around on the floor as if maybe he's dropped his wallet before he realizes it's in his hand. He turns in a complete circle and very nearly returns to his chair before he remembers why he got up in the first place. He stands there staring at my table, a monument to drunk indignation, then takes a couple of tentative steps. From the look of it, his legs are not entirely sure they each have the same destination.

"What would you like to drink?" The waiter looks first to her. He has excellent peripheral vision. He sees the man stumbling this way. Before she can speak, the waiter raises one hand and flashes a bright laser pointer toward the mirror behind the bar. He flashes it one more time and instantly two guys in black T-shirts, heavy-chested bouncers, come out from an area behind the bar. Like heat-seeking missiles they home in on the drunk staggering this way.

The girl says something to the waiter, but I don't hear it. I assume she's ordered a drink. She may have ordered the club's entire inventory of liquor for all I know. At the moment, my attention is drawn to the action on the other side of the room. The stumbling inebriate is scooped off his feet from behind. From the look of astonishment on his face, he seems to be questioning how it is that he can suddenly fly. He is carried like a stack of straw overhead and then soundlessly and within seconds disappears through a dark door that, for all I know, could lead to a coal bin on the other side of the room. For a moment I wonder if he might show up in Shanghai in a few months working cargo on some hobo-ridden, rusted-out freighter. I make a mental note not to find out.

None of this is lost on the Solemn Order of Head Ties, who suddenly temper their volume. A guy with his pants down quickly pulls them up, his gaze still fixed on the dark door of doom.

"And you, sir?" The waiter looks at me.

"What?"

"Would you like another drink?"

"Oh, ah, I'll just have another club soda—make that with a twist of lime this time," I tell him. "Oh, and a little something for you," I say. I palm him a scrunched-up hundred-dollar bill.

"Oh, thank you, sir! Much appreciated."

The move is not wasted on the girl, who takes in every detail and seems to smell the money from the scent still on my hand. "What is it that you do for a living?" she asks.

"I'm in business. I live in Omaha and I own a company that manufactures fertilizer." And at the moment I'm just full of bullshit. "My name is Warren. . . ."

"I thought you said your name was Paul?"

"Oh, ah, Paul Warren," I tell her. One thing is clear. She's going to need a lot more to drink if this is going to work. And I will have to insist on full rations, nothing watered down.

Ben, Crystal, whatever her name is, is absolutely knock-'em-dead gorgeous. Even if I stay sober, she is going to be a challenge. Alex was right. She is ether in the flesh, the stuff of which young men's dreams are made. She flashes a smile that is deadly, so stunningly beautiful that I want to stare, but I don't allow myself. I exercise restraint. I am here on business. I avert my eyes, look at something else, the candle on the table, the naked woman on the stage. I pretend to be cool. Suddenly I find myself sneaking a glance. She turns and catches me and I blush. What is worse, she knows it and it doesn't faze her. This should not surprise me. She has no doubt lived her entire life with this affliction. The usual dazed reaction from every paralyzed male she meets. She sizes me up from across the table.

"What brings you here tonight?" she asks.

"You do." My first truthful statement.

"Now I know you're lying." She issues a smile, generating enough heat to melt the male ego. "How did you find out about this place?"

"A friend told me."

"First time here?"

"First time."

"Bet it won't be your last."

"I'm not a gambler," I tell her. "But if I were, I'd never be fool enough to let you take my money on that wager."

"How sweet. You speak well, and so quickly," she says. "Words seem to come easily to you. Is that an essential skill in the fertilizer business?"

"Only if you want to sell it," I tell her.

The waiter brings our drinks, mine in a tumbler, hers in a mini cocktail glass not much bigger than a thimble. We tap the glass rims and two seconds later hers is gone. I can hear the cash register ringing over at the bar.

"Might I suggest a bottle of champagne?" says the waiter. "We have some excellent vintages." He smells a sucker on a roll.

"I'll bet you do," I tell him. "Why not? And two big glasses this time."

Eleven

Ana Agirre stepped off the plane, cleared immigration and customs, collected her bags along with a rental car, and was on her way headed south from LAX in less than an hour. She took a reading from her laptop before leaving the rental car lot using a portable hot spot she purchased at the airport. It worked off a 4G cellular signal and gave her access to portable Wi-Fi while she was in the States.

Once she located what she was looking for, she tuned the car's GPS to home in on an address just south of Mission Bay, a place called Ocean Beach. This was the location where the signal was coming from. They had moved a few miles since the earlier reading she had taken just before leaving Amsterdam on her connecting flight across the Atlantic. They were up to something. She didn't know what.

Each time they turned on the small satellite antenna connected to Ana's laptop, the one they were supposedly field-testing, it sent an encrypted signal from the antenna to the desired navigation satellite high in the sky overhead. It was like an electronic handshake between the computer's software and the navigation system. The software not only unlocked the vehicle's navigation and computer systems but also left data at a little-used online site operated by the French military to which Ana had access. It was former French military technicians turned high-tech mercenaries who had designed and built the system for her who had told her about this. The online data allowed her to track the location of the antenna on the ground through GPS coordinates. She could then track this with precision using Google Earth.

They had used her software in the desert east of town three weeks earlier. Ana knew this not only because she had read the news accounts, but because she had the tracking data to prove it. Now she was getting antsy. She wanted to know why the equipment hadn't been returned to the makers. She called the number the man had given her over the phone only to be told via recording that the number was disconnected. She wanted her stuff back and she wanted it now. She had a contract to complete. Her clients were getting nervous.

Twelve hundred dollars and two bottles of champagne later she isn't even showing signs of mild inebriation, while the end of my nose feels like it belongs to somebody else. Built like a bird weighing maybe a hundred and ten pounds, the girl who calls herself Crystal on the job and Ben on the street is showing all the signs of being able to drink me under the table. So I cut to the chase.

"You know, I was wondering if you might be up to a private party tonight?"

"And I was wondering if you were ever going to ask?" she says. "We can have them send another bottle of champagne upstairs."

"Oh, not here," I tell her. "I was thinking we could do it back at my hotel where we can relax."

"You were, were you?"

I nod and smile.

"Aren't you the fast worker? I'm afraid that won't be possible," she says. "If we're going to party in private, it would have to be here. It's perfectly safe."

"Yes, but . . ."

"I'm sorry. I don't go out. Not on a first date," she says.

"Next you'll be telling me that you don't kiss on a first date."

She laughs. "That all depends where you want it," she says.

"I want it in my hotel room," I tell her.

"I'm sorry. That's just not possible." She says it with a tone of finality. I don't want her to get up and walk.

"You mean they won't let you?"

"It's not that."

Good! At least it's not a house rule, something she can't violate.

"Then what is it?"

"It's just that I don't know you that well."

"What's to know?"

"For one thing, how do I know you're not a cop?" she says.

"Have you ever known a cop to come in here, under-cover, I mean?"

She shakes her head. "Not yet, at least. But then, there's always a first time," she says.

"Raise my right hand and hope to die," I tell her. I put up my left.

"I don't think you're really that drunk." She reads me like a book.

"Give me another bottle and I'll show you."

She turns toward the waiter.

"Let's do it in my room," I say. "I'll make it worth your while." The final resort.

"How much?" she says.

I take a deep breath. "Five hundred," I tell her. "Besides, how do I know *you're* not a cop?"

"If I were, I would be arresting you right now," she tells me.

The thought has never even entered my mind until this moment. What if she were working undercover? Stranger things have happened. Judges have been defrocked and lawyers pilloried for what I have just done, conversed about sex and money in the same sentence.

"You think I'm a cop, you can search me, see if you can find a badge."

"Sounds like fun." I try to keep her talking.

"But not for five hundred," she says. "For that we can go upstairs. If we are going to go to your room, I'll need more than that." The door is open, if only a crack. "Besides, if I leave early I have to buy my way out. The house will fine me. I have to pay them."

"How much?"

"Two hundred and fifty," she says.

"So how much do you need?"

"To go to your hotel room?"

I nod.

"Fifteen hundred." She says it without batting an eye, the price she already had fixed in her mind probably from the moment she sat down. She looks me up and down and figures from my pained expression that it's a no-go. "It was nice to have met you," she says, and starts to get up.

"No need to run away," I tell her.

"Time is money," she says.

I don't want her walking away. I need to find out what she knows. "Twelve-fifty!" I blurt it out so loudly that the guy at the next table hears me, whips around, gives me a smirk, and says, "Go for it!" He looks at her with lust in his eyes and licks his chops.

I wonder if I've just screwed the pooch. I lower my voice an octave. "You clear a cool thousand." My attempt at reason comes off sounding desperate, Milquetoast the bookkeeper sporting a green shade with a pencil behind his ear.

"I knew you weren't that drunk." She thinks about it. "Do you have a room?"

Maybe she likes vulnerable guys.

"I do. Down the street, on the beach. Place with the blue neon sign, says Hotel. Next to the tattoo shop."

"I know the place. I can meet you there," she says. "Give me a few minutes."

"And what if you don't show up?" I ask.

"Then you get to take a cold shower." She smiles.

"OK." I look at my watch. "See you in half an hour." I start to get up from the chair.

"Didn't you forget something?" She looks at me with a deadpan expression, like Bacall asking me if I know how to whistle.

"What's that?"

"Your room number," she says. "Unless you want me to knock on all the doors."

"Room number seven." The room Herman already rented in hopes we'd get lucky.

She stands. The top of her head doesn't quite reach my shoulder even in her platform spiked heels. She comes in close and gives me a soft kiss on the cheek, like the wings of a butterfly flicking my skin. Her hand on mine. There is a reason this stuff is against the law. I can smell her perfume, more intoxicating than the champagne. I open my eyes and all I see is her back, sensual curves and shapely legs as she floats away from me through ankle-deep fog on seven-inch heels.

This time he rang her at home, the brownstone in Georgetown. She picked it up and recognized his voice instantly, the chill up her spine, the hound from hell.

"I thought we weren't doing this anymore, conversing on the phone." It was after nine in the evening. Maya Grimes was in no mood to be jerked around. She'd had a tough day on the Hill. Her smile muscles ached from greeting people she disliked.

"As I recall, that was one of your rules, not mine," said the Eagle.

"What is it this time?"

"Got another job for you."

"Can't it wait until tomorrow?"

"No."

"Fine."

"I want you to call the White House," he said. "Talk to some people. The appointments section, judicial nominations. You know lots of people there."

"Go on," she said.

"There's two slots open, an open seat on the Federal District Court, Southern District, your state, as well as the Ninth Circuit Court of Appeals in San Francisco. I want you to put a bug in somebody's ear. Do it first thing tomorrow morning. Tell 'em you're pushing two candidates, one for each position. And as far as you're concerned, they're the only people for the jobs."

"Who are they?"

"I'll give you the names later."

"I can't tell them I'm supporting people and then refuse to give them the names."

"Sure you can. You're a US Senator. You can do anything you want. Tell them if they try to nominate anyone to fill either spot you'll use your office to stand in the way. You'll give them the names as soon as your staff is finished checking the candidates out. Tell 'em it could take a while."

"Senatorial privilege," said Grimes.

"You got it."

"You can't just leave these positions open. The one on the Ninth Circuit already has a short list of qualified candidates approved by the ABA, the American Bar Association."

"They have their criteria, I have mine," said the Eagle.

"I've already committed," said Grimes.

"Tell them you've changed your mind. Woman's prerogative."

"The White House will think I'm crazy."

"Tell them you're going through a change of life. I don't care what you tell them, just do it." He slammed the phone down in her ear.

What the Eagle wanted was to keep the positions vacant so he could use them when the time came. Under the ritual of senatorial privilege, the senior home state senator could effectively blackball a nomination to the federal courts in his or her own state. Or, as in the case of the Ninth Circuit, block any candidate coming from that state and then wheel and deal with other members of the Senate to get what he or she wanted. It was an unholy practice. But even members who didn't like it had to go along, part of being in the club.

Because the judicial nominations required Senate confirmation before they became final lifetime appointments, a hearing would never be set unless the candidate had the blessing of the state's senior senator. It was a corrupt custom dating back eons and had been used more than once to shake candidates or their supporters down for money, or to exact favors from other politicians and the White House.

The Eagle knew that if Grimes used her muscle, she could keep both positions vacant indefinitely. It was nice owning your own US senator. The Eagle possessed a stable of them, like racehorses, and with a single phone call he could work any one of them into an instant lather.

Twelve

The Tarnished Eagle wished he was in the bar, the private club with the lawyer and the girl. At least he could have had a drink. He could have used one, but there was no time for that now.

"Do we know what they talked about?"

"If I had to guess, I'd say he was trying for a date. We lost at least half, maybe sixty percent to background noise." The transcript was going to have major holes, train loads of blank white space labeled "Unintelligible." The gain on the mic from the lawyer's cell phone simply couldn't handle the constant blast of the bass from the music.

"Why couldn't they have met in a library?" said the Eagle.

"He's out of the building." The voice at the other end suddenly came alive.

"Where is he headed?"

"Hold on. Looks like the other man has joined him out in front of the building. They are both headed back toward the car. They've crossed the street. Yes, they're back in the car."

"Do we have sufficient assets to track them?"

"Got it covered."

"Are they moving?"

"Not yet."

"Keep an eye on them. Where is the girl?"

"One second. Looks like they're on the move, backing up."

"Where's the girl?"

The Eagle could hear voices conferring at the other end of the line.

"We think she's still inside."

"What do you mean, YOU THINK?"

More panicked voices at the other end. "No. No. She's inside." This seemed to be the consensus.

"Are you sure?"

"That is confirmed. Feet on the ground inside. She is still there."

The Eagle settled down. Maybe she had already told them what it was they wanted to know. At least she hadn't left the building with them. He thought for a moment and considered the options. Then again, maybe that wouldn't be so bad. "What do we have on the man's vehicle?"

"Plate number, aerial profile. Not to worry, we have it covered."

"That's not what I meant," said the Eagle. How old is it?" He was thinking about the target possibilities.

There was a delay at the other end. They were gathering the information. "That's a negative," said the other man. "Cannot be used."

The lawyer's car was too old. Their man on the ground had checked it out while the two occupants were in the club. Just his luck. More than a million lawyers in the country and they had to find the one riding around in a dinosaur.

"We could try to hijack a cue ball," said the voice from the other end. "That is, if they try to use his ride. But that is problematic."

"You think?" Sarcasm dripped from the Eagle's voice.

What the man at the other end was talking about was to electronically hijack another car or preferably a large late-model truck and use it like a missile to destroy the target vehicle.

"As I recall, that didn't work very well last time."

"We got the target."

"You got half a target. The reason we're doing the drill over again," said the Eagle.

"Not our fault."

"OK! All right!" said the Eagle. "Let's not be splitting hairs on an open line."

"We've got movement. The vehicle," said the man on the phone. "Moving slowly, westerly direction. Away from the building. They do not appear to be in a hurry."

"Any sign of the girl?" asked the Eagle.

"No. One moment." Seconds went by, almost half a minute.

"Talk to me," said the Eagle.

"They've stopped again. Half a block down heading west, stopped at the intersection. Looks as if they're not exactly sure . . . hold on. They turned left and picked up speed. Wait a second."

"What is it?"

"They pulled into a parking lot."

"Where?" said the Eagle. He was getting too old for this. The stress, the long days, it was taking a toll.

"One moment." More seconds passed.

"It's a motel."

"Damn it!"

"One of them is out of the vehicle, headed toward the front of the building. Looks like he's gone inside."

The Eagle knew it. They had set up a meeting. He wondered how much the lawyer already knew. A transcript with more holes than Swiss cheese, she could have told him anything inside that club. The girl was likely to remember him, right down to his silver-handled cane. She had commented on it, the fact that she'd never dated someone who carried a cane before. She called it "elegant." He wondered if she was putting him on or putting him down. What was an old man like him doing in a club like this? Business, if the truth be told. Champagne and a room upstairs, conversation and money changing hands. Services rendered, but not the usual kind. Sweet girl, and bright. She didn't miss a trick.

"Both men have now exited the vehicle and entered the motel. What do you want to do?" The voice at the other end of the phone roused him and set the adrenaline flowing again.

"Just hang tight. Keep an eye on them and call me the minute the girl leaves the other building. Do we know where her ride is?"

"One moment." There was a delay. He could hear voices in the background over the line. "The driver is on the road, just exiting I-5, en route."

"Headed her way?"

"That's affirmative."

All the pieces suddenly snapped into place. They were waiting for her at the motel. She called her ride and, depending on what they told her, how much she knew, she was either getting ready to meet with them or getting ready to run.

What he couldn't be sure of was how much she knew. She had very quick eyes and they seemed to be everywhere all at once, spilling over you like a flood. There was little that escaped her. She caught him up in two small lies in the first three minutes of their conversation the one time he met her. That and the fact that the story he gave her about a practical joke being played on a young friend, the prank invitation to a party, had not fooled her. She knew he was lying. There was more to it than that, but she didn't care.

She did it for the money. The mistake was in paying her too much. The high tariff would guarantee that she would remember him, right down to his argyle socks. Still, the cash couldn't be traced.

It was the note and the name he had given her that worried him the most, the name Ives was to use if he got stopped at the door. He told her not to write it down. He gave her the name and asked if she could remember it. She said: "Sure! Just like the Bishop at Canterbury." She might have worked in a strip club, but she'd read a few books and knew how to trigger memory with it.

He worried the instant she said it. For all he knew, she could have been a grad student at the university. He should have checked her out more thoroughly, but it was too late for that.

He wrote the address and a phony cell number out on a slip of paper and told the girl to wait for the kid outside his office at noon. He gave her a photograph so she could recognize him. The address would get him to the party. The name would get him through the door if anyone questioned him.

Now, as the man at the other end of the phone might say, the entire mess had become "very problematic." If the lawyer told her that Ives was used as cover in a killing, her nimble little brain would start turning over all the details. The man who gave her the note: What did he wear? What did he look like? The silver-handled cane. She would certainly remember that. What was on the note? The location of the party. She probably looked at it. Whether she would have committed it to memory was doubtful. But the one thing she was not likely to forget, the name, the one that gave Ives access if he was challenged, that she would remember.

Inside the hotel room I turn on the light, which consists of a single lamp on the nightstand by the bed. Herman pulls the curtains closed and we sit and wait.

I look at my watch. "Twenty minutes if she's on time."

"What did she sound like?" he asks. "She seem scared?"

"No reason to be. I didn't tell her anything."

"What's she like?"

"All business," I tell him.

"So she thinks she's coming here to polish the nob," he says.

"Wasn't my idea," I tell him.

"What you think she's gonna do when she sees me?" he says.

"Run like hell," I tell him. "That's why you're going to be hiding in the bathroom until she and I get through the preliminaries. Once she agrees to talk, I'll introduce you."

Moving headlights flash in the parking lot out front. The sound of gravel under tires.

Herman gets up off the bed and sneaks a tiny peek around the end of the curtains. He watches for a second. I notice the headlights moving around like someone backing into a space across the way. Then they go out. A few seconds pass.

"It's her, I think," says Herman. "Guy in a car. She walked up, started talkin' to him. Maybe a john, I'm not sure." He keeps looking.

"Be careful they don't see you."

I hear a car door slam. A second later the electronic beep and the flash of lights as the doors lock.

"She's comin'," says Herman, "and she ain't alone."

"What?"

"She's got a guy with her. Big dude," he says. He lets loose of the little pinch on the curtain and looks at me. "I'll be in the bathroom if you need me. Good luck." Herman heads into the bathroom, leaves the light off, and closes the door.

I sit there nervously tapping my foot on the carpet waiting for the rap on the door.

"What do you mean, you couldn't get her?" The Eagle was flummoxed.

"We couldn't. She never got in the car." The man at the other end was trying to explain. "She hoofed it," he said, "from the club to the motel. It's only a block. The driver went right to the parking lot. She met him there."

"Son of a bitch," said the Eagle. "Well, it doesn't matter now. They're gonna talk no matter what we do. It's too late to do anything about it." He thought for a moment. "Can you turn on his cell again?"

"I don't know. Depends how much battery is left."

"Well, try! And record it this time. I want one transcript, no copies, and when you're finished, destroy the audio. Is that clear?"

"Yes."

"And when they're done, you finish the operation. No ifs, ands, or buts, and no mistakes this time." The Eagle pushed the button on his cell phone and hung up.

Thirteen

When the knock on the door finally comes, I sputter and end up answering with a voice that sounds like Minnie Mouse. I cough and come down two octaves before I say, "Who is it?"

"Come on now, who do you think it is?" she says.

For a moment I consider sliding the security chain onto the door until I can find out who her friend is. But it probably wouldn't do any good. The door looks like it's made of cardboard. Besides, the chain might put her off, cause her to simply walk away. So I take a deep breath and open it, just a crack. "Hello."

She gives me a studied eye. "You're awful nervous." She is nearly lost in the shadow of the man Herman spied from the window. If I had to guess, I'd say he's about six foot five, sporting an upper body like a bull only with more hair on his chest. This seems to sprout up into a beard on a brooding face that would rival Neptune's. The only thing missing from this picture is the trident. "Aren't you going to invite us in?" she asks.

"Who's your friend?"

"He's my brother," she says.

"Yeah, I can see the family resemblance."

"He just wants to make sure I'm OK. Nothing to worry about," she says. "As soon as he's satisfied that I'm safe he'll wait outside."

"That shouldn't have too much effect on my performance," I tell her.

"Are you going to open up or not?" she says.

I ease the door open.

She smiles and slides around me through the opening and into the room while the guy's eyes scan me up and down like an imaging machine. When he's done with this, the big brown eyeballs do a quick roll around the inside of the room.

"Is he going to do a blood test?" I ask.

"That's not a bad idea." The guy says it with no humor in his voice. He just pushes past me, no ceremony, and heads toward the bathroom, the closed door with Herman on the other side.

"Hold on a second," I say.

He turns and looks at me. "You got a problem?"

"We're all going to have a problem if you open that door," I tell him.

"Is that right?"

"Yes. Just listen to me for a second. My name is Paul Madriani. I'm an attorney. I'm working a case." I reach into the inside pocket of my jacket.

"Keep your hands where I can see 'em," he says.

When my fingers come out they are holding a business card. I hand it to him. He looks at it and then hands it to her.

"Are you with the police?" she asks.

"No. I'm a private defense attorney, criminal cases, but on the other side," I tell her. "The man inside the bathroom is my investigator. We didn't want to scare you off."

"Yeah, right!" says her man.

Herman opens the door and steps out.

As soon as the guy sees him, the big black face staring back at him, he starts to bristle, spitting expletives, racial epithets about people hiding in woodpiles, while he flashes mean looks at Herman and me.

He squares up against Herman, tenses his body and widens his stance over the tactical boots on his feet, neck bowed as if he's readying for combat.

"Calm down! Relax," I tell him. "There is nothing bad going down here."

"Are you packin'?" he asks Herman.

"No."

"Lift your coat. I wanna see."

Herman does it.

The man looks down around Herman's ankles. "Lift 'em."

Herman pulls up his pant legs to show that he has no weapon strapped to his ankles. First one, then the other.

The man turns to me. "You?"

I shake my head. "That's not my gig," I tell him.

He doesn't bother to frisk me.

"What's this about?" she asks.

"We are prepared to pay you," I tell her. "For information."

"Is this about the club?" she asks.

"No."

"What then?"

"Can we close the door?" I look out through the open portal into the parking lot. "I'd rather not have the world looking in."

The guy looks at her. She nods. "Go ahead," he says.

I do it, walk over and close the door. "I admit it's not much of a room. Not a lot of places to make ourselves comfortable," I say, "but take a seat if you can find one."

She settles onto the edge of the bed. The guy remains standing, as does Herman. Contest of the bulls.

I grab a chair, pull it toward the bed, and sit. "About three weeks ago there was an auto accident on a highway out in the desert. A woman was killed. A young man was arrested. He's our client. You don't know his name but you have met him," I tell her.

She doesn't say a thing. She just looks at me, steely eyed, chewing gum.

"You invited him to a party. You gave him a note telling him where this party was to take place and you told him you'd meet him there. But you never showed."

The eyes start to shift and the chewing stops.

"Our client was drugged at this party and he was transported unconscious to the site of the accident." I don't couch it as belief, but fact, leading her to believe that we have more than we do. "The accident itself was staged."

"I don't know what you're talking about." Finally, a denial.

"Our client has identified you by photograph as the person who invited him to the party and who gave him the note with the location. He has said nothing to the police as yet. But if you refuse to cooperate, he'll have no choice."

"I . . ."

"Don't say anything, not yet. Just listen," I tell her. "Our client has also described in particular detail that tattoo on your leg." She looks down over the hem on the bottom of her micro-mini, one hand absently touching her naked thigh. "If you like, we can take the cops and have them talk to the artist who put it there. The man has a photograph of the tattoo with your name on file."

"So what?" she says.

Two bullets and she is still holding up. I am running out of ammunition. "Now if you like, we can take the fingerprints we lifted off the note, the one with the directions to the party, and give those to the police as well." I lie. It's a whopper, but it stops her in her tracks like a dumdum round.

"You know what the cops are going to think?"

She shakes her head rather nervously.

"That you were part of this from the beginning. If the evidence we have is accurate, the victim in this case was murdered."

The M word pushes her over the edge. "I don't know anything about any murder. I didn't drug anybody," she says.

I turn and look at Herman. "I told you so. Herman here believed you were part of it. I told him I didn't think so, that they probably used you just like they used our client. Hired you and didn't tell you a thing. Didn't I, Herman?"

"Got me there," says Herman. "Owe you ten bucks," he says.

By the look of relief on her face she would gladly front him the money for the wager right now. "That's right," she says. "He didn't tell me anything."

"Who?" I ask.

"The man with the cane."

"What was his name?"

"I don't know. He never gave me a name. If he did, I don't remember. Besides, everybody lies about that." She would be an expert on this.

"But he did hire you to deliver the note?"

If I listen closely I can hear the tinkle of crystal as she shatters.

"Yes, but that's all," she says. "He gave me the note and told me who to give it to. He said it was a joke . . ."

"Tell me about him, the man with the cane."

"I don't know. He was maybe sixty, sixty-five, older guy," she says. "Well dressed. Gray hair. He carried this cane, looked silver, you know, on the handle. Some kind of a bird. I don't know. He gave me the note and a picture of this young guy, your client, I guess. I mean, if anything happened, I'm really sorry," she says.

"Go on."

"Well, that's it," she says.

"How much did he pay you?"

She swallows hard enough that I wonder if the gum went down. "I don't remember," she says.

"Maybe if the police ask it might jog your memory."

"All right," she says. "Two thousand . . . twa . . . twenty-five hundred dollars."

Herman whistles. "FedEx is gettin' screwed," he says. "You think maybe their delivery people need shorter skirts?"

"We'll put it in the suggestion box," I tell him. "Where did you meet this guy, the older one with the cane? At the club?"

She nods, quick vertical head movements like the spring-bound head of one of those plastic puppies mounted on a dash.

"How many times did you meet him?"

"Once. Only the one time."

"Upstairs or down?"

She knows what I mean. "We went up into one of the private rooms. He bought some champagne. You have to do that if you're gonna go there."

"Mm-hmm, go on."

"We talked, that's all."

"He gave you the note, the picture of our client, and told you that you could find him where?"

"In front of the building where he worked."

"He gave you that address as well. Did he write it down?"

"No. I knew the place. Big plaza downtown. I shop there sometimes." She stops abruptly, glances toward the ceiling like a lightbulb just exploded and says, "You know, maybe you can get his fingerprints?"

"Whose?"

"The man with the cane," she says. "You know, off the note."

"I'll work on that," I tell her. "Did he say anything else?"

She thought for a moment. "Let's see. He told me to give him the note. Invite him to the party. Tell him I would meet him there." She ticks them off with her fingers counting them off like it's a checklist, your five basic steps on how to hook the horny male. "And, oh, yeah, I forgot," she says. "He told me that I was supposed to tell him that if anyone tried to stop him at the door, you know, the party . . ."

"Yes."

"That he was supposed to be seated at Mr. . . ." Her voice trails off. She freezes up for a second like she can't remember, then suddenly she smiles and says, "Mr. Becket. That's it. That was the name. That he was supposed to say that he was to be seated at Mr. Becket's table."

"That was the name he gave you? Mr. Becket?"

"Yes. That was it."

"Do you think he was Becket? The man with the cane?"

"I don't know." She says it with a lilt as if answering this is beyond her pay grade.

"You didn't know anything about this party?"

"No."

"Twenty-five hundred bucks seems like a lot of money," I tell her.

"Listen. He told me it was a joke, on a friend. I had no idea," she says.

"We're going to need a written statement for the police."

"The police?" she says. "I don't want to get involved with the police." She starts to get up from the bed.

I've said the P word—plague, police, it's all the same thing to her.

"It's the only way you can clear yourself," I tell her. If I couch it in self-interest maybe she'll sit down again. "Tell them what you know. That you had no idea what was going on. Otherwise they may think you're involved."

"I'm not talking to any cops," she says. "I do that, I'll lose my job."

"OK. All right. But you can give *us* a written statement."

THE ENEMY INSIDE · 143

She thinks about this. "I suppose. On condition that I don't have to talk to the police."

"Fine," I tell her, as if a signed affidavit under penalty of perjury won't have them knocking on her door.

"You said you were willing to pay." Brutus standing at the end of the bed inserts himself as her business manager.

"Only if we have to," I tell him. "It would be best if we didn't. For our client as well as for Ben."

She shoots me a startled look, surprised that I know her name.

"For legal reasons it would be better if no money changed hands on this."

"No. That ain't gonna work," he says. "You're gonna have to pay. Don't tell them anything more and don't sign anything. Not 'til we see the color of their money."

"Who am I talking to, you or her?" I look up at him.

"Right now you're talking to me," he says.

"And what is it exactly that *you* can tell us that might be helpful?"

"I can tell you to jam it up your ass," he says.

"Hey, hey. None of that," says Herman.

"Tell your monkey man here to put a cork in it." He looks at Herman and rolls the bow in his neck until it looks like a python crawled under his jacket.

"You know, we can go outside and monkey man here can get a hammer and fix that for ya," says Herman. "What you need's a good spinal adjustment and a colonic."

"Who's gonna do it? You?"

"Jeff, that's enough!"

He looks at her. The muscles in his jaw relax just a hair so that he is no longer crushing his molars.

"I know what he wants. How much are you willing to pay?" she asks.

We're back to this.

"What we talked about earlier."

"Twelve-fifty?"

I nod.

She looks at him.

He gives her an expression as if to say, "it ain't much" even though he was willing to sell her body for it ten minutes earlier. "Where's the money?" he asks.

"At my bank," I tell him. "The ATM."

"See? They don't even have the cash," he tells her. "How were you gonna pay her for her services?" He turns this on me.

"I wasn't." He still doesn't get it.

Fourteen

"A pimp and his ride," says Herman. He is glaring at the shiny new black sports car that Ben and her boyfriend slip into out in the parking lot as we get ready to leave the motel.

It grinds on Herman as we settle into the worn seats of my beat-up Wrangler to lead them to the office. I have called ahead. Brenda, who was working late, is waiting for us so she can type up the affidavit. It is best that we get this done now, without any delay. The longer the girl thinks about it, the greater the danger that Ben may come down with a case of second thoughts and disappear. That or Midas her manager may get greedy and up the price. We need to strike while we still have the scent of money to hold their interest.

"First the bank," I tell Herman.

He is driving my car, leaving his Buick parked back by the club. We can pick it up later. Herman hasn't had anything to drink. Besides, I'd rather not make it a parade to the office.

We loop around and head east on Narragansett, back toward the airport and I-5. Herman glances in the rearview mirror every few seconds to make sure they are following us.

"You think you can find this guy Becket?" he asks.

"I am hoping that maybe we won't have to."

"Told you," says Herman.

I am starting to fall under the sway of his original notion, that if we give the police a strongly worded affidavit and then lead them quickly to the witness, that she may go to pieces in front of them, enough to convince them she is telling the truth. If that happens, the entire case may disappear. They will dump the charges on Ives and we can go back to afternoon naps in the office.

"What do you think a car like that runs?"

I look over and catch Herman checking out the sleek black luxury sports car in the mirror. There is a look of lust in his eye and it is not for the woman in the front seat.

"I don't have a clue," I tell him. "Never shopped for one. As you might have guessed, I'm not into cars."

"I'd like to be," says Herman. "That one, the series, the wheel package, leather interior, navigation . . . think it comes in a convertible hardtop?"

"Beats me."

"I think that one's a convertible hardtop." Herman convinces himself. "Fully tricked out, trip the meter, I'm guessing six figures. You're talkin' a hundred, maybe a hundred and ten thousand you get the little brass cup holders. We're definitely in the wrong business."

"You don't have to convince me," I tell him.

"I wonder if he pays any taxes."

I don't say anything.

"You know, that's not a bad idea."

"What?"

"You know he's takin' all the money from the girl, don't you? Probably got a stable of 'em to boot. He can afford a car like that, she's gotta be givin' him beaucoup bucks."

"And your point is?"

"Say we feed him to the IRS?" Herman looks over at me with a gleam in his eye. "No. No, listen," he says. "They tell me you get ten percent of whatever the wolf man gets in back taxes and penalties. That's probably more than you make in a year. More than I make in a decade. Besides, what's he gonna do with a car like that, they ship him to Terminal Island. What I hear, they don't let you drive there. He ain't gonna need that car," says Herman. "Pick it up for chump change. And besides, you be doin' her a favor."

"You know, Herman, that's what I like about you the most."

"What's that?"

"You've got such a big heart, always looking out for orphans and defenseless women," I tell him.

He laughs.

"Let's not forget the bank." If he blows past that stop there is going to be a lot of gnashing of teeth and noisy disappointment from the car behind us.

We work our way toward Harbor Drive, swing onto it and head toward downtown. As we approach the airport, we pick up speed. By now the rush hour is ebbing. We roll along in front of the airport doing forty, catching all the lights. Herman has them timed.

"Where'd they go?" He's looking in the mirror.

"What?"

"They're gone."

I turn and look. "No, they're not. They're in the inside lane." They are just behind us in the lane to our right, the hood of the dark sports car moving up on us, sitting in Herman's blind spot, in the gap between the rearview and passenger-side mirrors. Herman keeps stealing glances into the glass but he still can't see them. "What're they doin' out there? Why don't they stay behind us?"

As he says it, the car pulls forward until it is even with us. Herman is gaining speed. I glance at our speedometer. He is doing fifty.

"Slow down!"

I look over at the other car and the hulk behind the wheel is looking down trying to do something with one of the controls on the dash while he steers with the other hand. Suddenly he turns and looks directly at me through the driver's-side window. There is a quizzical expression on his face, something between surprise and panic. He yells at me, but I can't make out what he's saying.

The girl in the passenger seat is terrified. She looks at me, her eyes two huge ovals as she struggles for a handhold on the leather seat. The roar of the accelerating engine as it's jammed into passing gear sounds like a jet heading down the runway. The girl's hair streams back around the headrest, her body thrust deep in the seat by the sudden force of the acceleration. The last vision I get of either of them. They rocket past the entire line of cars in our lane.

"What the hell?" says Herman. "Is he crazy?"

"Stay with them," I tell him.

"Are you kidding? He's gotta be doin' ninety."

"Follow him!"

Herman jerks his head to check the blind spot and gooses the Jeep into the right lane. He picks up speed, weaves in and out of a few cars.

I watch the black car as its taillights fade into two dim red specks in the distance. Herman is getting up on seventy by the time I see the traffic light up on the Pacific Highway maybe a quarter of a mile away. The light is red. There is a growing line of cars stopped in both lanes. I can't tell if Ben and her boyfriend are there.

Suddenly a huge flash erupts off to our left, a billowing ball of orange and yellow flame. It lasts for a few seconds and is quickly engulfed in dark black smoke. I can't tell where it's coming from, somewhere off in the distance.

"Airport runway," says Herman.

It's the right location. It appears to be in the area of the blast deflectors at the end of the runway where the jets turn up their engines for takeoff. But as we approach the area I can see a large passenger jet sitting there waiting for clearance. No problem.

The smoldering flames, the smoke that is now several hundred feet in the air, are beyond the airport, just to the other side.

Herman takes a left on Laurel and races toward the smoke. Another left on Pacific Highway and there it is. The flaming remains of a fuel tanker truck, both trailers ablaze.

Herman brings the Jeep to a stop in the middle of the road. Traffic is shutting down. People are running frantically away from the gas station where the truck is parked. A fueling hose already on fire snakes from the front trailer into a hole in the blazing concrete apron of the station fed like a burning fuse into one of its underground tanks.

Under the center section of the truck's rear trailer, its crumpled nose embedded and flaming, almost unrecognizable, is what is left of the black sports car. Herman was right. Its hard convertible top has been opened and peeled back either by the force of the collision or the blast that followed. The searing heat generates its own wind. In the dancing flames, two figures still strapped in their seats, little more than bobbing skeletons, seem to dance in the heat waves that rise up from the blistering asphalt pavement under the car.

Without warning, the blast hits us, a gust of searing heat so intense that I don't even hear the sound of the explosion as the shock wave passes through us. I shield my face with one hand and turn away as Herman and I try to huddle, taking what cover we can below the dashboard of the Jeep. The concussion rocks the car and leaves us momentarily stunned. I can hear nothing but the pounding of my own heart, as if I have been immersed in a sea of instant silence.

As I raise my head above the dash I see that most of the truck is gone. Only the frame of the tractor with its engine block and dual rear axle remain, the melted rubber from its tires still flaming as black smoke rises from the wreck. There is no sign of the car or its two occupants, only a massive molten hole in the ground where moments before I had seen it.

Fifteen

Ana Agirre methodically tracked the location of the signal as she drove south down I-5. She continually glanced across to the passenger seat of her rental car as she watched the beeping signal on the map overlay from her open laptop. The signal was being fed by a small satellite antenna on the car's dash that was wired into the computer.

Just as she passed under Interstate 8, less than four miles from the city center, she looked back up at the road and saw a massive ball of fire as it erupted in the distance somewhere off to the right of I-5. Whatever it was, she guessed that it was no more than two, maybe three miles ahead. The ball of flame continued to roll high into the sky as if in slow motion, brilliant yellow turning to orange until it was enveloped in a thick veil of black smoke. Both hands on the wheel, she glanced back over at the computer and its beeping signal. The location of the explosion and the signal on the map caused the muscles in her stomach to tighten.

She veered to the right onto the shoulder of the freeway and gunned the small car, passing a line of slower vehicles. Traffic on the highway began to pile up as she got closer to the column of smoke. The roiling black cloud, like an evil genie out of its bottle, reached several hundred feet into the air as it drifted across the elevated freeway ahead. She could see cars, their front ends dipping in a parade of red lights, as drivers stomped on their brakes.

Agirre took an exit and found herself emerging down a long ramp from the freeway onto a broad surface street. It was three lanes in each direction divided by a raised curb and the cylindrical concrete pillars supporting the overhead freeway. There were signs to the airport ahead. She followed them and within minutes found herself driving through a dense fog of black soot. She turned the fan of the air con to the off position on the little car's dash to keep the acrid smoke from filling the passenger compartment.

Ana began to wonder if they had used her equipment to bring down an airplane. If so, she would be running for cover for the rest of her life. The US authorities would turn over every rock to find out who was responsible. If they found any trace of the equipment it would lead back to her. She navigated blindly for three blocks until the breeze off the ocean began to clear the air, pushing the smoke to the east, toward downtown.

As she eased into an intersection behind traffic, Ana saw the burning wreckage off to her right, the smoldering remains of a truck. Next to it was a cavernous hole in the ground belching smoke and flame, the odor of gasoline wafting in the air. The electronic baying of emergency vehicles in the distance could be heard as they approached the scene, first responders. She looked for burned bodies on the ground. She couldn't tell how many might have been killed.

Ana hesitated for only a second. She knew it was now or never. She had to recover the equipment. She was furious, seething with anger. They had used her equipment in a garish display of pyrotechnics that was certain to result in dramatic news coverage. She could see cameras on some of the light poles along the street. This meant that authorities would have videotape of the seconds leading up to the crash and its resulting explosion. These pictures would make international news. Depending on the body count, the images would spur authorities to dig deep looking for the answers as to the cause.

Cars were stopped on the road ahead of her. Ana didn't care. She drove up onto the sidewalk to get around them. She kept going, one eye on the bleeping signal still emitting from her laptop as she approached the location. It was now less than two hundred meters ahead. Ana knew that if they turned off the equipment she would lose the signal and, with it, any hope of recovering her equipment.

Bright graffiti covered part of the exterior of what had once been a spit-polished building owned by the military. A man in his early thirties wearing a blue hardhat and white coveralls climbed down the shaky steel ladder fixed to the structure's rear wall, a kind of fire escape. The place was an old warehouse once used by the navy to mothball supplies. It had been turned over to the city during one of a series of base closures designed to bring down government costs. Instead, costs skyrocketed and the building lay largely abandoned, used mostly by vagrants who lit fires inside its crumbling walls on chilly nights.

As soon as the man reached the bottom rung he jumped the four-foot gap to the ground, then looked back up to his colleague. "Send it on down!"

The man on the roof was similarly attired. He passed a sealed case the size of your average rolling luggage over the parapet on the roof and lowered it quickly on a rope to the man on the ground. Anyone seeing them would think they were doing maintenance, except that it was getting late, already well past dusk.

The man down below unfastened the rope from the handle on the case and lugged the heavy ribbed, stainless-steel box toward a car. The case contained a laptop, an external power pack, and two large batteries, enough energy to operate the computer and the small antenna for three hours.

The man's car was parked a few feet away next to a white utility van they had rented to carry the larger part of the load. It took maybe thirty seconds to open the trunk of the car and load the box inside. When he was finished, he headed back toward the ladder. By then the rope had disappeared once more up onto the roof of the building.

Blaring horns and the sound of sirens could be heard in the distance. The man at the bottom of the ladder looked nervously in the direction of all the commotion, about three blocks away. He cupped his hands to direct a restrained shout up to the man on the roof. "Hurry up!" It was getting dark. With all the squad cars descending on the area, headlights coming from an abandoned building might draw attention.

Up top, the other man stuck his head over the edge of the roof and looked down. "Gimme a second. I don't want to drop it." He disappeared back to his task. A few seconds later, a large heavy tubular tripod was eased over the edge of the roof and lowered to the ground.

The man down below undid the rope and carried the tripod toward the van. By the time he returned there was no sign of the rope or his compatriot up top. "Get a move on. We've got to get out of here."

"Go ahead!" said the man on the roof. "I can handle the rest."

"You sure?"

"Yes! Go!"

The man on the ground wasted no time. He jogged toward the car. In less than a minute he was out on the road, headed the other way, away from all the flashing lights and the high-grade action down the street.

His partner on the roof had only two more items to load up, the fourteen-inch satellite antenna and the coil of cable that came with it. He strapped these together with a cable tie, wrapped the end of the rope through a metal bracket on the back of the antenna, and lowered the whole package over the edge of the roof and down. As it settled onto the ground he dropped the rest of the rope over the side. He climbed up and over the parapet onto the ladder and down. By now it was nearly dark. He moved quickly to gather up the antenna, cable, and the nylon rope as he headed toward the van.

The double doors at the back were already open. He skipped up into the cargo area and carefully deposited the antenna onto the floor. He secured it with a tie-down so it wouldn't fly around.

As he stepped out of the back of the van and closed the doors, he was busy searching for the keys in his pocket. He barely noticed the brief red flicker of the laser-guided broad head as it rocketed toward him. In less time than it took to blink, the rotating razor-sharp edges at the arrow's tip tore into the center of his chest. The momentum of the arrow carried it through his body as the glowing tip just missed his spine and came out his back. Skewered like a piece of meat, he dropped to the ground like a sack of flour. All of it without a sound, the difference between Ana and the people who abused her equipment.

She moved quickly across the graveled pavement behind the building. She looked in the back of the van and quickly realized that only part of the equipment was there, the antenna and some cable.

By the time she reached the man on the ground, the muscles in his legs were still twitching. A froth of bloody bubbles emerged from the corner of his mouth carried on a shallow breath. He was still alive, but he wouldn't be for long.

She laid the bow on the ground and got up close to his face. "Where's the rest of it? The box with the computer?" She grabbed him by the hair and pulled his face up to hers so he could see her in the darkness. "Is it up on the roof?"

She realized he couldn't speak and watched as the life went out of his eyes.

Agirre took a deep breath and then allowed the man's head to settle back onto the ground. She reached around behind him with gloved fingers and quickly unscrewed the broad tip of the arrow from its shaft. She examined it to make sure that no part of the razor's steel had broken off to become embedded in the wound.

Ana then dropped the arrow's tip into a small plastic bag and slipped this into her coat pocket. Then with enough force to raise his back off the ground, she stood and pulled the fletch end of the shaft with both hands until it slipped from his body. She made no effort to wipe the streaks of blood from the shaft on his coveralls. She wanted no telltale signs offering any clue as to what had killed him.

The rotating flared razors on the tip of the arrow would have made a massive wound obliterating any pathologic evidence as to its cause. The frayed threads of cloth where the arrow had pierced the coveralls, front and back, might offer a hint to a bow hunter. But most pathologists were used to dealing with gunshot and stab wounds, where they would collect ballistic evidence or measure the shape and depth of a knife wound looking for toolmarks on bone. In this case they might venture a guess, but there was nothing left behind from which to form any real conclusion, no toolmarks or ballistics that could be matched to a weapon.

By morning, the removable razor edges of the broad head would be dancing in the sandy surf beneath the ocean off the end of some pier. The wooden shaft would be burned. The light compound takedown bow would be reduced to its three component parts and slid back into their plastic tube, less than a foot in length. Checked with other luggage at the airport, it had cleared both security and customs coming from France, as had the arrows after they were reduced to pieces to be assembled on arrival.

Ana found the keys to the van on the ground next to the dead man's left hand. First she climbed up onto the roof of the building where she had seen him coming down. There was nothing there.

She had arrived at the corner of the building just in time to see the first man jump into the car and drive away.

There was no sign of the large steel case. Maybe he had put it up in the front seat. She picked the bow up off the ground and went around the vehicle toward the driver's-side door. When she opened it, her heart missed a beat. There was no sign of the box, the computer, or the one-of-a-kind software inside it, items that she feared could be traced back to its makers, and from them to her.

By lowering the front passenger seat of her rental car, Ana was able to load the antenna, cable, and tripod into the vehicle. She would rent a storage locker to stash the stuff until she could find the rest.

Sixteen

The ragtop on my old Jeep is singed and the passenger-side Mylar window is partially melted from the heat of the blast. Whatever took control of the flashy high-end car that carried Ben to her death, it was clear from what I saw that her boyfriend who was driving was helpless. The fact that Alex was unconscious, and from everything we know couldn't operate a car in his condition, raises the obvious question: Was Serna killed in the same way? Was Alex just the passenger payload in a guided missile?

My ears are still ringing as Herman and I settle into two high-back wicker plantation chairs on the patio behind Norman Ives's home. It is on a bluff overlooking the Pacific in La Jolla.

Herman and I didn't waste time going back to the office following the inferno near the airport. Instead, we drove directly here. I called ahead and then phoned Harry and asked him to meet us. He is on his way. It is time to pick up the pieces and regroup.

Norman and Sharon Ives are Alex's parents. It is in their house, a stately white Dutch gambrel-style home on an acre of manicured grounds high on a bluff over the ocean, that Alex has been staying since his release on bail. A large oval pool in the backyard, the reflection of its submerged lights dancing in the trees overhead, offers the illusion of an oasis. Beyond the yard, off in the distance, a few dotted points of light mark the dark horizon, boats at sea on a moonless night.

Sharon Ives offers us a drink, iced tea. We decline. Norman offers something stronger and Herman takes a scotch on the rocks. Herman's hand seems to be shaking, a slight palsy, the effect, I suspect, of the blast. I fill them in. Harry arrives and I replay the revolving tape of the evening's grisly events for him.

Any hope of evidence that might cause the D.A. to drop the charges against Alex Ives went up in flames with the girl named Ben. I can still see her eyes, the aspect of her face as I stare down at the intricate woven surface of the rattan coffee table around which we are all now huddled.

"I don't understand. Why can't you just tell them what she told you?" Sharon Ives doesn't get it.

"Whatever she told us is hearsay," I explain, "inadmissible in a court of law. Besides, it's not likely that the prosecutor would take our word for it."

"We needed her," says Herman.

"A writing would have helped," says Harry.

I talk to Alex about the little bits and pieces I got from the girl before she died, the silver-handled cane with the bird on it, the description of the man, gray hair, sixty to sixty-five, well dressed, wearing a suit. "Could be anybody," he says, "but it rings no bells." Not until I mention the name Becket, the man whose table he was supposed to be seated at the night of the party. "That was it. I remember now," says Alex. "Becket. But I never needed it because no one asked."

"So where do we go from here?" Norman, Alex's dad, asks the question.

"That's the problem," I tell him. "After what happened tonight, our biggest dilemma is no longer a legal issue. We must now be concerned for your son's safety."

"What do you mean?" With this, I have Mother Ives's undivided attention.

"It pains me to tell you this, but whoever killed the girl probably wants to kill your son," I say.

"I think you're being overly dramatic," says Alex.

"Bullshit," says Harry.

Sharon Ives looks at Harry as if he has just defecated on her best china.

"You can double that for me," says Herman.

"Only reason you're alive is some Good Samaritan pulled you from the flames the first time," says Harry.

"Why would someone want to kill Alex?" she asks.

"You better ask your son," I tell her.

She looks at him. "Alex, tell me! What have you gotten yourself involved in? I want to know, and I want to know now!"

"Mom!"

"Tell your mother!" Norman Ives piles on. "Son, we need to know what's going on if we're going to be able to help you."

Alex looks at me with an expression like I've ratted him out. "All right!" He's had enough. Everybody, including his parents, beating on him, and now two murders. "I'll tell you what I know," he says. "Not that it's going to do any good. I can't see any connection. You have to promise not to tell anyone else."

"Get him a drink," says Harry. "I have a feeling it's going to be a long night."

Over Jameson on the rocks, the kid unloads what he knows. "A few years ago, if you remember, there were news stories about the Treasury Department, the IRS, and some offshore banks. Internal Revenue was cracking down on overseas banking. They were chasing US citizens who had money deposited in confidential offshore numbered accounts. One estimate was there was two hundred and fifty billion dollars in back taxes and penalties owed on what was hidden offshore. Pick a report and they'll give you a different number," says Alex. "Nobody knows for sure how much. According to the US politicians who were leading the charge, these people with the numbered accounts were dodging US taxes, either by shifting funds offshore before paying taxes or depositing income earned overseas and not reporting it."

"I remember," says Harry. "As I recall, the Swiss bankers were screaming that the fakers in Washington had them stretched out on the rack. The powers in D.C. were turning the screws. Threatening lawsuits."

"To the Swiss, banking was a cornerstone industry, and confidentiality was its foundation. It was the principal reason many people banked with them, especially the wealthy," says Alex. "In many cases these were not interest-bearing accounts. The well-heeled were often willing to deposit money and pay fees for privacy. Uncle Sam had fallen on hard times."

"Not hard to see why," says Harry. "Forty years of profligate spending by American politicians pissing

168 · STEVE MARTINI

away other people's money had them searching cup-
boards for loose change."

"Somebody suggested the idea of shaking down the
overseas banks to get them to cough up the names of
American taxpayers," says Alex. "After all, most of
these were foreign corporations, and Washington was
wallowing in class warfare. Hating the rich was in
vogue," he says.

"And it wasn't just civil lawsuits. Some of the
European officers of these banks were threatened with
criminal prosecution here in the United States. Charges
that they had knowingly conspired to assist US customers to commit fraud and tax evasion. And our government had a big hammer. International wire transfers,"
he says. "If you want to send money by wire to another
country, something that is done daily by businesses
around the world, many transactions require that you
convert it into US dollars because the dollar is the world
reserve currency. That means that these transactions
have to go through the Federal Reserve System in New
York. The US Treasury Department let it be known
that overseas banks refusing to cooperate with the IRS
by failing to disclose the identity of US account holders
might have their wire transfers blocked by the Fed in
the future. In effect, this could put foreign banks out of
business."

"T. R. said to carry a big stick, but nobody ever said anything about a cudgel," says Harry. "Still, I guess if they owe the taxes."

"That was true, as far as it went," says Alex. "But then some strange things began happening. Stories started to crop up around Capitol Hill that the Treasury and the IRS were beginning to soften on the issue. Evidence started to surface that they were cutting deals, outlining a plan that wasn't nearly as forceful as the words and accusations they were spouting in front of the cameras."

"Pushback from foreign governments?" asks Harry.

Alex shakes his head. "There was that, but there was something more. We were told that identification of some accounts was being treated as out-of-bounds, off-limits. There was something called the 'PEP Office' that had been set up at one of the foreign banks that had a branch office in Washington. PEP, we were told, stood for 'Politically Exposed Persons.' These are people with power in public office. It's one of the things banks look for as a red flag in terms of possible money laundering. Typically it involves third-world dictators who might be looting their national treasuries. But not always. It could also involve politicians from developed countries who have suddenly acquired funds offshore and they want to hide it in a numbered account."

"Funds from where?" says Harry.

"That's the question," says Alex. "Nobody knows. What was more interesting was that when this information surfaced, that there might be US PEPs out there, politicians with numbered accounts, a lot of them seemed to lose interest in the offshore banking issue. Some of the people pounding loudest on the table suddenly got very quiet."

"Your government at work for you," says Harry.

"Go on," I tell him.

"Because the Swiss banks were being hammered by the IRS and the Treasury Department, they decided to use a random selection method for picking several thousand US account holders at one bank headquartered in Switzerland. The identity of the account holders and the account information for the unlucky ones who were picked was to be turned over to the IRS for audit. The account numbers were to be drawn at random in hopes that the fear of exposure would force other Americans to come clean, file returns with the IRS, and avoid enforcement actions should their accounts be selected for audit. But according to Tory, a source working at the bank told him that there were a number of accounts that were never placed in the pool for selection."

"Who told him this?"

"I don't know. It happened on our first trip when we were in Switzerland. But I didn't go to the meeting. He wanted to go alone.

"There's more," says Alex. "We were told there was a whistleblower, a man by the name of Rubin Betz. He had been arrested by the FBI for tax evasion and money laundering some years earlier. I can't remember exactly when. He claimed he was being set up, that the government had built a case against him because they wanted to shut him up. At the time they arrested him, he worked for one of the offshore banks. I can't remember which one.

"He claimed to have the goods on a number of powerful people, including some American politicians who he said held sizable numbered accounts in banks overseas, accounts that were never disclosed either to the IRS, to Treasury, or on public disclosure forms that are required to be filed under federal law. He said that these people were being allowed to skate while others were being hammered by the government."

"Did you talk to this guy Betz personally?" I ask.

"No. That's the thing. He's in a federal penitentiary, maximum security. Bunking next to one of the ayatollahs who tried to blow up the World Trade Center before they knocked it down. That's what I was told."

Harry and I look at each other.

"For a white-collar crime, I'm told that this is unusual," says Alex. "You're both lawyers." He looks over at Harry and me. "You tell me."

"So if you didn't talk to him, how do you know all this?" asks Harry.

"The only one Betz was allowed to see was his lawyer. So I talked to him."

"And he told you all this?" I ask.

I can tell by the body language that Harry is already starting to discount this. Disgruntled lawyer who lost a case.

"He told me that he and Betz tried to cut a deal with the government. They made what you call a proffer. You know what that is?"

I nod.

"Betz and his lawyer supplied a list of names to the deputy US Attorney handling the case, names of people that the whistleblower, Rubin Betz, said held secret offshore accounts. This list went up the chain at Justice. I was told by the lawyer that some of these names you would recognize. Prominent people," says Alex.

"Did he supply you with any of the names?" asks Harry. "This lawyer?"

"No."

"Then what happened?" I ask.

"According to Betz's lawyer, the government not only refused to deal with them, they piled on more charges. They claimed that Betz was not dealing honestly and that he was withholding information from the government. The attorney admitted that his client was no choirboy. But he claimed he wasn't withholding anything either. He said that the government used this as an excuse to put the man away. It also chilled anyone else with information from coming forward. It was almost as if they didn't want to know. The lawyer said that Betz wasn't dangerous. There was no history of violent crimes in his past, what the lawyer called mostly minor white-collar stuff. And no reason for maximum security. He said they charged Betz with things that they never charge in other cases. Stuff they always let slide, especially if you were willing to cooperate, which Betz was."

"Lesser included offenses," says Harry.

"I don't know. Probably. All I know is that they threw the book at Betz," says Ives.

"Prosecutorial discretion," says Harry. "Government can do whatever it wants, kick the crap out of their political opponents while ignoring the crimes committed by their friends. Given the current political divide it could become the next national pastime."

"Betz's lawyer told me that at sentencing the government asked for a term of fifty years. Even the judge went ballistic. He sentenced him to twelve."

"He must have done something," says Harry. "Still, goes to show you, you never want to get crossways with the government."

"This lawyer, do you have his name?" I ask.

"I do. But it won't do you any good."

"You mean he won't talk to me?"

"He won't talk to anybody," says Ives. "He's dead."

"Don't tell me . . . a traffic accident?" says Herman.

Ives shakes his head. "Plane crash," he says. "About a year and a half ago. Just after his client went to prison. He owned a small private plane. They said it was a mechanical problem."

"Alex, I want you to quit that job right now," says his mother. "Who are these people you've gotten yourself involved with?"

"I thought it was our government. But I'm not so sure anymore," says Ives.

"Why would they kill the lawyer," says Harry, "when they went to all the trouble of prosecuting Betz? Why not just kill them both if the mission is to shut them up?"

"That's a good point," I say.

"The answer to that may have died with Olinda Serna," says Alex.

"What?" Harry looks at him.

"It's how we got on to Serna," says Ives. "She and Betz knew each other." It sounds as if we are about to go full circle.

"Betz and Serna used to work together."

Harry and I look at each other.

"Back in the day when she worked campaigns before she went on Senate staff and later became the hotshot lawyer, I was told she and Betz were an item. They lived together. He handled the money. Her name was on the campaign finance statements. She was paid. He was a volunteer. They ran a business. At least that's what I was told. He did most of the legwork, the collections," says Ives. "I also heard that a lot of the checks that came in went through his fingers. Campaign contributions and maybe other things I don't know about. Some of this is in Tory's files. He would have more details," says Alex.

"These campaigns. Do you know who they were for?" asks Harry.

"Members of Congress. She was working in D.C. at the time."

"Aren't campaigns usually handled in the district, back home?" I ask.

"Apparently not this stuff," says Ives.

"Which members of Congress?" says Harry.

"I don't know. Again, that's probably something Tory would know. I think he's got the records."

"What about the trip to Switzerland?" says Harry. "You told us before that you and Graves went to Switzerland looking for something?"

"We did. Tory had some information. A contact, he said, in Lucerne. We went there to meet with him. But when it was time to see the man, Tory went alone. He told me it would be best. The guy might be less nervous if he approached him by himself."

"What else did he find out?" says Harry.

"Just what I told you. If there's anything more you'd have to get it from Tory. When he came back from the meeting he was very tightlipped. It was strange. Tory seemed to have changed about that time. Before then, he shared a lot of what he knew. After that, he seemed to play everything close to the vest. Kept it to himself like maybe he didn't trust me. Not just me but others as well."

Tory Graves, the name keeps popping up. He is climbing up the list of people I want to meet.

"So what do we have?" says Herman. "A dead lawyer. Another woman and her significant other burned to death in front of us. Some guy doin' time for cheatin' the taxman. And lots of money moving around overseas. What's the connection?"

"I don't know," I tell him. "But one thing's for sure. It's not safe for Alex to remain here any longer."

"Listen, I can take care of myself," he says.

"Yeah. You proved that the night of the party," says Harry.

"I wasn't expecting anything. They surprised me."

"Yeah, and they'll do it again," says Herman.

"Besides, the longer you stay here, the greater the risk for your parents," I tell him.

"I hadn't thought about that," he says.

"You should. The three of you will be safer if Alex is someplace else," I tell them.

"Why can't we just go to the police?" says his mother. "Aren't they supposed to help in cases like this?"

"They might believe us. Or they might not," I tell her. "Either way, their only recourse will be to put Alex back in jail. If they believe he's in danger, they'll go to court and tell the judge he's a flight risk, and the judge will probably revoke his bail. If they put him back behind bars, I can't vouch for his safety."

"Oh, God!" His mother doesn't want to hear this.

"It's OK. It'll be all right," I tell her. "We'll find a place for him where it's safe." Even as I say this I know it's an idle promise.

"Where?" says Harry.

"I don't know. I'll work on that."

"You know what it sounds like to me?" says Herman.

"What's that?" I ask.

"Sounds like they couldn't afford to kill Betz cuz maybe, just maybe, he hid a pooper in the chute."

Ives and his mother look at me as if this is some foreign regional dialect and I'm the local interpreter.

"I think what Herman's saying is that Mr. Betz may have hidden documents or other evidence as security against a violent end," I tell them.

"Pooper in the chute, how quaint," she says. "So what you're saying is that if he died unexpectedly, this information, the pooper as he calls it, would be revealed—made public? Is that it?"

"That's it," I tell her.

"And cause quite a stink," says Herman.

"It's only good," says Harry, "if the other side knows about it but can't find it."

"Maybe they did," says Herman, "know about it, I mean."

"That would be very smart." She nods approvingly as she looks over at Alex, the weight of this night's anxiety hanging heavy on her brow, the thought, I am sure, running through her mind at the moment: "Why can't the lawyers, if they know so much, secure one of these bulletproof 'poopers' for my own son?"

Seventeen

Lang-Jian Cheng sat behind the large ornate desk in his office at the Central Military Commission in Beijing. Wrinkled and bald, with a fringe of gray that wrapped his head above the ears, General Cheng was a career soldier in the People's Liberation Army.

He was head of Second Bureau, China's overseas foreign intelligence unit, where he was known as "the Creeping Dragon" by subordinates. He was renowned for his practiced patience, his willingness to wait for just the right moment before acting, often to the consternation of younger and more aggressive officers.

This morning, Cheng was busy reading the latest intelligence communiqués along with the daily briefings from the bureau's burgeoning overseas offices and operations.

He smiled after reading one of them. There were reports that an American CIA station in Central California had christened Cheng "Long John," apparently in reference to the pirate in Robert Louis Stevenson's novel *Treasure Island*. It tickled his fancy, since he had earned this alias by thoroughly penetrating America's high-tech industries in Silicon Valley. The place was believed to have so many of Cheng's spies working there, gathering information and sending it back to Beijing, that some in the US intelligence community now referred to it not as "Chinatown," but as "Cheng's Town."

For a moment he considered framing the report for his wall, and then thought better of it. He put it facedown on the pile of documents already read and reached for his coffee.

If the truth be known, they would realize that Cheng's network was far more pervasive, so much so that it had drilled into the very core of the American government in Washington.

The FBI didn't know it because it was wielded through a Western intermediary, a man Cheng knew he could not always trust. But then, Cheng wasn't sure he could always trust his own children, let alone his subordinates, such was his nature and the nature of the Chinese power structure. Trust was a weakness he couldn't afford.

He sipped his coffee as he considered the man code-named "Ying." He was not in the strictest sense what you would call a "Chinese asset," a spy who was handled by agents out of the Chinese embassy in Washington or one of its consulates in the far-flung United States. In fact, Cheng's people knew only his code name and nothing more. Because of his unique position Cheng protected him and dealt with him directly.

Their dealings were grounded not in ideology, but pragmatic common interest—the seeds of which were money and power. The money came from Chinese investments made through the Hong Kong and Shanghai stock exchanges. These were certain coveted military-industrial stocks normally not made available to Western investors by the Chinese government. Profits taken from these were deposited in Ying's numbered accounts in private banks in Hong Kong, none of which were accessible to American taxing authorities or law enforcement. There was nothing they could do.

As far as Cheng was concerned, the Americans had no one to blame but themselves. Their open society was riddled with leaks, leakers, and unlocked safes. If it continued, China and Russia would have to erect walls just to keep out the growing number of disgruntled American defectors with their computerized mountains of top-secret information.

American technology, which had exploded in the 1980s with the personal computer, had grown so fast and in such a turbulent fashion that US industrial security was a joke. America's ineptitude invited other enterprising powers to steal everything that wasn't locked down. Even their own government didn't know how many priceless jewels they possessed. Under such a system, how could anyone protect them?

He picked up the next report and began reading. Before he had completed three lines of Mandarin characters Cheng was reminded that the West and, in particular the United States, had far deeper problems than industrial or even military espionage.

America's greatest dilemma was not with China, Russia, Pakistan, North Korea, or the stateless terrorists of the Middle East. Its most serious problems were internal, part of the nation's own political genetics.

Reflections of this could be seen in the partisan divisions and the take-no-prisoners domestic political warfare that had become part of the daily news cycle in modern America. This constant infighting was largely intended for the acquisition of personal power by a handful of political celebrities fawned over by the American media. The process consumed vast financial and political resources, none of which took the country any closer to a single perceptible national goal.

In Cheng's view a sound dictatorship was far more efficient.

To American politicians partisan disputes were a purely domestic matter. It was no one else's business, and certainly beyond the purview of any foreign power. Yet, what they failed to realize were the foreign intelligence implications of this conduct, the toxic opportunities that it afforded to America's adversaries abroad.

As far as Cheng was concerned, democracies started wars they could not finish because they lacked the long-term political will that would allow them to complete what they had started. A war begun in one regime would result in failure and defeat when the troops were withdrawn in the next. The Fates often hung on the whim of voters who had no idea of the consequence of their votes and whose actions were often rooted in lies from ambitious politicians willing to deceive in order to attain higher office. But in Cheng's mind, democracy was not a rational method for making sound policy.

In modern China, lies, as an instrument of maintaining power, were unnecessary because there was no one to lie to. The people had no power, as long as they were controlled by the government. And once you fell from power, lies were futile.

In America, politicians and the media, including the news outlets that pretended to cover government affairs, downplayed this near full-time exercise in deceit by calling it "spin." This seemed to excuse it from the more serious lies committed by ordinary citizens who would pay dearly if they tried to deceive the state.

Cheng found the justification for this American anomaly interesting. The rationale was that if you punished those in power with prison every time they lied, no one would run for public office. Cheng found it surreal that in the United States, supposedly the gold standard of modern law and justice, with its hundreds of thousands of lawyers, millions of statutes, and armies of judges, there was not a single penal law punishing officials who intentionally and repeatedly lied to their people on important issues of state.

You could no longer shock the average American, no matter the scope of the scandal or the damage that it caused. They had come to expect this from their leaders.

Eighteen

For a lawyer worth his salt, defending a case in any court of consequence, there are two things that will generally keep you up nights: unexplained coincidence and the serpent of surprise raising its ugly head in the courtroom.

The fact that, of the countless millions of vehicles garaged in Southern California, Ives managed to smash into the one occupied by Serna, an object of inquiry in one of his stories, would test the limits of serendipity to the mind of any normal juror.

The only answer we have for this is the theory that Ives was drugged and that the accident was staged by others—a preplanned murder. But here, there's a problem. Between now and trial there is more than a fair chance that the D.A. and his investigators will kick over a rock and discover what Ives was up to, that he was working on a story involving Serna.

Even if they don't, it is likely from what Alex has told me that Tory Graves, his boss, being the hard-core muckraker that he is, will not hold the story. He will publish whatever he has before we can get to trial. If this happens, the prosecutor could easily jump on our theory, turn our own shield into a weapon, and beat us to death with it.

As I think about this I am searching the Internet looking for something, some clue as to how an external force might take control of a vehicle moving at high speed. This might give us some lead as to how Ben and her boyfriend died, and perhaps how Serna was murdered.

Something catches my eye, an online article: "How Stuff Works: Are Modern Cars Vulnerable to Hackers?" I read it and search further. I find more, another item: "Hackers Reveal Nasty New Car Attacks." And more: "How Modern Cars Can Be Hacked." On top of this is a mountain of other material, recent news articles concerning how carmakers are on the verge of developing driverless vehicles, the dream of the future. Maybe we should be more cautious about what we dream of.

As I read on, the small hairs on the back of my neck begin to stand up. High-tech controls have been growing under the hood and inside the passenger compartments of automobiles for more than two decades. They operate the cruise control, setting the car's speed. They can activate anti-collision avoidance systems, throwing on the brakes. Computer sensors fire airbags. They are used to lock car doors. There are literally scores of tiny "electronic control units" installed in modern passenger vehicles, and more were being added every year.

Most people, like me, paid no attention. Government safety agencies encourage these developments. Sometimes they mandate them. The problem is, as with everything else that is high tech, there is a downside—loss of human control.

One of the articles talks about a high-tech black-bag government agency that had already found ways to crack these systems, to hack them from outside the car, ways to turn them into weapons. There are sensors that, if they are hacked, can be used to turn off airbags, cut off the engine, or bleed the brakes so they no longer work. Some software could actually take over the navigation system of the vehicle involved. You could lock the doors so that the occupants could not escape, screw with the antilock brakes so they no longer worked, turn off the power steering, or limit the car's turning radius.

And then in the middle of one of the articles, the bombshell. Among the top-end luxury cars was the automated self-parking systems now available on some of the latest models. People love these because the built-in sensors control automated front-wheel movement and make it possible for them to parallel park between cars by pushing a button and merely touching the brake when the car was done. The system was only supposed to work at slow speeds, three or four miles per hour, and in reverse. But according to the article it was now believed that the black-bag computer nerds working for the government had been able to turn this to the dark side. They had managed to trick the car's speedometer and transmission so that you could hijack the parking system to control the car's steering and do it remotely at high forward speeds. The theory was that this could be used to turn a vehicle into a veritable deathtrap. It made it possible to orchestrate head-on collisions. I am beginning to think this is more than theory.

I print out the articles, and as they pile up in my printer I turn my attention back to the crisis at hand. The question prosecutors will try to answer if they find out that Alex was working on a story involving Serna. Could they cobble together a theory as to why he might want to kill her? Give the cops an hour and they will come up with a dozen theories, warp their evidence around the best one and run with it. This is likely to be more plausible and certainly more satisfying to the jury than our own—that some other dude did it, but we don't know who it is.

The answer to this riddle may lie in whatever revelations lurk in the details of the dirt dug up by Tory Graves. This is the surprise package we don't want exploding under our case in front of the jury.

Harry and I have managed to stall the preliminary hearing in Ives's case, the question of whether he should be bound over for trial in Superior Court. The outcome of these proceedings is preordained. Alex will have to stand trial. But we have waived time in the interest of delay, the perpetual strategy of every criminal defendant and their lawyer. But in this case we had a better reason than most, something we chose not to share with the judge or his clerk when we did the little dance in chambers to waive time.

If pushed to the wall and asked to produce our client, Harry and I will have to say that we don't know where he is. That's our story and we're sticking to it, at least until our asses are thrown in jail, at which time Harry says he reserves the right to reconsider.

Alex's parents actually don't know where he is. We have kept them in the dark. We thought about posting a sign on their front lawn telling whoever wants to kill him that they don't know where their kid is, just as a precaution. But we didn't.

This morning I made two phone calls. The first was to Tory Graves in D.C. He took the call, then dodged about on the phone for a while telling me how busy he was. Graves did not seem terribly concerned about Alex or his current predicament. In the end he agreed to see me, but only after I suggested that we might need to subpoena him as a witness unless, of course, I could find out what I needed to know in some less formal way. That seemed to soften his hide. It also fed his curiosity. He wanted to know what I was after. I told him it was better discussed face-to-face. We scheduled a meeting on his turf.

The other call was to a lawyer in Los Angeles, Cletus Proffit, the managing partner at Serna's old law firm, Mandella, Harbet. I wanted to at least plumb the depths with a few of the people she worked with.

I knew Proffit, but only by name. He was one of the pillars of the local legal clique in the state. He had done all the chairs at the county bar up in L.A. and found a place to squat on the state bar's board of governors when the music ended. He spent a few years, his spare time, doing the bar's good works, peddling bills to protect the average Joe from the malevolent clutches of scheming lawyers. The test of legal leadership was always the same, to rat out the fraternity. One was expected to do this. It was the lawyer's equivalent of a priest sporting sackcloth and ashes outside the church door. Your way of saying that you were repenting, but only for the sins of others.

Proffit's wife, who was also a lawyer, sat on the federal bench. She was mentioned periodically as a likely nominee to the Circuit Court of Appeals in San Francisco.

When I finally got through to his office, Proffit's secretary told me that her boss was back east, in their Washington office on business. She said that he was likely to be there for some time. I got the number and called it.

When I told the receptionist what it was about, that I represented the man who was involved in the accident with Serna, my call was instantly routed, the transcontinental express from my lips to Proffit's ear in a nanosecond.

The man was full of jovial good cheer, what you might expect from a leader who'd spent the last several years screwing over other lawyers. He told me that Serna's death was a great loss to the firm, that she was a very special person, and that he would have an exceptionally difficult time finding someone to fill her shoes. He called it a tragedy at least three times in two sentences, and said that he hoped that my client was not too seriously injured.

For someone who had lost an irreplaceable cog in the firm's wheel, Proffit didn't seem terribly perturbed that I was calling him on behalf of the drunk, at least according to the early news reports, who had turned his partner into a piece of crisp bacon.

I told him that Ives was fine, but that he was facing some serious charges. I asked him for a meeting.

He wanted to know why.

I told him that I wanted to discuss Serna's involvement with the firm, the nature of her practice. What she was like, any volunteer activities in the community in the event that we might ultimately have to deal with "victim impact statements"—that is, if my client was convicted. Just general background stuff, I told him. The information any prudent lawyer might gather regarding the victim in such a case.

There was a long pause at the other end of the line. Proffit then suggested that perhaps it could wait until he returned to Los Angeles. He told me that with Serna's sudden death and all the reorganization in their Washington office that, at the moment, he was simply too busy.

I told him that I already had a ticket to fly to Washington on Thursday morning. Three days from now.

Proffit said he was certain that wouldn't work. He couldn't fit me into his schedule. It was impossible.

Besides, he hated to see me travel all the way across the country on such a mundane matter.

I told him that I wasn't, that I already had a meeting scheduled in Washington with another party on Thursday afternoon to gather other information in the case.

In the breathless pause that followed I might have thought Proffit had wrapped the coiled wire from his phone's receiver around his head. Such were the palpable brain waves resonating at my end: "What other party?" "What information?"

He asked me to hold for a moment. When he came back on the line, it was to tell me that he had conferred with an assistant and that, as a courtesy to me, to avoid inconvenience, they would rearrange his calendar to fit me in. The first step in this process was to find out what time my other meeting was.

I told him that, if necessary, I could probably reschedule it. Nonsense, he said. It was clear that he wanted to meet with me after I had met with whomever else I was seeing. It sounded as if Proffit might want to tie me to the wall in his office and work me over with his stapler to find out who I was meeting with and what they had to say.

When I told him my other appointment was set for Friday afternoon, Proffit immediately said he was busy all morning. Would it be possible for me to hold over or to meet that evening? We set the meeting for seven, at a restaurant near his office. He gave me the name and address, said he would have one of their secretaries schedule the reservation in his name. I thanked him, and we hung up.

I couldn't be sure whether Proffit knew anything or if he had something to hide. But I could smell the worry on his breath, even over the phone. There was something about a silk-socked lawyer in the midst of an organizational meltdown in his firm who takes the time to turn on the charm for a perfect stranger. Adjusting his calendar for my convenience. It makes you want to grab your wallet and hang on.

Something was bothering him. Whatever it was, it had Serna's name all over it. And unless I missed my bet, it had nothing to do with filling her high heels at the firm. Proffit wanted to know what I was looking for in Washington. More to the point, he was desperate to find out who the other party was I was meeting with.

Ana Agirre had lost her ability to track her equipment or the people who had it. With the death of the man near the van and the discovery that the vehicle contained only the satellite antenna and its tripod, she was at a dead end. The van was a rental. She knew that would lead nowhere.

The people she was looking for had the computer and the software, but without the antenna they couldn't use it. And without a signal, Ana couldn't track them. She wanted it, all of it, and now. Time was running out on the European contract.

She thought about it for a while, racked her brain. The only lead she had left, and it was a long shot, was the original accident out in the desert. One of the parties had survived. She knew this because she had followed the news surrounding the accident from the moment the tracking signals told her that her equipment had been used and where. She knew Ives's name because she had taken notes. He was charged with the death of the woman who had no doubt been murdered.

Ana headed to a local library. Online she checked the local newspapers going back a few weeks. There she found the name of the lawyer representing Ives—Paul Madriani. She Googled the name and found the location, the law firm of "Madriani and Hinds," an address on Orange Avenue in Coronado. She set up to watch the place, at first from a distance from her car in a parking lot across the street, and later from a table in a restaurant very near the entrance to the office where she could see people come and go.

It was probably just another dead end, but if anyone knew anything about the accident that might give some clue as to who had her equipment, it would be either the local authorities or the lawyers involved in the case.

What she saw was a guy who came and went regularly and who occasionally stopped in the restaurant where she was seated having coffee. The waitresses always greeted him by name, Harry. This she assumed was one of the lawyers, Harry Hinds.

She watched and waited. For two days there was no sign of his partner, Paul Madriani. Ana considered her options, whether to approach them under some false guise to see what she could learn about the case, or to try to enter the office at night to look for notes or files that might give her more information. She started casing the office at night, checking the routine of the janitors, taking notes on who worked late.

Ana was hunched down at the office door in the shadows of the small garden plaza fishing for the set of lockpicks in her bag. It was after two in the morning. Dressed in a navy blue sweater, dark pants, and a pair of black running shoes, she blended easily into the night. She was preparing to break into the law office. The restaurant and its bar were closed, everything dark, when she heard the noise behind the building. She moved quickly without a sound along the path, toward the gate leading to the service area behind the office.

Through a crack in the gate she saw him. One man, all alone inside the garbage bin, rooting around, occasionally scraping against the inner steel walls. At first she thought maybe he was some transient. But as she watched she realized whoever it was wasn't hunting for discarded cans or bottles or other treasures of the destitute. He had taped a large trash bag to the outside lip of the bin. Whenever his hand emerged over the opening it was to stuff papers, what looked like documents, into the bag. He was looking for something, and it wasn't recyclables.

Ana's eyes were glued to the action in the bin. After a few minutes the man hoisted himself up out of the large container, over the edge and down to the ground. He grabbed the trash bag from the open edge and quickly headed out toward the street.

She was behind him in a flash. She watched as he entered the passenger side of a car parked halfway down the block toward Orange Avenue. It was a large dark cross-country vehicle, what the Americans called a four-by-four. The driver had the engine on in a second and they pulled away from the curb.

Ana turned and ran for her own car parked just down the street. In less than half a minute she was after them. At this hour there was almost no traffic, only one other vehicle on Orange Avenue that she could see,

and it was well out ahead of the 4x4 she was following. Keeping them in sight was not a problem. They
crossed over the bridge from Coronado and headed
north up I-5.

Ana hung back, following from a distance so as not
to alert them. They took the interchange at 94 East.
From there they headed north, up 805. They took the
exit at Miramar Road. They drove some distance east
before taking a right.

As Ana approached the intersection where they
turned she saw a sign: MCAS MIRAMAR. It was a military base. As she looked off to her right she could see
the car with the two men in it stopped at a kiosk in the
center of the road, a small guardhouse. A few seconds
later they passed through. Ana didn't take the turn.
She couldn't follow them there, but to her it all made
sense.

The fear growing in her mind was the possibility
that the American military, or one of their intelligence
agencies, held the equipment that the French techs had
designed for her. If that was the case, the authorities
already had it. If somehow they used it to their own
embarrassment, they might decide to tie it to her. She
had to get it back, but she couldn't go here.

Nineteen

Early morning, and the Eagle was back on the phone. This time it was an encrypted and scrambled line, but the headache coming over it was just as bad.

"It seems we've lost him," said the man on the other end. The "him" he was talking about was Alex Ives. "We've got a blanket over the house. According to the information from the surety who wrote the bail bond, that's where he's supposed to be. We see the old man and his wife. They keep coming and going, but no sign of the kid."

The Eagle thought for a moment. This can't be happening. "Maybe he's hunkered down inside the house, doesn't want to come out," he said. Always think positive.

"I don't think so."

The Eagle was almost afraid to ask why.

He didn't have to, the man on the other end volunteered it. "This morning we waited 'til the parents left, and we entered the house. The place was empty. Nobody there," said the man.

"Son of a bitch!" said the Eagle. "You're sure? You checked the entire house?"

"Top to bottom," said the man.

To the Eagle, the answer was simple. The idiots working for him were too busy cleaning up the mess they'd made at the gas station in San Diego, too distracted by their own fireworks to bother watching the house until it was too late. The damn lawyers had spirited the kid away. Where was anybody's guess. "What about the parents? Did you follow them?"

"Yeah! They went to the store. She got her hair done. They dropped off the dog at the groomer . . ."

"Great!" said the Eagle. "Next time I need a good groomer to clip your ass, you can tell me where to go. What about the lawyer? What's his name?"

"There's two of them," said the other man. "Madriani . . ."

"That's the one."

"And Hinds."

"Anybody bothering to watch them?" Sarcasm dripped from the Eagle's voice.

"We're on it," said the guy. "One of them is at the office in Coronado as we speak. Hinds. The other one, Madriani, boarded a plane early this morning headed for Washington."

"D.C.?"

"He wasn't goin' to Seattle," said the guy on the phone.

"I take it it's too much to ask whether you might know what he's up to? Could it be he's going on vacation?"

"We don't know. I doubt it," said the guy. Sometimes it was hard to know when the Eagle was serious and when he was just screwing with your head. "We think whatever arrangements he made he probably did them over the landline from his office."

"And I take it you didn't have a tap on the phone."

"No."

"Why not?"

"Most people don't realize," said the guy, "it's harder to get a tap on a landline these days than a cell phone. First off, you have to find somebody old enough who knows how to do it. Not as simple as you think. We're working on it. We'll get it done."

"Some time this century, I hope," said the Eagle. "Stay on top of the lawyers, especially the one on the plane. I want to know what he's up to."

"Got it!" It was the way the guy said it, such certainty and assurance. The last time they voiced such confidence they blew up half a block of San Diego and burned down the other half. It prompted the Eagle to stop and reconsider.

"On second thought," he said, "leave the lawyer, the one named Madriani, to me." He collected the name of the airline and the flight number from the man on the other end along with the ETA, estimated time of arrival, looked at his watch, and told him, "I'll take it from here. You! Your job is to find the kid. Get on it! Find him!" Then he slammed the phone down.

The rippling thermal currents rising off the sidewalk made it look like the griddle on a stove. The small shopping center with its bright-colored walls reflected the intensity of the sun so that it heated Herman's body like a tanning bed. It felt good. He was happy to be back in a place that was so familiar.

Wearing a tank top, shorts, and flip-flops, Herman trudged down the burning sidewalk and toward the two-story white structure with the red-tiled roof. The red and yellow sign out front read DHL. Inside, the air conditioner was humming, the temperature a good forty degrees cooler than on the cement outside.

Herman wiped the sweat from his face with a handkerchief, then gathered the supplies he needed from the shelf against the wall. He took four of the cardboard letter packs so that if things got dicey, he could seal up any future message on the run and, if he had to, ship it on the fly from the front desk of any of the resort hotels in the area. DHL, for a price, would pick up.

He took the pen from his pocket along with one of the blank forms, an international air waybill, and completed the information on the form. He entered his name as "H. Diggs" and used the address of the DHL office as the sender's address. He didn't want to use the actual location of the condo. He entered the law firm's DHL account number to pay for it.

He completed the customs portion of the form, declaring no value, then completed the rest of the form and signed it. Then he took the note from his pocket and checked it one more time. It was obscure to the point of being bland, the length of a message from a Chinese fortune cookie. "Package arrived safely. All well this end. H."

It was written in Herman's scrawl with a pen on a piece of otherwise blank paper. He folded it up once more, put it in one of the open letter packs and sealed it. He slipped the waybill inside the plastic window on the outside of the envelope and got into a line behind two other guys. Herman folded his broad arms across his barrel chest and waited.

204 • STEVE MARTINI

The trio, Paul, Harry, and Herman, had worked out the details over the kitchen table at Ives's parents' house the night the girl named Ben and her driver were killed. They kept his parents out of it, so they would know as little as possible, sent them to the other room where they could not hear. If questioned by authorities, they could honestly say they had no idea where their son was. Besides, the fewer people who knew, the better, less chance for a mistake.

The two lawyers took their lead from Herman as to the selected location. Given the history of narco-terror and the violence of the cartels, American tourists might shy away from Mexico. But as a place of refuge to hide out with Alex Ives until things cooled down, it was perfect. For Herman, it was like going home. He had connections and contacts in Mexico going back more than a decade, to the time when he worked corporate security and executive protection in Mexico City. It was where he first met Paul Madriani.

Herman called his contacts from a pay phone in a hotel not far from the Iveses' home. His friends gave him the name of a small condo near the beach in Ixtapa. They had used it once or twice as a secure location for corporate executives when traveling on the coast. They gave Herman the address and told him to check it out online. Herman didn't want to do that for obvious reasons. He trusted them. He discussed it with Paul and Harry, gave them the address in case of an emergency, and gave his friends in Mexico the green light to set it up.

Norman Ives came to the rescue to solve one of their problems, his son's lack of a passport. Through his business, Norman had extensive connections with a number of air transport companies and private pilots. He was able to secure help from a small air freight company that owed him a favor.

Late that night, Herman took over and worked out the destination with the company and its pilot so that Norman Ives would not be involved in any of the details. The carrier agreed to fly Alex and Herman to a small dirt strip, thirty miles from Zihuatanejo on Mexico's Pacific Coast, about an hour north of Acapulco by air. They filed no flight plan and avoided radar over the border by flying well out to sea before heading south down the Mexican coast. The landing strip sometimes used by drug dealers had no control tower, customs, or immigration. Herman had used the place years earlier in his prior employment, once when it was necessary to bring in a special cargo of American firearms needed for security.

Ixtapa was a small community just a couple of miles north of Zihuatanejo, its sister village. Both were perfect. Low-key tourist destinations nestled in the hills over the ocean where no one would ask any questions of two Americans relaxing on vacation.

The only real wrinkle was communications, how to stay in touch with the office and keep track of what was going on.

It was the mysterious manner in which people kept dying behind the wheel of their cars that gave Madriani and his friends pause. It had the distinct odor of high tech about it. Especially after witnessing the startled look on the face of the driver and the girl next to him as their vehicle launched them down the road toward eternity, their destiny at the gas station.

It wasn't a far reach to imagine that whoever was doing this might have the technical savvy to invade the firm's electronic communications, to say nothing of their cell phones. Hackers were doing it all the time. Most people didn't care, but for those who did, recent developments in the news made it clear, you could no longer trust your cell phone or your computer when it came to personal or professional privacy. And they weren't dealing here with mere matters of legal etiquette, feared breaches of the sacred seal of lawyer-client. Anyone probing these communications was probably looking to kill Alex and anyone else unlucky enough to be near him at that moment.

There was no sure way to protect against the penetration of communications and no time to look for encrypted phones. Even if they could find them, it was hard to know if they were equipped with the latest scrambling software.

The trio, Paul, Harry, and Herman, after thinking about it, decided that the best option was the one used by the Unabomber. He had managed to stay off the radar screen of the most technologically advanced government on earth for more than a decade—by going primitive. No computers, no telephones, no wires leading to his shack in the woods, not even electricity. They agreed not to use e-mails, the Internet, or phones, either cell or landlines, to communicate.

Any messages would go by snail mail or private delivery services, and even then they would not be delivered directly to the condo unit, unless it was an emergency. They would be collected by Herman, if sent by mail, at general delivery in the post office. If sent by private carrier he would pick them up at the carrier's local office. It might take a few days longer to get there, but they believed that the risk of its being intercepted and read were far less. They would keep the content of any messages short and cryptic, giving away as little information as possible.

The clerk behind the counter took the envelope from Herman. He put it on the scale, checked the waybill, completed his portion of it, and then entered whatever information was needed into the company's computer. This produced a stick-on barcode. He peeled the sticker from its backing, slapped it onto the envelope, handed Herman his copy of the waybill with its tracking number on it, and dropped the envelope into the mailbag for shipment to the airport with the next delivery.

Herman turned and headed for the door. He would hop in a cab and in a few minutes he would be back under the cabana with Ives, fondling a cold bottle of Dos Equis.

Twenty

The headquarters of the *Washington Gravesite* are located on K Street in downtown D.C., just a few blocks from the White House. The offices are in a high-rise office building between a dairy trade association and a door with a brass plaque on it bearing the name of a lobbyist and his associates.

Inside the smoked glass doors of the *Gravesite* there is a front counter with a receptionist. Behind her in an open area the size of a basketball court is a small army of employees chipping away like inmates on a rock pile at the keyboards in front of them. Some of them are wearing headsets, talking on the phone as they type. The place has the appearance of a boiler room, no art or pictures on the wall, no indoor plants. Just steam coming out of the ears of the people working.

210 · STEVE MARTINI

If the markets and their analysts are correct, the old world of newsprint is breathing its last, being replaced by flickering screens and stories that are updated by the second, faster than the human brain can absorb them.

Most of the people working here are young, in their twenties, burning with the fervor of a new generation of journalists. You can smell it in the air and see it on their faces. For them it's the Wild West. They are finding their feet in a new industry. Hard news blog sites are cropping up on the Internet like iron printing presses and fixed type on the old frontier. Some of them have their own brand of journalism and their own rules. It's a changing universe and one with a lot of downsides for the dinosaurs.

Many people are scared, especially those in their middle years. The pace of change has many of them terrified. If you work in a paper mill or a warehouse, drive a truck, or deliver newspapers, you have to wonder what the future holds.

On his website, Tory Graves claims to be watching over government because many in the traditional press and television have given up the ghost. "No longer reporting hard news, they are now in the propaganda business, depending on which side of the partisan divide they stand and who is in power. WE PRINT

THE NEWS!" These last four are words that might have spilled from the mouth of William Randolph Hearst or his fictional alter ego Charles Foster Kane in another age.

They are splashed on a banner in bold black type and hang above three sets of doors on the far wall. It is toward one of these, the double doors in the center, that I am directed.

He offers me a Coke or something else to drink. When I turn him down, he cuts to the chase. "I don't have a lot of time. We're approaching deadline. I've got another meeting with my staff in forty minutes, so whatever it is you want, could you make it quick? I would appreciate it," he says.

Tory Graves appears to be in his mid-fifties. Beady little eyes but otherwise not bad looking. Tall, slender, disheveled, a wrinkled dress shirt that looks as if it's been slept in for a couple of days. He wears a pair of wire-rim glasses propped on his forehead atop a full graying mop of hair that has the look of an overdue meeting with a set of shears.

He flops into the chair behind his desk that has the same cluttered appearance as the man, stacks of papers and books, a half-eaten apple on a napkin on the back corner nearest him. Looking at the frenetic soul seated there, I suspect this may be his lunch.

212 · STEVE MARTINI

"I'm sorry," he says. "I don't mean to be rude. How is Alex? I have been meaning to call him. I just haven't had the time. I hope he's all right. Is he making out financially?"

Ives has been off payroll, on leave now for a month. Graves, for some reason, docked him immediately following his arrest. He didn't fire him, but instead told him in a letter that had the scent of a lawyer's hand on it that Alex was suspended without pay pending the disposition in his case.

"He's all right," I tell him. "Worried, of course, but he's doing OK, at least for the moment." I leave a little wiggle room, since "OK" in this case embraces hiding out in Mexico as insurance against being killed.

"How can I help you?"

There is no sense trying to dance around the pink gorilla sitting in the middle of his desk, so I go right to the furry beast. "I take it you knew that the victim in this case, the person killed in the accident with Alex, was Olinda Serna?"

"Emm." He runs his hands through his hair, pulling it over the crown of his head. It immediately flops back over his ears the instant his hands leave it. "I'd heard that," he says.

"And you know who she is?"

"I know she worked for a law firm here in Washington."

"I believe you also know that she figures prominently in a major news story that your publication is currently working on."

"Where did you hear that?" he asks.

"I don't have time to play around," I tell him.

"We may be on the trail of a hot story, but then we work on a lot of big stories," he says.

"This one, I'm told, is a capper."

"So?"

"So you don't think it's strange that Serna, who was being probed and poked in the journalistic sense by one of your reporters, ends up dead, killed in an automobile accident three thousand miles away on the other side of the country? In the middle of nowhere? And the car she collides with is being driven by that same reporter?"

He looks at me, turns his nose up, and glances up at the ceiling. You can tell from his expression that the thought has crossed his mind. "How much did Alex tell you?"

"Enough to know that this is no coincidence."

"My first thought," he says, "was perhaps that he was following her a little too closely. Then I saw the news reports that said he was drunk. Mind you, I never knew Alex to drink. And certainly not on the job," he says. "You need to know that the *Gravesite* had absolutely no knowledge as to any history of prior alcohol or drug abuse on Alex's part. If that's what this is about, I'm going to have to end the conversation now. Because I'm going to want to bring in my lawyers."

"What?"

"If Serna's heirs are pushing Alex and looking for deep pockets behind him," he says, "they're barking up the wrong tree here."

"What? You think I'm here looking for cover in a tort case? Some whacked-out theory of agency? That the *Gravesite* might be liable for monetary damages if Alex was on the job when he killed her?"

"You tell me," he says.

"Furthest thing from my mind," I tell him. Though I hadn't thought about it until now, this could be another headache down the road. "That's not what this is about. Alex wasn't drinking at the time of the accident. At least he wasn't drunk. The police report shows only a small amount of alcohol in his system. No more than one drink."

"If that's true, how did the accident happen? What does Alex say?"

"He was unconscious. He doesn't remember anything."

"You mean he has amnesia?"

"No. Not in any ordinary sense," I tell him.

"What then?"

"We believe he was drugged. Driven out to the site by someone else and used to stage the accident."

He gives me a look like I'm a man from Mars, smiles, and says, "Are you serious?"

I nod. "Very much."

"You're telling me Serna was murdered?"

"Looks like it. What's more, we believe that two other people besides Serna have now been killed because one of them was unlucky enough to have been used to set up the accident. She knew too much, and for this reason we believe she was killed."

"You *are* serious!" he says. The expression on his face is not so much one of shock as that of a prospector who's found gold.

"I need to know what's going on. What it is that you're investigating, and how Serna fits into the picture."

"Holy . . . I always suspected they were hard-core," he says, "but I never envisioned this."

"Who?"

"What kind of evidence do you have?" He grabs a pencil and starts fishing on his desk for a fresh piece of paper. "Tell me," he says. "Can you give me the names of these two other people? The ones who were killed? You do have evidence?" Our meeting is suddenly turning into my interview.

"We're unable to prove the presence of drugs in Alex's system. We think they used what are called roofies . . ."

He stops his scribbling long enough to look up and say, "You mean the date rape drug."

"That's the one."

He writes it down.

"It works its way out of your system very quickly and leaves you with no memory of what happened during the time you were under. None of this is for publication," I tell him.

"Of course. Of course," he says. "Have you told anybody else about this?" Graves wants an exclusive.

"Not yet. But I may be forced to tell a jury, and to do it sooner than I would like, given the sparse evidence we have. That's why I'm here talking to you."

"Ah, I see," he says. "So you don't have any hard evidence." He puts the pencil down.

"Circumstantial only. I may not be able to prove any of this unless I can show a compelling reason why someone else might have wanted to kill Serna."

"I'm not sure I can help you," says Graves.

"You said these people are hard-core. Who are you talking about?"

He shakes his head. "There's nothing I can tell you," he says. "I'm sorry."

"I know you're working on a hot story. Alex told me so."

"What exactly did he tell you? He didn't give you any documents, did he, anything in writing?"

"No. But I know that Serna was involved. I know it has to do with offshore banking and private numbered accounts. I know it all started a few years ago with the campaign by the Treasury and the IRS to identify American taxpayers who were believed to be evading US taxes by hiding money in undisclosed foreign accounts. I know that some funny things started happening when Uncle Sam got too close to powerful people believed to hold some of these accounts. Perhaps some politicians?" I wrinkle an eyebrow and look at him, a human question mark.

"Alex has been talking out of school," he says.

"Alex is in trouble," I tell him.

"Still, you really don't know anything," says Graves.

"So enlighten me."

He tilts his head, looks at me, a pained expression. "I wish I could." Hands back in his hair. "I wish I could. I really do. But I can't."

"If I can't tell a judge and a jury what's going on here, Alex is very likely to end up in prison. A long stretch," I tell him. "You do understand that?"

"I'm sorry. I wish I could help. But the story is no longer mine."

"What do you mean? Alex told me you knew everything."

"Well, he was exaggerating," says Graves. "There are still things we don't know and some important details we haven't been able to confirm."

"But you can tell me what you do know."

"Can't do that either," he says.

"If you force the issue, I can drag you in front of a judge, subpoena your records and notes. You know as well as I do the court will compel you to turn them over. There is no shield law that's going to protect you in a case like this. A man's liberty is at stake. The court will balance the equities and I got news. You're going to come up short."

"I understand and you're probably right. But you still won't get anything," he says.

"The judge could put you in jail," I tell him. "Contempt for refusing to comply with a court order."

"Hell, you'd probably be doing me a favor," says Graves. "All that publicity would serve to increase the value of the *Gravesite*. Besides, there are forces at work here you don't understand."

"Enlighten me," I tell him.

"I don't know how much I should tell you," says Graves. "Maybe we should just let everything fall where it may."

"Aw, come on, be a pal to your employee," I tell him. "A hint or two might keep Alex out of the slammer."

"I doubt it," he says. "Problem is, I don't own the story any longer, the stuff involving Serna."

"What do you mean?"

Graves takes a deep breath. "Alex doesn't know about this. Nor do any of the people out there." He gestures with a nod toward the outer office. "If they knew they'd all be looking for other jobs. You see, I own the *Gravesite.* I started it twenty years ago. I tried to root it in the old traditions—Drew Pearson, Jack Anderson. You know. But between you, me, and that wall over there, the entire operation is heavily in debt. It's the problem with e-journalism, the problem with changing technology, with many of the businesses operating on the net. It's the question of how you monetize your product. How to get people to pay for it."

"That's interesting. I sympathize. But what's that got to do with Serna and why the world caved in on her?"

"Everything," he says. "Do you know who Arthur Haze is?"

"Who doesn't?" Haze is in his eighties, a billionaire media mogul with a chain of newspapers, radio and cable channels that span a good chunk of the globe. Most people want to be rich and famous. Haze, from a young age, wanted to be famous for being rich. And he succeeded.

"In the last four years, I've entertained two offers to buy the *Gravesite* outright. Both of them from Haze. I turned both of them down. It wasn't the money," he says. "I don't want to sell. The *Gravesite* isn't for sale to anyone and especially to someone like Haze. He would turn it into a tiny cog in a massive media machine. It would get lost.

"But then a year ago I ran into difficulties. I could no longer meet overhead. I cut some jobs. Didn't want to, but I had no choice. All I was doing was buying a little time. I thought about moving out of the high rent district. But even with that, the writing was on the wall. I could make payroll for maybe a few more months and that was it. I needed capital. I needed a loan, a big one.

"I went to the banks. They turned me down flat. The financial value of the *Gravesite* is in its future, which, like everything else on the web, is highly speculative. They weren't willing to take the chance. There was only one place I could go—Haze," he says.

"He had mountains of cash. When I first approached him, he thought about it and said no. All he had to do was sit back and wait until I went under. Then he could pick up the *Gravesite* for pennies on the dollar. I had to find something that would force him to change his mind. And I did. It was the story that involves Serna," says Graves.

"It was the biggest story we've ever had. I reduced everything we knew, all the evidence we had, our research files, the entire story, to writing and copyrighted it. I talked to my lawyers and, only after they were satisfied, I shared one copy of the materials with Haze.

"He's an old newspaper hand. It was where he cut his teeth when he was a kid. He knew a hot story when he saw one. He realized that with the copyrighted materials and the fact that the story was so big, that if we succeeded in getting to publication we could sell it all over the world. And everybody would be buying because if they didn't, they would be locked out of some of the details on the biggest story since Watergate— bigger!" he says. "The revenue stream would be sufficient to carry us for years. Haze might not get another chance to buy the *Gravesite*, and he wanted it, wanted it badly."

"So Haze bought the copyright," I say.

Graves nods. "So now you understand why I can't talk. Even if I wanted to. We have the exclusive rights on first publication, so the *Gravesite* gets attribution everywhere the story appears. But eighty percent of the revenue goes to Haze. The money he paid will keep our doors open for at least two more years. If we can publish in that time, and I think we can, the money from the story and the global publicity will carry us over the hump."

"In the meantime, Alex goes to prison," I tell him.

"If I talk. If I told you anything specific as to the story, Haze would sue me seven ways from Sunday. He'd get the *Gravesite* and everything it possesses, including the story," says Graves. "I just can't help you. I'm sorry."

"What about Rubin Betz?" I ask.

Graves's little eyes grow wider with the mention of the name.

"What can you tell me about him?"

"What did Alex tell you?"

"He said that you referred to Betz as the Holy Grail. The key to your story."

"What exactly did he tell you? Did he use those words?"

I smile and play along. "He said that Betz held the key."

With this he gives me a quizzical glance.

"Come on, at least give me a clue."

"Then you don't know, do you?"

"Know what?"

"Never mind," he says.

"Alex called Betz the whistleblower. Said he was in a federal prison. Maximum security to keep him quiet. He told me that Betz knew things about powerful people. That he claimed to have the goods on some prominent politicians with undeclared numbered accounts offshore. That Betz and Serna were, in a word, 'acquainted.' And that the government was doing everything in its power to keep him there, to shut him up."

"I've never talked to the man. Nor has anyone from the *Gravesite*," says Graves. "What we know about Betz is pretty much in the public domain. Everything except his ancient history with Serna. You can look it up," he says. "Stories on the Internet. Stuff in the newspapers. Most of it unconfirmed. Now if you could get to Betz, talk to him and find some way to confirm what he knows, being that you're a lawyer, you might be able to find out what we can't. In that case, we might be able to work out a deal. Sharing information," he says.

"You think the stuff on Betz is true?"

"What I think doesn't matter," says Graves. "All that counts is what we can confirm."

"And what about Switzerland? Alex says the two of you took a couple of trips there looking for some information? And that you went to meet someone, alone."

"No comment," he says. "I can't talk about that."

"Give me a break," I tell him. "Can't you at least give me something? I assume you don't want Alex to go to prison?"

"I don't," he says. "He's a good reporter. Dogged. I like him. I like him a lot." Graves looks like a man who's trapped. Worried and perhaps feeling like a heel at this moment, at least I hope so, anything would help. "Let me think," he says. He wheels around in his swivel chair, turns his back to me for a moment, and looks out the window, the wall of glass behind him toward the buildings across the street.

When he turns back, the fingers of both hands are steepled under his chin as if he is deep in thought. "I don't know a lot about the law or copyright," he says. "But I assume that if you were to discover what I know on your own, from other sources independent from any information we have here at the *Gravesite,* without any assistance from me or my staff, that Haze would have no claim against the *Gravesite.*"

Of course, this ignores what Alex has already told me. I nod. "That's true."

"Did you ever read the Bible?" he asks.

"I have."

"Then you know that Jesus spoke in parables."

I nod again.

"I make no pretense to be the Son of God," he says, "but listen to my parable and see what you can draw from it."

"Can I take notes?"

"No! Do you remember Abscam?"

"I remember the movie."

"That was *American Hustle*. This was the real thing," he says. "It may be that's where they first got the idea."

"Who?"

He gives me a face and shakes his head like that's out of bounds. "You wanted a clue. I'm giving you one. Abscam was a political scandal back in the late seventies, early eighties. It started as an FBI undercover sting involving stolen property and corrupt business types in the Big Apple. It lasted for two years.

"Then in the last few months somebody at the FBI got the bright idea to take it in a different direction. It morphed into a probe of political corruption and migrated from New York to Washington. By the time it got here it had grown into a couple of musta-chioed Arab oil sheiks throwing money to members of Congress willing to do official favors in return. In the end, by the time the FBI pulled the plug and shut it down, they had netted six members of the House and one US senator. There was one member of Congress who, when offered the money, actually said 'No' and another who mumbled sufficiently so that they couldn't bring charges.

"When they finally went public, the FBI got ham-mered from every side. Some claimed it was a setup, that otherwise ethical politicians were induced to commit crimes because they were entrapped. Others said the FBI folded their tent and shut down the show because of fear that the political class, those who sur-vived, would get their revenge by crushing the bureau when the dust settled. The FBI's official version is that it all came to a sudden end because one young lawyer at the Justice Department who was privy to the details left his briefcase containing sensitive undercover infor-mation on a train. You can take your pick. I like the second one," said Graves.

"You'll notice that was thirty-five years ago and there hasn't been another sting aimed at politicians in Washington since. That tells you something. The rumor was that had they let it go on for a few more months, they might not have been able to find a quorum for either house under that great big dome. The place would have been empty." With this, the story stops and he looks at me.

"Your point is?"

"If you look closely, you'll see there are several lessons here. One," he says, "is that most politicians are oversize. They have massive egos and appetites to match. They are always testing to see if they can game the system. And monkeys learn from past mistakes."

"OK." I have no idea where he's going with this.

"You don't get it, do you?"

I shake my head.

"If people are getting stung, sent away for acts of corruption committed here, what's the answer?" he says.

"Go straight?"

"Remember these are people with big egos," he says.

"Do it offshore?" I say.

"Bingo."

"OK, but I still don't get it."

"Second parable," he says. "A lesson from J. Edgar. Very brief. Then I gotta run. Got a meeting and I'll see you to the door," he says.

"You remember back in the seventies, maybe before your time, J. Edgar Hoover, the director of the FBI?

He died in '72, I think. But he was director for almost forty years. They couldn't get rid of him. They tried, believe me. Several presidents wanted to fire his ass. He was an irascible bastard with a lot of vices. Years after he died, we found out that the mob had been paying his gambling debts at racetracks for years. So according to Hoover's Bureau, the official position of the FBI was that there was no such thing as organized crime in America. The next time somebody looks at today's FBI and tells you this ain't your daddy's FBI, you tell them you sure as hell hope not.

"Anyway, they couldn't fire the son of a bitch. Hoover had a card catalogue in his closet at home filled with all kinds of embarrassing information. For years he'd been using the bureau's agents to dig up dirt on politicians all over this city. Not only here but back in their home states. If you were an aspiring politician with some dark skeleton under your bed you could be sure J. Edgar would find it and take pictures of it for his files. Anybody who was anybody had a file in Hoover's closet. If you were important, you had two or three. And if you even dreamed about making a move on him, he let it be known that your life story with every wart highlighted in headlines would spread out all over the wires and in every newspaper in the country by the next morning. As you can imagine, he didn't need to do a lot of arm twisting on Capitol Hill when it came to the bureau's budget. Some people call it extortion. But I once heard a very wise man refer to it as 'the Hoover Effect.' Now you go home and you think about it, these two parables. Put 'em together and see what you come up with. I'm sure it will come to you."

He opens the center draw of his desk, takes something out. Something small, because when he closes his hand it's gone, I can no longer see it. Instantly he's out from behind his desk, easing me out of my chair, his arm around my shoulder, guiding me toward the door while I'm still trying to close up my briefcase. "It was nice talking to you," he says. "Perhaps we can do it again sometime under happier circumstances." He waltzes me out through the computerized rock pile in the boiler room outside, past the receptionist, through the smoked glass doors, and into the public corridor outside.

He reaches out to shake my hand, then looks down as he does it. "You dropped something," he says.

Before I can say anything Graves reaches down to pick it up. Without looking at it he hands it to me. Then he shakes my hand, smiles, and before I can say a word he is gone back into his office.

He disappears behind the counter and through the sea of workstations beyond. I look at the item in my left hand. It's a business card, very stiff, raised lettering, something expensive: "Gruber Bank, A.G." The information on the card appears to be printed in German, telephone numbers, a street address in Lucerne, and the name "Simon Korff, Auslandskonten."

Twenty-One

W e know where he is. We know the general area. And we're on top of it. Give us twenty-four hours, we should have him." They had located Alex Ives.

"Where is he?" asked the Eagle.

"Mexico, a small resort town on the Pacific coast. Not a lot of places for him to hide there."

"Are you sure?" The Eagle wasn't convinced. "Ives didn't have a passport. He was out on bail. The court would have forced him to surrender his passport as a condition of release."

"Yeah, we thought about that," said the other man. "Then it hit us. Ives's old man has connections through his business. What if they chartered a flight and flew to a small strip where there's nobody to check for a passport?"

"Go on," said the Eagle.

"We haven't seen him, but we know he's there. All we have to do is hang tight. The man with him will lead us right to him."

"Good job," said the Eagle, ". . . if you're right."

The guy at the other end smiled as he explained how they did it. They had been using the cell phones belonging to the two lawyers, not only to listen in on their conversations and phone calls, but to track their locations.

Then suddenly both phones went dead, almost at the same time, as if someone had removed the batteries. It happened the night the girl was killed at the gas station, almost within minutes of the event. There was one quick call between the two lawyers and that was it. Both phones remained dead for almost twenty-four hours.

At the same time, incoming calls to the office from an investigator who worked for the firm, a man named Herman Diggs, whose cell was also being tapped, and who generally called in at least once or twice each day, dried up completely. They knew where the two lawyers were. One was in Washington. The Eagle confirmed that. The other was at the office in San Diego. But the investigator, Diggs, had disappeared.

Connecting the dots wasn't hard. Diggs was baby-sitting Ives. The question was where?

About the same time that the cell phone traffic fell off, there seemed to be more frequency in the number of deliveries from private mail services to the office. It was hard to miss. DHL, in particular.

One of the more enterprising eaglets decided to go Dumpster diving in the trash bin behind the firm's office late at night to see what he could find. Among the piles of trash he brought back, they looked for messages but found none. These they figured must have been shredded. But among the items pilfered were the various account numbers for the firm's private delivery services, DHL, FedEx, and United Parcel.

Account numbers usually appeared on waybills that customers using the service often simply tossed into the trash when they were finished tracking packages that had already arrived at their destination. None of the waybills looked as if they had anything to do with Ives or where he might be.

It was the account numbers for the various carriers that turned out to be the key. With the cutting-edge software they possessed, the Eagle's minions were able to marry up the Madriani account number for each carrier with the tracking number for each delivery paid for under that account. They didn't have to go back very far, only a few days to the time when Ives disappeared.

The linkage of account numbers with individual tracking numbers on packages was accomplished by a stick-on barcode slapped on every package by the carrier when the item was first dispatched. The barcode allowed the carrier to use handheld scanners at each point along the delivery route to instantly collect the identifying information and show the location of the package. This information was fed wirelessly to a central computer system and could be used by the company or a customer who possessed the tracking number to go online and track the progress of the delivery from its point of origin to its ultimate destination.

It was the item from Zihuatanejo on the Mexican coast, a place some of the gringos and locals called "Zihua," pronounced "Zee-wah," with the name of the sender, H. Diggs, that instantly caught their attention.

For the Eagle, this was the sign that his crew had finally done something right. Before he could ask, they told him that they had already dispatched two men down to Mexico to hang out near the DHL office at that location. They had a picture of the investigator from the P.I.'s state licensing agency so they could easily identify him. If authorized, they were prepared to "scrub" Ives as well as the investigator if he got in the way, the latest in a long line of euphemisms for murder.

Mexico was the perfect cover. You didn't need a traffic accident to do it down there. Make it look like a drug hit and even if they had to kill both men, it would draw less attention than death by natural causes in most other places. The Eagle didn't bat an eye. All he said was: "Do it!"

Having gotten what he wanted, the man at the other end hung up.

The light on the Eagle's smartphone went dark as his eyes returned to the picture window across the street. He was parked, seated in his car in Georgetown across from a small restaurant. Inside he could see the lawyer, Madriani, and another man at a table. They were talking over drinks. Through the open window of his car the Eagle took several pictures with a long-lens camera. He didn't know who the other man was, but he intended to find out. He wanted no more loose ends.

Before our drinks arrive I realize that Cletus Proffit has been doing his homework, probably burning up the computer cables to LexisNexis, the lawyer's crystal ball into the unknown. He is not only familiar with my client's name, he knows that Ives worked for the *Gravesite*. On Nexis, if you punched in Alex's name and did a search, no doubt you would find every story ever published under his byline. I am guessing that this must have rattled Proffit's brain when he first saw it.

"What a coincidence," he says, "that two people who worked here in Washington should be involved in an accident there."

I play it down. I tell him that Ives actually worked for the *Gravesite* out on the West Coast, but still it is a small world.

"Indeed," he says. If he knows about the story involving Serna, he hides it well. Any thought that his firm was under the glass being studied by Graves for prominent mention in the scandal sheets I would think would have curled his socks right up to his eyeballs. Instead, he changes gears and asks me whether I do very many drunk-driving cases.

I tell him no.

"I was wondering about that," he says. "Because it would seem to be a very strange case."

"Why is that?"

"From what I understand, your client's blood alcohol level was well below the legal limit."

The only way he could know this is if he had ordered up a copy of the police report. It answers one question: Someone at Proffit's firm is keeping tabs on our case. That could be a problem if they decide to wade in, to push the prosecutor for sterner action.

"That's true," I tell him. There is no sense lying about it.

"Then how do you account for it? The accident, I mean?"

"It's a mystery," I tell him.

"Emm." This sets him to chewing on a sliver of ice from his highball.

"What can you tell me about Serna?" I ask.

"Wonderful woman," he says. "Hard worker. Always there when you needed her."

"What type of work did she do?"

"You don't know?"

It's an irritating practice that some people develop, answering questions with a question. Proffit has it down pat.

"No."

"Mostly she worked legislation. Up on the Hill. Sometimes the White House but mostly Congress. She did some admin law, appearances before the regulatory agencies when we needed it. Mixed bag." He says it like this is a description of the woman herself. "She'll be missed."

Yes, but not by Proffit, unless I miss my bet. "You make her sound dynamic."

He looks at me over his drink, chuckles a little, and says, "She had her moments."

"What did she do before she came to the firm?"

"Legislative staff." He takes a sip, Jim Beam over ice. Like a deposition, he offers nothing more.

"What did she do there?"

"Worked for the Senate Finance Committee. Later I think, if I remember right, she went to Senate Banking. She seemed to have a good head for figures. And a photographic memory. Everything she read she retained instantly," he says. "A mind like a steel trap."

"The way you say it, makes it sound like perhaps you got caught in it?" I smile at him.

"No. No. On the contrary, we got along very well. In fact, I was the one who put her up for partner," he says.

"How long ago was that?"

"Two years," he says. "And there was no opposition. Everyone agreed she deserved it. She lived for the firm."

"No family life?"

He shakes his head. "Lived alone, I believe."

"Did she have many friends?"

"Oh, she belonged to her share of organizations. Women's groups mostly. Professional associations. So I'm sure she had friends."

"But you didn't know any of them?"

"No. We weren't that close. Not socially," he says.

"I'm told she had a boyfriend at one time."

This gets his interest. "Really?" he says. "Where did you hear that?"

"I don't remember," I tell him. "But somebody I was talking to mentioned it."

"Emm." He sits there waiting for me to offer more. When I don't, he says, "Do you remember the guy's name?"

"What guy?" Two can play this game.

"The boyfriend," he says.

"Oh, that. It was a while back. Betz, I think was the name. Yeah, Rubin Betz."

If he recognizes it, he doesn't show it.

"Do you know what she did before she was on congressional staff?" I ask him.

He shakes his head. "No. That's going back a ways. Before my time."

"I doubt that," I tell him.

"What I mean to say is that was some years before I met her."

"I see."

I am beginning to think that we have exhausted all the topics when suddenly he looks up at me and says, "Do you know whether they knew each other?"

"Who?"

"Your client and my partner," says Proffit. "Had they ever met, before the accident, I mean?"

"I don't think so. What would make you think that?"

"I don't know, I'm just wondering," he says. "They ran in the same circles. Washington politics. Maybe they knew each other."

Suddenly it hits me. What Proffit is concerned about is the chance that Ives and Serna might have been meeting at some remote location so that she could feed him information on something. Maybe she was one of his sources. I begin to wonder if Ives has been straight with me.

"I'll have to ask him," I say.

"I'd be curious," says Proffit.

I'll bet he would.

"Do you know what your client was doing way out there?"

"You mean where the accident happened?"

"Yeah."

"Says he can't remember," I tell him.

"Really? Musta been one hell of a collision."

"It was."

"What about her? Do the police know why Olinda was out there?"

"If they do, they haven't shared it with me," I tell him. "Do you know?" I turn it on him.

He shakes his head vigorously.

"What was she doing in California?" I ask.

"We're not sure," he says.

"So she wasn't there on business?"

"It's possible," he says. "She pretty much ran her own operation. From the firm, I mean."

"So she didn't have to clear travel with anyone?"

"No."

"What about her calendar?" I ask. I look at him and realize from his expression that this is getting too close to the corporate bone. No doubt if I subpoenaed her calendar, Proffit's firm would object on grounds of attorney-client privilege.

"I'm not sure. I'd have to look," he says. "Funny thing about Olinda. I don't think she used a calendar much. Kept everything pretty much in her head."

I'm getting the sense that if there was anything on a calendar, Proffit's probably going to go home and burn it.

"I take it she didn't have any family in that area?"

"Not that we know of," he says. "We're still checking. How did your other meeting go?" He slips it in without missing a beat.

"Oh, fine. Fine," I tell him.

"It's good you were able to get so much accomplished on one trip," he says.

"Yes."

"I hope Mr. Graves was able to help you."

I look at him, son of a bitch! "How did you know who I was meeting with?"

"In this town," he says, "it's impossible to keep anything secret."

I sit there looking at him, wondering if he had Graves's office bugged.

Twenty-Two

Early the next morning, on the flight home, I settle back into my seat, close my eyes, and drift into that netherworld between consciousness and sleep. The pulse of the jet engines drowns out the idle chatter around me as I think about Graves and his silly parables. The ham-handed antics in the hallway with the German business card. He must think I'm some rube.

He has what we need. He admitted as much. His copy of the document he prepared for Arthur Haze with all the details of the story they're working on. The item he copyrighted in order to secure the loan. It was probably tucked into one of the filing cabinets in his office as we sat there talking.

But Graves is no fool. You can bet it's not there this morning. It would be too easy to roll into his shop with a subpoena and grab it before he or Haze could act to stop us. He would have moved it by now. Why couldn't the man make it easy on all of us and just tell me?

After talking to Graves, I'm convinced that we already know almost everything there is to know. His statements to me to the contrary, I believe, were bravado, an attempt to cover for the fact that Alex had already lifted the curtain on his show. What else could Graves say? *Then you really don't know anything, do you?* Nice try. I think the only thing we're missing are the details. But then, of course, the devil always lives there. What we need is a name, dates, account numbers, and perhaps a few other hard verifiable facts that we can present to a court.

Serna was blackmailing somebody. Of that I am certain. Whoever it was either killed her or had someone else do it. From what Alex told us, it was probably some powerful pol in Washington who had an offshore numbered account. How much is in it or where the money came from is anyone's guess. But if I had to, I would say that it's not their failure to pay taxes that is the problem. God knows that enough appointed and elected officials have "forgotten" to pay tax on earnings they made overseas in recent years and have received nothing but a slap on the wrist from the IRS, collection of back taxes, and payment of a penalty at most.

But what if the source of the funds is a foreign bribe? That's an entirely different kettle of fish. With the IRS and Treasury stomping around in the weeds looking for American taxpayers hiding money overseas, a high-profile politician with a hidden slush fund in a Swiss bank would be in a highly agitated state.

Somehow Serna found out. Perhaps she was given the information by the whistleblower, Betz, before he went into the slammer. That would make sense. The reason they couldn't kill Betz was because he had something buried, insurance against accidental death, information that kept him breathing. But it wasn't enough to keep him out of prison. He tried to cut a deal with the feds, and they weren't buying. I make a mental note to find out when he was sentenced, where he's serving his time, and to check for any news stories surrounding his trial. Whoever Serna was extorting killed her. This makes perfect sense.

It's the other piece of the puzzle that gets clumsy. Why did they go after Alex and try to rope him into the accident? If Graves was the one with the details, killing Alex wouldn't solve their problem. Then again, people act on what they know or what they think they know, and sometimes on what they see. If it was Ives who was assigned to investigate Serna, and we know that it was. If that's what they saw, then going after

Alex made sense. This would be true especially if they couldn't be sure how much he knew.

With my eyes still closed, I finger the small business card nestled deep in the side pocket of my suit jacket. I pull it out, open my eyes, and look at it again. For once I wish I'd taken German in high school instead of Spanish. The long unintelligible word under the man's name "Auslandskonten." I wonder what it means.

Proffit stepped off the long escalator into the crowded underground cave that was the Washington Metro station at Crystal City. Early-morning rush hour and the place was mobbed. Under the high honeycombed arch of the ceiling, civil servants and sexy young secretaries in short skirts moved like a herd of wildebeest toward the platform and the rails that would take them downtown to work.

Ten minutes earlier Cletus had left Vicki Preebles back at her apartment, told her to sleep late and come into the office around noon. One of the perks of banging the boss.

He sipped on his Starbucks cappuccino through the little hole in the cup's plastic cover. Somebody jostled him from behind and he burned his lip. He looked down and saw three or four dots of milky foam as they dribbled down the lapel of his suit coat.

"Shit!" He stopped in midstride, shifted the cup from one hand to the other, shook the burning liquid from his fingers, and tried to brush the foam off his jacket. Like Moses parting the waters he forced the flood of people behind him to flow around if they wanted to get to the train platform.

This morning the place was like a game of bumper cars. Proffit would have preferred to use one of the firm's hired limos with a driver to run shuttle between the office and Vicki's place, but to do so would have left a record of his sleepovers. He didn't need any wagging tongues at work, or anonymous e-mails to his wife from pissed-off secretaries who had to show up for work at eight. Better safe than sorry.

Proffit's marriage at this point was more business than pleasure. His wife, a federal judge, was pleasant enough in a social setting, but alone with Cletus she was a stone-cold idol. She knew what he was up to. To rub her nose in it was to play with fire. Press the issue and she could probably show him that she still knew her way around in a divorce court. He didn't want to find out. They tolerated each other because it suited their purposes. Besides, Proffit knew that she had been sleeping with one of her clerks for almost a year now, taking nooners at a local hotel whenever the docket was slow. Leave well enough alone. He could ride the Metro with the unwashed.

He glanced down to check the folded silk handker-chief in his chest coat pocket, to make sure it wasn't stained with coffee or wrinkled, then proceeded on his way. He held the cup out and danced around a cluster of commuters in order to move toward the edge of the platform.

People jostled back and forth in front of him like cross traffic at an intersection looking to position them-selves toward the front or back of the train when it came. A man in a dark trench coat packing a briefcase shot across his path like a comet just inches in front of him. Proffit had to come up short just to avoid shower-ing the guy with hot coffee.

"Excuse me!" said Proffit.

"You're excused." The guy turned and looked over his shoulder as he said it.

Proffit did a double take.

The man quickly disappeared into the mob. To Proffit, he looked like the original mad professor, a shock of messed-up graying hair on his head. He recognized him immediately from the photographs e-mailed to his office the day before. Photographs from the investigator Proffit had hired to track the lawyer, Madriani, from the airport when he arrived, to his meeting the previous afternoon.

It was Tory Graves. Small damn world, thought Proffit. Too small. He was itching to get back to L.A., a town big enough you didn't have to worry about running into people you didn't want to see. His mind on other things, he didn't even notice the other man, the one moving around behind him carrying the tarnished bird's head cane.

Proffit felt the wind coming out of the tunnel, the singing steel of wheels on rail as the train approached. People pushed toward the edge of the platform. Clete found himself carried along in the swell of this human sea. His feet seemed to float across the rubberized mat toward the strip of concrete at the very edge. The round embedded red and yellow warning lights in the concrete strip began to flash.

In the distance he could see the lights on the train as it barreled through the tunnel speeding toward them. People kept pushing inexorably toward the tracks. All along the platform they jockeyed for position, the train getting closer, the wind on his face. Cletus felt himself leaning as someone pushed him from behind, another hit his hand.

Suddenly there was the screeching metal as the brakes shot on. Women were screaming as a dull thud echoed through the cavern like the sound of a melon smashing on concrete. The cup flew from Proffit's hand and splattered across the window on the leading car just above the spider of shattered glass and blood. The train shook and rattled, then stopped abruptly several hundred feet from its normal position.

Proffit realized that someone had been shoved off the platform in front of the train. It's what happened when you dallied with the unwashed. He straightened his suit coat, turned around, and plowed through the sea of humanity headed for the escalator and a taxi up top.

Seventy feet down the tracks the Eagle polished the silver handle on his cane with his handkerchief. There were times when a long narrow stick came in handy. After the Venusian eruption at the gas station in San Diego he had decided to take care of this loose end himself.

Twenty-Three

By the time I step off the plane and make my way to the baggage area, Harry is already there waiting for me. He looks flushed, out of breath. He's probably double-parked out in front hoping the cops won't tow his car or worse, blow it up.

"Let's go."

"Gotta get my bag," I say.

"Why did you check it?"

"Wouldn't fit in the overhead. They downsized the flight, the plane was full. Two people got bumped, so you're lucky I'm here," I tell him.

"Apart from that, how did it go?"

"OK, I suppose. I'm not sure what I accomplished. The good news is Graves has what we need. The bad news is he won't share it with us, at least not willingly. Instead he wanted to speak in parables."

"Maybe he was having premonitions," says Harry. "Tory Graves is dead."

My head snaps around to look at him.

"He was killed this morning in the underground at one of the Washington Metro stations."

"How?"

"An accident," says Harry. He pushes his nose off to one side with his thumb as if to say, "for anyone stupid enough to believe it."

Harry had set the browser on his computer to capture any news from or about the *Washington Gravesite* and feed it to his e-mail. This morning, about an hour after I took off from Dulles he tells me that the little bleeping telegraph message tone on his iPad started going crazy.

"According to the reports, Graves fell off the platform directly into the path of an oncoming train. Very convenient," says Harry. "Perfect timing."

"At least whoever did it didn't blow up the station," I tell him.

"We wouldn't even know it was him," he says, "except somebody who saw it happen recognized Graves and called it in to the *Gravesite*. All the other news blogs are reporting that authorities declined to identify the victim pending notification of next of kin. Did he tell you anything?"

Before I can answer, Harry says: "Hold that thought. I gotta cover the car. Grab your bag and I'll meet you outside."

Back at the office we settle into the conference room as I continue to update Harry.

"You think he was telling the truth about the deal with Arthur Haze?" he asks.

"I don't know. But I have to say he made it sound plausible."

"Haze is no fool," says Harry. "If he forked over as much cash as Graves claimed, they must be sitting on one hell of a story. Which raises one other question."

"What's that?"

"Do you think whoever killed Graves knows about the deal, the fact that Haze has a copy of the story, at least as it stands?"

I hadn't considered this until Harry mentions it. "Good point." I think about it for a few seconds before I tell him: "There's no way to be sure, but I'm guessing they don't."

"Why is that?"

"Graves told me that Alex didn't know about the Haze deal, nor did any of his other employees. He was afraid if they knew the business was on the skids they'd be out looking for other work. So unless I'm wrong he held that information very close."

"Why did he tell you?"

"The only purpose I can think of is to scare me off. Graves wanted to let me know that if we issued a subpoena for records and notes we'd be up against deep pockets, swimming in a pool filled with sharks . . ."

"Meaning Haze's lawyers," says Harry.

I nod. Alex's parents are comfortable. But in a drawn-out battle in court, Arthur Haze could buy and sell them a few million times over and not even feel the pinch. His attorneys could probably tie us up for years if we tried to go after the copyrighted draft of the story.

"What about this stuff on Abscam and Hoover?" says Harry. "What was the point? What do you think he was trying to tell you?"

"Your guess is as good as mine." I tried to go over it all with Harry in the car on our way in from the airport. Without any notes, I struggled to recall the exact words used by Graves. Now that he is dead and no longer available I'm forced to think more seriously about what he said.

I reach out and grab a legal pad from the table and try to make some notes while at least part of it is fresh in my mind.

"Politicians being people with big egos and appetites," I say it out loud as I write so that Harry can follow along.

I make each one a bulleted point on the page with my pen. "Always testing the water to game the system."

"Learning the lesson of going offshore."

Little nuggets that probably lead nowhere.

"And finally, last but not least, the Hoover Effect. J. Edgar's torrid card catalogue and how he used it."

I look up at Harry. "Put it all together and what do you have?"

He shakes his head. "To me? It's a lotta crap," says Harry. "I don't want to take anything away from the dead but the fact that most politicians have big egos ain't gonna make it as a hot news flash anytime soon. Now if he found one that didn't, that might be a story. Nor is the fact that they game the system. The offshore part maybe," says Harry, "but only if we can get the specifics. Who's got what and where."

"Do me a favor. Check something over there on the computer for me."

Harry goes to the desktop in the corner.

"Google up one of their language translators."

He does it.

"German to English," I tell him. Then I spell out the word, the one with fourteen letters that I can't pronounce under the man's name from the business card given to me by Graves. When I'm done I tell him: "That's it."

Harry punches the return key and waits.

"What does it mean?" I ask.

"Foreign accounts," says Harry.

It was late in the afternoon on the fourth day when Ana finally saw the man she thought might be Madriani. Her car was parked at the curb as Ana sat at one of the tables at an outdoor café watching the entrance to the parking lot behind the law office.

She wasn't interested in the lawyers. What she wanted was more information about the people going through their trash. Who they were and whether they were connected with the man she had killed near the airport, the one who had her tripod and the satellite antenna.

She had been following the lawyer named Hinds for three days. She knew where he lived, an apartment on the other side of the bridge in San Diego, his name on the mailbox downstairs. She knew where he hung out, a small restaurant nearby where he had dinner each night and breakfast on two successive mornings. He always picked up a newspaper from a small cigar store on his way to work each morning. He had a dull routine and a life to match. No women. Lived alone. You could set your clock by him.

On the road she always stayed far enough behind him to allow anyone else who was tracking him to pull in front of her, but no one ever did. This made her nervous. The fact that the Dumpster divers disappeared into a military base meant that these people might well be looking down on both of them from an eye in the sky.

This morning she chose not to follow Hinds from his apartment into work and instead went directly to the office. He didn't show up. She didn't know why. Maybe he was sick.

She backtracked to his apartment, but his car was gone. Perhaps he was in court. If so there was nothing she could do but wait for him at the office. She sat at the table under the umbrella and watched the entrance to the alley behind the plaza that led to the parking lot. Hours went by and he never showed.

Ana kept an open paperback in front of her. Occasionally she stood to stretch her legs looking both ways up and down the street to see if anyone else was sitting in their car studying the alley entrance. Nothing.

She was about to pitch it in when, just before four, she saw Hinds's car pull around the corner, pass by, its left blinker already flashing as it turned into the alley and disappeared. There was a man sitting in the passenger seat next to Hinds.

Ana grabbed her book, paid for her coffee, and made a dash down the street the other way. She circled around the front of the building, entered the small plaza, and down the path past the door to their law office.

She could hear them talking back by the parked car. Ana stopped. One of them was coming this way, a gravelly sound like something being dragged on the pavement.

"Paul, why don't we lock your suitcase in the trunk? No need to take it into the office."

"You're right."

The other man had to be Madriani, first name Paul. She heard him turn and go back, then the pop of the trunk as it opened.

"Did Graves have any idea that Serna was murdered?"

"No, but when I told him, he was all ears, pen at the ready. He wanted all the details."

Ana made a note on the inside cover of the paperback in her hand, the name "Graves."

"He wasn't worried?"

"He didn't seem to be."

She heard the clatter of the suitcase as it was dropped into the trunk.

"But it got his journalist juices flowing."

"Did you tell him about the girl? The explosion at the gas station?"

"Yeah."

"And that didn't bother him either?"

The trunk slammed closed. Ana didn't hear the response, then: "Knowing what he knew you think he'd be worried."

"Knowing what *we* know maybe *we* should be worried."

What she heard was shoe leather on gravel coming this way. She turned and walked briskly in the other direction out toward the plaza. When she got there she turned just in time to get a look at Madriani.

He was tall, dark haired, a little gray around the ears, worry lines in the forehead and the beginnings of a five o'clock shadow. His suit coat slung over his shoulder and rumpled shirt made her think that he'd just gotten off a long flight. As soon as she got back to her hotel room she would run a news search for the name "Graves."

Twenty-Four

The Creeping Dragon nearly glowed with pride. His people had launched three small objects into orbit around the earth, antisatellite devices intended to blind and deafen America and its allies if and when the time came for war. The weapons had been hurled into space atop a Chinese launcher and were already conducting maneuvers as they circled the planet.

One of the weapons was equipped with a long extension arm capable of attacking American military and intelligence satellites and literally tearing them apart. It was part of the growing Chinese Star Wars program, a program that the current American administration pretended did not exist.

US satellites that had allowed America to dazzle the world with its military prowess through two Gulf wars were vulnerable to any adversary possessing the technology to destroy their eyes in the sky.

China not only had the ASAT (antisatellite) technology, but believed itself to be further advanced in this field than any other nation. More to the point, at a time when China was increasing its military and scientific research budgets, the United States was going in the opposite direction. America was reducing the size of their military to a level not seen since before the Great War, what the Americans called World War Two.

Cheng would meet up with Ying, his American asset, in little more than a week in Hong Kong, where the man came occasionally for quick trips to visit his money.

The bureau's assessment had already been delivered to the Chinese premier and to the standing committee of the Politburo. It was without question far more candid and certainly more realistic than the American president's last State of the Union message.

China had identified the problems of a budding cancer in the US body politic forty years earlier, even as the Cultural Revolution and the Red Guard were turning their own country toward chaos. Leaders in China and within the Chinese Army had reacted with an uprising of their own, deposing the "Gang of Four," Mao's wife and her cadre, who had given rise to ideological chaos.

A new generation of leaders pulled China back from the brink and set it on a rational course toward modernization. It was a program that required hard work, discipline, and a firm controlling hand by those in power.

Theirs, the new China, was not to be an open and unbridled democracy with its fits and starts and messy course alterations dictated by elections. Modern China would be a nation with vision and a program capable of taking the country and its people into the future.

Most of all, it would possess what America lacked—a well-designed, long-term strategic plan for the direction of the nation, but equally important, the sustained political will to carry it through.

The irony was that many in America thought of China as a socialist state. Yet it was America and its current crop of leaders who promised not only an open and free society but also a national government that was the planet's ultimate nirvana. A place where if power was transferred to them, these politicians would guarantee a flawless social safety net for all.

The problem was they could not pay for it. They financed it by plundering the surplus trust funds of other programs that they had been bleeding for decades, and in more recent years by selling US Treasuries to Cheng's own government.

The United States had been digging a deep hole for itself for at least three decades. American leaders sat by watching as vast sectors of their heavy industry hemorrhaged and ultimately fled offshore. Factories that didn't leave closed down. Some politicians actually assisted these industries in their departure. Many Americans didn't understand why. The politicians created cover for themselves claiming that this was all part of the "new world order."

The next round of leaders seemed stunned when they woke up to realize that many of these corporations, multinational American giants, were no longer paying taxes on their overseas income. Wonder of wonders! To cap it off, these selfsame leaders couldn't agree on a feasible method to encourage or force these companies to bring the money home. To the contrary they passed tax laws that actually discouraged this.

Cheng smiled. The bomb that was killing the United States was not hydrogen, atomic, or neutron. It was either stupidity or corrupt leadership, or both. And in Cheng's view it was sucking the air out of America. China had become America's banker for a simple reason. The United States needed ever-increasing infusions of cash.

Americans were told they could have it all. They were, after all, a rich nation!

Some US leaders invited the destitute of the world to cross their leaking borders with assurances that they would be entitled to the same. All that was required was political acquiescence to the politicians making the promises. They extolled America as the "great melting pot" and in the next breath engaged in dangerous games, pitting one group against another, then summed it all up by saying that "Americans needed to come together!" The nonsense made Cheng's eyes water with laughter.

The reality was that in America the truly rich had regiments of lawyers and accountants with numberless schemes to avoid taxes. And when that wasn't possible, they could hide their money offshore. There were members of Congress who knew that, because that's where they hid theirs.

It was irony indeed that in the late 1980s as Beijing edged closer to reclaiming control over the island of Hong Kong and its adjoining territories, many wealthy Chinese abandoned the island, seeking refuge in the West. This despite the fact that Chinese leaders gave firm assurances that they would not interfere with the financial gold mine that comprised international trade in Hong Kong.

Recently there had been difficulties in Hong Kong, demands for democracy. But Cheng knew in the end that Beijing would win. The answer, as always, was patience.

Land prices in Hong Kong were higher than ever, the highest in the world, and business thrived. The reality was that those with power and wealth always thrived, no matter the nature of the political process. To Cheng it was ironic to watch the wealthy capitalists in Hong Kong side with the Communist government in Beijing. Both wanted the same thing, stability. Democracy was expendable. Money could still be made. China needed capital from the West to fuel its modernization on the mainland. Accordingly they did what was necessary to carry the nation forward.

Why slam the door closed in Hong Kong when you could filter the message of libertine freedom from the West and use the open door of commerce and China's favorable wage rates to bleed your adversary dry? And besides, what better place to do business if your craft was espionage than your own island of economic avarice?

Twenty-Five

One of Herman's friends in Mexico supplied him with a local SIM card for his unlocked cell phone when he first arrived with Alex. The Telcel card allowed him to make local calls that could not be traced to Herman by name.

Each SIM card carried its own phone number. Throw the old one out and you could disappear and start over again with a new number. Mexico was now requiring some form of identification such as a passport to buy a SIM card, and to Herman, this was a sign. Every government on the globe was crawling up your behind to keep tabs on you like you were their puppet.

He used the local card each morning to check with DHL to see if any messages had come in under the name H. Diggs. This morning he was told there was one.

He trudged a few blocks before waving down a cab and did the drive, about four miles to Zihua and from there to the DHL office in an industrial area of town. He picked up the envelope at the counter and stepped to the side near the supplies as he opened it and read. The message caught him by surprise. He read it twice to make sure he understood what they were saying. Tory Graves, Alex's boss, was dead.

Herman didn't need the details to know that the man had been murdered. In the note, crafted by Harry, Hinds referred to it as "another accident."

The lawyers had cut Alex off from the Internet when he headed south to Mexico with Herman. They made sure that he left behind all of his electronic paraphernalia. His cell phone, computer, and iPad were in storage, at least until he returned and things were safe. They didn't want him leaving digital bread crumbs behind for the killers to follow.

Now with Graves dead, Madriani and Hinds worried that Alex might see it on the television in Mexico or read it from some other source and panic. They sent the short message south by DHL to Herman, an over-nighter, to alert them and to tell them both to just sit tight and wait.

As far as Herman was concerned, the lawyers' recommendations on something like this, where to stay and how to hide, were just that, recommendations. That's why they paid him. Herman would be guided by his own senses, and at the moment they were setting off uncomfortable vibes exploding like sky rockets. Four people murdered in accidents three thousand miles apart in little more than thirty days. Whoever was after them wasn't wasting any time.

Herman's first instinct was not to tell Alex about Graves's death. The last thing he needed was a kid in panic. Perhaps later. For the moment he decided just to pick Ives up and move, a new location, somewhere not too far, north or south, up or down the coast, simply telling Alex that this was all part of the original plan.

To Herman, the fact that they had murdered Graves meant that whoever was after them would now double down on their search for Alex. These were people with resources. They had proven that. It was possible that they already had a lead on the kid. Even if the chances of this were slim, the smart thing to do was to cut all the threads and force them to start looking all over again. If nothing else, it would buy time.

Herman fingered the cell phone in his pocket, thinking to call his contacts in Mexico, some quick help to relocate, but then thought better of it. He could call from the condo.

He crumpled up the message in his hand, but he didn't throw it out. Instead he stuffed the wrinkled ball of paper back in its envelope, tucked it under his tank top, and headed out. This time at a faster pace. He moved quickly along the street under the blazing morning sun looking for a taxi, anxious to get back as quickly as possible to the condo and Alex.

Becket is not an altogether uncommon name. Making it even more difficult is the fact that the girl, Ben, did not give me a first name, nor did she tell me if it was spelled with one *t* or two.

It's even a longer shot because of the question of whether Mr. Becket actually lives in the area at all. He could have been a guest at the party, perhaps buying a table. From what Alex described, the gathering sounded a lot like a fund-raiser, the older upper caste in tuxedoes and evening gowns, catered food and drink, all under Chinese lanterns.

We have issued a subpoena for information from the navigation satellite company supplying the equipment in Alex's car, but the company's legal team is dragging their feet.

So I've had my secretary and another assistant working on trying to find Mr. Becket for the better part of a day, and so far they have come up with forty-seven exact matches for the surname Becket under one of its two spellings in San Diego County alone.

Using the information given to us by Alex as to the general location of the party we have narrowed it to three exact hits showing that name with Del Mar postal addresses. This is, of course, assuming that Ives paid enough attention to know where he was when he got out of his car that night. He said it was somewhere up near Del Mar.

I had my secretary run a data check on the three Del Mar hits. One of them was quickly dissolved, a woman, fifty-eight, living in a rental unit in the village. The other two both show unlisted telephone numbers with addresses on the bluffs above the town center. I know the area. These are large homes, some of them bordering on estates, with oversize yards and pools.

If Alex was here, it would be a great help. A simple drive-by and he might be able to recognize the place.

As it is, I do the next best thing. A Google Earth satellite check of both addresses shows one of them to be a definite possibility. It has a very big yard, what you might call grounds, much of it covered by the canopy from trees and a large pool in the backyard, oval in shape, same as Alex described when we questioned him. If I could only zoom in and look through their windows I would know more. I will have to wait for the next generation of Google for that one.

I head out by myself in the car, a task I would usually assign to Herman. But then he's gone, too.

By the time he got to the steps leading up to the condo, Herman was sweating like a bull and was out of breath. He had done the three blocks since stepping out of the cab in record time. He didn't want the cab pulling up to the front door. He rested for a few seconds at the foot of the stairs, if for no other reason than to regain his composure. Body odor was one thing, anxiety was another. It wouldn't do for Alex to smell the scent of panic on the man who was hired to protect him.

He climbed to the second floor and used the key in the door.

"That you?" Alex was in the second bedroom down the hall to the rear.

"Yeah, it's me."

"Did you get it? What'd they say?"

"Nothing special," Herman lied. "Just checking in. They do have a new location for us, however. We're gonna have to move."

"Why's that?" Alex popped his head around the open door and looked down the hallway at Herman standing in the entry. "Jeez, you're all sweaty. Why don't you take a shower? At least get comfortable. Why are we moving?"

"They found a better location," said Herman.

"Where is it?"

"I'll know in a few minutes. I've gotta make a local call, some arrangements. But you can start getting your stuff together."

"OK." Ives disappeared back into the bedroom. "Won't take me long."

They were both living out of suitcases. Herman went into the front bedroom and closed the door. He took out his cell phone, pushed a few buttons, put it to his ear, and waited for somebody to answer. On the third ring there was a pickup.

"It's me," said Herman. "I need some help now! We gotta move and do it quietly and quickly, quick as we can."

"Where?"

"Anywhere but here," said Herman. The problem was that the arrangements for the condo had been made before Graves was killed, in the panicked hours following the fiery crash at the gas station in San Diego. There was no way to be sure what kind of surveillance they might have been under, even at the Iveses' house. The only way to be certain was to move to a new location where no one knew where they were, not even Paul or Harry. There was a reason why fugitives, narco kings, and the rest never slept in the same location two nights in a row. Herman was beginning to feel that same urge now.

The guy on the other end asked Herman if there was some emergency.

"I don't know. For now I'm just tryin' to be safe. Fill you in when you get here. How soon?"

The man told him twenty minutes. Herman said, "See you then," and hung up.

He went into the bathroom, grabbed his shaving gear and a shirt that was drying on a hanger. He looked in the mirror and realized that Alex was right. He needed a shave and a shower. His face was drawn, tired. In his hand was the skull shaver he used to maintain his shiny dome. Herman wondered how much gray would appear if he allowed it to grow out again. He didn't dwell on the thought. Instead he went back into the bedroom and put the shaving gear in his bag, folded the shirt and laid it in the open suitcase on the floor.

He started to walk away, stopped for a second, thought about it and went back to the suitcase. He reached under a stack of shorts and felt around until he found what he was looking for. He pulled it out— Springfield Arms .45 semiauto pistol, the ultra-compact with the short barrel. The whole thing, from hammer to muzzle, was no more than six inches. Flying in a private plane and landing on a dirt strip had its advantages.

He unzipped the mesh bag mounted along the inside of the suitcase and felt around until he found the heavy clip. There were two of these. Fully loaded, they carried seven rounds each. Eight, if you popped one in the pistol's breech after sliding the clip into the gun's handle.

Herman quietly slipped the clip into the gun and gently pushed it home until it clicked. He didn't rack a round into the chamber as he didn't want the telltale sound traveling through the common wall into Alex's room. He put the loaded gun under the top pair of shorts in the open suitcase and headed out toward the kitchen to grab a bite to eat while they still had time.

Twenty-Six

The residence belonging to Rufus Alexander Becket is indeed lavish if its outward exterior is any indication. I can see where this might have put Alex off from the instant he stepped out of his car. From the street, it sits behind an immense southern live oak tree that must be at least two hundred years old. Its sprawling and arching branches cover what looks like half a football field of front yard, some of them touching the ground.

Around the tree in a semicircle are boxed hedges lining a circular driveway. Behind all of this is what looks like a two-story French provincial house, though I cannot see all of it. It appears to be something right out of Burgundy or the Loire Valley, as if it might have been plopped down here from a hot air balloon

276 · STEVE MARTINI

complete with its slate roof. The roof alone is something I am guessing would cost close to a million dollars, given the sprawl of the place.

If I had to guess, I would say none of this is new construction. From the look of it, it probably dates back to the thirties, one of the old estates still left from the golden age when a handful of tycoons developed the area and built the Thoroughbred horse racing track that is, as the crow flies, little more than a mile away.

I park on the other side of the street and study the place for two or three minutes from my Jeep. I don't dare sit here for long. This old vehicle with its partially singed and now-discolored ragtop is certain to raise eyebrows in this neighborhood.

I step out, quietly close the door, and cross over to the driveway on the other side. There is a brass plaque near the edge of the curb. It's a historical marker. "This Diegueño Oak is believed to be nearly five hundred years old and is thought to have stood on this spot in 1542 when the Portuguese explorer Juan Cabrillo landed at Point Loma."

I was wrong. It is more than two hundred years old. And from the looks of it, the cables supporting the branches and the carefully manicured and tended ground around its trunk, it may be here long after my bones have turned to dust.

I head up the driveway. A long walk. It takes several minutes to make it to the front of the house, up the white brick steps to push the brass knob for the doorbell. I don't hear a thing. I am guessing that the oak on the front door may be older than the tree out front, and perhaps thicker. Finally it's opened by a man in livery, formal attire not seen in many places these days.

"I'm here to see Mr. Becket." I hand him a business card.

"Is he expecting you?"

"I don't think so."

"Can you state your business?"

"It's private," I tell him.

"Just a moment." He closes the door all the way until I hear the heavy lock snap shut.

I wait for what seems like forever, standing on the stoop with my hand in my pocket trying to look casual so that no one will think I'm waiting here to hold someone's horse should they come trotting by. Finally the door opens again.

"If you'll come this way," he says.

I follow the manservant into the house, down a long broad entry of gleaming dark hardwood. There is a massive crystal chandelier overhead, doors on both sides trimmed out in white antiqued paint. Or perhaps it's just authentically old, I think. He leads me to the second door on the left and knocks.

"You can come in." The voice on the other side.

He opens it and I step through. Inside is an ornate study, two levels of walls lined in books on shelves with a narrow catwalk on the second story. There is a banister all around this and a wooden spiral staircase trimmed out in bird's-eye maple leading to the upper level.

Before I can take it all in, the man behind the desk has already moved around it. He has a smile on his face and his hand extended. "Hello. I'm Rufus Becket. How can I help you?" He is short, maybe five foot six, what you would call rotund, chubby cheeked with jowls cropping up below his jawline. His face tan, the only giveaway that he probably doesn't spend all of his time in this room. Probably a golfer, I am guessing.

"Paul Madriani, and I'm sorry to bother you."

"No problem," he says. "Can I offer you a drink? Something cold?"

"No, I'm fine."

"Some iced tea," he says. "I can ring the kitchen."

"Sure. Why not." An excuse to sit down.

He pushes a button on the phone, orders up two iced teas, and is back to me in a flash. "Have a seat," he says.

I take one of the client chairs on this side of the large partner's desk, something European and old. He settles into the other client chair and turns his jovial eyes on me as if, perhaps, whatever he was doing before I arrived was not as interesting as my interruption.

"The reason I'm here is that I have a client who is in some difficulty at the moment."

"What lawyer doesn't?" He laughs and looks at my business card. "What type of law do you practice?" he asks.

"Criminal."

"Ah." This sobers him up a bit.

"My client says he was at a party, that the location was a large home in this area. He was given the name Becket. My client is out of town right now but I'm sure he'll be back in a few days. If I were to bring him by he might recognize the house," I tell him.

"When was this party?" he asks. "We have a number of events each season."

I give him the date.

"There's no need to bring him by. Does he work in the industry?"

"What industry is that?"

"Defense," he says. "We had a large gathering here at the house that evening for one of the trade associations. Part business, part fund-raiser. You know, candidates pressing the flesh, working the crowd for money come campaign time. It's not exactly fun, but necessary. If you understand my meaning."

"Of course."

"Must have had three or four hundred people here that evening. Parking was a madhouse. Pissed off some of the neighbors. I can tell you that. We invited most of them to the event to try and keep them happy. But then you always miss a few. What's your client's name?"

"Alex Ives," I tell him.

He thinks for a moment. Shakes his head a little. "I don't think I know the gentleman. But then I didn't know two-thirds of the people who were here."

"What type of business are you in?" I ask.

"Contracting. My company does work for the Defense Department, the military, other government agencies. They have needs, we supply them."

"That's a broad field." I'm hoping he will narrow it.

Instead he says, "Some of it is classified," and slams the subject shut.

"Looks like it pays well." I gaze about at the cache of leather-bound books, the house and its palatial furnishings.

"I have no complaints."

There's a rap on the door.

"In," he says.

A waiter in a white linen jacket enters with a large silver tray, a full pitcher of iced tea, and two tall glasses already iced. The waiter drops a linen cloth along the edge of the desk and puts the tray on top of it. He pours two glasses. Becket takes one. I take the other. Becket thanks the waiter and the man leaves.

"Sugar?" he says.

"Not for me."

"You'll like this tea. That is, if you're a tea drinker. I am," he says. "And you're right, sugar ruins it. It's an herbal black currant. I think you'll enjoy it. What exactly is this difficulty your client is having? I hope he didn't drink too much? The night of the party, I mean?"

"No. That's the one thing I can certify. He wasn't drunk. But he does have a problem. It seems that when he left here he was not functioning under his own power, you might say. And he can't remember anything after that. Not for some time anyway."

"Does he have some kind of health issue? A medical problem?" Then Becket's eyes suddenly light up. "He's not the young man?" he says. "The one who passed out?"

"Then you saw him?"

"No. No. But I heard about it," he says. "That's what this is about." He says it like he's relieved. Puts down his glass and slaps his hands together. "I thought it was something serious. I didn't see it happen, of course. But I heard all about it," says Becket. "I was in the house when it happened. My assistant told me that a young man went down over near the rose garden in the back. Toppled over like a cement statue, according to what I was told. They assumed he just had too much to drink. Some friends apparently helped him up and out to his car. I didn't know who he was. By the time I got outside he was gone. So I never actually saw him. My assistant took care of it."

"Is your assistant available?"

"As it happens, he's on vacation."

"Do you know who helped him out to his car?"

He shakes his head. "Apparently they left with him. I don't imagine he was in any shape to drive. From what I was told, I was led to believe that they all came together. That they knew one another. I assume no one was hurt?"

I don't tell him about Serna and the accident out in the desert. Or our belief that somebody slipped Alex a roofie. If he hasn't read about Serna in the newspapers by now, I suspect the minute I leave he'll be doing research under Alex's name. At which time he'll clam up, thinking, like Graves, that I'm here to spread the benefits of civil liability.

"What about your wife? Maybe she saw something?"

"I'm afraid not. She was with me."

"The household help?"

He's shaking his head. "Other than my assistant, I doubt anyone else was involved. They were all in the house. The only people working the party that night were the caterers."

"Do you recognize the name Benjawan Tjahana?" I change the subject. "I think I'm pronouncing it correctly. Her nickname was Ben, I believe. A young woman, very pretty, probably Indonesian. I think she went to school in the area. May have worked in a club down in San Diego?"

Before I even finish the question he is casually shaking his head once more. "No. Should I? Was she here that night?"

"I don't think so. You didn't tell anyone that they could invite strangers to the party, did you? I mean people off the street."

"What do you think I'm running, a frat house?" he says.

"I didn't think so. Who catered the party?"

"I'd have to check. I can't recall who it was that night. We use several different companies depending on the size of the crowd. I'm sure my wife would have that information. Give me a moment." He gets up and goes to the phone. Makes a call, I suspect on the intercom since he only presses one button. Hushed voices as he explains to her why I'm here and asks for the name of the caterer. "Ah, yes. That's right." He writes it down on a Post-it note from his desk. "Thanks, dear. Listen, I'll be up in just one minute. I know. I know. I'm running late." Then he hangs up.

"What would we do without wives?" he says. "Are you married?"

"My wife died some years ago."

"Oh, I am sorry. I don't know what I'd do without Doreen," he says. "Here it is. Trousdale and Company. They're a very good firm. We've hired them before. Do a great job. They set it all up. Clean it up when they're done. A few hours after the crowd leaves you wouldn't even know anyone had been here. They show up with two or three large trucks and an army of help. Chairs, tables, food, beverages, everything, the linens and glasses, the works."

"I don't imagine you have a list of the personnel working with them that night?"

"No. You'd have to get that from them," he says. "Listen, I'm sorry. I wish I could stay and talk longer, but I have to go. My wife's upstairs and I'm on the clock. We have an engagement this evening and I'm running late."

I take a gulp of tea. He takes the glass from my hand and sets it on the tray. It's obvious the meeting is over. "I hope you understand." He starts ushering me out of the chair and toward the door.

"Of course, and I want to thank you. You've been very helpful."

"I hope so," he says. "Anything I can do, just call." Then he says, "Oh, here." He reaches for a card on the desk and hands it to me. It has his name and number on it. No address, no e-mail, nothing else.

"What's the name of your company?"

"I own several different entities. None of them are publicly traded," he says. He offers nothing more.

"Just one more question. Would it be possible to get a copy of the guest list for the party that night?"

He stops in midstride and looks at me, the smile fading from his face. "Oh, I'm not sure I can do that," he says.

"Is there some problem?"

"Well, sure. There were all kinds of people here that night, members of Congress, people from some of the regulatory agencies, state and local elected officials, registered lobbyists, a lot of candidates looking for campaign money. You know how that goes," he says.

"No, I'm afraid I don't."

"Well, be glad of it," he says. "I get twenty envelopes a week with invitations to fund-raisers. Buy a table here. Buy a table there. If you bought every table they wanted you to, you'd be bankrupt. People will drive you crazy. And if you don't give, they'll slam the door in your face the next time you show up to try and do business. Take a political science course at the university and they tell you the money only buys access. Spread enough of it in the right places and it buys a hell of a lot more than that. But giving you a list of those at the party could be a problem. You see, it's up to them to report their activities. I wouldn't want to get crosswise with any of them. If they fail to report to the appropriate regulatory agency, and I show them as being here, they're in trouble, and so am I. Besides, I'm not even sure we have the list anymore. I'd have to check with my assistant when he returns from vacation."

"Your wife wouldn't have the list, by any chance?"

He smiles at me and says, "No."

"I'm not interested in outing any of these people," I tell him. "All I want to know is whether anyone there that night might have seen what happened when my client passed out. Did they know any of the people who helped him to his car? Names," I tell him. "That's what I need."

"Why? What do you need them for?" he asks.

"It's part of the case. It's confidential. I really can't discuss it."

"Well, I guess we all have our secrets," he says. "Let me think about it. I'll talk to my assistant. See if we still have the list. But, like I say, I'm not sure I can give it to you."

He is affable, a little slick, perhaps a sales background if I had to guess. If he has the guest list and I issue a subpoena he will probably shred it and claim it was discarded long before the subpoena was issued. For the moment I may have to depend on the man's goodwill, as much as I hate to.

He leads me to the front door, shakes my hand, gives me a broad smile, and two minutes later I'm back in the Jeep headed south toward the office.

The good news is I have now found the location of the party and confirmed that Alex passed out and was helped off the premises by person or persons unknown. The bad news is that this is all hearsay, none of it admissible in a court of law. We still have no percipient witnesses. No one who saw any of it. More to the point, I have no names or descriptions of any of the people who shanghaied Alex and dragged him off into the desert that night.

Twenty-Seven

The tempered glass pitcher sat steaming on the hot plate under the Mr. Coffee. Two ham and cheese sandwiches with plenty of sliced tomatoes were on plates on the countertop in the kitchen. Herman was already chowing down on one of the sandwiches.

"Come and get it! Coffee's ready!" he hollered down the hall to Alex.

"Be there in a sec!"

Herman mopped down the countertop where he'd assembled the food as he chewed. He would do the dishes and put everything away the minute they finished eating. He didn't want to waste time cleaning up once his support crew arrived. Herman's rolling suitcase was already zipped up, sitting in the entry hall ready to go.

After thinking about it for a while Herman had calmed down. He was reasonably confident that their location had not been blown, at least not yet. If the people tracking Alex already knew where they were, they would have made a move by now. He and Ives had been camped here for three nights.

"Hurry it up!" Herman yelled down the hall again. "We don't have all day."

"Coming." Alex dragged his wheeled suitcase out of the bedroom and down the hall. He stood it up next to Herman's by the front door.

"Got everything?"

"You wanna check my room?" said Ives. He wasn't used to the hustle.

Alex grabbed the plate with the sandwich, skipped the coffee, and headed into the living room to turn on the TV.

"No time for that," said Herman.

"Just want to see what's on CNN."

"Be the same bad news tomorrow," said Herman. "You can catch it then. We don't have time."

Alex dropped the TV controls back on the coffee table. "You act like you been in the army."

"How's that?"

"A drill sergeant."

"Could be your generation lacks discipline. Ever think of that?" said Herman.

"Well, I know you can't be talking about me," said Ives. "Cuz when I was a kid I walked six miles in bare feet in the snow in the middle of winter to school and back, both ways uphill."

"Sounds like my school district, except we didn't have any feet," said Herman.

Alex laughed.

"Tell you about the army I was in. Long as we're telling whoppers," said Diggs. "Four older brothers who'd kick my ass in a heartbeat if I didn't jump fast enough to do what they said." He rinsed off his plate and started drying it. "But even then they had to wait in line to get their kicks in, behind my mama. And she wore big boots."

"Good old days in the hood," said Alex.

"And you want me to believe you weren't born suckin' the silver spoon? If I didn't get you outta bed in the morning you'd sleep 'til dinner."

"Actually, if I could, I'd sleep through dinner. Don't want to hurt your feelings, but anybody ever tell you you're a terrible cook?"

"You're eatin' my food."

"It's either that or starve," said Alex.

"And here I was thinking you liked Cheerios and milk."

"And as for sleeping late, there isn't much else to do. You won't let me go down to the beach."

"Too easy to drown," said Herman.

"I'm a good swimmer."

"Not if somebody chains an engine block to your foot."

"Here's an idea. Why don't you do something useful and get me a woman?" said Ives.

Herman laughed. "You wouldn't know what to do with a woman. Besides, do I look like a pimp?"

"Now that you mention it."

"Just cuz I beat your ass at rummy last night."

"Let's not talk about that," said Ives.

"What would your mother say?"

"No, not my mother," said Alex. "You can get any other woman but her."

Herman started to laugh. The kid had a quick lip. "You're awful. No wonder these people want to kill you. Now hurry up and eat before I have to slap you around."

"You hurt me and the lawyers are gonna be very unhappy," said Ives.

"Yeah, but think of all the fun I'll have."

Ives laughed. Something went down the wrong way and he began to choke.

"Have another bite," said Herman. "Sit tight. I'll come over and give you a Heimlich hug."

Between choked words: "You leave my heinie alone."

Herman busted up. Three days and they had already

come to this. Another week and they'd be throwing food and lighting farts on fire for laughs.

"True what they say," said Herman. "Familiarization does breed contempt. Maybe best if I just let 'em kill ya."

"You couldn't do it." Alex was coughing, still clearing his throat.

"And why not?"

"You'd have nobody to play rummy with."

"Well, there you go, something to do tonight."

"You already took all my money," said Ives.

"Four dollars and twenty cents? You're not worth much."

"You're right. I'm gonna have to talk to my boss about a raise when I get back."

Herman didn't touch it. The smile on his face evaporated. He turned his back and started sponging the countertop again. "Hurry up and eat, we gotta go." Graves's death and the fact that he hadn't told Alex suddenly wrung all the merriment from his voice.

"Something wrong?"

"No. We just gotta go. I'm gonna—"

Before he could finish the thought there was a rattle at the door, almost like someone was knocking but not quite. Herman wasn't sure. Maybe it was the wind.

But Ives heard it too.

They both looked at the front door.

"You think it's them?" Alex whispered.

Herman shook his head and put a finger to his lips.

There it was again. This time there was no question, three clear knocks.

"Must be your guys. I'll get it." Alex was closer. He started to get up.

Herman's right hand shot out like a traffic cop, freezing Ives in place. He moved a finger to his lips and listened for a second. Then a couple more knocks. He motioned for Alex to take his sandwich and the plate and head to the bedroom.

Ives looked confused. But he didn't say a word, not even to whisper. He picked up the plate and slipped quietly down the hall.

What bothered Herman was the lack of noise outside. Whoever was at the door had not come out of a vehicle in the parking lot. Otherwise he would have heard the engine as they pulled in, and a slamming door as they made their way to the stairs. Even with all the laughter, Herman had one ear primed for the van.

He bent down low so that any light streaming in from the back of the condo wouldn't cast his shadow against the peephole in the front door. He moved quickly across the entryway, down the hall to his own room and into the bathroom. The small six-inch window high on the wall with its sliding translucent glass was open just a crack. Up on his tiptoes Herman peeked out.

There was one man at the door. Herman could see all the way to the end of the balcony in that direction. There was no one else there. He couldn't see in the other direction unless he slid the window open further and pressed his head into the corner to look back.

The man was wearing a bright red polo shirt with a yellow collar and trim down the three buttons at the center of his chest. There was a small DHL logo on the shirt. He was wearing tan shorts. Black hair, dark complexion, Herman assumed he was Mexican. He carried a flat box, yellow and red like his shirt and a clipboard in one hand. He knocked on the door with the other.

Herman wasn't buying it. If there was a package, why didn't they give it to him at the shop? Still, the only people who knew he was here were Harry and Paul. They had agreed not to send anything to the condo unless it was an emergency. Maybe it was. With Graves dead perhaps they thought there was something Herman needed to know. But why a box? There was only one way to find out.

He moved back to the front door, stayed low and moved toward his suitcase. *"¿Quién es?"*

"DHL. *Entrega.*"

He might have been making a delivery, but his tongue was paralyzed. There was no trill to the word as he spoke. Whoever he was, Spanish was not his first language.

Herman zipped open his suitcase, reached inside, and found the Springfield Arms .45. He slid the pistol out of the case. But he hesitated to rack the first round. The guy outside the door would hear it.

"Who is it for?" Herman figured why play games?

"Ah, *señor*, you speak English. Delivery for Mr. H. Diggs."

"Who is it from?"

"Ah, *¿cómo se dice?* Ah, how do you say, *abogado*?"

"Lawyer," said Herman.

"Ah, *sí, señor.*"

"The name, what's the lawyer's name."

"You open the door, I show it to you."

"Just read it to me. I'm not sure I want it."

"You want, I could take it back to the office."

"You do that," said Herman.

"The name is, I could spell for you if you like."

"Go ahead."

"First name Pablo, how you say?"

"Paul."

"*¡Sí!* Last name M-A-D-R-I-A-N-I. How you say?"

"Madriani," said Herman.

"Then you know the man?"

"Just leave it outside the door. I'll get it in a minute. I'm not dressed. Taking a shower," said Herman.

"Cannot," said the man. "Requires a signature."

Herman didn't answer. Instead he slowly stood up, off the side of the center of the door and looked through the peephole. The fish-eye lens gave him a panoramic view of the man's face, pockmarks and a ruddy complexion. "Hold up the waybill. I want to see it."

"*Señor,* I don't have time for this."

"I guess not, you're making deliveries and you're on foot. Where's your truck?"

"We don't use a truck here, *señor.* Here we use automobiles. We don't have the equipment you have up north." As he spoke he held up the waybill so Herman could see it through the glass lens. "Hold it still," said Herman. He could see the law firm's name and address neatly printed in the "Sender's" block. But this could have been gotten by anyone with access to the Internet. Then he saw the firm's account number printed in the block. And near the bottom the clincher, Brenda Gomes's signature, the "gate watcher" at the firm. Nothing went in or out of the office without her seeing or touching it. Herman had seen her scrawl her name enough times to know it.

He stuck the gun in the front of his pants and covered

it with his shirt. Then he swung open the security latch on the door and opened it.

The guy outside was all smiles. He handed the box to Herman and laid the clipboard on top of it, then gave him a pen and showed him where to sign.

Herman clicked the pen, went to fix his signature, and discovered that the ballpoint was dry.

"Ah," said the man. "I don't have another pen."

Herman fixed him with a stare. The guy was still smiling. "I've got one in the kitchen. Stay here." Herman handed everything back to him. As he turned for the kitchen, Herman slipped his right hand under the front of his shirt and grabbed the handle of the pistol. With his left hand he knocked Alex's empty coffee cup onto the floor. It shattered on the tile, sending bits of glass everywhere.

At the same time Herman turned quickly and dropped down behind the island in the center of the kitchen as if retrieving some of the broken pieces. Instead he pulled out the pistol and racked a round.

When Herman stood up the guy was still standing in the open doorway, holding the package and the clipboard, tapping his foot on the cement outside the door like he was in a hurry.

Herman felt like a fool. Fortunately he'd kept the gun below the counter where the man couldn't see it. He laid it on an open shelf down low. "Where is that pen?" Herman saw it over near the sink, went over, and picked it up.

He signed for the package and a few seconds later the guy was gone.

Herman closed the door and swung the security U-bolt back into place.

Twenty-Eight

This morning I look at the documents open on my desk. Harry has already read them. It's a court-ordered status conference, early on to see where the case is going. It's set for the end of the month. The prosecutor has offered Alex a plea bargain, what in California is called a "wet reckless."

Like a camel without humps, it's a strange animal, reckless driving but with some alcohol involved, perhaps smelling the cork. Because the level of blood alcohol in Alex's system is well below the presumptive limit of intoxication, the D.A. has doubts about his own case. If he only knew the half of it. The problem is we can't tell him, not without hard evidence, and we have none. Still it's a crazy offer because of the vehicular manslaughter charge. You can bet that ain't going away. Which means this camel won't hunt.

But that's not the problem. The judge has ordered us into chambers to discuss the matter. He has also ordered that we bring our client to sit outside in his courtroom so that we can run any offer by him in hopes of a deal. Judges are often the most optimistic people in any room. They can afford to be. This one ought to be wearing white robes and singing in a choir.

Yesterday I checked out the caterers, the name given to me by Becket for the company that worked the party that night. Trousdale and Company. It was a dead end. No one remembered a thing. My guess is that when you're paid to work that many parties serving alcohol, discretion requires a flexible memory. The company could be on the hook if they overserved.

I step out of my office and head down the corridor to Harry. He is chipping away at the computer inside his den when I peek in.

"You want to grab some coffee?" Harry is still looking at the computer screen. I am standing in the open doorway.

"Did you see it?" Harry means the notice-of-status conference.

"Yep."

"What do you want to do?"

"I don't know."

"Where you want to go for coffee?"

"I was thinking Lucerne, maybe by way of Amsterdam."

Harry turns to glance at me with a grin, then back to his computer. He thinks I am joking. "Why don't we just go sit outside under one of the umbrellas at the Del? It's a lot closer." Somehow the silence tells him I'm not kidding. When he turns around again, Harry is no longer smiling.

"In case you haven't noticed," he says, "business is way down. Half of our client load has disappeared. And one of them is hiding out in Mexico last time I looked. Some judge about to kick our ass if we can't produce him at court in what? Ten days, is it?"

"Nine," I tell him.

"Well, there you go."

"Can you think of a better time to travel? Besides, I'm told the weather in Lucerne is beautiful this time of year. Pretty city too. Certainly better than the ambience in the lockup downtown."

Harry gives me an arched eyebrow, Ahab looking for the white whale. "What's in Lucerne?"

"A banker," I tell him.

"Is he gonna loan us money?"

"I could go alone," I say.

"That's a good idea. Why don't you do that?"

"Fine. You can stay here and handle the pretrial."

He stops typing.

"If things blow up while I'm gone, you end up called to the courthouse, me out of town, and Herman not around, who's gonna spring you from the metal box downtown?"

"I've got friends," says Harry.

"I know. One of them is looking at you right now."

There is another reason I want Harry with me. It remains unstated, but neither of us are oblivious to the danger around us—the accident at the gas station, the sense that I am a carrier of death like a contagious disease after meeting with Graves.

I noticed, two days ago, a loaded pistol in the center drawer of Harry's desk, a snub-nosed hammerless thirty-eight. I was looking for some Advil. Harry always keeps it there. His drugstore, and I stumbled over the thing. I hadn't seen it for years. I thought he had sold it. But he hadn't. Like Harry, the old brass bullets in the gun are probably corroded, but it gives him a sense of security. I am not leaving him here alone.

Twenty-Nine

"Who was it?" Alex came out of the room. "DHL. Delivery from the office."

"Open it," said Alex.

Herman grabbed a knife out of the drawer in the kitchen, laid the box on the counter, and used the knife to peel back the glued-down tab sealing the end of the box.

The brilliant flash was blinding. The concussion threw both of them against the wall, where they lay dazed for several moments listening to the hissing sound as the gas filled the room.

The choking sensation was finally what wakened them. Herman came to, crawling around on his hands and knees, coughing, sputtering up green slime, feeling his way through the billowing fog until he finally fell over Alex who was just beginning to move.

Ives was in a panic. He couldn't breathe. He struggled to his feet and tried to make it to the door. Herman had to restrain him.

Ives was pumping so much adrenaline that it took almost the full reserve of strength left in Herman's body to bring him down. Alex clawed at him with his fingers, trying to get away, scraping the skin from Herman's arm as they fought. They fell somewhere near the island in the center of the room. Herman knew it because he hit his head on the corner of the counter as they went down.

He felt around with his hand, found the open shelf and the weighty steel of the pistol, grabbed for it, and brought the gun down hard across the back of Ives's head near the base of his skull. Even with this, the kid was still trying to get up. Herman knew he couldn't fight him much longer. He was coughing trying to catch his breath. He was trying to yell at him to stop. But he couldn't get the words out.

He hit him again, a glancing blow off his shoulder. Then one more time. The gun caught Ives near the crown of his head. He went down onto the floor hard and didn't move.

Herman wondered if he'd killed him. But he didn't have time to find out. The CS gas was overwhelming him. It burned his skin, scorched his lungs, and turned the sockets of his eyes into fiery liquid pools.

He crawled on his hands and knees away from the front door toward the back of the unit, the ocean side.

He found a chair and threw it with all of his strength toward the light. The crash of glass told him he found his mark. The large picture window facing out toward the Pacific shattered. Shards of glass fell from the window frame up near the ceiling.

The pressure of conditioned air inside the unit forced enough of the gas out the opening that Herman could finally make out some details in the room. Through a veil of tears he could make out the lump on the floor, Ives's motionless body lying there.

Herman stumbled toward the front door. He reached with his thumb until he found the safety, clicked it off, and pulled the hammer back. He swung the safety bar, dropped to his knees, and threw the door open as he went down onto his stomach.

The instant he did it, a volley of bullets ripped through the open door, the subsonic crackle of a silencer as the rounds slammed into cabinets in the kitchen somewhere behind him. A cloud of tear gas driven by the ocean breeze through the smashed window billowed out through the open front door. Another volley of shots, this time fired blindly, smashed into the doorframe above Herman's head. Bits of concrete and drywall drifted down like flakes of snow.

Herman could see red. He thought it was blood in his eyes from the tear gas until it moved. It seemed to float among the clouds of gas running out of the room. It was no use trying to line up the sights on the pistol, his vision was a blur. Instead he took aim with both eyes open along the top of the pistol's return, adjusted to fire low so he wouldn't fire over the top, and squeezed off three quick rounds at the bottom center of the moving red object. When he wiped his eyes and looked again it was gone.

He crawled out through the open door along the balcony outside. A cross breeze cleared the cloud of gas enough for Herman to make out the lifeless body of the deliveryman lying on his back, still wearing his red shirt. A submachine gun was now strapped across his chest, the fat tube of a silencer protruding from the end of the barrel.

Herman got to his feet. He moved like a drunk and started to stumble forward. The moment he did, another volley of shots stitched the outer wall of the building a few feet in front of him. He looked over the railing down into the parking lot. All he could see was a blur, a hazy figure in the distance, what looked like jeans and a white T-shirt. Then another flash of fire from the muzzle of the man's gun. Rounds ricocheted off the steel railing in front of Herman. Some of them splintered, sending tiny pieces of copper shrapnel buzzing into his body like burning wasps.

Herman wavered in a daze, standing there on the balcony, silhouetted against the building waiting for the inevitable. He watched the blue and white blur as it danced in the distance. He knew it was too far away for the pistol in his hand even if he could take aim, which he couldn't.

He waited for the muzzle flash when suddenly a large white object streaked into the parking lot. It obliterated everything in its path like an eraser on a blackboard. It took out a small light pole, caromed off another car, and rolled like a rocket sled into the man with the gun. When it finally came to a stop, Herman's eyes fixed on the white van that was coming to pick them up. They were late.

Thirty

For all we knew, our computers and cell phones had been hacked and our landlines tapped. Harry has called in a security company to run a sweep of our home and office phones. The rest of it might take longer. But it's likely Harry still won't trust any of it. It took him two years to finally start using the computer. Now he's addicted to it.

After Graves's death we were compelled to disconnect everything from the server in our office and pull the plug on the Internet. Our computers are now little more than glorified typewriters. The only signals they emit are Bluetooth wireless to the printers, and even that Harry is talking about shutting down and reverting to cables.

"Two coach seats. We can't afford business class." Harry has a notebook in his hand writing down the details.

"How long's the flight?" I ask him.

"Fifteen hours here to Amsterdam. After that it's a cakewalk."

"I get the aisle."

"You're the one wanted to go," says Harry.

"OK, you can have the aisle." Better that than having to listen to him complain for fifteen hours. "Try to get a decent hotel at least."

"Two nights, right?"

"Right."

"In the meantime, you try to see if you can get some lead on this guy," says Harry. "The banker. What's his name?"

"Korff. Simon Korff. I called the bank, the one on his business card."

Harry shoots me a look, arched eyebrows.

"I used the phone at the bar in the Brigantine, paid for the call with my credit card," I tell him.

"Good. We don't want the man dying of an accident, at least not before we talk to him."

"They say he doesn't work there anymore, but they've seen him around town. They're pretty sure he still lives there. I'll check online to see if I can find a listing for White Pages in Lucerne. Do it at the library on my way home."

"Gimme the name again," says Harry. He writes it down. "I'll look and see what I can find when I'm over at the Del. Concierge is a sweetheart," says Harry. "She'll let me use the computer in the business center."

"Good. It would help if we could use LexisNexis. Better search engine."

"But we can't. OK, I'm outta here. Back as quick as I can," says Harry.

He may be trudging back and forth across the street. Any questions or problems as to the reservations, Harry can't call for clarification because of the phones. And the secretaries can't do it because we're trying to keep them out of the information loop. Nobody in the office knows where we're going. Only that we'll be back in four days. This includes travel time.

Harry heads out the door.

Herman was right about one thing. It didn't take them long to get into the van and on the road once it arrived. With the help of his friends they grabbed Alex and the two suitcases and stuffed them into the back of the vehicle. Then hauled the two bodies in after them. With a few neighbors looking on, the van rocketed out of the parking lot and down the road. It looked the worse for wear, a broken windshield and a badly dented front panel on the left side in front of the driver.

Herman figured the only reason the killers didn't use a larger explosive device was they couldn't be certain that Alex was in the condo. The only way to be sure of that was to flush them and kill them outside. They probably would have taken photos of Ives's bullet-riddled body to prove the kill to whoever hired them.

As it was, Herman very nearly did the job for them. Ives's head was still bleeding from where Herman nailed him with the heavy barrel of the pistol. Herman held a compress to it as one of his friends poured water from a canteen over Ives's face trying to wash the residue of tear gas from his eyes.

"Hurts like hell," said Alex.

"Hurt a lot more if you'd gone out that door," said Herman.

"What you're saying is you saved my life."

"Looks that way."

"Next time could you do it a little more gently . . . OW! Watch the head."

"Sorry. If it don't stop bleeding soon, we're gonna have to get you some stitches."

"Jeez, do we have to ride with them?" Alex looked at the two dead bodies piled up in the back of the van as the vehicle bounced around on the highway.

"How much farther?" Herman yelled to the driver.

"Few miles."

"This would be a whole lot better if I had some milk." Herman's buddy with the canteen continued to dribble water down Alex's forehead and over his eyes. Ives jerked a little, brought one arm up. "Don't rub it with your hands, son. Only make it worse," said the man. "Water is OK, but milk neutralizes the CS. Stops the burning faster."

"Let's stop and get some milk," said Alex.

"Not 'til we get rid of our passengers." Herman gestured with his head toward the two bodies in the back. The one hit by the van looked like a rag doll. Herman had already gone through their pockets looking for anything that could identify them. They were clean, not a thing. Even the labels on their clothes had been removed. They were ghosts, the sign of professionals.

Even their weapons, MAC-10 machine pistols, bore no marks or serial numbers. They had been taken off by a grinder, probably in a machine shop, and the metal etched with acid. Even the FBI crime lab would have had a hard time lifting the serial numbers. The guns were cheap enough to be cartel pieces, but to Herman it was suspect. Still, the short barrel had saved his life. Designed for close-quarters combat in confined areas, the man shooting from the parking lot had missed Herman with several bursts because he couldn't track him down with the short barrel. He was spraying and praying until he was turned into jelly by the front end of the van.

"Rental agency's gonna be pissed," said Herman.

"Take it your firm has insurance," said the driver.

"Not for this, they don't. Probably not good in Mexico in any event."

They may have been Herman's friends, but they were on the clock. The firm was paying them and the bills were mounting. Now they could add to it the cost of a new vehicle. Herman was hoping that Alex's parents were good for it. After all, it had saved their son's life.

"We could just drive it off a cliff with the two bodies," said the driver.

"What do we do for wheels?" said Herman.

"Good point. We'll pick up another rental, sort it out later," said the guy.

Ten minutes later, both of the shooters were sleeping with the fish. Their bodies pitched off a cliff into the Pacific at the end of a dirt road just south of Zihuatanejo. They threw the machine pistols in after them. If they were stopped they didn't want the cops finding them in their possession. Herman could always toss his small pistol into the brush at the last minute. Killing someone in Mexico was a venial sin. Packing a gun, especially if it originated in the States, carried a maximum load, heavy time in a Mexican hole that passed for a prison.

As for the bodies, Herman's folks could have propped them up on a bench at a city bus stop the way it was done a few years earlier when one of the cartels wanted to make a statement. But they decided this would not be good for tourism.

Back on the road Herman struggled to change his clothes. He rifled through his suitcase for a clean pair of shorts, some underwear, and a fresh T-shirt. His skin burned from the gas that saturated his clothing.

"We stop, get some baking soda," he told the driver. "Lots of it." Baking soda on the skin would neutralize the chemicals in the gas and stop the skin irritation until they could get to a shower, where cold water and soap could be used to wash it away.

"And milk," said Ives. "My eyes are still burning. Where are we gonna go?"

"For now that's just what we're gonna do, go," said Herman. He wanted to put distance between them and the police back in Ixtapa, who he knew would be looking for them by now, taking descriptions of the van and the men in it. If they were lucky, none of the neighbors milling in the parking lot would have thought to take down the van's license plate number. Hopefully too scared to think about it.

Herman changed, then went to open Alex's suitcase. As he did he noticed that one of the rounds from the machine guns had ripped a hole into the ballistic fiber of the luggage. He zipped it open and starting sorting through it to find a change of clothes for Ives. Between a pair of shorts and some denim jeans he found a spent bullet perfectly formed, as if it had been fired into a baffle by a ballistics expert trying to match up the lands and grooves. It was a .45-caliber ACP round. Not many people used them, not in silenced fully automatic pistols.

"Coming up on the airport," said the driver. "Let's get rid of it." He was talking about the van. "I'll drop you off, close as I can to one of the rental agencies." The guy with the canteen worked his way up and back into the passenger seat. "You may have to walk a bit. I don't want to have to do the circle through the airport. Security's too tight. Pick up a four-by-four if you can. Something big and we'll meet up on the road, head out to the highway, and go south. Find a place, some quiet dirt road, where we can dump this thing into the ocean."

"No," said Herman. "Better idea." Herman was looking skyward through the back window of the van as he talked. "There's a resort a few miles back on the highway. They got a parking garage, free parking, big sign on the road."

"Saw it," said the driver.

"Then you get the rental, let him drive." Herman gestured toward the man in the passenger seat. "The two cars will meet up inside the garage under cover, not out on the road. We go in separately," said Herman.

"Got it."

Thirty-One

S he saw him leave on foot and wondered where he was going. It was the middle of the afternoon. They had already gone to lunch and returned. So Ana followed him.

Harry Hinds crossed over Orange Avenue and walked south along the front of the old hotel with its cone-shaped red roof and white siding. She wondered what her young niece and nephew would think if they saw this glittering place at night. When it was lit up, Ana thought it resembled an old-fashioned carousel.

Hinds took the curving cement walkway toward the hotel's main entrance. Ana followed, far enough behind so that he wouldn't notice. He might have been going to a meeting, except he wasn't carrying a briefcase or wearing a coat.

He walked under the portico leading to the entrance and disappeared inside. Ana followed.

As she entered the lobby she lifted her sunglasses in order to see. Hinds was approaching an alcove off the main area, across from the reception counter. Under the alcove were two desks. One was empty, its plate-glass surface shimmering, not a scrap of paper on it. A woman sat at the other.

The moment she saw Hinds she stood, smiled broadly, and greeted him, not formally, but by his first name. "Harry! How have you been?" Ana couldn't hear her, but she could read the woman's lips.

She couldn't make out what Hinds said. His back was to her. They chatted for a couple of seconds and the woman said, "How can I help you?"

"Oh, sure. Have a seat."

They sat down at the desk.

Ana had her book. She plunked herself down in one of the striped club chairs against the wall in the lobby. She opened her novel and peered over the top, sharpening her listening eye.

Hinds handed the woman a folded piece of paper and they talked. "I see. I see." The woman looked at the paper. "I see that. I can try. It's short notice. But I'm sure we can find something. Let me take a . . ." The woman swiveled around toward the computer at the side of her desk. Ana lost the half of the conversation she was able to pick up. The screen was too far away to make out anything.

The woman worked at the keyboard for two or three minutes as Hinds settled back into the chair. When she finally swung around toward him again she said, "Two coach seats. Last minute, they're expensive." She pulled a piece of paper from a printer under the desk, lined on it with a marker, and slid it across to him.

He looked, said something. She shook her head. And finally Hinds nodded. "Hotel's no problem." She said something about reservations this afternoon.

He said something else.

"Oh, sure, no problem. Feel free." She pointed to something across the lobby. "They ask you for a room number, just tell them you talked with me," she said.

Hinds got up and headed across the lobby, past the carpeted oak staircase, and through a door on the other side. The sign overhead read: FEDEX OFFICE CENTER. As soon as he left, the woman got up from behind the desk. For a moment Ana thought she was going to follow him, then the woman turned and disappeared under a sign that said LADIES.

Ana got up and made a beeline for the desk in the alcove, with Hinds's note and the printout spread out on top of it. When she got there she hesitated only briefly, looked around, then down at the desk.

The note said "Lucerne," what looked like the name of a hotel and some dates. Ana lifted her cell phone from her pocket, made sure the flash was off, and with one eye on the reception desk and the other on the ladies' room, snapped three or four quick pictures of the note and the single page computer printout.

Satisfied that no one had seen her, she drifted away across the lobby and toward the business center where Hinds had disappeared. Through the glass door she could see inside. He was seated at one of the computer workstations chipping away at the keyboard. Why would he come over here to use the computer? she wondered. Then she thought about the man going through their trash behind the office. The lawyers knew they were being monitored. Ana made a mental note to be more cautious.

The gleaming black Town Car with Senate plates pulled up in front of the low metal building at Reagan National Airport. They were only three miles from the Capitol. The driver and another staffer, each wearing stiff dark suits, opened the doors and quickly stepped out of the front of the car.

The driver ran to the back to get her luggage from the trunk. The other young man opened the back right passenger door. Grimes set one foot onto the sidewalk, a forty-five-hundred-dollar Christian Louboutin Croc pump, took the young man's hand, and exited the car.

She took a couple of seconds to assemble herself on the sidewalk, fluffed up her hair and straightened the long cardigan scarf so that it draped properly down the front of her dress, a one-of-a-kind Dior casual fashioned exclusively for travel.

The driver hustled her luggage up the ramp and into the building. The two men had been to this place enough times by now, almost every Thursday afternoon, to know the drill. They would pick her up at the same location Tuesday morning.

Grimes's Gulfstream, the one she and her husband owned, was parked in a hangar on the other side of the building. She walked up the steps while her assistant carried her briefcase and computer and held the door open for her.

There was no TSA screening here, nobody sticking a hand up your crotch or x-raying your body, and no lines, no screaming children or bumping up against the unwashed. Though today Grimes had to suffer the inconvenience of a late takeoff.

She was waiting for two House members whose session was running a few minutes late, people from her own party who were hitching a ride home with her. She had hoped they would be here by now. They would, of course, have to pay for the privilege, or at least the taxpayers would, this to keep the seam on their ethics straight.

Air travel on private jets for members of Congress had become an issue a few years earlier when corporations started using it to gain access. The way to avoid the conflict of a gift was to have the members pay at least part of the cost. Now for a few thousand dollars of the taxpayers' money, funds from their office budget, they could party all the way across the country. No problem.

But today there was a problem. Her driver, coming the other way from delivering her luggage to the plane, stepped up close. "Senator. There's someone waiting to see you."

"Where?"

"Outside. He wouldn't give me his name." The assistant stepped off to the side so that Grimes could see past him through the glass door leading out into the hangar.

The Eagle was standing on the gleaming concrete just this side of the stairway leading up to the open door of the plane.

"He said that you would want to talk to him." The look on Grimes's face told the kid that something was wrong. "Do you want me to call security?"

"NO! It's all right . . . not a problem."

"Would you like us to stay?"

"Ahh, no . . . put my computer and the briefcase on the plane. Then take the car and go, both of you, back to the office."

"Are you sure?"

Grimes snapped her eyes toward the kid and froze him with a cold look. "I wouldn't say it if I wasn't. Now go!" One of them headed for the plane with her brief-case and computer in hand. The other one disappeared out the front door back toward the car.

She looked at the Eagle, who just stood there staring at her through the closing glass door, a simpering smile on his face. Whatever it was, he'd better make it quick. She wanted him out of here before her colleagues arrived. It wouldn't do to have them seen together.

"What do you want?"

"Perhaps you'd like to talk up in the cabin," he said.

"We can talk right here."

"I could use a ride out to the coast." He had his own plane, but he wanted to talk to her on hers.

"That isn't happening!" said Grimes. "I have other passengers today."

"Really?"

"Yes. Two other members."

"That's great. I'd love to meet 'em." He headed toward the stairs and started to climb.

"And my husband's meeting me at the other end."

"You can introduce us," said the Eagle.

She looked toward the building, hoping the other two members wouldn't come walking through the door any second.

"Aren't you coming?" He stood at the top of the stairs in the plane's open door, looking down at her.

She had no choice. Grimes climbed the stairs as quickly as she could. Once inside, she was greeted by the copilot. "Hank, this is Mr., uh . . . Mr. Black. He'll be flying with us today." She looked nervously over her shoulder. "We should take off immediately."

"I thought there were two today. Another passenger?"

"He canceled at the last minute," said Grimes. "I'd like to get moving as quickly as possible."

"You got it." The copilot whistled. Two guys came out and rolled the stairs away. He closed the door and threw the lever to lock the pressurized seal. Then went forward. A few seconds later the engines started.

The Eagle settled into one of the cream-colored overstuffed executive swivel seats in the cabin. It was a nice plane, but not as nice as the one he owned himself, which was a later model.

The Gulfstream moved slowly out of the hangar onto the taxiway and started out toward the runway. Grimes leaned over and looked back through one of the windows.

"You might want to sit down, buckle up," said the Eagle. "But then I guess you own the plane, you make the rules. You wanna become jelly on the rear bulkhead, you paid for it, why not."

She dropped into one of the chairs on the other side of the cabin, buckled herself in, crossed her legs, crossed her arms, and glared at him.

"Blue Crocodile." He looked at her shoes. "Do they come that way? I mean snapping up out of the bayou? Or do they have to dye 'em?"

"What do you want?" She said this through lips stretched tight as a drum.

"I'll bet those are a real hit with the green-granola set. But then they probably don't know about the airplane either, do they?" He lowered his head a little and leaned forward so he could see out through the little porthole window just behind her. "Hey, isn't that Jim Bellows? Maybe we should wave."

She turned around in the chair. Bellows, a congressman from the Bay Area, was standing out in front of the hangar waving his arms frantically, motioning for them to come back.

Suddenly the door to the flight compartment opened. The copilot stuck his head out. "Looks like your other passenger showed up after all. You want to go back?"

"No!" said Grimes. "Just keep going."

The guy shrugged his shoulder and closed the door.

"My attitude entirely," said the Eagle. "Man wants to fly, he ought to be here on time."

"I don't know what I'm going to say to him next week," said Grimes.

"Tell him he got bumped."

"What do you want?"

"Oh, yeah, business. Well, let's see. It's going to be a long flight. We've got a lot of time. What is it, five hours?"

She ignored him. "I suppose the next thing you're going to want is a drink."

"Wouldn't hurt," he said. "Is there a flight attendant on board or will you be serving?"

"Get on with it." One of the blue high heels was now tapping the floor.

"Well, if you're gonna be that way, fine. Let's talk business. I take it you took care of the two judicial vacancies? Called the White House?"

"Is that what this is about?"

"Among other things," said the Eagle. He looked around, noticed the door at the rear of the cabin. "This thing got a bed back there? I could use some Zs later."

"Yes, I made the call! Just like you asked."

"What did they say?"

"They weren't happy. I'll tell you that. They wanted to know the names of the people I was leaning toward."

"And what did you say?"

"I told them I'd let them know as soon as my staff was finished checking them out. Exactly what you said."

"And?"

"What could they do?"

"Exactly," said the Eagle. "See? You have more power than you think."

"Against my better judgment."

"Well, I wouldn't worry too much about that," said the Eagle. "It wouldn't be the first time that let you down. Now what I want you to do . . . I think you know a lawyer out in L.A. by the name of Cletus Proffit?"

"Never heard of him," said Grimes.

"Mandella, Harbet, Cain. You know, Serna's old partners?"

"OK, maybe I know the name. I may have met him once or twice. I can't remember."

"Well then, it's time to get reacquainted. I want you to call him, ask him for a favor."

"I don't even know the man."

"That's all right. He knows you. He was a giver to your last campaign. Of course, he gave to your opponent as well. What you call an equal opportunity opportunist. When you talk to him, use his first name. Call him Clete. When he calls you senator, tell him your friends call you Maya. You know, polish his apple. Get his head in the trough with you. Make him think he's part of the club. He'll do whatever it is you ask. Tell him you want him to act as an intermediary on some highly sensitive pending judicial appointments. If you do it right, he'll be flattered," said the Eagle. "Now here's what I want you to tell him. . . ."

Thirty-Two

"So what did you find out?" A half hour out on the flight and Harry and I settle into the coach seats and listen to the drone of the jet engines. We're on our way to Amsterdam, the first leg of the trip.

"It's a moving target," says Harry. "Some of the numbers Alex gave us at his parents' house that night are dwarfed by more recent news accounts." Harry has been living at the Del's business center for the last three days. Doing research.

"One Swiss bank alone claims there are fifty-two thousand Americans with secret numbered accounts."

I shoot him a glance. "You're kidding."

"We're obviously in the wrong business," says Harry. "But I have to say, the IRS played hardball. They turned the screws on the overseas banks. Threatened

them with heavy withholding taxes on their US operations if they didn't cooperate. Threatened some of
them with criminal sanctions for aiding and abetting
tax evasion. Most of the banks were forced to make
concessions to open their books. One bank alone paid
fines totaling seven hundred and eighty million dollars
to the US Treasury," says Harry.

I whistle low and slow. This is probably a measure of
the value of their American operations. The fine is likely
a drop in the bucket compared to their US business.

"Plus the disclosure of forty-five hundred names,"
says Harry. "American depositors and their account
numbers to be drawn at random and delivered to the
IRS. That's intended to scare everybody else into dis-
closing offshore assets on their tax returns."

"That would do it for me," I tell him. "But then
I wouldn't have enough money to open a numbered
account in the first place. What about this guy, Korff?
Any lead on him?"

"I have a few addresses in and around Lucerne. It's
not an uncommon name. Strange thing is," says Harry,
"Lucerne is not a big banking center. Zurich, Bern,
even Geneva, but not Lucerne. There are a few of
what they call cantonal banks, local provincial institutions. But why this one, Gruber A.G., is in the middle
of Graves's story, I don't understand. Doesn't make
sense."

"We'll have to ask the man when we find him," I say.

"Also the whistleblower, Betz. There're a number of articles about him online. And it's true what Alex said. He did claim to have information about American politicians with secret numbered accounts in Switzerland. I printed some of the stuff out. It's in my briefcase. What's more," says Harry, "there doesn't seem to be a lot of interest in finding out who they are."

"Don't you think that's strange?" I ask.

"Maybe. I don't know. Then again, not necessarily," says Harry. "Powerful people in D.C. are often allowed to skate. We always think of ourselves as head and shoulders above any banana republic. In the end, are we really that different? Human nature being what it is," says Harry.

"Never thought of it that way."

"You should. That's not to say everybody's corrupt. There are, no doubt, a lot of good people there. Like everywhere else, about five percent of any population account for most of the problems," says Harry. "Usually the same five percent, and they'll do it over and over again if you give 'em a chance. It's just that people with power have a much greater opportunity for mischief, and they probably get away with it more.

"Every once in a while they'll nail some guy in Congress, indict him, convict him, and send him away just to let the rest know that there are some limits. It hasn't happened for a while. Probably overdue," says Harry.

"For years there have been stories of insider trading by members of Congress," he tells me. "You have to figure these people are privy to a lot of secrets. Potential investments nobody else in the world could get near. The temptation would be great to pass the information on to friends, and relatives. The last time they bailed out the banks," says Harry, "word is that there were key members of Congress who knew who was getting what and when, long before it was ever made public.

"Later there were charges that family and friends, distant relations went out and jumped on the stocks for the banks getting the money. If so, some of these people could have made a cool killing on the back of the taxpayers who picked up the tab," says Harry. "I'm not saying it happened. Nobody was indicted. But there were accusations."

"Sounds like you think Martha Stewart ought to complain," I tell him.

"I would if I were her," says Harry. "Not that it would do her any good. It's what I told Alex that night, remember? Prosecutorial discretion? Nothing you or I can do about it.

"But here is something I do want you to think about. And when you do, I want you to worry," says Harry. "Promise me?"

"Ok, I'll worry," I tell him.

"I'm reading between the lines, so take it for what it's worth. Remember the term Alex told us about, PEP—politically exposed persons?"

"Yeah."

"Well, it's a term of art. It's all over the literature on private numbered accounts. And it's highlighted in red letters. It's a major cause for concern," says Harry. "Everybody from the UN on down."

"Go on."

"There's an article, I printed it out. According to this piece—and I can't vouch for its accuracy, it's from one of the US financial networks—they're reporting an undisclosed number of US political figures, maybe past, maybe present, they don't know for sure. But it's pretty certain that they are account holders who possess offshore numbered accounts and who have not disclosed or paid taxes on the funds in those accounts."

"How do they know?"

"Because some information slipped out in the random selection process. If I had to guess, I'd say it was probably a mistake. And it's certain that there are more."

"Why doesn't the IRS go after them?"

"They don't know who they are," says Harry. "All they know is that they are sufficiently prominent to show up on the bank's PEP list, not by name, only that they are American political figures who have undisclosed accounts. Worse than that. The IRS can't be sure how deep the swamp is. Or for that matter what's swimming in it."

"What do you mean?"

"Bits and pieces of information," says Harry. "But if you put it all together you get a mosaic."

I start to smile like he's putting me on.

"Listen to me. I spent three days looking at this stuff because you asked me to. I looked at the tea leaves and now I'm telling you what I read in them. No one knows how much money is on deposit in individual accounts for these so-called PEPs, or how many officials are involved. Nor do they know where the money came from. And that's the key, the source of the funds. IRS and Treasury tripped over this when they started shaking down the foreign banks. And now they can't be sure how bad it is."

"Go on."

"There's no way to know," says Harry. "But according to one of the articles, a scholarly piece, that's one of the major fears. It's why PEP deposit holders, politicians, their family members are great big red flags for these private banks. And the banks don't always know because the account is probably opened in the name of some other straw man. This is not money these politicians would want the world to know about."

I sit there listening, my brain reeling like an empty spool, to what Harry is saying.

"What are you talking about? You mean bribes?"

"Shh, not so loud," says Harry. He gives me an exasperated look. "It's one thing to be bought off by some lobbyist in D.C. representing poultry producers in Iowa. Or, for that matter, even if the chickens are in Poland. But what if some of this money is coming from a foreign government, the recipient may not even know it," says Harry. "He knows he's being bought. But if he fulfills the quid pro quo, he may also be committing an act of treason." Harry looks at me. He is stone-cold serious.

"Take that and multiply it by a dozen other members, and ask yourself, does the IRS or for that matter any other government agency really want to roll that rock over? Given the low public esteem of Congress or government in general?" says Harry.

"Holy sh . . ."

"Shh. Quiet," says Harry. "It could be nothing. Maybe somebody popped a window and I'm feeling the

336 • STEVE MARTINI

effects of the thin air. Then again that might explain why so many people have been dying in accidents lately."

Four rows back and on the other side of the aisle, the dark-haired woman holding the novel tried to listen to what the two men were saying. Their heads kept moving closer to each other as they spoke. The engines were too loud and their voices too low.

When they landed she would wait for the other passengers to unload, then check the seats of the men for any scraps of paper they may have left behind. There was a two-hour layover in Amsterdam. They weren't going anywhere. Ana knew she'd catch up with them again, on the connecting flight to Zurich, and if not then, on the train to Lucerne. It was going to be a long trip.

Thirty-Three

G reat Britain held possession of the island of Hong Kong and the southern portion of the Kowloon Peninsula since the mid-nineteenth century. They acquired the area known as the New Territories later. The British had seized them in two successive opium wars, first the Island and then Kowloon across the narrow waterway, the harbor they would later name for Queen Victoria.

Both wars were fought against fading Chinese dynasties by the British Empire, which at that time was at its zenith. It stood alone as a world power with the largest navy on earth.

The Opium Wars, while adorned by diplomacy with the trappings of state policy, were in fact little more than naked acts of economic aggression by a powerful nation against a weaker one.

Britain wanted Chinese goods, silks, spices, tea, and other valuable commodities. The problem was that it had nothing to trade in return, nothing that China wanted or needed. What they wanted was to be left alone.

British business interests struck upon the idea of selling opium to the Chinese, which was then abundant in the far-flung British Empire. They reasoned that the Chinese would become addicted, thereby feeding future demand for the product.

When the Chinese government resisted by seizing loads of opium entering their country on British ships, war followed.

The Chinese were quickly defeated. In 1842 Britain took as part of its prize the Island of Hong Kong. In 1860, following the Second Opium War, the English took Kowloon. By the terms of treaties signed under the muzzle of British cannons, Great Britain took and held both of these possessions in perpetuity.

Western historians would call it "the opening of China." The Chinese would refer to it as the time of the "unequal treaties." Regardless of the name, it marked the beginning of China's colonization by Western nations, spheres of influence that would over time be seized for concessions by the world's other major players.

During the early years of British administration, what had been a sleepy fishing village on the eastern shores of Hong Kong was transformed into a thriving center of British colonial commerce. The island's population grew geometrically. It became a magnet for trade. Development and construction on the island spread. When Kowloon was added to the British possessions, it too prospered and grew. By the end of the nineteenth century the explosion of commercial growth and construction in what was a limited area had taken its toll. Economic success had its price. It placed a strain on the domestic water supply as well as the arable land available to grow food for what was becoming a densely populated British colony.

In 1898 Britain once again approached a fragile and increasingly unstable Chinese government. This time, rather than using force they used their diplomatic muscle to negotiate a ninety-nine-year lease for an area adjacent to Kowloon. The lease embraced 368 square miles of the mainland as well as numerous small islands.

What would become known as the New Territories would total more than eighty-six percent of the entire area of the Hong Kong colony. Its lease would also become the straw that broke the lion's back. In time, with patience and changes in geopolitics, China would force Britain to surrender its infinite hold on the commercial prize, the skyscrapers of Hong Kong and Kowloon, and the bustling harbor that separated them.

The Creeping Dragon alighted from the small Chinese Army executive jet inside a military hangar at what most residents of the island still called the new airport—Hong Kong International. It has been built on reclaimed land not far from Kowloon in the New Territories and was considered by many to be a marvel of modern engineering.

Built under British administration, it took six years to complete, cost twenty billion dollars, and was turned over to the Chinese government one year after Britain ceded Hong Kong back to China in 1997.

Cheng considered it a coup. Icing on the cake. Into the early nineties the British had dragged their feet. They tried to negotiate a joint-sovereignty agreement, seeking to keep their hand in Hong Kong. They saw no rational reason why the Chinese government would want them out. British colonial administration was a model of efficiency. Besides, without the British government to ensure stability, might China not be killing the goose that laid the golden egg? What if foreign investment fled Hong Kong? China would be left holding a bag of bones.

The government in Beijing wasn't buying any of it. What made the British think China couldn't administer Hong Kong at least as well as they had? After all, most of the residents were Chinese. To them the argument was an insult.

Added to this was the fact that Chinese history was a bitter pill, fruit from a poisonous tree. They reminded the British of the inequitable treaties that allowed them to take Hong Kong and Kowloon in the first place. And of the wars that led up to them, wars that ultimately left a legacy of Chinese opium dens fostered by British mercantile interests.

Britain claimed an obligation to look after the interests of their Hong Kong subjects. Beijing told them that if they felt strongly about it they should give these people British passports. This was a prickly domestic issue back home in Britain, what to do if there was a panic. Millions of Chinese immigrants flooding into the British Isles.

There were many meetings over months and years between various leaders. Sometimes there were hostile words and threats. If China wanted to, it could simply have taken the colony. Geography was on its side. With the largest standing army in the world there would be little Britain could do to stop them. But why do it if it wasn't necessary? Patience!

In the end, it was not threats but a practical argument that won the day. Beijing made it clear that on July 1, 1997, the ninety-nine-year lease would end. On that day, the New Territories would revert to China. Britain had no right under international law to extend the lease. Beijing wouldn't hear of it. All access to the Chinese mainland beyond Kowloon would be cut off. If Britain wanted to remain on the island of Hong Kong or the tip of Kowloon, they did so at their own peril, because chaos would follow.

The unstated question was, Where were they going to get the food and water necessary to support the more than six million people then living in what was left of the British colony?

It was a question for which the British government had no answer. They had run out the string. They had no desire to leave China with feelings of open hostility between the two countries. The handwriting was on the wall. After one hundred and fifty-seven years, Britain would go as they had done from India a half century earlier. The difference being, Hong Kong was not going to become part of the British Commonwealth. It belonged to a sovereign country already, China.

Cheng was right, to those with patience came the fruits of victory. China established a Special Administrative Region for Hong Kong with assurances that it would remain that way for at least fifty years. It was business as usual. Unless you followed the news you might not even realize that the British had left except for the recent disruptions, which had already fallen off the front pages of most newspapers around the world. The democracy movement was dying largely because the lawyers and businessmen who made the island hum with commercial activity were so busy making money that they couldn't be bothered to attend the protests.

The well-monied movers and shakers told the movement's leaders, mostly disorganized college students and a few professors, that they would try to show up if the organizers could reschedule the "demonstrations" for a weekend. Such was the practical nature of the Chinese mercantile mind. As far as Cheng was concerned, any thought that this might evolve into a real revolution died of embarrassment.

This morning Cheng had his own business to attend to. The government limo whisked him along the highway and threaded through the crowded downtown streets. Twenty minutes later it dropped him under the portico at the entrance to the Intercontinental Hotel, overlooking the water at the tip of Kowloon.

Thirty-Four

O n the way to the airport to pick up the second car in Zihua, Herman's head finally cleared enough that he was thinking once again.

He was confident there was no one following them on the highway. But whoever was tracking them and was able to find them at the condo probably possessed high-end assets. Merely looking in the rearview mirror or backtracking to trip up anyone following on the road wasn't going to cut it.

Depending on who they were, they could have been watching the condo by satellite or using one of the small remote control drones. For a few hundred dollars anybody could buy one of these little bastards and equip it with cameras. If they were flying high enough, people on the ground couldn't see or hear them. With three or

four they could conduct twenty-four-hour air surveillance over a building and watch anyone fleeing from it.

Whoever it was could have been tracking the van as
they fled south along the highway and Herman knew
it. He needed to change out vehicles, but do it in a way
that it could not be seen from the air.

The parking garage at the resort on the beach was
perfect. Inside there were enough cars already parked,
with traffic moving in and out that anyone watching
overhead would see only the van going in and never
coming out.

A half hour after entering the garage, Herman, Alex,
and the other two men emerged in a dark blue Range
Rover, but instead of heading south, they went north.
With enough time to think they came up with the perfect location, the fishing resort of Manzanillo.

A few hours north on the coast highway, Manzanillo
had an airport where, if they needed to, they could
rent another vehicle. It was a sport-fishing mecca,
sailfish capital of the world, blue marlin and dorado.
It was large enough with plenty of tourists so that four
American men looking for fun would not be noticed.
It also had a very active cargo-container port and was
only a few hours by car from the dirt airstrip where
Herman and Alex had flown in. For anyone on the run
it offered multiple means of transport and escape.

It was their second night in the seedy hotel at the south end of town near the container port. The air conditioner didn't work and there was enough grease and dirt on the windows that no one could see in or out.

Herman couldn't sleep. In the morning they would move again, just to be on the safe side. Though he was certain that if they got away clear in the car there was no way anyone could have tracked them here. They were cut off from the world.

For Herman that was part of the problem. He wanted to get word to Madriani and Hinds back in Coronado that he and Alex were all right. But he didn't dare. An incoming call even from a pay phone to the office on Orange Avenue might alert anyone listening in as to their location in Mexico.

Herman couldn't be sure if Madriani even knew about the attack at the condo in Ixtapa. He might have seen it on the news. Then again, with the level of narco violence in Mexico, a shooting with blood in the parking lot and no dead bodies was not exactly a hot international bulletin back in the States.

The bigger fear were messages from the law firm coming south. There was no one in Ixtapa to receive them. But Harry and Paul didn't know that. It was clear from the shooter's uniform shirt that their method of communication was compromised. Anything coming this way might be read by the people chasing them.

Finally he couldn't wait any longer. About midnight Herman roused one of the other men and the two of them headed into town. They purchased a small stack of international calling cards at a shop on the main drag, then drove fifteen miles farther north up the main highway to a pay phone at the airport.

Herman hoped that anyone intercepting the call might assume that they were traveling on through, headed north up the coast to Puerto Vallarta or, better yet, catching a chartered flight.

He placed a call to the unlisted number at Paul's house. There was no answer. One o'clock in the morning in Manzanillo, midnight in San Diego. Where was he? Perhaps burning the midnight oil?

Herman called the back line at the law firm. What he heard this time alarmed him: a recording telling him that the office phones were temporarily out of order. What the hell was going on? He wondered if whoever came after them in Ixtapa had also attacked the office. Herman immediately called Harry's number. Again there was no answer. This time he left a message.

"Where the hell are you guys? Your office phones are out of order. There was a serious problem at the condo here, repeat serious problem, but we are all OK. Repeat OK! Do not . . . repeat, do not use previously established method of communication. It is compromised. Will contact you again when I have time." Herman went to hang up, then stopped. He lifted the receiver back to his lips and said, "Headed east on charter flight, Tampico. Will contact you from there." Then he hung up. At least this would give anyone listening something to waste their time on.

He called Paul's house and left the same message. Herman didn't have home numbers for any of the other office staff. He considered calling Sarah, Paul's daughter up in L.A. He desperately wanted to know if her father and Harry were OK and, if so, where they were. But he didn't want to get Sarah involved. Calling her number could present problems. There was no way to be sure just how sophisticated the people trying to kill them were, or what kind of eavesdropping or tracking software they might have. Herman knew that if anything happened to Sarah he wouldn't have to worry about the people trying to kill him, Madriani would do it himself.

He slipped the calling cards back in his pocket and the two of them headed back to the dingy room near the port.

Thirty-Five

This morning Cheng was not in uniform. Instead he wore a stylish dark blue sharkskin suit, starched white dress shirt, gold cuff links, and a striped silk tie.

Two security men followed behind him in a separate car, also dressed in civilian clothes.

None of the local authorities in Hong Kong had been alerted to Cheng's presence. He would slip in and out of the city unnoticed. To anyone looking at him, Cheng could easily pass for an affluent Chinese businessman. His face was not known to the public. In fact, most officers in the Second Bureau made a point of staying out of the media. If you took their picture there was a good chance you would have your camera smashed.

He walked into the lobby of the Intercontinental. Under his arm he carried a small leather folio.

350 • STEVE MARTINI

One of the security men stepped out of the car and followed behind at a discreet distance.

The Intercontinental was one of the more expensive hotels in town. The Presidential Suite would run you almost fourteen thousand dollars a night. Ying, the man he was coming to meet, liked to live well. Cheng knew he was also careful. He wasn't staying in the hotel. He was merely taking a room as cover for the meeting. He did this each time they met in Hong Kong.

Ying owned a luxury condominium high up on the island on the other side of the harbor. It was a very expensive address. Ying thought he had covered this well, but Cheng knew about it. Title to the estate was held in the name of a corporation registered in Andorra, a tiny principality and banking haven tucked in the Pyrenees Mountains between Spain and France. Hong Kong might be a Special Administrative Region, but it was not exempt from Chinese Intelligence.

Ying had a lot of houses. He could afford them. When you did business with other people in Cheng's line of work you always wanted to know what they did with their money, how they spent it, what they bought, and if they made investments, how they hedged their funds. It told you a lot about their goals and ambitions, their tolerance for risk, character, and sometimes their weaknesses.

He checked his watch, ten thirty-five. He was five minutes late. Cheng went to the house phone, picked up the receiver, and when the operator answered, he gave the name Joseph Ying and asked her to ring his room. Cheng knew this was not the man's real name. He used a number of aliases. Given his government connections he possessed bona fide passports in all of them. Ying was the name he used when doing business in Asia.

Three minutes later Cheng walked into the blue-tinted lounge with its angled walls of floor-to-ceiling glass looking out over the harbor. He walked over to one of the low cocktail tables, laid the leather folio down, and waited. A few seconds later one of his security men walked in and took a seat at the bar. The place was nearly empty. By noon it would be getting busy. Cheng hoped to be out of there by then.

He sat down at the table. Ying kept him waiting. Five minutes, then ten. Cheng looked at his watch. He wondered if Ying was sending him a message. Perhaps he had appeared too anxious. Finally, after fifteen minutes the American sporting a Chinese name came through the door. Cheng stood up, reached down, and furtively wiped the perspiration from his right palm onto the back of his slacks so that by the time Ying reached him he was ready to shake hands.

352 • STEVE MARTINI

"Sorry I'm late. Right after we hung up I got an urgent call. I had to take it. I couldn't get them off the phone."

"Of course. No problem," said Cheng. "I was just sitting here enjoying the view."

Ying turned and looked out through the wall of glass at the sparkling waters of the harbor. "It is gorgeous, isn't it? Every time I come I am amazed. It becomes more beautiful with each passing year."

"Unlike us," said Cheng. They both laughed.

Ying was taller, older that Cheng, and he wasn't Asian. Round-eyed, gray hair, he was always well dressed, three-piece pinstriped power suit set off by a conservative club tie. He would have fit in well at the British colonial clubs of an earlier era.

"How was your flight?" asked Cheng.

"Fine."

"Did you come in this morning?" Cheng tested him.

"Ah, no. I got in last night, about eleven," Ying lied.

He had been in Hong Kong for three days, closed-door meetings at his house on the island. Cheng's men had him under surveillance. They were also monitoring his calls. They were unable to get content because Ying's cell phone used high-end encryption and the man was careful to keep conversations brief. But they could track the location of incoming calls.

"Perhaps we should get down to business," said Cheng.

"Let's do it."

They sat and ordered drinks, Scotch and soda for Ying, a Virgin Mary for the general.

"One might think you were Catholic," said Ying.

"Not unless the pope is Communist," said Cheng. They laughed. Drinking on company time, especially when the business being transacted was critical, was not conducive to advancement in Chinese leadership circles.

"Saw your man at the bar." Ying glanced at the security man sitting there by himself drinking a club soda. "I suppose you don't go anywhere without them."

"No," said Cheng. Even if he wanted to. It was unwise for government officials to meet with Westerners unless they had at least one credible witness present. Cheng's masters in Beijing, while increasingly modern, could still be gripped by pangs of paranoia. The security man might not be able to hear their conversation, but he could at least attest to the fact that the meeting took place in open view, plain sight, and was business-like in its conduct.

"I have a number of questions," said Cheng. "I trust we can have a frank discussion."

"Of course."

"I am interested in information as to your firm's Western political assets?"

"By Western you mean . . ."

"The United States," said Cheng.

"What do you mean by assets? Do you mean consultation on political matters?"

"I thought we agreed to be frank?" said Cheng. "What I mean is, how many of these people do you actually possess? And at what level?"

The older man looked at him from across the table. "May I ask where you get your information?"

"You can ask," said Cheng.

"If by 'possess' you mean own in a way that I can order their actions," said Ying, "none. It doesn't work that way."

"Of course not." Cheng smiled. "I understand it is much more complicated and subtle. I didn't mean to imply anything improper."

Saving face was just as important in America as it was in China.

"I can reason with a significant number of them," said Ying. "Some of them in key positions. Others may follow their lead. Depending on the level of controversy. On a good day I can persuade a dozen, perhaps more, as to the wisdom of my suggestions on any given issue."

Cheng looked at him and read the gleam in his eye for what it was, Irish bullshit. "Your calendar must be filled with good days. I say this because your persuasiveness is legendary. Surpassed perhaps only by your modesty?"

"What can I say?"

"Let me put it another way," said Cheng. "Have you ever been refused?"

Ying smiled. "The secret, General, is never to allow yourself to be put in that situation."

"I see. Your logic is too compelling, is that it?"

"What is it exactly that you have in mind?"

At one time Ying was reputed to have worked for US intelligence, though information was sketchy as to which agency. Nor was it clear whether he was directly employed or hired under contract. Either way, his work was not as a field agent. It was technical.

According to his Chinese dossier, Ying's holdings were extensive. His businesses, and there were several of them, specialized in resource consultation, commercial intelligence, and international security. Over the years he had branched into other sidelines, some of which were obviously unmentionable. Ying appeared to have no loyalties except to his own pocketbook. He played both sides of the street, and every corner at the intersections. Along the way he sold intelligence services to clients and often used the information to buy up valuable resources, oil contracts as well as other commodities. Oil was his specialty. In the process he had acquired immense wealth, though no available published source seemed to know exactly how much. He was sufficiently shrewd to stay in the shadows, well below the political and media radar.

His companies could go where the US military and the CIA could not due to the hypersensitivity of the political disease the Americans now referred to as "boots on the ground." For this reason, Ying was privy to information his own government could not get. Cheng wondered how long it might be before Ying ended up the wealthiest man in the world. If and when it happened, and it may already have, Cheng knew that Ying's name would never appear in *Forbes*.

By profession he was not a soldier, but a geological engineer trained in locating oil domes and substrata petroleum resources. It was this fact that made Cheng particularly nervous when, during their last meeting, Ying's conversation drifted into the subject of the Spratly Islands. For Cheng this was like an iron ship striking a magnetic mine.

The Spratlys were a chain of largely uninhabited atolls in the South China Sea. They were known to be rich in oil, natural gas, and valuable fishing rights. Half the nations of Asia were now claiming them. But China, being the biggest bully on the block; was at the head of the line. Beijing was busy drumming up international support for the geologic fable of an ancient subsea land bridge connecting the islands with the Chinese mainland a thousand miles away.

This was the diplomatic Chinese fan spread open to cover the cudgel in its other hand, the largest standing army in the world and a growing navy. Beijing wanted the islands. Nothing was going to stand in their way. Cheng's job was to do everything in his power to get them. Failure was not an option.

"The matter we talked about the last time we met," said Cheng. "Do you remember?"

"You mean the question of territorial rights?"

Cheng nodded.

Ying's eyes gleamed. Plant the seed, tend it, and it sprouts, he thought. "I remember." China was desperate for allies, anyone who might bless their claim that the South China Sea was a Beijing swimming pool. What Ying wanted were oil and gas concessions, investments in exploration rights. He didn't care who got the islands, as long as his company was hip-deep in concessions when the fight was over.

"Then you know what I'm talking about," said Cheng. "Are you familiar with the United Nations Convention on the Law of the Sea?"

"I think I've heard of it," said Ying.

"There is a vote being scheduled on a resolution in the Security Council."

"Yes, as I recall, it's about four weeks out. Doesn't give you much time. I take it you want to influence the outcome?"

"Of course. China would like to convince the US administration not to exercise its veto. If certain domestic political pressure could be brought to bear on the president. What we would like . . . what Beijing wants . . ."

"You want the United States to disengage on the question of the islands. To put a leash on its navy in the South China Sea so that China might be the only big player," said Ying.

"I could not have said it better myself," said Cheng. "It is, after all, a matter outside their sphere. It does not concern them. What we seek is simple and fair."

"You don't have to convince me," said Ying. "There may be a few US admirals and a general or two."

"All we want are quiet bilateral negotiations with our Asian neighbors. We want to avoid a multilateral circus in the UN with bright lights and Western news agencies hanging from the chandeliers."

"I understand. You want to go one-on-one. Get your neighbors behind closed doors where you can cow them into a corner and fence off the Spratlys behind a Chinese wall. You don't have to dress it up for me."

"No, that's not . . ."

"It doesn't matter," said Ying. "Imperialism pays. It's a proven fact. Whether the boot doing the kicking is on a British, American, or Chinese foot, it makes no difference to me."

Cheng started to get up. To an avowed Communist schooled in the system, these were fighting words.

As the general rose to the bait, eyes blazing from across the table, Ying smiled at him and winked. "I'm sorry. It was a bad joke. In extremely poor taste," he said. "I apologize. I hope you will forgive me. My sense of humor sometimes gets the better of me. "

Cheng caught himself. He smiled nervously as he glanced over at his security man, who had come off the stool and was moving toward them. Cheng raised his hand and motioned the man away. He was still angry, uncertain as to whether the American wasn't still playing with his head. He settled slowly back down into his seat. "Are you willing to help us or not?"

"That would depend on how much you are willing to pay, and in what form?"

Their drinks arrived just in time to chill Cheng's anger. Ying hung his silver-handled walking stick, the sharp metal beak of the bird's head catching on the wood at the edge of the table. The imagery was not lost on Cheng: the fact that the alias *Ying* in Mandarin, translated into English, matched the code name often used to identify the American by Western intelligence agencies—the code name "Eagle."

Thirty-Six

Harry and I checked into the Hotel des Alpes in Lucerne. It is situated on the old quay near the north end of the medieval wooden- covered walking bridge, the Kapellbrücke, Chapel Bridge. Here Lake Lucerne closes to a narrow waterway and empties into the Reuss River.

We waste no time unpacking our bags. Instead we head out while it is still light, trying to track down Simon Korff, the banker questioned by Tory Graves and whose business card Graves dropped on me before he was killed.

Harry located four addresses online for the name Korff in and around Lucerne. Three are in town. The fourth appears to be some distance outside the city on the other side of the lake. None of them show the first name of Simon or the letter S. Harry is worried that his search may have been incomplete because of the limitations on the computer search engine he used.

This proves to be the case when we check the local phone book in the room. We find two more listings for Korff but again no match on the first name.

I start dialing using a Swiss SIM card in my unlocked cell phone. Harry and I purchased four of these at a shop at the airport in Zurich when we landed. We'll use them and toss them as we move.

The first two calls are dead ends. Both are answered in German, which quickly changes to English the minute they realize I don't speak German. No one at either address has heard of or knows a Simon Korff.

The third call, I hit pay dirt. A woman answers. When I mention the name she says, "Ya. Simon Korff is my father-in-law."

"Is he there by any chance?"

"May I ask who's calling?"

"My name is Madriani. I'm an American lawyer. I represent some banking interests in the United States. We have been informed that Mr. Korff is knowledgeable and experienced in Swiss banking. We are looking to hire."

Harry gives me a pained expression.

I shrug. It's the best I can do on short notice.

"Just a moment." I can hear her talking in German to someone at the other end.

A few seconds later a man comes on the line. "Hello!"

"Hello, sir. Are you Simon Korff?"

"I am."

"The Simon Korff who worked for Gruber Bank here in Lucerne?"

"Ya. That is correct."

"We would very much like to talk to you," I tell him.

"What does this regard?"

"I would much prefer to discuss that in person if you have the time to meet with us."

"Of course. When would you like to do this?"

"Tonight, if that's possible."

"I could do that. Where are you?"

I give him the name of our hotel.

"I know the place. I could meet you there," he says.

"Have you already had dinner?"

"No."

"Why don't we talk over dinner?"

Harry nods, gestures with his hand like he's drinking from a glass. My partner is offended that I lied to the man about a job. But he has no difficulty at all plying him with liquor.

"There's a very nice restaurant here on the second floor. Why don't we meet there, say seven o'clock?"

"Ya, good," he says.

I give him my name. As he writes it down I tell him to have the front desk call me when he arrives and we'll meet him in the lobby.

"Good. See you at seven," and he hangs up.

"He's gonna be angry when he finds out there's no job," says Harry.

"What else could I say? If I told him how I came by his business card and what happened to Graves he'd hang up in my ear and run. Your job is to keep his glass full."

"My kind of work. It is, after all, a business deduction," says Harry.

"I go away for five days and the entire damned world falls apart," said the Eagle. He was talking to one of his lieutenants from his hotel in Manila in the Philippines. He had one more piece of business to attend to before returning to the States. "What happened?"

"We don't know. Our people located them. There was a shootout, a lot of damage, blood at the scene, but no bodies. And everybody disappeared."

"What do you mean, they disappeared?"

"Our people never called in. It's pretty clear they're dead."

"Who did it?"

"We have to assume the P.I. The one with Ives."

"Was he armed?"

"We don't know. Mexican police have the building all cordoned off. But according to reports, they found no one inside."

"What about satellite surveillance? Don't tell me that you weren't watching in real time?"

"We were," said the man, "but there was a problem. Too much smoke. The CS gas clouded out the overhead cameras. And the pavement was too hot to pick 'em up on the thermal. All we saw was a lotta smoke and white light. A white van raced into the lot in front of the place. We lost it in the smoke for maybe a minute, minute and a half. When it popped out again it was doin' like ninety out of town headed south down the highway."

"And you didn't follow it?"

"We did. That's how we know our people are probably dead. The van stopped along the coast and dumped what looked like two bodies in the ocean."

"Who were they?"

"Johnson and Hayes."

"Andy?"

"Yeah."

Andy Hayes was one of his most reliable operatives. Special Forces trained, he had at one time been part of the army's Delta Force unit headquartered at Fort Bragg. It had cost the Eagle a bundle to recruit him.

"We lost the van in a parking garage down the coast. They pulled in and never came out," said the guy at the other end. "Musta had another car stashed. When we checked we found the van, broken windshield, dented front end, and a lot of blood inside, and no clue as to where they went."

"That means whoever was in the van knew they were being tracked overhead," said the Eagle.

"That ain't the half of it," said the other guy. "They've also gone dark at the law office in Coronado. Landlines are all out, cell phones down, and their link to the net, it's disconnected."

"What about the two lawyers?"

"They're in Europe."

"Where?"

"Switzerland. Lucerne." The man would have told the Eagle that they had 'em covered, but he didn't dare. Instead he said, "We brought in assets from Libya. Two guys under contract. They're very good. In the meantime we're set up overhead. They checked into their hotel and haven't emerged."

"Those are narrow winding streets," said the Eagle. "I know that town. A lot of ancient buildings with a dozen ways in and out. Do you know what they're doing there?"

"No."

The Eagle could guess. It was clear that they had some kind of a lead. Who or what it was, that was the question. "You're going to lose them on the satellite. You do know that?"

"Our people will be on the ground in less than an hour. We brought 'em in through Diego Garcia the minute we found out where they were headed. From there to Zurich. Then we chartered a chopper. We wired them photos of the two lawyers and the name of the hotel."

"They know what to do?"

"Yes."

"I hope they do a better job than the crew in Mexico," said the Eagle, and he hung up. He checked his watch. He was already running late for his meeting at the white gingerbread structure on the Pasig River downtown—the Malacañang Palace.

Thirty-Seven

P rivacy is the main rule. It is as old as the industry in Switzerland. And unlike other restricted relationships, the lawyer-client, the priest ah . . . what is the word in English?"

"Penitent?"

"Ya, that's it. Unlike those, violation of bank secrecy is a serious crime with large fines and prison in Switzerland. Unlike the movies, there is no total anonymity. To open an account you must identify yourself, produce a passport if you are not a citizen, and the account number is attached to your name."

"Here, have another drink," says Harry. "Let me fill that mug."

Simon Korff pushes the stein across the table, his fist the size of a sledgehammer gripped tightly around the handle. He has a smile on his red face, cheeks with so many tiny broken blood vessels they look like ground beef. He is a prototypical German; you could put his smiling face and naked body on a poster and children would instinctively dress him in lederhosen. A large man, rotund, probably blond at one time, what little hair he has left has now turned gray. He is older than what I might have pictured. I am guessing late sixties.

"Not even the Swiss government can get this information except in special cases."

Harry lifts the pitcher of dark lager with both hands and fills the stein almost to the brim. "There you go."

"You are a good host," says Korff.

"I like to listen to what you have to say." Harry lifts the nearly empty pitcher, taps the glass with his finger as he looks at the waiter to bring another.

We have been here a little over two hours. Four pitchers of beer, enough food to feed an army, and Korff is still sitting upright lecturing us on banking. Strangely enough, he hasn't asked a single question about the supposed job offer.

"You say the government cannot even get this information?" I ask.

"No. No. NO!" He grips the stein in one hand and waves his finger in front of his nose with the other. "Only if there are serious crimes," he says.

"For example?"

"Money laundering, drugs, evidence of organized crime. It used to be that even for tax evasion the government could not find out who had what on deposit. Now," he says, "that has all changed."

"In what way?" I ask.

He takes another large gulp from the stein and wipes his mouth on the back of his shirt sleeve. "Well, tax evasion was not a crime in Switzerland. At least not a serious crime. It was what you call, umm . . ." He searches for the term.

"A misdemeanor?" says Harry.

"That's the word."

"I'm beginning to like this country," says Harry.

"Anyway. Because it was not a serious crime in Switzerland, other governments could not pursue their citizens for tax evasion on money deposited here. The Swiss government would not cooperate with them. Now that has all changed."

"Go on," I say.

"Your government has caused a lot of problems," he says. "Hurt the banks. People lost jobs. All because they want the money." He takes another drink.

"What was your job at the bank," I ask, "at Gruber?"

"Oh. I was an officer at Gruber for twenty-two years. The last three I was what they call the anti-money-laundering compliance officer. A very important position," he says. "It was my job to detect money laundering and to report it to the bank president and to the authorities."

"I see. Was there much money laundering that went on?" I ask.

"Not in the beginning," says Korff. "But toward the end before I retired, yes. It was very serious."

"Really?"

He takes another drink and Harry fills the stein from the fresh pitcher.

"Yes. It was bad."

"I'd be curious to know, how does a . . . uh . . . anti-money-laundering compliance officer discover such things?"

"Usually cash," he says. "When someone brings large amounts of cash to deposit, that is usually a problem. Especially small denominations. It's often drug money."

"Are you familiar with the term PEPs?"

"You must be reading my mind," he says. "That was the problem at Gruber. You know what it means? This PEPs?"

I nod. "Yes. Politicians, their families, people associated with them."

"Well, when people like this, some PEP shows up at the bank and he or she has cash, sometimes suitcases full of it, you know you are in trouble. You cannot take that money, no matter how much it is."

"And this happened at Gruber?" says Harry.

"Oh, yes." He takes another drink. A little bit of it sloshes down onto his belly. "It was the reason I was fired. That and your government."

"I don't understand," I tell him.

"Let me tell you." He leans toward the center of the table like he wants to whisper some secret.

Harry and I join him halfway.

"The Americans wanted to go after their citizens for taxes. They pressured the big banks. Not the ones here," he says. "The ones in Zurich and Geneva, Bern. The banks with overseas offices in the United States. After so many years of threats, the banks and the Swiss government finally said enough. They agreed to some plan to release information so that the American government could go after these people, American citizens with accounts in Switzerland. But then," he says, "they had a problem. The PEPs." He looks at us and wrinkles his forehead until the furry mice of brows above both eyes begin to dance.

"They had too many," he says. "These people had accounts in banks all over Switzerland."

I shoot Harry a glance.

"As you can imagine, this was embarrassing, hmm? They already told the press back in America that they were going to deal with these tax cheats. Now they find out there were powerful American politicians involved. And not just a few. So what to do?"

"What did they do?" says Harry.

"Consolidation," says Korff. "They allowed the depositors, the PEPs, to move these accounts from the big banks where most of them were deposited to a handful of small banks in more remote areas. In the cantons. Because these transfers were inside Switzerland, they went unnoticed by the central banks in Europe and the United States. I don't know whether they were informed or not. Probably not.

"What made it worse was that many of these transfers were made in cash. Large, large amounts of cash. Big bills. In the United States the largest denomination is the hundred-dollar bill. But in Switzerland we have the thousand-franc note, worth almost eleven hundred US dollars. The PEPs, the American PEPs, were showing up with multiple trunks, you know . . ." He gestures extending his arms way out.

"Steamer trunks," says Harry.

"Ya. That's it. The steamer trunks, filled with thousand-franc notes. Truckloads of them."

"Why not just wire the funds?" asks Harry.

"They did not want any record of the transaction other than the deposit at the bank."

"You know, a friend of mine mentioned something about this." I look at Harry. "You remember, what was his name? Ahh . . . Graves."

"Tory Graves," says Harry.

"That's it."

"You know him?"

"Oh, yes."

"He came to visit me," says Korff.

"No, what a small world."

"Yes. He was very interested in what was happening. In particular, where this money came from and how they would be able to use it."

"Yes, we'd be interested in that as well," says Harry. He pours more beer.

"Sure," says Korff. "I will tell you."

Thirty-Eight

Cheng settled into the seat on the Chinese Army executive jet as it sped toward the Dabie Mountains. He was halfway along on his journey, the two-and-a-half-hour flight from Hong Kong back to Beijing.

As he looked down on the sprawling foothills he could see another dam under construction, one in a vast series of projects.

China had come a long way. Cheng may have been a godless bureaucrat, but he knew that his nation had been blessed more than once by Joss, the ancient Chinese god of good fortune. They had but one great adversary left in the world, America, and to Cheng's thinking, based on every measure available to him, America was in decline.

While the United States was distracted with its Mideast adventures and its myopic focus on terrorism, China was busy investing in long-term infrastructure and industry, grabbing up critical global resources—oil, metals, and rare earth among others. Even the fabled iPhone and the Apple computer were assembled in China.

As America's wars dragged on with no long-term political solution, voters grew weary. Cheng's analysts in the Bureau predicted this result years before it actually occurred. They based their predictions on an earlier model, the war in Vietnam. The perceived American enemy was different, but the result was the same.

America, once in a war stance, had a tendency to perceive its enemy as a vast unified monolith. Cheng couldn't be sure whether this was driven by military strategy or political ideology. But he and his analysts could see its effect. In Vietnam the monumental enemy was international communism, toppling dominoes that would consume the world if Vietnam was lost. In fact what was being waged was a war of nationalism by a country the size of California with an economy that was struggling to become third world.

Now the United States was gripped by an Islamic wave of jihad, hostility that transcended national boundaries, launched by a multitude of splintered sub-national groups, many of them with different motives and grievances. There were so many of these that they defied identification. Even here, in the tribal chaos and ancient feuds of the desert, America had managed to inflate the balloon of a large unified enemy, an army of Islamic radicals. The violence was real, but the army, if it existed, was unified by only one thing—its hatred for the West, Europe and America. To Cheng and to China, this was a huge boon. They couldn't have invented anything this beneficial if they had designed it themselves.

Cheng had to wonder if decades from now historians might look back and realize that what was actually in play were numerous wars of nationalism being waged across an entire region in the Middle East. Cheng suspected that this was the result of artificial boundaries drawn by the Western powers in the Hall of Mirrors at Versailles at the end of World War One. These boundaries had completely ignored ethnic, religious, and tribal factions. Instead, colonial spheres of influence were carved out of the desert for the Western powers who won the war so that they could plunder the oil reserves just then being discovered. In a place where tribal blood feuds were millennial in duration, this was like planting the seeds of poison to be harvested in the future.

In America, after more than a decade of desert warfare in Afghanistan and Iraq, the party out of power won election and took control. America reversed course and withdraw its forces. Chaos ensued.

The American faction now out of power claimed that the winner so hastily abandoned the field and withdrew that they were now the authors of anarchy in a growing number of places in the Middle East. America's partisan divide went global. Its allies began to question US resolve. From everything Cheng could see, all of this played into China's hands. American allies who already had doubts concerning US military and political resolve began to double up on them, including many of the Asian nations that were China's neighbors, its competitors in the race for the Spratly Islands.

One of these was the Philippine Islands. It was to this that Cheng now turned his attention. He was troubled by a report he had just received, the cable still in his hand.

Cheng knew that Joe Ying possessed his own private jet. It was a modern Gulfstream G650, a plane costing almost sixty million US dollars. It had a range exceeding eight thousand miles. More than enough to fly nonstop from Hong Kong to the American West Coast.

And yet upon leaving Hong Kong, Ying's Gulfstream didn't fly to California. Chinese radar and overhead surveillance showed the plane diverting to the Philippines. Cheng wondered why.

He alerted the Chinese embassy in Manila, and two agents were dispatched to see what was happening. As it turned out, Ying wasn't topping off the Gulfstream with fuel. Instead, a limousine picked him up at the airport and transported him to one of the five-star hotels in downtown Manila.

Ordinarily this might have been a matter of little or no consequence, except for the fact that two hours later another dark Town Car was seen chauffeuring Ying to Malacañang, the white gingerbread building on the Pasig River that served as the Presidential Palace.

This was no coincidence. The Philippines had become China's most serious rival in the increasingly contentious and sometimes heated conflict to win the Spratly Islands.

There was never any doubt among Chinese leaders that the government in Washington coveted the Spratlys because of their rich treasures. US oil and gas interests salivated at the thought. America no doubt regretted the fact that it had not claimed the islands as part of its vast Pacific "protectorate" in the days immediately after the Second World War, when American power went unchallenged. But at that time no one knew their value.

Now the United States was hobbled by new realities: the government in Beijing was a rising power, the waters around the islands were becoming a Chinese lake, and Washington could make no colorable claim to the islands due to their location remote from any US territory or possession.

For this reason they needed a game piece. Chinese intelligence, Cheng's bureau, now believed that the Philippine government in Manila had become just that—America's pawn in the battle for the Spratlys. If the United States could muscle the islands into Philippine hands, they would no doubt receive their share of the treasures.

Ying knew that his own intended prize, a generous slice of the rich oil and gas concessions, required that he be on the winning side. If he backed the loser, he stood to gain nothing.

The stakes in this contest were sufficiently high that Cheng couldn't afford to take a chance. What was Ying doing at Malacañang Palace? If the United States prevailed, and it was later determined that Ying played a hand, Cheng's association with him would be more than enough to take the dragon down. He would end his days chopping wood in some mountainous frozen gulag, or worse, tied to a concrete post already pockmarked by bullets.

It was near midnight. Proffit was back in L.A., lying in bed wide awake, listening to his wife snore through the wall in the adjoining bedroom. Home two days and he was already missing his liaisons with Vicki Preebles. The supple secretary may have been manipulative, but she didn't snore.

Yet that wasn't the reason Proffit couldn't sleep. He was wondering whether to tell his wife about the phone call he received earlier in the day. He was afraid if he did, she would rip his head off. More than that, he was petrified that whatever he was now caught up in might take the firm down, or himself. He knew it had to do with Serna, but how? Until he had the answer to that, he had no choice but to keep it to himself.

Proffit was in his L.A. office and had been on the phone with Cyril Fischer, his number two in D.C., when the call was interrupted by a breaking tone from the intercom.

"Just a sec." Proffit pushed the button on the phone. "I left instructions not to be disturbed!"

"Sorry, but I thought you might want to take this one," said his secretary.

"Who is it?"

"An assistant to Senator Maya Grimes, says his boss would like to talk to you."

"She's on the line?"

"Extension six."

"Tell him I'll be right with her." Proffit punched the button to Fischer. "Gotta take another call. I'll get back to you in a few minutes." He hit extension six. "This is Cletus Proffit."

"Just a moment for Senator Grimes."

A few seconds later the familiar voice came on the line. "Mr. Proffit?"

"Hello, Senator. How are you?"

"I'm good. I hope I didn't catch you at a busy time."

"Not at all."

He wondered what she wanted. If it was a campaign fund-raiser, his firm's dance card was already punched full. Since Serna's death he had a drawer full of these, all of them bundled and mailed from the Washington office to his personal attention in case there was something Serna had been up to that he should know about.

"To what do I owe the honor?" said Proffit.

"It's not about money, if that's what you're thinking."

She must have had a crystal ball. But then, these days why else would any politician be on the phone?

Proffit knew her, of course. Who in the state didn't? They had met a few times, just in passing at crowded political and social events. But they were not intimates.

Proffit was a Democrat, a dyed-in-the-wool liberal who, when necessary, wore it on his sleeve. His specialty was entertainment law. He did enough work in and around Hollywood that his liberal credentials were as necessary to survival as breathing air.

Grimes had once been a Republican, a former state legislator, and was elected secretary of state for California. She had parlayed this into a successful bid for the US Senate almost twenty years ago. As the state turned increasingly blue, Grimes saw the fiery finger etch its warnings on the wall. She switched parties, but only halfway. She went Independent. That was twelve years ago.

This was about the same time that she and Serna had become tight, doing the women's thing up on the Hill. At least according to the information that Proffit was able to dredge up. Grimes now caucused with the Democrats. Serna had taken bows for this. She claimed to be the instigator of Grimes's conversion. Now there were growing rumors that the senator might actually become a Democrat before the next election. The world was full of opportunity for those who were sufficiently flexible.

Proffit wondered if that's what the call was about. "What can I do for you?"

"Actually it involves an important matter of Senate business. I need help from someone who is knowledge-able and somewhat connected with the organized bar in our state. You come highly recommended."

For a moment Proffit was flattered. "Of course, assuming it's something I can do, I would be happy to help."

"It is," said Grimes. "You're aware there are some vacancies on the federal courts in the state, for both the Southern District as well as the Ninth Circuit?"

"So I hear." Proffit's wife, who sat on the District Court in Los Angeles, was in fact a candidate for the appellate slot on the Ninth Circuit. According to information, she was on a short list in the White House, people who had already cleared all the non-binding hurdles at the American Bar Association and the State Bar. Proffit had put his own shoulder to the wheel, if for no other reason than to get his wife out of town. Once nominated and confirmed by the Senate, she would spend at least four days a week in San Francisco. Paradise to Proffit.

"The fact is, I am getting tremendous pressure from the criminal defense bar back there to the effect that they are underrepresented on the Ninth Circuit," said Grimes.

"Is that so? I hadn't heard."

"I have talked to people in the White House and it seems there is some sympathy for this position there."

Proffit thought about asking who at the White House, but he knew she wouldn't tell him. His wife had been a civil practitioner before being appointed to the bench. Proffit could smell a rat. She was about to be passed over. Still, why would Grimes be calling him? Perhaps there was some way he could turn it around.

"One name keeps popping up," said Grimes. "A criminal defense lawyer in Southern California by the name of Madriani. I'm told that you know him."

Proffit's heart skipped a beat. Couldn't be the same one. Not the lawyer representing the driver who killed Serna?

"Where's he from? What city?" said Proffit.

"San Diego area, I believe."

"Paul Madriani?"

"That's the one."

"Somebody must be walking in my shadow," said Proffit. "I met him one time. Couldn't have been more than two weeks ago. If you're looking for an endorsement or a review, I couldn't recommend him. From what little I know, he doesn't have the background." What Proffit meant was the pedigree, hailing from a small firm outside the cloistered club of the organized bar. "Do you mind my asking where you got your information that I knew him?"

"I'm not at liberty to say. But he does have significant support in certain quarters, and according to these people he appears to be highly qualified," said Grimes.

"Beyond that, my office has already conducted a thorough background check. And I've notified the White House of my endorsement."

"Then you didn't call me for a personal review?"

"No," said Grimes.

Proffit wasn't stupid. Whatever was going on, he could smell Serna all over it. The fact that Madriani represented the man accused of killing her in an accident was no coincidence. He was curious to discover the connection so that the firm could tiptoe around it, avoid any fallout. At the same time he didn't want to become personally involved.

"If you don't mind my asking, can you tell me if Mr. Madriani has formally applied for the Ninth Circuit position?" Proffit was familiar with all the contenders. He didn't remember seeing his name. If he had, he would have put the word out to his friends on the various reviewing panels to deep-six him. Two or three black balls were usually all it took to finish off somebody who didn't have the horses in terms of political pull with the appointing power.

"The people who recommended you told me you had a way of coming directly to the point. That's exactly what we were hoping you could help us with," said Grimes.

"What?"

"We'd like you to approach Mr. Madriani and tell him that my office is inviting him to apply. We would like him to do so as soon as possible, unless of course he is not interested. But we think there's a good chance he will be."

"Wait, wait, wait! This is all very awkward," said Proffit. "You do know . . ."

"That your wife is a candidate for this position as well? Yes, I wanted to talk to you about that," said Grimes. "I know this must be very disappointing for you, but you are aware of the custom known as senatorial courtesy? Sometimes they call it privilege."

"Go on."

"The fact is, for that vacancy, because it's assigned to California, no other candidate can be scheduled for confirmation before the Senate without my consent." She listened to him breathing on the other end of the line. "Just to let you know, I am already committed to Mr. Madriani's appointment. I have advised White House staff to that effect. So you see, it would be to your benefit to use your best efforts to persuade Mr. Madriani to apply."

"Just how do I do that?" Proffit was beginning to lose his temper. Smoke coming out of his ears.

"We have something that I am told will help. But before we get to that, you need to understand that there are currently twenty-nine active seats on the Ninth Circuit, and several judges who are nearing retirement. We expect at least two, possibly three vacancies in the next two years. Just so you know, your wife would be in an excellent position for any one of those other appointments. I would give you my assurance in those regards."

For a moment Proffit wondered whether Grimes and Madriani might have been meeting together, in the sack. He took a deep breath. Grimes was putting him in a box and nailing the lid on. If he refused or failed, Grimes was in a position to block his wife's nomination for higher appointment for as long as she was in the Senate. If so, and his wife found out, she would make Proffit's life miserable, or worse, divorce him and take half the value of his partnership in the firm. She could ruin him.

"Of course this is assuming he's inclined to do so. Not everybody wants to be on the bench," said Proffit. "You say you believe he's interested, but he hasn't filed. I don't get it."

"Good. If you're curious, then I'll assume you're on board," she said. "Now this is all confidential. You do understand that?"

"I haven't said I'd do anything."

"But I'm sure you will. Right?"

Proffit thought about his options. "I suppose."

"You don't sound enthusiastic," she said.

"I'll have to work on that later," said Proffit.

"Of course. Take your time. But don't take too long. So that there is no confusion later," said Grimes. "I will be sending you a check in today's mail, a retainer. Be kind enough to send me a fully executed retainer agreement, signed by you, to my office here in Washington."

There was no response from the other end.

"Are you there?"

"You want to treat this as a legal matter?"

"Absolutely. I'm asking you for your assistance and advice as a lawyer."

"On this?"

"You haven't heard everything yet."

"What else?" said Proffit.

"On the retainer agreement, if you have to describe any of this, just call it general legal advice. No need for any specifics." She was being careful to cover her tracks.

Establishing an attorney-client relationship would seal Proffit's lips, prevent him from talking to anyone else about their conversation without her prior, expressed written approval.

"There's a case, a federal appeal. Well, actually, it's more of a negotiation at this point, or will be shortly. In any event, the case is *United States versus Rubin Betz*."

The instant the name was mentioned, Proffit sat bolt upright in his chair. He'd heard it before. In fact, he had scoured the Internet search engines at the office looking for anything he could find on Betz. Rubin Betz was the name Madriani had given him the night they met in the restaurant in Georgetown. The name of Serna's old boyfriend. The synapse in his brain sent a jolt of adrenaline to his heart. Now Grimes was calling with the same name. Whatever it was, Serna was in the middle of it. Shit was about to rain down on the firm. Proffit could smell it.

"Mr. Betz is in the federal penitentiary at Florence, Colorado," said Grimes.

"Supermax!" Proffit almost said, "I know," but he didn't. Instead he bit his tongue. Florence was dubbed the "Alcatraz of the Rockies," where the feds sent the worst of the worst, tight controls, stories of complete isolation. From everything that Proffit had read, it was the one thing that didn't make any sense.

Betz was a banker. At one time he worked for one of the large Swiss banks with branches in the United States. That was what got him in trouble, the charge that he had conspired with some US deposit holders to conceal overseas profits from the tax man. It was a white-collar crime, but he was doing time in the tightest maximum security prison in the United States.

"What did the man do? This guy Betz? You've got to do something bad to get sent to Florence." He was hoping Grimes might tell him.

"You don't need to be concerned about that. You can look it up later." Grimes knew he would. She also knew that Betz wasn't in Florence because of anything he'd done. The government put him there to prevent any harm from happening to the man, and not because they loved him. It was to avoid the public fallout that they believed would occur should he die in prison. Florence was the only place of incarceration within the federal system where they could adequately protect him and, at the same time, keep him from talking to anyone else. Betz had what a few of her colleagues on the Hill were now calling the Midas key. They were trying to deal with him, to put closure on the entire affair. The fear was that sooner or later some federal judge might cut him loose, or worse, reduce his term and send him to a minimum security institution, where if he got into an argument or crosswise with one of the gangs, another inmate might kill him. Even the fear that he might fall down a flight of stairs had some members of Congress walking the floors at night.

"Mr. Betz requires the assistance of a good criminal lawyer," said Grimes. "He doesn't yet know it, but he's about to become involved in some rather complicated negotiations."

"What kind of negotiations?"

"As they say in the military, that's beyond your pay grade," said Grimes. "All you have to do is carry the message. We want Mr. Madriani to offer his services. Betz has no lawyer at the moment. Tell Madriani he will be well paid for his services, if he cooperates."

"What makes you think he'll do it?" said Proffit.

"Trust me. He will."

"How much is he being paid?" said Proffit. "He may want to know."

"He won't. We have it on good authority that he's been dying to talk to Mr. Betz for some time. This is his chance."

"And because of this you think he'll file for the judgeship?"

"Even if he doesn't, he'll talk to Betz." With that, Grimes hung up in his ear.

Thirty-Nine

"You asked about the source of this cash." It is getting late, nearly midnight and Korff is still telling us about the dealings of his old employer, Gruber Bank.

"When you are talking about the PEPs, politically powerful people who are carrying cash to the bank, there are generally two sources that you look for. Either the person has looted his country's treasury, which happens more often than you would like to think. But usually that is limited to the third world. Or the PEP is being bribed by some foreign entity, a corporation, perhaps a wealthy individual, or some other country.

"It is the reason why the PEPs are so much trouble. They show up with cash. You don't know the source. Even if they claim it is legitimate, how do you know? There is no way to prove it."

"But you said Gruber allowed these PEPs to make large deposits in cash?" says Harry.

"Yes. That's why I complained. As the bank's anti-money-laundering compliance officer I knew what would happen. The minute they deposited the funds they would start to launder it."

"How do they do this?" I ask.

"There are a number of ways," says Korff, "but the most common is to purchase a legitimate business that deals in large amounts of cash, high volumes. A casino, for example. They are notorious as currency laundries. Or what happened in one case involving one of your American PEPs, he bought a chain of coffeehouses.

"The way it works, they use clean money, funds for which taxes have already been paid, to buy the business. They start small. Then if the business makes, say, two hundred thousand dollars the first year, they report income of two million. They take dirty money from the secret bank account to make up the difference."

"But they'd have to pay income tax on the full two million?" says Harry. "Doesn't make any sense."

"On the contrary," says the banker. "That's the point. The money in the bank was free money. They didn't have to do anything to earn it, other than the corrupt act. But they can't spend it until it is laundered. They report it as legitimate income and pay the tax.

What is left is clean. The entire purpose is to legitimize it by paying the tax.

"Then the next year they take the laundered money and expand their business. Now they have five coffeehouses. That year they earn a million dollars in actual income and report five million. You can see how it would grow very quickly. At some point you stop expanding the business and instead use the laundered profits to invest in other things. When you are done, you end up with a business worth a fortune and a pile of clean cash invested elsewhere."

"Like I said before, we're in the wrong business," says Harry.

"Did you know any of these PEPs? Were they people you recognized?" I ask.

"Oh, yes, of course," he says. "There were a number of prominent politicians. Some from Europe. Some from the United States. Many of them I didn't know. Some from South America. They would come in speaking Spanish, sometimes Portuguese. And the Russians, of course, they were always there."

"You mean to say Russian politicians are corrupt?" says Harry.

"Does a Frenchman speak French?" says Korff.

They both laugh.

"The Americans," I say. "I'd be curious to know who some of them . . ."

"I really shouldn't tell you that." Korff is weaving in his chair, halfway through the latest pitcher of lager. "It could get me in serious trouble."

"Just between us," says Harry. He upends the pitcher of beer over Korff's stein one more time. "Would you like another?"

"I would not say no." The banker laughed.

"Come on, a few names," says Harry. "Between friends."

"OK. A lady, a woman. One of your senators. Her last name is"—he whispers—"Grimes."

"Maya Grimes?" I look at him.

"You said it, not me. She made trips over several months. Enough cash to fill a cargo container," he says. "This was maybe four years ago. And there were others."

Before I can ask who, Korff gives up eight more names, every one of them recognizable, fixtures with long tenures in the House and the Senate. And he tells us that one retired member of the Senate now sits on the board of directors of Gruber Bank. The names include members of both political parties. If what we are being told is accurate, corruption may be the only thing that is still bipartisan in Washington.

He says there are more, but he can't remember all the names. I recall the comment by Graves concerning

Abscam and the FBI sting, that if the feds hadn't pulled the plug and brought the undercover investigation to an end they might have had trouble finding a quorum to do business in either house on Capitol Hill.

"How much money are we talking about here?" says Harry. "In broad numbers, I mean. Do you have any idea?"

Korff starts to nod. "That was what worried me, part of the reason I complained so much. Before all of this, Gruber was a small regional bank with local deposit holders, mostly individuals and small businesses. It had assets of a little more than half a billion francs. All of a sudden, in less than two years, we had accounts in excess of one hundred billion."

Harry looks at me. I know what he is thinking. It's time for me to start worrying about what he told me on the plane on the way over.

"Not all of these deposits were from Americans, you understand. Some came from Europe, Latin America. As I said, we had deposits from almost everywhere. Money from the larger Swiss banks was being moved to smaller banks where it wouldn't be noticed. Banks without branches overseas where your IRS and Treasury would have less leverage. We even had diplomats from the United Nations with PEP accounts at the bank." Korff looks at both of us. He starts to laugh.

"These people were on the news at night complaining about corruption in the third world, telling poor countries they had to clean up their act if they wanted help from the IMF, the International Monetary Fund. And during the day they were making PEP deposits in cash, large amounts into their numbered accounts at Gruber."

"Makes you wonder about human nature," says Harry.

Not if I know my partner. Harry's been convinced since shortly after escaping the womb that the angels of our better nature took flight the instant Adam had his ass tossed from Eden.

"You wouldn't by any chance have any documents concerning any of this?" he asks.

"No, of course not. But the bank has them. They would have all of the names and the account numbers."

"You said there were exceptions to the bank secrecy laws in cases where there was evidence of criminal wrongdoing, money laundering. If that's the case," I say, "what's to prevent a foreign government or some private party from accessing the banks' files on these accounts?"

"Ordinarily I would say you are right," says Korff. "But not in this instance. You see, there was a kind of informal understanding between the Swiss government and the other countries involved. What you might call a 'safe harbor.'"

"Go on."

"If the money was moved, transferred from the large Swiss banks that had international branches, during the window of time that was agreed upon, the United States agreed not to pursue it. Other countries followed the American lead. They would make no inquiries and the Swiss government would not be asked to relax the rules of secrecy concerning any of the PEP accounts. Once they were transferred, they would be untouchable."

"Why would they do such a thing?" I ask.

"Because no one wanted the information to be made public," he says. "There were serious concerns that disclosure would threaten political stability in a number of countries, not the least of which was your own. There was also concern as to the effect on financial markets," says Korff.

"He's got a point," says Harry. "How do you explain to the common folk who are grubbing for a living that half of their leaders are on the take?"

"Precisely," says Korff. "It was a very big problem. But still there should have been other ways to deal with it. I became a thorn because I kept pointing that out. Because, you see, I had no choice. As the bank's compliance officer, if I said nothing and suddenly the news

400 · STEVE MARTINI

came out as to what was happening, I would be the one who was responsible. Gruber's president and his friends on the board would claim they knew nothing. So what else could I do? I papered their walls with my complaints. When it was over they fired me. So there you have it. How I became unemployed. Now, what is this job you are looking to fill?"

"Why didn't you take the information to the media?" I ask.

"This is not the United States, my friend. If I said anything they would have had me in jail, charged under the bank secrecy statutes."

"But the statutes didn't apply because of the criminal acts," I tell him.

"They do if the Swiss government says they do. And the banking industry in Switzerland is very powerful."

"Let me see if I understand what you're saying." I lean over the table. "The bank has all the information on these PEP accounts, numbers as well as the identities of the clients holding those accounts?"

"That is correct."

"But the bank can't be forced to give up the information, even though there is clear evidence of money laundering and probable corruption, because they're shielded by secrecy. Not because it's covered by Swiss law, but because other governments have decided not to challenge the issue since their own politicians are involved?"

"There you have it. Now you understand," he says. Korff takes another swig from the stein and swallows it.

"And a private party seeking this information, bringing suit from outside the country . . ."

"Would have no chance at all," he says. "Without support from their own government, Switzerland would simply refuse to cooperate. Secrecy is the first rule. The only reason it has been relaxed is because of outside pressure from other governments. Take that pressure away and we go back to the first rule."

I shake my head. If he's right, Harry and I have hit a stone wall. A long trip for nothing.

"Excuse me," says Korff, "but I'm getting the sense that you're not really here to offer me a job. Instead, you're looking for information. Am I right?"

"Yeah," says Harry. "But you have to admit that the beer in this place is pretty good."

"I thought so." The German's happy expression collapses. "Yes. The beer was good. And I enjoyed the meal," he says. "And it is good to get out of my son's apartment, to give them some time alone. So for that I thank you. I have enjoyed the conversation. When you get to be my age, it is good to be listened to by people who, at least for the moment anyway, think you have something important to say."

I am feeling like a heel.

"It is difficult to lose one's job when you get old," he says. "There are not a lot of opportunities."

"I'm sorry that ours was a lie," I tell him. "Sorry that we had to deceive you. If there had been an easier way we would have taken it."

"I understand," he says. "I'm not going to ask you why you're doing what you're doing. Looking at your faces, listening to your questions, I assume that your motives are proper and correct. For whatever reason you are doing this, I hope you get them."

By "them" I am assuming he means the PEPs. That's not our mission, but if they should happen to tumble along the way, neither Harry nor I would shed any tears.

"So do we," says Harry.

"All of this, the money, the PEPs, the corruption, it troubled me greatly." He uncouples his hand from the beer stein, looks down at the table for a moment. When he lifts his head there is a tear running down one cheek.

"It is difficult, very difficult to do the right thing, and to end up as I do. I had worked for Gruber for twenty-two years. I knew the original owners. Nice men. To watch and see other people do what these people have done. To see them prosper. And to watch as society cloaks them with protection. . . ."

I reach across the table, grab one of his fat hands before he can say anything more. "I'm not going to lie to you again and tell you that I feel your pain," I say. "But I do understand. We both understand," I tell him. "You need not have any doubts. You did the right thing. I think you know that and so do we. And if your family is any judge of character, and my guess is that they are, they know it as well. Whatever these other people did, they have to live with it. Take it to the grave with them."

"I may not be much of an audience," says Harry. "But I've been around long enough to know that it wasn't the beer talking tonight. Sometimes life sucks," he says.

"Yes, it does. But not always." Korff lifts his head and wipes the tear away with his sleeve. "Sometimes you get lucky, as you have tonight."

"How's that?" says Harry.

"Because you see, there is another set of records."

"What do you mean?" I look at him.

"I had to be sure I could trust you," he says. "I am not the good person you think I am. I want my pound of flesh. The American PEPs used a broker. He would have his own set of files, account numbers, names, all of it. I assume he was a broker, at least that's what I was told."

"How do you know this?"

"Because I saw him. Everything about the way these accounts were handled was unusual. Normally an account is opened and funds are deposited, everything done between the bank and the client. No one else involved.

"But this, the transfer of all these accounts, the use of cash so that there would be no paper trail. To say nothing of the amounts involved. That and the fact they had such a short period of time to complete everything. That is probably why they used the broker. In fact, there were two of them. The actual broker and his lawyer. They were in the bank every day for almost two months."

"Did you know them?" says Harry.

"No. They were both Americans, US passport holders. I know that. I was told that the broker was an acquaintance of Gruber's president, that they had done business over the years, that the broker once worked for an American branch of a large Swiss bank headquartered in Zurich. They kept most of the staff at Gruber away from them, including myself. Only those in direct support had any contact."

"Can you remember any names, anything about them?" I ask.

"You know, after he left, I thought about it, and I

realized I forgot to tell your friend Graves about the woman, the lawyer. I only saw her a couple of times and always at a distance. I never heard anyone call her by her Christian name. They referred to her only as Fraulein Zerna."

"You spell that with a Z?" says Harry.

"No. First letter S."

"You mean Serna." Harry looks at me.

"My English is not always good," says Korff.

"Can you describe her?" I ask.

"As I say, I didn't see her up close. I would estimate she was maybe . . . a hundred and seventy centimeters in height."

"In feet and inches?" says Harry.

He thinks for a moment, a quick conversion, banker's brain. "About five foot seven in inches. She had short dark hair. Medium build. She spoke both English and Spanish. I remember that. Oh, and she worked for a law firm in Washington, D.C. I'm sorry I don't know the name."

"Well, we won't be talking to her," says Harry.

"Why not?"

"She's dead," I tell him.

"Oh." Korff flashes a look at Harry, then back to me, weighs what is left unstated and says, "How did she die?"

"Officially?"

He looks at me and nods.

"An accident."

"But you don't think it was?"

"We know it wasn't," I tell him.

This doesn't seem to surprise him. "I wondered," he says, "how long it would take before this kind of thing began to occur. With that much money and these kinds of clients, it was certain to happen."

"Why is that?" I ask.

"It's the nature of the animal," he says. "The thing about PEPs. They commit bad acts, they take money, and because of it they are highly vulnerable to extortion. It's how they got the name 'Politically Exposed Persons.' Depending on the power they possess, there is a high correlation to violence. From what you're saying, I take it then you knew these people, the broker and his lawyer? I expect that he is probably dead as well."

"Do you have a name?"

"Yes," he says. "Rubin Betz."

I think about it for a moment and suddenly it all makes sense. The whistleblower. It was little wonder they had him locked up. It was probably the only reason he was still alive, that and the radioactive pile of information he had salted away.

Forty

The two Libyan mercenaries took turns watching from a rooftop across the river with a pair of 20×80 binoculars, powerful field glasses that brought everything up close. The location five stories up gave them a good line of sight through the windows along the second-story balcony into the restaurant.

They had located and identified the American lawyers earlier in the day from photographs soon after their quarry had checked into the hotel. In the evening the lawyers were joined by another man, an older European who arrived on foot. They saw him cross the wooden bridge and head toward the hotel until finally all three ended up in the restaurant.

The Libyans had been fully briefed on what to do. Anyone meeting and talking with the lawyers was in their cross hairs. But now they were getting stiff lying out in the open air on the cold hard roof. Whatever the three men were discussing, it was taking far too long to suit the Libyans out on the roof.

Finally the man with the field glasses observed one of the lawyers as he paid the bill. "Wake up. They are getting ready to leave."

The other Libyan stirred, cleared his eyes, and started to get up.

"Wait." They spoke in Arabic.

Across the river the three men got up from the table. They shook hands and walked toward the back of the restaurant, where they disappeared.

"All right. You know what to do?" The man with the field glasses looked at his partner.

"Yes."

"I will stay and watch to make sure the other two go to their rooms. If they follow the old man I will call to warn you."

"Good."

"Check your phone. Make sure it's on."

The one holding the glasses said, "Go!"

The other Libyan scurried across the roof and clambered down a fire escape at the back of the building. There was no reason to hurry. He knew that the old man would cross the wooden footbridge moving toward

him. All he had to do was get to the end of the bridge
on this side of the river and wait.

He reached the ground, walked briskly toward the
bridge, and checked his watch. It was after one in the
morning. The narrow winding back streets of the old
town were almost completely deserted. The shops
along the way were all closed, the interiors dark. The
open-air street vendors had long since shuttered the
stalls, hauled away their perishables, and headed for
home.

Occasional traffic could be heard on the four-lane
auto bridge a hundred meters or so to the east, where
the waters of Lake Lucerne flowed into the river.

The Libyan quickly found a position near the end
of the wooden footbridge. He hunkered in the shadows near one of the closed stalls on the curving cobbled
quay along the riverbank. He waited as he listened
to the lonely whine of a motor scooter somewhere off
in the distance as it shifted gears until it was swallowed
by the silence of the night.

We left Korff in the lobby. He was a few sheets to
the wind, uneasy on his feet. Still, for a man who had
downed an ocean of beer, the fact that he was standing
at all was itself an Olympian feat. We gave him some
cash, three hundred Swiss francs, for his time, for

the information, and to hire a taxi to take him home.
Harry and I offered to go with him. But he said no.
He took the cash, thanked us profusely, and headed to
the counter to call the night clerk to get a cab.

Harry and I headed up to our rooms. European
style, each of the adjoining rooms has a tiny bath with
a shower and a window overlooking the river, comfortable but small and very expensive.

Tonight I don't care. I could sleep in a tent. I'm
exhausted, finally losing the battle over the nine-hour
time difference between the West Coast and Lucerne.

In the hallway outside his door Harry stops, looks at
me, and says, "I just had a thought. Why don't we head
back?"

"What?"

"Home," he says.

"What, you mean now?"

"Why not? We stick around, we're just gonna swallow a big load of jet lag. If we head back now, we stay
on California time and we'll be fine. We sleep on the
train to Zurich and all the way home on the plane. You
heard the man. There's nothing more we're gonna get
here."

"I'm tired. I want to sleep. We paid for the rooms,
let's use them. Besides, how can you be so sure there's
nothing more?"

"Unless you think he was lying," says Harry. "What else is there? We need hard evidence and there's only two sets of records. The bank has one. The other is buried somewhere, probably stateside, and the only man who knows where is locked up in a federal pen.

"You think he was lying?" says Harry.

"You mean Korff?"

"Yeah."

"No. I think he told us everything he knew."

"So then we know almost everything there is to know. We just can't prove any of it." Harry puts the key in the lock and opens the door to his room. Harry disappears inside, but he keeps on talking and doesn't close the door. Harry's wound up. He wants to chat. "What else is there? Tell me?" he says.

I ignore him, open the door to my own room, and flip on the light. I can hear him still jabbering away in the other room. I yawn, cover my mouth, and make my way around the bed toward the window on the other side. When I get there I pull the curtains closed. All I want to do is collapse on the bed and sleep. I'll shower in the morning.

"I'm talking to you," he says. "Where'd you go?" I hear him hollering, top of his lungs in the other room. If he doesn't tone it down they're going to throw us out. I stumble back around the bed into the hallway toward his room. When I get to his open door I tell him as much.

"Good," he says. "They throw us out, we can go home." Harry has his back to me, opening the window, taking in some fresh air. With Harry, a few beers and he gets a second wind. He pulls the curtains closed as he turns to look at me. "If we stay here we're just wasting more time. You heard the man. There are no records to be had. Not here at least."

"There is the bank," I tell him. "It's a shot."

"You mean Gruber? Yeah, right through your head. You don't actually think they're gonna share anything with us. You heard him. Swiss banking secrecy is carved in stone. Put there by the fiery finger of God. We go wandering over to Gruber asking questions about any of the information he gave us tonight, they're gonna throw our asses in the Swiss pokey until we tell them who ratted them out. Then the three of us can share a cell," says Harry.

He may be right. But at the moment I'm not thinking too clearly. "OK, but why don't we get some sleep first?"

Harry stops talking. Instead he is looking down at something with the kind of expression you might save for a snake.

"What is it?"

"That."

"What?"

"My comb. On the bed."

"Jeez, you had me scared." There's a small pocket comb lying near the head of the bed halfway under one of the pillows.

"I didn't leave it there," he says.

"Maybe you did and you forgot."

"No. I didn't open my bag." He lifts the rolling piece of luggage up and tosses it onto the bed. Harry unzips it and throws back the cover. He looks but he doesn't touch anything.

"Is everything there?"

"I don't know. But it's not the way I packed it," he says. Harry would know. He is phobic about such things.

I head to my room and check my bag. Before I even get it open I realize he is right. The running shoes I'd packed in the side pocket are no longer there. When I unzip the bag I find them inside, on top of my other clothes.

I leave the bag unzipped on the bed and head back to Harry's room. When I get there he is folding up a piece of paper, something from his travel folder.

"We can sleep on the train," he says. He's already chugging around the bed toward me. "There's one that leaves for Zurich at two." He grabs the comb, tosses it in the suitcase, and zips it up.

Before I can say another word, Harry has the lights off, pulling his suitcase behind him. He closes the door to his room and ushers me down the hall to get my bag and lock up.

At this point the adrenaline has kicked in. I am no longer arguing with him. My weariness seems to have fled, driven off by my natural instinct of flight rather than fight.

The ancient covered footbridge was lit by incandescent lights high up under the gable of the wooden roof. The bright light seemed trapped inside the long span over the dark water.

But even with the illumination it was difficult from outside to see much on the bridge at night. There was only a small gap between the eaves of the roof and the solid plank walls that lined each side of the walkway. If a person fell on the bridge, unless you were walking on it yourself, you would not be able to see them.

The Libyan hiding in the shadows on the other side realized this almost immediately. He had been waiting almost ten minutes by the time he saw the old man stumbling along the quay across the river. In that time not a single soul had crossed the footbridge. The man was getting tired of waiting. Besides, from the look of it, the old guy might pass out before he got across.

About fifty meters out from the Libyan's side of the river there was a large six-sided stone tower with a matching hexagonal roof. It appeared to be part of the bridge structure. At the tower the bridge angled sharply to the left. To that point the Libyan would have complete cover from the old man moving toward him from the other side of the river. He considered moving out onto the bridge at least as far as the tower. Then he looked at the cold, dark water flowing by, and decided against it.

If someone entered the bridge behind him when he was engaged with the old man he would have to run to the far side of the bridge to escape. The river was less than a hundred and twenty meters wide at this point. But the old wooden bridge, because it ran at a diagonal across the water, was more than two hundred meters from end to end.

If someone saw him, called the police, and they closed off the two ends of the bridge, he would have nowhere to go but over the side and into the water. He was not a good swimmer. Just downstream a few hundred meters the river washed over the baffles of a small dam, and the water was swift. The Libyan wanted no part of it.

Besides, here on dry land, he had an advantage, not only darkness and surprise, but the steps leading down from the bridge. The old man would have to navigate those. In his present state he might fall and break his neck even if no one touched him.

The Libyan moved out toward the steps leading up to the wooden bridge, passed into the shadows beyond them, and huddled down low near the ground. He would wait.

Up on the roof, his partner watched the lights in the two rooms across the river through the field glasses. The lawyers were getting ready for bed. He had seen them come to the windows and close the curtains.

Earlier in the evening as the two lawyers were having dinner, his compatriot now down by the bridge stole into their rooms at the hotel and went through their luggage. As instructed, he was looking for any documents that might be important. He found nothing. Neither one of the lawyers was carrying a computer. That seemed strange. The man doing the search was young but highly efficient. When he finished the search of the first bag he casually deposited everything back inside the suitcase, zipped it closed, and put it back on the floor. Then he locked up the room and went next door.

Here he had a separate task to complete. When he finished searching the suitcase he laid out his tools and materials on the bed and went to work on the inside of the case.

He placed a sizable package wrapped in a single thin layer of plastic on the bed next to him. It was about the size of a small laptop computer and approximately one inch thick. It weighed a little more than half a kilo. He knew it wouldn't take much to break the plastic covering. Any sharp impact or rough handling would do it.

He worked swiftly, his fingers and hands nimble. In less than three minutes he was done. He checked to make sure that everything was dry and then tossed the American's clothes and other personal items back into the bag. He added one more little touch, then zipped the bag closed and stood it back down on the floor where he had found it. Then he exited the room and locked the door.

Now as the Libyan watched through the field glasses his compatriot scurried near the entrance to the bridge and disappeared into the darkness.

All was going well. A few seconds later the two lawyers turned out the lights in their rooms. He knew they would be tired. They had traveled much farther to get here than either of the two Libyans. Weary from their trip, within minutes the Americans would be sound asleep.

He lowered the field glasses from his eyes, pushed himself back from the parapet along the edge of the roof, and made his way toward the fire escape at the back of the building.

Forty-One

Simon Korff fingered the crisp bank notes in his pocket. The three stiff one-hundred-franc bills felt as if they just came off the press. They even felt warm from the lawyer's pocket. He hadn't seen that much money at any one time since losing his job at the bank.

He knew that he had promised his dinner companions that he would take a taxi home. He had intended to do just that. But when he got to the hotel's front counter the night clerk wasn't there. He hit the bell twice but no one showed up. As he stood there waiting he considered the cost of the taxi and had second thoughts. With the money in his pocket he could buy a nice present for his son and daughter-in-law. They had been so good to him. For once he would be able to do something for them.

He turned and headed out the front door. As he navigated his way around and over the cobblestones on the street the cold night air seemed to have a sobering effect. The tingling sensation at the tip of his nose began to lessen. The walk would do him good. This way by the time he got home he could slip into the apartment without stumbling and waking everyone up.

Slowly he made his way to the bridge, up the two broad steps, and onto the old wooden concourse. He steadied himself against the railing and looked down the long straight tunnel. Under the gabled roof with its massive beamed supports, the bright overhead lights showered the entire path with a yellow incandescent brilliance.

The glare may have made him feel safe, but the pounding in his head had the old man wishing for a little less radiance. Besides, Lucerne was a tourist town. No one worried about walking at night. The crime rate here was almost nonexistent.

He trudged along under the glowing lights, stopping every so often against the railing and the solid wooden walls. A few times he wondered how he had gotten from the railing on the left side of the bridge to the railing on the right without intending to do so. At one point he stumbled into a huge curved laminated support the size of a tree trunk. He reached out and slapped the solid wood as if it had assaulted him. Then he collected himself and moved on. In the distance he could see the outline of the tower at the side of the bridge. He steeled himself and moved toward it as if it were a waypoint on GPS and he was on autopilot.

By now I am starting to get irritated with Harry. "Let it go!" I tell him. "We'll sort it out when we get home."

"I'm not gonna let it go. Eight hundred bucks," he says. "We'll pay for tonight but not for tomorrow night." Harry has hammered on the bell at the front desk long enough to rouse the night clerk, and is now arguing with the man across the counter.

The clerk is half asleep. "Sir! I have told you. Cancellation requires forty-eight hours' notice. That is hotel policy."

"And, as I told you, we have an emergency. We have to leave, and we have to do it now," says Harry. "You know as well as I do the place is full up. We had to pay a premium for the rooms to get them on short notice. You'll rent them in the morning within an hour, and for the same price. So why don't you just print out a cancellation form and we will leave. Unless you want to wake up the entire hotel."

"I'm sorry, but I cannot do that."

"Then perhaps you can give me a list of the names of all the people who had a key to our rooms?" says Harry.

"What do you mean?"

"What I mean is that somebody let themselves into our rooms during dinner and it wasn't to turn down the covers or leave chocolate kisses."

"Was anything taken?"

"We don't know and we don't have time right now to stop and find out. Tell you what, why don't we call the police?" says Harry.

"No. No," says the clerk. "No need for that. I'm sure we can work this out."

"I knew you could," says Harry.

The clerk wipes the sleep from his eyes as he shuffles his feet toward the computer to work up the form.

I look at Harry. "Please tell me you're not gonna do the same thing for the plane tickets."

"Let me think about it."

It didn't take Ana long to realize she wasn't the only one tracking them. Her senses had been attuned to this since first setting up outside their law office in Coronado.

Whoever had her equipment still had an interest in their client, the one named Ives. Otherwise why go diving in the trash bin behind their office? If she had any doubts concerning this, they were cured when she saw them disappear onto the Marine Corps Air Station at Miramar. Sooner or later, Ana knew she would get lucky. And like bees to honey, they would come back.

She watched the lawyers long enough to see them settle down to dinner with a third man, an older guy, European from the cut of his clothes. Then she peeled off from the lawyers and keyed instead on the two men watching them from the roof across the river.

Ana carried a large quilted shoulder bag. It looked handmade because it was. She had fashioned it herself—one of her hobbies, sewing. It had little pockets stitched inside. One of them contained a small 4X minimonocular infrared night scope. With this, from three hundred meters away, in the shadows on the other side of the river, she was able to light up the two men on the roof as if she shot them with a flare.

She watched as one of the men left the roof. Ana thought about going after him but instead sat tight. She needed only one of them. If she could take him alive and had enough time, she could squeeze him for everything he knew. Find out who hired him, a name and a location. With that she could go get her stuff.

Three minutes later she saw movement on the other side of the river. The man from the roof emerged from one of the darkened little lanes between the buildings across the way. She watched him through the night scope as he hunkered against one of the vendor stalls near the far end of the wooden footbridge.

He remained there for a while. It was obvious they were stalking someone. She figured it had to be one of the lawyers. Perhaps both of them. Ana didn't care. What she wanted was information. She kept flashing the night scope between the one on the roof and his partner near the end of the bridge.

Finally the guy on the ground moved. She watched as he went past the entrance to the bridge. Suddenly the night scope flared. A blinding orange flash from the bright lights on the bridge caught her directly in the eye. The man had moved to where the scope was useless. There was too much light. She blinked, then closed her eyes until the glowing orange spot on her retina receded. She closed her eye, rubbed the lid, and blinked a few more times. Finally she brought the scope back up to her eye. She trained it up toward the rooftop, away from the lights. This time the man, the one on the edge of the roof, was gone.

"Damn." She quickly capped off the ends of the scope, slipped it back into the pocket of her large shoulder bag, and began to move. There was another footbridge, a wrought-iron one that crossed the river about eighty meters downstream, to the west. She moved as fast as she could toward the bridge and the other side of the river. If she could circle around behind them fast enough she might catch one of them before they disappeared.

As the old man made his way across the bridge it seemed to the Libyan who was waiting for him that his footfalls became less lumbering, more regular and steady. He seemed to pick up his pace.

The Libyan began to wonder if he might have a fight on his hands by the time the old man reached this side. Either way it had to be done. There was no time to waste. He pulled out the coil of four-hundred-pound monofilament fishing line from his pocket and looped one end of it around the post next to the steps leading onto the bridge. He tied it off.

Then he scurried across and did the same on the other side, pulling the line taut about eight inches above the second step. In the bright light from the bridge the white line shimmered like a spider's web in the morning dew. There was nothing to be done about it. Who could have expected this much light?

He pressed the button on the side of the knife and the six-inch blade snapped open. He cut the line with a single stroke from the razor-sharp blade. Then he unwound another four feet of line and cut it.

He put the unused coil back in his pocket and at the same time fished out two small wooden handles. The handles, each about four inches long, were cut from the branches of an acacia tree. They were harder than oak. He doubled the line and wrapped one end around the center of one of the handles, then took the other end of the line and did the same with the other handle. He crossed his hands, one over the other, then gripped the handles tight in his palms so that the doubled-up line passed between the second and third fingers of each hand.

As he uncrossed his closed fists, the line of monofilament formed a loop about the size of a man's head. As he pulled the handles farther apart the loop closed until the garrote narrowed to the diameter of a man's neck. Pulled tight with the full force and leverage of a man's arms, it would slice through flesh like a cheese cutter, and almost as fast.

The Libyan could hear the shuffling of shoes on the wooden planks of the bridge as the old man drew near. Every once in a while he peeked over the steps leading up to the bridge to see if he could see him coming. But the angled elbow at the tower cut off his view.

Finally the old man cleared the turn. When the Libyan saw him he realized he was moving faster and with more coordination than before. He seemed to have sobered up. And now that he was close, he looked much larger.

The man may have been old but was big and barrel-chested, with shoulders and arms like a blacksmith. The Libyan weighed a hundred and sixty pounds soaking wet. The man coming at him looked as if he might tip the scales at three hundred pounds.

He began to wonder if he could hold him down long enough for the garrote to do the job, and if not, whether the blade on his knife was long enough to penetrate something vital. The Libyan began to have doubts. If only his friend had come to help him. The two of them would have no problem. Alone, he wasn't sure.

Ana made her way as quickly as she could across the metal bridge. It was a straight shot perpendicular across the water. But she was afraid to run for fear that the rattling footfalls on the bridge would draw attention.

At the far side where the wrought-iron bridge met the quay, the distance between it and the end of the wooden bridge where the man was lurking was only about forty meters. This was the result of the diagonal line taken by the old wooden bridge as it crossed the river.

428 · STEVE MARTINI

As she came off the bridge Ana had only two options. In front of her was a building blocking her way. She didn't dare turn left along the quay. If she did, within seconds she would run right into the man waiting at the end of the wooden bridge, assuming he was still there. Instead she went right and walked as fast as she could away from him.

The second she cleared the large building on her left and saw the cross street, she turned the corner and started running.

She ran a little, then walked briskly, then ran again. She had to work her way east back to the wooden bridge. It was no more than a large city block away but from where she was, she couldn't see it. Behind the buildings along the waterfront was a labyrinth of small lanes, arcades, and narrow streets. None of them seemed to run in a straight line.

She stopped, reached into her bag, and placed her hand firmly around the composite grip. The streets were deserted. Everything was dark. Ana glanced about to make sure no one was looking before she lifted it from the bag. She pulled it out, then felt around in the bottom of the bag for the small cranking device until she found it. She kept walking, one eye ahead of her into the distance, as she lined up the crank and wound it with the small stem handle, turning it like a coffee grinder.

Forty-Two

The Libyan watched from the shadows off to the side of the bridge as the old man reached the steps. When Korff got there, he steadied himself with one hand on the heavy beam that formed the handrail on one side of the stairs and began to step down.

Holding the open-bladed knife in one hand, the handle of the garrote in the other, the Libyan waited for him to tumble. Instead the old man came down the steps slowly, sideways, until his lead foot hung up on the line he never saw. For a second he leaned off balance, looked as if he might go down, then grabbed the heavy timber that formed the banister and pulled himself back. He stood there one-legged on the step, the other foot somehow hooked, hung up on the fishing line as Korff tried to regain his balance.

It was now or never. The Libyan came out of the shadows behind him, stepped gingerly over the taut line and plunged the blade of the knife deep into the lower right side of Korff's back. He probed with the point, moving the handle, searching for the kidney. The second he did it he realized that the blade was too short. He pulled it out and jammed it in again.

. This time he hit a nerve. Like a wounded bull the old man lashed out with his left arm. It caught the Libyan on the side of the head with the force of a wooden log and drove him down onto the stairs. The old man's foot came down with such force that it snapped the line strung across the steps.

The knife still in his back, the old man thrashed about, turning in circles as he tried to reach behind to grab the handle. But he couldn't get it. The blade was buried in a blind spot beyond the angle where his elbow simply didn't bend.

The Libyan lay on the steps nearly paralyzed with fear as he watched the hulking form lashing out madly at the empty air above him.

The old man tried to reach the knife with one hand as he swung blindly overhead with the other, all the while yelling and shouting in a language the Libyan couldn't understand. He bellowed like a bull, enough noise to wake the dead. He struggled to find the handle of the knife as he bled onto the stairs.

Lights on both sides of the river started coming on. If the old man got a hold of his knife and could pull it out, the Libyan knew he would cut him to pieces. He pulled himself to his knees and grabbed the garrote from the steps where he dropped it.

He came up behind Korff just out of reach of his swinging arm, looped the double strand of monofilament over the old man's head and dropped it quickly around his neck. With the full force of both arms he pulled, using every ounce of strength in his body. The loop snapped closed. Instantly the yelling stopped, the last German syllable cut in half.

The old man went down, the Libyan riding on his back as he pulled the two wooden handles with all of his might. He could see the top of the man's ears as they turned a cyanotic blue. His fingers tore at his neck trying desperately to reach the line now cutting deep into his throat, closing off his air.

Suddenly the two wooden handles jerked. They moved several inches apart as if the line joining them had snapped. But it didn't. Instead it held. Instantly the old man's hands fell away and his body went limp as he slid down the stairs headfirst onto the cement below, blood and aerated bubbles pouring from the deep crevice cut into his neck. The Libyan let loose of the handles. The garrote had done its job, severing the windpipe and the jugular.

He stood up, grabbed the handle of the knife, and pulled it out. He wiped the blood from the blade and the handle on the back of the victim's coat, cut the handles from the garrote, and quickly disappeared into the darkness, snapping the blade closed as he went.

Ana made her way around the buildings and back to the cobbled walkway along the river. She approached the entrance to the bridge from upstream just in time to see the man step away from the body on the ground. She watched as he quickly walked in the other direction away from her, headed west along the river, back toward the metal bridge she had just crossed.

Ana cursed herself for her lack of patience and then followed him. As she passed the pile of death lying at the foot of the steps she realized it wasn't one of the lawyers. It was the other man. The one they dined with. She wondered who he was, but there was no time to find out, not now. As she looked up she noticed that the killer was walking swiftly along the river, opening the distance between them.

She picked up the pace and moved, her soft-soled shoes glided silently over the rough stones. The man in front of her seemed oblivious.

Ana stayed off to the left, toward the building side of the quay, away from the water. Each time the man looked back she was in the shadows, lost among the stacked chairs and canvas-shrouded stalls of the closed-up riverside bistros. After a while he seemed to slow down, but he still hugged the river's edge.

She wondered if he was moving toward a rendezvous with the other man she'd seen on the roof. Ana stayed with him, searching for some way to get out in front so she could take him by surprise. He passed the wrought-iron bridge. Thirty meters farther on he walked by the intersection that Ana had taken in her circuitous course to get around him. It was a tactical blunder that now left her scrambling to catch up.

She watched as he crossed a small open plaza with a broad concourse of steps leading down to the water, geese squawking in the dark distance. She waited until he cleared the open area and then raced after him.

She saw him for a fleeting instant before he disappeared around a bend where the broad quay narrowed to a paved footpath. The slender track seemed to thread between some ancient buildings stacked up against the river and the water's edge.

For a moment Ana hesitated. The path was dark, constricted, and dangerous. If the man stopped along the way she might run right into him before she realized. She looked down, gripped the handle of the object in her hand more tightly, and moved on.

Thirty seconds further along, the path intersected
with another bridge over the river, this one quite wide,
open, and well lit. For a moment she wondered if he'd
taken it. But as she studied the broad span over the water
and the straight road it connected to across the way, she
realized he couldn't have, not unless he ducked into one
of the buildings either here or on the other side. If he
was walking on the open road she would still see him.
Both the bridge and the street beyond were deserted.

Ana continued along the water, picking up speed,
moving fast, throwing caution to the wind. But always
the object in her hand was pointed forward. She passed
the swift running water at the dam as it coursed
around the concrete baffle, a running rapid against the
stone embankment on her side of the river.

Then just as she edged around a closed cheese vendor's stall she saw him. He was maybe fifty meters out
in front of her, walking at a steady pace but not rushing. He entered an area where the path narrowed once
more, this time to the point where it formed a veritable
catwalk suspended over the water. In places it appeared
to be barely wide enough for two people to pass. The
walkway clung to the side of several buildings that
formed a cliff at the water's edge.

Ana saw her chance. An intersecting street dead-
ended at the river just at the point where the catwalk

began. She ran toward it, wheeled to the left away from the river, and raced along the street. It skirted around directly in front of the line of buildings edging the water. Ana ran down the broad lane in front of a three-story structure. The sign mounted in front read: MUSEUM.

She continued running past the complex of buildings, a hundred and twenty meters in all. When she rounded the corner of the last structure, she raced toward the river once more.

By the time she got there, Ana's heart was pounding. She was breathless, her back pressed against the white plaster wall of the building as she waited.

She looked down and checked the feathered fletches on the bolt to make certain they hadn't become detached or frayed. The custom-made crossbow was compact, silent, and powerful. Fashioned of fiber composite materials, it featured two concentric cams mounted on the detachable split limbs of the bow.

The cams multiplied the power of the thrust from the string once it was wound tight by the small cranking device she carried in her bag. It could launch a projectile at three hundred and fifty feet per second.

The weapon could shoot both longer arrows and shorter bolts. Depending on the weight of each it could deliver more than a hundred pounds of kinetic energy to the victim at fifty yards. In a word, at close range it was deadly.

Tonight Ana was hoping she wouldn't have to use it, that the medieval appearance of the device might be enough to hold the man in place and frighten him senseless so that he would tell her what she wanted to know. There was no need to kill him if she didn't have to.

A second later she heard what sounded like shuffling footfalls mixed with the rushing water of the river. Ana snapped a quick peek around the corner and stepped out away from the building, moving quickly to the center of the walkway. She pulled the curved rear shoulder stock tight into her body to steady her aim and sighted down the barrel over the bolt until it was pointed at the center mass of the man's chest.

At first he didn't even see her. For someone who had just killed another man he seemed unfazed, his attention gripped by the splendor of the river. The unremitting sound of the cascading water seemed to have drowned his senses. His attention was focused on the other side. Maybe he was meeting his companion over there.

He was maybe twenty-five feet away and closing on her. Any second he would turn and see her. She stood stone-still.

He was young, maybe early twenties, slender, well-muscled, and wiry. She guessed he was probably quick and dangerous because of it. He had a dark complexion and short dark hair. If she had to guess she would say North African, perhaps Egyptian or Lebanese. But he could have been from anywhere.

When he finally turned his head to the front, the startled expression that washed over him seemed to drain the blood from his face. It froze him in place, fifteen feet directly in front of her with nowhere to go, the river on one side and the solid wall of the building on the other. A look of panic filled his eyes. Instantly his knees flexed, his arms extended out from his sides ready to fight as he turned his head first one way, then the other, looking for any avenue of escape.

The last thing she wanted was a rabbit. Ana knew if it turned to a footrace she would never be able to catch him. He was young, lean, built like a runner. She was winded, still recovering from her sprint around the building.

She tried talking to him in French. When that didn't work, she tried English, then Spanish.

Whether he didn't understand her or chose not to, she couldn't be sure. But it seemed to relax him. Slowly he came out of his crouch, relaxed his arms as he studied her from a distance. He put his hands on his hips, struck a bold pose, murderous male model strutting the latest in soiled T-shirts and shredded jeans.

She motioned for him to put his hands up.

He didn't do it. Instead he just stood there looking at her. The message? She had only one arrow. Did she really want to burn it over something like this?

Ana kept the crossbow trained on him as she backed off a couple of steps. It was a mistake.

The kid suddenly smiled. He mistook her movement for fear. It told him all he thought he needed to know. If she wanted to kill him she would have already done it. She was probably just some pain-in-the-ass citizen trying to be a hero. He had already made enough miscalculations to fill a book.

She motioned with the crossbow for him to get down on the ground.

This time he shook his head and the smile broadened. He motioned with his hands toward one thigh, challenging her to shoot him in the leg. He'd be on her with the knife in an instant, cutting her throat. Besides, she'd probably flinch at the last second and miss. This time he winked at her and said something in a language she didn't understand, at least not the words.

Ana got the message. The eruption of manliness, the seeping arrogance. Not only was there a single arrow, but the person behind the trigger was a woman. She could read it in his eyes. Ana had known that look since she was a young girl. If he wasn't careful this machismo was going to get him killed.

When his feet suddenly started to move and he backed up just a short step she said, "No!" He was getting ready for something. She could tell.

He stopped momentarily as his right hand slowly went toward the back pocket of his jeans. The smile never left his face.

Ana knew he was reaching for the knife.

"Stop!" She shook her head, looked at him with a stern expression, tightened her grip on the crossbow, and leaned into it as if she was about to pull the trigger.

His hand slowed but only for an instant before it disappeared behind his hip. The sound of the water covered the snap of the blade as it opened.

He may have concealed the knife, but his faltering smile and the fixed concentration in his eyes told Ana all she needed to know.

The spring in his legs launched him toward her. Two strides like a long jumper and he closed the distance. She pulled the trigger.

The needlelike point of the knife lashed out toward her throat as the momentum of his body quickly carried him forward.

The bolt met him in midair. It entered his chest and disappeared for a fleeting instant before Ana glimpsed it again in the distance as it skipped like a stone across the surface of the river.

His outstretched arm holding the blade reached her just as she turned her body and stepped to one side. His lifeless form flew past and collapsed in a heap on the cement a few feet beyond where she stood.

A fraction of a second sooner and even as deadweight his body would have planted the knife in her chest.

Forty-Three

Harry and I hoof it toward the traffic bridge where the lake pours into the river. On the other side of the bridge is the main Lucerne train station, a modern glass and steel structure.

In front of it in the distance I can see the freestanding remnant, the high arching stone façade of the entrance to the nineteenth-century station. That building was lost to a fire in the early 1970s.

In the dead of night there is almost no traffic at all on the bridge. It is nearing two in the morning. Harry and I walk briskly without saying a word, dragging our luggage over the rough cobblestones as we go. The two bags bounce all over the place. Off to the right I see banks of flashing lights just across the river near the entrance to the old wooden footbridge a few hundred yards away, downriver.

"They must be doing some work," says Harry.

Four minutes later as we approach the other side of the bridge we see that a small crowd has formed near the stone walkway leading along the river. There are a dozen people or more, all looking down the river toward the flashing lights.

By the time we get there, the contagion of curiosity has infected us. We stop for a moment and look down the river along the quay on this side. It is not construction. I can see police vehicles, several of them, and a larger crowd near the end of the wooden bridge. "I wonder what happened," says Harry.

A fellow standing in front of us hears him. He turns, looks at us, and says, "Someone murdered an old man coming off the bridge."

As shocking as it is, ordinarily we might not have thought anything more about it, except that Harry and I were instantly troubled by the same question. We look at each other.

"No," says Harry. "Couldn't be. He left almost an hour ago. You heard him. He was gonna take a taxi back to his son's apartment. We gave him the money." Still, the rash of accidents leaves us both wondering.

We are going to miss the 2 A.M. train. By the time we drag the rolling cases the hundred and eighty yards or so down along the river, Harry and I convince ourselves that it can't be Korff. It isn't possible. Some other poor soul.

Harry had given him the money and extracted the promise that he would take a cab home. I was standing right there. I saw the whole thing. This image of the three of us in the hotel lobby makes it even more surreal when I see the back of Korff's jacket. The collar is still wet with his blood as he lies facedown on the concrete, a few feet beyond the steps leading up to the bridge.

Standing in the crowd holding our suitcases and looking at his dead body on the ground, Harry and I feel as if we've been sucker-punched.

Police officers are standing around, a couple of them in plain clothes—detectives, I am assuming. One of them is taking pictures with a large SLR camera, moving in for different angles around the corpse. The flashes of the strobe light up the cold night air each time he snaps the shutter and fires. The uniforms are telling the crowd every few seconds to step back.

"Why didn't he take the cab?" says Harry. "He said he would."

"Maybe he needed the money," I tell him.

"The cost of a taxi wasn't worth his life."

"I'm sure he knows that now." What is troubling to me is not just the violence of the act, but its utter futility. "Why? Why do it at all?"

"What do you mean?" says Harry.

"Why bother to kill him?"

"Obviously because he knew too much," says Harry.

"Yes. But he'd already told us everything he knew. Whoever killed him had to know that. They were either tailing him or . . ."

"Or what?" says Harry.

"Or they were tailing us. Either way they had to know he already met and talked with us. If the purpose was to silence him, why not kill him *before* he talked instead of after? It's the pattern. The same thing happened with the girl, remember?"

"I wasn't there," says Harry.

"That's right. It was Herman and me. They waited until after we talked to her in the motel room. And then they killed her. Killed both of them, Ben and her friend. And Graves. I met with him at his office. We talked. Next morning he's dead in the underground. Each time they waited until after they talked to us, and then they killed them."

"Kiss-of-death syndrome," says Harry. "Maybe we need to stop talking."

"But we're still alive."

"We may not be if we stick around here much longer." Harry checks his watch. "We can still make the three o'clock train if we hurry."

We make it to the station, Harry checks our tickets, three-day rail passes, good for another two days. He squats down to tie his shoelace. As he does it he sees something on his bag down near one of the rolling wheels.

I turn to check the illuminated sign showing departure times and cities to make sure we get to the correct platform.

When I turn back Harry has his finger to his nose. Seems he's rolled his bag through something foul.

"What is it, errant dog?" I say.

He ignores me, stands up, grabs the handle of the rolling bag, and walks away.

"Where you going? The platform's the other way," I tell him.

Harry doesn't say anything. He just keeps walking. He pulls his bag over against the far wall inside the station, away from the crowd. I follow him.

"What's wrong?"

"Do you have anything valuable inside your suitcase?" he asks.

I shake my head. "Some clothes, underwear, extra pair of shoes, my shaving kit. Just the usual."

"Anything with your name on it?"

I think for a moment. "No. I don't think so."

"You want to be sure," he says. "You can replace everything when we get home. In the meantime, tear the ID label off your bag." Harry is doing this with his own luggage as he talks.

"What?"

"Just do it," he says. "And while you're at it make sure there's no stick-on barcodes from the airlines on the outside, anything that can identify you."

"Why?"

"How much time did you have to carefully go through your bag before we left the hotel?"

"What are you talking about? None. Neither did you."

"Exactly!" says Harry.

He turns his head and looks at me, and suddenly it dawns on me that maybe it's not what they took out of our bags we should be worried about. Harry knows something he's not telling me.

"Is there something on board?" I ask.

"You bet."

"Is it dangerous?"

"Could be."

A cop in a uniform with a dog on a leash forty feet away is sniffing bags. Suddenly this has Harry's full attention. "Right now I'm wishing it was more crowded. Rush hour or something," says Harry. "If he starts to come this way"—Harry nods toward the cop—"just walk away and take the bag with you. Don't run. Go out the way we came in."

"Listen, why don't we roll them into the bathroom, use the handicapped stall," I tell him. "Open 'em up and check them out."

"Unless I miss my bet we're not gonna find anything unless you can come up with a sharp knife. I'm thinking they slit the lining and slipped it between the inner lining and the outer case. I've seen it done," says Harry. "Super-glue the cut . . ." Harry suddenly looks down at his shoes and smiles. "I don't want to keep looking at him. If I do, I'm gonna look guilty and he'll come over here with the dog. In which case we won't need a knife," he says.

"What is it, explosives?"

"No. If they wanted to do that they would have left the bags alone and slipped a couple of devices under our beds," says Harry. "I think you're right. I don't think they want to kill us. At least not yet. At the moment I think they have something else in mind."

"I'm listening."

"The suitcases in the room. The comb on the bed. Everything tossed and put back so carelessly inside the bags. No one is that stupid. What they wanted was to send us a message," says Harry. "Let us know they'd been in the rooms."

"Why?"

"My guess is so we'd panic and run."

"And here we are," I tell him.

"Yes, but we've had time to think. That and some really fine luck," says Harry.

"What are you talking about?"

Harry's eyes keep tracking the cop with the dog as the canine and his master move toward the platforms. "My bag. I'm gonna hate to lose it," he says. "I've had it at least ten years. It's been everywhere with me. Thing like that grows on you."

"You make it sound like a family pet."

"Well, it just did me a favor no dog at the airport is ever going to do."

"What?"

"It told me what I had in my bag. About a month after I bought this case it got hung up on one of the convey jobs at one of the airports. Brand-new case and suddenly it has a small rip in the outer canvas down near the left wheel. You can imagine how angry I was."

"Yeah, I can imagine."

"Well, between the little rip and the bouncing ride over the cobblestones, if that dog over there picks up the powder trail I'm leaving, he's probably gonna OD," says Harry. "I'm surprised he hasn't already found it. If he does, you'll want to get out of my way, 'cause I'm gonna have to outrun him dragging the suitcase all the way to the river."

"What? You mean cocaine?"

"No. Hell," says Harry, "over here that's a party favor. Get caught and you gotta say ten Hail Marys and write 'pardon my sinuses' eight times on the blackboard. No. Don't look now but I think that snow coming out behind from my wheels is China White."

Harry is talking heroin. "Why kill us," he says, "when they can dump us in some European dungeon for a few decades? In the meantime, everybody who's chatted with us is turning up dead."

"So what do you want to do? We could just leave the bags here and walk away."

"We do that, two abandoned bags, they'll find them before we can get halfway to the platform." Harry is looking at the cop with the dog again.

"We could take them back to the river and dump them," I tell him.

"Not a bad idea," says Harry. "I wish you'd come up with it about five minutes ago. You might want to take a gander at the door."

When I turn to casually look I see another uniformed cop with a dog on a leash standing there. Two more come through one of the side doors. Beyond the glass doors I see at least three police cars outside with flashing lights.

"One might think there were a lot of druggies that come through here in the middle of the night," says Harry.

"No. It's overflow from the crime scene. They're thinking whoever did it might be trying to take a train out of town."

"Well, aren't we lucky," says Harry. "We're gonna get busted, but for the wrong reason."

We watch as the cops all gather by one of the doors. They hold a conference. For the moment, at least, the way to the platform is clear.

"Won't do us any good." Harry reads my mind. "They're sure to search the trains before they leave."

Six more uniformed cops come through the doors as we're talking.

"Did you notice on the trains they have no porters? Everybody does their own thing with their bags."

"What about it?" he says.

"Follow me." We grab the bags and roll toward the platform halfway across the station. The train leaving for Zurich departs in ten minutes, assuming the authorities don't delay it.

Along the way there are trains parked at almost every platform. Some of them are dark, the doors locked, waiting for the morning commute.

When we get to Platform 36, there are two trains, both of them hot: the one to Zurich and the one directly across from it headed to Bern. The doors on both are open.

"Follow me."

"Where you going?" says Harry. "That's the wrong train."

"I know."

A couple of seconds later I step onto the train for Bern and pull my rolling bag on behind me. Harry follows me but with confusion written across his face.

There is already a pile of bags inside the barred-off area for luggage at the bottom of the stairs. We lug the two rollers and toss them on top. Then we climb the stairs to the passenger area on the upper level. I walk down the aisle, Harry following behind me. There're only four people in the car, lots of open seats. But Harry and I don't take any of them. By the time we reach the front of the car one of the conductors is climbing the steps coming up the other way toward us. When I see him I smile. "I wonder if you could help us?"

"If I can, monsieur."

"Is this the train to Zurich?"

"No, no, the train to Zurich is over there." He points toward the other side of the platform.

"Ah, stupid Americans," I tell him.

"No, not at all." He smiles.

He steps to one side and Harry and I quickly brush past him, down the stairs and across the platform.

Six minutes later we watch through the windows from our seats as one of the German shepherds goes apeshit trying to eat our bags over on the other train. The cop trying to hold him on the leash looks like he's about to go waterskiing behind the beast.

"Catnip for dogs," says Harry.

I'm praying the animal doesn't bite through the ballistic fabric on the outer bag. If he does, the blizzard of white powder will have them shutting down the entire station.

Our train suddenly lurches, cars bump together. It starts to move, slowly at first. It rolls along the platform picking up speed, moving past the pillars that support the transparent arches of the roof high overhead. As the train accelerates the pillars begin to look like pickets on a fence until they suddenly disappear.

We roll out of the station and through the rail yard. Harry wipes the sweat from his forehead. "Next stop, Zurich, and the plane ride home. Do me a favor," says Harry. "The next time I say let's not go, let's *not* go."

Forty-Four

After decades of isolation, broader economic opportunity finally came knocking at China's door. It was 1972, détente, what the Americans called "Nixon's opening of China." People in the United States were euphoric. The first real signs of warming in the Cold War.

Cheng realized even then, as a lowly officer in Chinese intelligence, that Americans as a group were naive. Chinese leaders politely nodded, smiled, and showed the man they called "Tricky Dick" the Great Wall.

There were times during American trade missions to China during the last two decades when things were so bad, so obvious, that Cheng and his subordinates hoped they weren't caught blushing. As when entire air wings of the US Air Force found themselves grounded for lack of parts that were back-ordered from Chinese factories. Even then US leaders failed to take notice, or if they did, they took no action.

The quaint theory that all America had to do was demonstrate its pluralistic democratic republic with its freedoms and liberty, coupled with America's massive engine of industry, and the world would follow was to Cheng the great American lie.

Americans had been told so often by their leaders that it was this, the tale of freedom and success that brought down the Iron Curtain and toppled the Soviet Empire, the mystique of Ronald Reagan. That if they waited long enough, it would do the same to China.

What ended the Soviet Union was precisely the trail that America was on now, a financially bloated central government and a faltering domestic economy that could no longer support it.

The Americans had clung to the railing longer than the Soviets for one simple reason. Unlike the now-worthless Soviet ruble, the Americans could print more dollars and the world would still accept them. The US dollar was, after all, the world's reserve currency. But its days were numbered. To Cheng, America was living on Chinese money and borrowed time.

The man known to his subordinates as the Creeping Dragon could only hope that he was not. This morning

Cheng's fears concerning Joe Ying were compounded. A series of four cables—two from a cultural attaché at the Chinese embassy in the Philippines, one from London, and one from the Chinese embassy in Washington—painted a picture with an ominous image.

Ying had been seen coming out of the Presidential Palace in Manila not just once, but on three separate occasions during the last four months. If this wasn't enough, Chinese agents had photos of him dining with a gentleman named Raymond Ochoa. Mr. Ochoa was an undersecretary of energy in the Philippine government.

Ochoa's name appeared prominently in the second cable from the Chinese embassy in Manila. Two weeks earlier he had awarded a competitive tender to an Indonesian firm known as Petrobets, Ltd.

The tender allowed Petrobets to explore for oil and gas in a region known as Area Seven. These were waters near the Spratly Islands, waters that China claimed as its own, even though they were almost seven hundred miles from the nearest point of undisputed Chinese territory.

What Beijing and much of the world called the South China Sea, the government in Manila called the West Philippine Sea. The Chinese military didn't care what anybody called it. They were too busy building aircraft super-carriers, two of them, both nuclear powered, and capable of matching anything the United States had in their Nimitz Class carrier fleet.

American intelligence knew about it. How do you hide two aircraft carriers, each more than three hundred and seventy meters in length? But the current administration in Washington kept it under wraps.

Russia was eating everybody's lunch in the Ukraine. Islamic radicals were running wild through the Middle East, promising to bring their jihad to Europe and the United States. This while they rattled the nerves of America's oil-producing allies in Arabia and Kuwait.

The last thing the American president needed was news that China was about to erase his airpower edge in the Western Pacific.

Cheng knew about problems. At the moment he had one of his own. It was the third cable, the one from their embassy in London, that started to light a blaze in his belfry.

An obscure British holding company headquartered in Bermuda, Aeries International, had just purchased a sizable interest in Petrobets, Ltd., the oil and gas concern that was gearing up to poach in Chinese waters off the Spratlys.

Researchers at the London embassy were still trying to run down the names of all the investors in the Aeries firm. But on the list of known shareholders there was one name that jumped out and grabbed Cheng by the throat—Cormac Llewellyn Grimes.

He looked at it several times, checked the rest of the names, and then came back to it again. Joseph Ying had connections with an American politician, a prominent member of the US Senate. Her name was Maya Grimes. It was the only name that Cheng was ever able to extract from Ying regarding Ying's contacts. It came as a result of a slip of the tongue during one of their conversations.

Ying guarded this information jealously. He once referred to her as the fastest horse in his stable. Grimes and her husband were wealthy in their own right, and powerful.

The second he got her name, Cheng had some of his people begin to collect information for a dossier.

Grimes's husband was a noted capitalist, an investor who went by the initials C. L. Cheng was looking at the open dossier on the computer screen in front of him. This was too much to be mere coincidence.

Cheng went to one of the search engines on the computer and ran the word "Aeries," the name of the holding company in Bermuda.

What came back on the screen was not what he was expecting. "Aeries Student Information System—Eagle Software. . . ." He was about to scroll down the page when the word hit him, like a bullet, right between the eyes.

It took him three more minutes to run it down. "Aeries" was one of two spellings for the same object in the English language. The other more preferred spelling was "Eyries." But of course the Bermuda corporation couldn't use that because there already existed another company using the name, Eyries International. The answer was found in the meaning of the word. An aerie is an eagle's nest.

Cheng leaned back in his chair and thought about it. He couldn't help but smile. Even though the man with the eagle-headed cane had crossed him, he had to admire his audacity. It was, in fact, brilliant. He might have lasted much longer had he stayed away from the feathered themes.

Ying was using the politicians he bought as well as some of their spouses to front for him on investments. He didn't have to trust them because he owned them. They did his bidding because they had no choice. Cheng wondered how much of the wealth that showed up on these people's financial statements was actually owned by Ying. Golden opportunities for special investments no doubt came his way, because of who they were. He probably had secret agreements signed by them tucked away in a safe somewhere, not that he would ever need them.

Ying, a.k.a the Eagle, clearly possessed elements of genius, but like anyone else wielding such power he also had his share of enemies. There was, in fact, one at the moment who was quite active. In anticipation of this possibility Cheng already had his agents with their ears to the ground. He made a note to pass the word.

Cheng's intelligence bureau had worked for years using cutouts, front corporations and sham companies in a program designed to compromise members of the US Congress. You would run out of digits trying to compute the amounts of money they had spent. The approach was always the same. Shower the politicians with cash, campaign contributions if you had to, outright bribes if you could convince them to take it. The goal was to compromise them so that the Bureau might extort official acts and secret information—to own them.

The Chinese thought their program was unique. In fact rogues from the US intelligence community, people who had left the government in some cases decades earlier and who went private setting up their own companies, were doing the same thing. Only they were doing it on a much larger scale and with much greater success.

In the last eight years, China had managed to net three members of Congress, people who were fully hooked. Two of them lost their next elections and the third died in office. Cheng and the bureau spent vast sums pursuing many more, mostly in the form of campaign contributions. All of this disappeared down a rat hole. When his agents, all hired occidental cutouts, went calling to ask for favors, they were told in effect to get lost. It was what the American lobbyists called "being paid for, but not staying bought."

By contrast, Ying, the Eagle, had compromised and as a consequence owned nearly a third of the key positions in the House and almost as many in the Senate. Cheng knew the approximate numbers, but he had lost years of sleep trying to figure out who they were. In the end it became easier and cheaper to deal through Ying, though the Bureau couldn't always get what it wanted, either in terms of information or the performance of official acts.

Cheng concluded that there must have been some vital element of the American political process that no matter how hard they tried, the Chinese simply could not comprehend. Perhaps it was cultural. One thing was certain: at least in the battle to seduce and corrupt their own leaders, Americans had clearly trumped their foreign adversaries.

Forty-Five

B y the time Harry and I get home I find a message left on my phone at the house from Herman down in Mexico. Something has happened. He doesn't say what. He tells me they're both fine. Then something about a charter flight and Tampico. Says he'll call back from there.

I listen to it again, this time taking notes, but before I can finish, the phone rings.

It's Harry. "I got a message from Herman."

"So did I."

"What do you make of it?"

"Well, they're alive. At least they were when he called. Did you get a time and date?"

"Sorry," he says. "I never set the feature on my phone."

"Same here." The fact is my telephone system at the house is so old it probably wasn't available on the handset when I bought it. It's a relic I brought with me from Capitol City on the move when I came south almost twenty years ago.

"They must have found them." Harry means the people chasing Alex.

"Sounds like it."

"Did you catch the part about the courier?"

"I was about to when you called."

"Says it's compromised. No more messages."

Harry is thinking the same thing I am, but he doesn't want to say it over the phone. This is probably how they found them.

"The place they went," he says. "Do you know it?"

Harry means Tampico. "No. Never been near the town. I don't have a clue as to where they might go. Herman has contacts in Mexico but I don't have any names, numbers, nothing. They're off the edge of the earth for all I know." If anyone is listening I want to get this part crystal clear.

"The phones are back up and working at the office," he says. "I just called. Told them we're back in town. Why don't we meet up there, say in an hour?"

I look at my watch. It's ten thirty in the morning. We flew standby, a red-eye out of Amsterdam, chasing the sun across the Atlantic. It lapped us and won. "What day is it?"

"Friday," says Harry. "Least that's what the calendar in front of me says."

Even with some pretty good winks on the plane, I'm dead. "Let me take a shower, get some coffee," I tell him. "Gimme an hour and a half."

When I get to the office Harry is already there. There're a handful of messages waiting for me in the little carousel on the reception counter. There would have been more, I'm sure, except the phones were down.

Sally, the receptionist, hands me another one. "This guy's called three times in the last two days. Says it's important."

I take the slip and look at it. "Clete Proffit." The pillar of the bar who had me followed to Graves's office in D.C. He wants me to call him back. I'm wondering what he wants.

I check the other messages. Nothing from Herman.

Sally is back talking on the headset, taking a call. I

whisper over the counter, "Did Mr. Diggs call by any chance?"

She shakes her head.

"If he does, put him through immediately. Even if I'm on the phone."

She nods. Gives me the big OK circle, finger to thumb.

I head to my office. When I pass Harry's open door I see him sitting behind his desk swung around in his chair with his back to me. At first I think he's laughing. Then I realize Harry is crying. Sobbing like a baby.

"What's wrong?"

He turns and looks at me, his face all red. "Oh, I'm sorry," he says. "It's nothing." He grabs some Kleenex from a box on the credenza behind his desk.

I close the door so that no one else can see. "What is it? What's wrong?"

He shakes his head, wipes his eyes, puts his hand out, like maybe I should go away. "It's nothing," he says.

"It must be something," I tell him. I've never seen Harry cry before. This is a first.

"I guess . . . I don't know. I guess it's just every-thing," he says. "All of a sudden it's just catching up with me. The other night. The old man."

He's talking about Korff. His body by the bridge.

Harry is suffering a delayed reaction. Post trauma. "Listen, why don't you go home and get some sleep? We're both tired. That's where I'm going in just a few minutes. As soon as I check my desk and take care of a few messages."

"I couldn't sleep," says Harry.

"You sure?"

"Yeah, I'm sure. Wasn't able to sleep at all on the plane."

I sit down in one of the chairs across the desk from him. "Why don't you tell me about it?"

"What's to tell? You were there. You know," he says.

"Sometimes things affect people in different ways. Tell me."

"Jeez," says Harry. "You're gonna make me say it?" He lifts his shoulders. When he drops them he starts crying again. "We got him drunk!" says Harry. "I can't help thinking that if I hadn't kept pouring, maybe he'd still be alive. Maybe he wouldn't be dead. Don't you get it?"

"No! No, you have to stop thinking like that. He didn't die of alcohol poisoning. He died because somebody murdered him. Giving him beer had nothing to do with it. We tried to put him in a taxi. We offered to take him home. Don't you remember? He said no. He wouldn't hear of it."

"I know," says Harry. "But I still can't help thinking . . ."

"He told us he'd take a cab. We both saw him. He walked to the counter and hit the bell. What were we supposed to think?"

Harry nods.

"Besides, the man had a tolerance for beer. I'm not saying he wasn't drunk. But if you or I had consumed anything near what he had, we wouldn't have had to worry about a taxi. They would have taken us away in an ambulance."

Harry looks at me red-faced and laughs. He wipes his nose.

"You can't blame yourself for what happened. Sometimes it's just fate. If JFK had been ten minutes earlier in Dealey Plaza he probably would have served out his term and, who knows, done another four years. If Lennon had come home an hour later at the Dakota, maybe he'd still be making music. And if Korff had gotten into a taxi at the front door, outside that hotel, my guess is they would have never even seen him," I tell him.

"You think so?"

"The fact they killed him on the far side of the bridge tells me they were probably waiting for him there."

"Maybe you're right."

"Nobody in their right mind is going to want to track Korff across that bridge under all those lights. He was a big man. And if he turned to fight maybe they get trapped out there."

Harry nods.

"So try not to think about it. We did everything we could."

"Yeah, but if we'd known . . ."

"But we didn't. We took him at his word. Sometimes that's all you can do."

"Still," he says. "We should have thought about it. I mean after the girl and Graves."

"We did think about it. That's why we told him to take the cab. It wasn't just because he was drunk."

"Yeah. I suppose."

"He knew that Serna didn't die in an accident. We told him as much. He was well aware of the dangers. He had to be. He knew more about what was going on than we did."

Harry nods. "You're right."

"Listen. Tell you what, when we're done here, why don't you follow me to the house. We'll sit and talk," I tell him. "We need to relax and unwind. A lot of stress."

"Yeah, I'm OK. Go do what you have to do."

"I will. But not until you give me that rusted piece of crap in your center drawer," I tell him.

"What were you doing in my drawer?"

"If you must know, I was looking for drugs."

"And you saw the gun?"

"You bet I did. How could I miss something like that?"

"What do you think, I'm gonna . . ."

"Not at all," I tell him. "I'm just worried that if you go and pull the trigger with the corroded bullets you've got, it's gonna blow up and take your hand off. I don't want you running around the office trying to hit the keyboard with a stump. That's all."

"Get out of here," says Harry. "Go make your phone calls."

I smile.

He looks at me and winks.

I head to my office.

Forty-Six

"Hello, Mr. Madriani," he says. "You called?"

"I did indeed," says Proffit. "How is everything going?"

"The usual," I tell him. Why trip his curiosity telling him about four murders and a burned-out gas station?

"How's your case going?" he asks.

"Which one is that?" I can play stupid too.

"Mr. Ives, of course."

"Oh, that! Moving right along. What is it you called about?"

"It appears you have friends in high places," he says.

"How's that?"

"Senator Maya Grimes called me the other day. Do you know her?" he says.

The second he says her name, the hair on the back of my neck stands up. Grimes, my home state senator, the woman Simon Korff saw at Gruber Bank with a boatload of cash. I could tell him I never heard of her, but I don't. "I know of her. Who doesn't?"

"That's funny," he says. "I was sure the way she talked the two of you knew each other."

"What did she say?"

"It seems she thinks very highly of you. So highly, in fact, that she asked me to give you a call."

"Why would she do that?"

"Well, it seems there's a vacancy on the Ninth Circuit Court of Appeals. You are familiar with the court? Sits in San Francisco, twenty-nine active judges, I believe. One step below the US Supreme Court."

"I'm familiar with it."

"Have you ever appeared before any of its panels?" he asks.

"Haven't had the pleasure," I tell him.

"Well, that is strange," says Proffit. "Senator Grimes seems to think you're highly qualified to fill the vacancy. So qualified, in fact, that she's already talked to the White House to inform them that you have her unqualified support for the position."

"And why would she do that?"

"I was hoping you could tell me," says Proffit.

"I have no idea. Are you sure you have the right Madriani?"

"Oh, yes. No mistake about that," he says.

"Why didn't she call me herself?"

"Well, you know politicians," he says. "They always want to keep some distance."

"You make it sound like a Mafia hit," I tell him.

"I'm glad you said it and not me. I'm just carrying the message. She would like you to file an application for the position as soon as possible."

"What's the rush?"

"As I said, I'm just conveying the message. Are you interested?"

"Let me think about it."

"Do you want some advice?" he says.

"I don't know. But it sounds like you're itching to give me some."

"Grimes is in the position to block other competitors for this spot, which she can do by using her position in the Senate to prevent the scheduling of a confirmation hearing if she doesn't approve of the candidate. It's called senatorial courtesy. However," he says, "she can't help you dodge the slings and arrows at a hearing if members of the Senate Judiciary Committee decide to come after you. Say if, for example, the candidate seems to be lacking certain qualifications."

472 · STEVE MARTINI

"You mean like me."

"Well, I didn't want to say it," he says. "I like you. I like you very much."

I suspect this makes me part of an exclusive club, fraternity of one. Maybe it will last until the end of our conversation, if he gets what he wants.

"Allow me to save you the pain," he says. "They would eat you alive. Why don't you let me call her back and tell her you're not interested? Save yourself a lot of grief."

Or, I could just ask him for a map through the mine-field. I'm sure Proffit climbed on his bulldozer to start laying them the minute he hung up the phone from Grimes.

"Did she say anything else?"

"There was one other thing. But it's somewhat distasteful."

"That's all right, I've got some mouthwash in the other room."

"I'm not sure I feel comfortable repeating it."

"Steel yourself," I tell him.

"Just remember you're the one who asked," he says. "She made it sound as if this, what I'm about to tell you, and the judicial appointment are somehow linked. In other words, you don't get one unless you do the other."

And this offends him.

"You mean like one of your contingent fees. You win, you take fifty percent of everything."

"We don't get fifty percent," he says.

"We can split hairs later. Cut to the chase," I tell him.

"But this does trouble me," he says. "We're talking a significant judicial appointment here. There should be no quid pro quo. You know that." What he's talking about is bribery. I suspect Proffit would know all about that. For all I know, he holds an advanced degree from Serna.

"You haven't told me what Grimes wants me to do yet. Who knows, maybe I've already done it."

"You haven't," he says. "Trust me."

That'll be the day.

"So why don't you tell me? Then we'll both know."

"I don't know. I'm not sure." He starts hemming and hawing.

"Tell you what," I say. "I'll take you off the hook. Why don't I just call Grimes at her office and she can tell me herself?"

"No, no, there's no need for that. I'll tell you."

"Good. Now that we're past all that."

"There's a case, a federal matter. She'd like you to get involved. You do federal work in the criminal courts, don't you?"

"On occasion."

"The trial on this is actually over," he says. "First she said it was an appeal. Then she said something about negotiations. I'm not sure of the actual details. And I'm not sure I want to know."

His nose is growing at the other end. If he keeps going on like this it'll be poking me in the ear any second.

"She said she was sure you'd be interested."

"And why is that?"

"It seems this man is incarcerated at a Supermax near Florence in Colorado. His name is Rubin Betz. At the moment, according to the senator, Mr. Betz has no legal representation. She would like you to represent him."

"Did she say why?"

"All she said was that she had reason to believe you were dying to talk to him. Her words exactly," says Proffit.

"That's it?"

"That's everything. But . . ."

"But what?"

"You should think very carefully about all of this. Especially this thing in Florence.

"I got to thinking," said Proffit.

Yeah, that's always dangerous.

"I remembered our conversation over drinks in Georgetown that night. Do you remember?"

"How could I forget? You had me followed to Graves's office."

"Yeah. Terrible what happened to him," he says. "How'd it occur, anyway? Do you know?"

"Why don't you get to the point? Our conversation in Georgetown?"

"As I recall, you mentioned that Serna had a relationship with a man some years ago. Unless I misunderstood, you said the man's name was Rubin Betz."

Serna was not the only one with a titanium memory. But then the fact that Serna had bedded a man at some point in her life seemed to come as a real shock to Proffit. How could he have missed that boulder when he was furiously turning over every pebble in her past?

"I thought to myself, now that is a real coincidence," he says. "It is indeed a small world. I mean, Ives smashes into Olinda way out in California. You talk to Graves and the very next day he gets hit by a train. And now this."

And unless he's just being discreet, Proffit doesn't know the half of it.

"As you say, a small world."

"I really don't want to get you into any trouble," he says. "If you like, I can call Grimes back and tell her you can't take the case."

"And why is that?"

"Well, don't you see it?" he says.

"See what?"

"Conflict of interest, of course. You represent Ives. Ives is involved in Serna's death. Serna had a relationship with this man, Betz. Plain as the nose on your face," he says. "You can't represent both of them."

"You're assuming their interests are adverse."

"Well, aren't they?"

"You know, Mr. Proffit, for a man who's supposed to be at the top of his game, the managing partner of one of the biggest international law firms in the country, you don't seem to have a very good handle on what's going on in your own offices."

"What's that supposed to mean?"

"If you don't know I can't tell you."

There is nothing but silence on the other end of the line.

"Are you there? Hello?"

"I'm still here," he says.

I give him a few seconds of silence to mull it over. Finally he can't stand it anymore. "Why don't you just tell me?"

"Not my job. Let's just say you should have kept a closer rein on her."

"On who?"

"No. I'm not playing that game anymore. I don't want to mention her name because I wouldn't want to disparage the dead. Besides, you never know who's listening in."

"*What?*"

"You haven't been watching the news lately. Tell you what. Why don't you let me worry about any conflict of interest. Call Grimes. Tell her I'm interested in talking to Betz. Ask her if she knows how I can make contact in order to set up arrangements to see him in Florence."

My guess is she'll pick up the phone and call the director at the Bureau of Prisons. They'll probably pick me up in a government jet and whisk me out there in hopes that I can clean up their mess.

"Oh, and so that there's no misunderstanding in terms of communication, I will confirm all of this in writing to Grimes's office."

"I wouldn't do that if I were you," he says.

"Well, that's the point. You're not me." And I hang up.

Forty-Seven

"They've shattered the vestiges of my idealism," says Harry. "The thought that Washington and Wall Street are corrupted by rapacious schemers." He's planted himself on the sofa in my den next to the kitchen.

"You're saying I shouldn't take the appointment?"

"Let's not be hasty," he says. "Why don't you call Proffit back, see if there's something in it for me?" If Harry had a cigar he'd be puffing on it, holding it between his fingers and flexing his eyebrows.

"OK, so we can both assume that the judicial thing is nothing but a distraction," I tell him.

"And if it isn't, it should be," he says.

"Thanks."

"Oh, it's not that I don't think you're capable." Harry looks at me. Another puff on his mythical cigar.

"Question is, how can they think we're that stupid? I'm insulted," he says.

"They didn't make you an offer," I tell him.

"Yes, but they know we're associated. It's a joint insult to our cumulative intelligence," he says.

"Yes, but look at it from their point of view. They needed a carrot to offer in order to offset the burden of representing Betz. You know, some plausible consideration to lure me to Supermax so they can probably stick a shiv in my back."

"You think that's the plan?"

"Not in so many words. Maybe not right there, but the ultimate objective, you bet."

"I've been wondering when they were gonna get around to that."

"You can be sure we're on their agenda."

"What do you mean, 'we'?" he says. "I wasn't invited to Supermax."

"No, but as you say, we're associated. I'd be surprised if you're not in their thoughts and prayers."

"Bastards!" says Harry. "If they're gonna kill me, they at least owe me a spot on the Supreme Court."

"We'll talk about that later. For the moment it looks like I'll be going to Colorado."

"You know they're not gonna let you talk to Betz unless they're listening in. That's a given," says Harry. "In that place the closest you're going to get to him is a window of solid acrylic eight inches thick, talking on a wall-mounted mic with the world listening in. The man may as well be a fish in an aquarium."

"Probably. But it's the only chance we're going to get."

"How do you know he'll even talk to you?"

"I don't. Except for one thing."

"What's that?"

"Proffit said something about negotiations. He said he didn't know the details, but that Grimes first referred to the matter as an appeal, then said no, it was a negotiation."

"So maybe they've made him some kind of an offer?"

"Or getting ready to. If you think about it, it makes sense. They hit Betz hard, too hard. Alex said Graves called him the whistleblower. Betz was trying to cooperate with prosecutors, and, in fact, he did. He turned over information on taxpayers with offshore accounts from his old employer, the Swiss bank he worked for. But they were small fry. Then suddenly he becomes a little too helpful. Betz tries to put a cherry on it by telling them he had information on powerful political figures with offshore accounts."

"The PEPs. What Korff told us," says Harry.

"My guess is prosecutors were probably pretty excited about this at first. But then remember what

Alex said? Betz, through his lawyer, the one that died flying his plane, made a proffer. They would have asked for some kind of a solid offer from the government, a short stretch in one of the federal country clubs or maybe straight probation. Who knows? But in order to get it, they had to make the proffer and show their hand."

"And when whoever was supervising at Justice saw the scope of the thing, they probably had to pick him up and dust him off," says Harry. "How do you go to your boss and tell him you want to indict half of Congress?"

"That's when they started loading up the charges in order to keep Betz quiet, lock him away as long as possible. But one of them, either Betz or the lawyer, and I'm guessing Betz because he's the only one still alive, took a look and realized that this was a problem."

"Because of the scope," says Harry.

"Exactly. If it went public with this many officials the political consequences alone could be catastrophic, to say nothing of the economy. Government goes down, markets tumble. Then think about what Korff told us. If investigators started looking at where this money came from, chances are some of it may track back to foreign governments. That goes public, it's pretty hard to sweep it under the carpet. The implications get serious in a hurry, depending on what was sold."

482 • STEVE MARTINI

"And if European Union officials get drawn in, it grows like a cancer," says Harry.

"So the deal with Betz was off, at least for the moment. Somewhere along the way he took out an insurance policy. Buried something somewhere. If anything happened to him it gets sent to a million sites on the Internet, every news outlet they can think of. So now the government is invested in making sure nothing happens to him. He's OK for the moment. The reason he is where he is. It's the only place they can keep him safe and at the same time keep him from talking."

"They could try to defuse it," says Harry. "Prosecute some of them. Put the fear of God in the rest, force them to resign or face the consequences."

I shake my head. "If the government tries to cherry-pick the worst offenders, the defense lawyers will eat them alive. They'll be demanding to see all the documents, unredacted, and asking questions about why Senator Smith was prosecuted when Senator Jones got a pass. They'd be arguing that the entire prosecution was nothing but politics at play. Worse than going after them all. Once the prosecution starts down that path they won't be able to control the mess any longer."

"Then why would the government offer a deal now, assuming they are?"

"Maybe they have no choice. They know they've overreached. If you check the charges and look at the guidelines you're probably going to find out they've overcharged the case for sentencing purposes. And how do they justify holding him at Florence if at some point he decides to appeal, gets tired of sitting in a hole by himself. The writing's on the wall. He's like a grenade rattling around, waiting to go off. If he steps out and gets killed, whatever he has tucked away gets published and broadcast. So they want closure. Some deal."

"What could they possibly offer him by way of a deal that would protect him?" says Harry. "Witness protection?"

"They may offer it. But in this case I'm afraid it would be an illusion. The problem is, no one can be sure who's involved. For witness protection to work, you have to be able to trust the government. A mole buried in the Justice Department or some other agency and they'd have Betz's location and his new identity before you could sneeze. He wouldn't last a week."

"Then what's the answer?"

"I'm not sure there is one."

"Then why would you go to Florence to talk to the man?"

"Because I don't think we have a choice any longer."

"What do you mean?"

"I wouldn't want you to stay up nights worrying, but . . . I'm afraid you and I are in the same fix Betz is, only we don't have a prison cell to hide in."

"You mean what you said before? Being in their thoughts and prayers?"

"You know they got pictures of the two of us shimmying out of that hotel, tripping over Korff's body. And Ben at the motel, me with Graves. We may not have all the answers, but we know too much to be allowed to live. Don't you think it's strange we made it out of Lucerne?"

"We were lucky," says Harry.

"No. I don't think so. I think they could have killed us probably half a dozen times. But they didn't want to. You said it, remember? The question is why? And we know the answer to that as well. Kiss of death," I tell him.

"They were following us."

I nod. "Right to Ben, to Graves, Korff, and they tried to get Alex twice, but they missed if the voice mail from Herman means anything. The kid must lead a charmed life."

"It's what I told you," says Harry. "You said no."

"Changed my mind this afternoon."

"Why?"

"Proffit's phone call. Why would Grimes want me to talk to Betz? I mean, knowing what we know. She has to know he has information. Graves called him the Holy Grail. Now we know why. Everybody else with any information is dead."

"Because we led them right to their front door," says Harry.

"The problem they're having with Betz is they know where he is, but they can't get at him."

"So what do they want you to do?"

"They want me to get him out."

"So they can kill him."

"No, so that they can kill all of us. You, me, Herman, if they can find him, and Alex. You see, once we deliver Betz we will have completed our mission. I can't imagine what other chores they might have for us."

"So who's doing all the killing?" he says.

"If I knew the answer to that, I wouldn't be sitting here. I'd be downtown spilling my guts, everything I knew, to the D.A. But Graves gave me a clue. At the time I dismissed it. I don't mean to say he named the perpetrator, but he identified the motive. The bad thing is it's institutional, built into the system, dangerous," I tell him.

"How do you mean?"

"Remember what Korff said about the PEPs, politically exposed persons? He said they presented special problems because they were susceptible to extortion, which in turn leads to violence."

"That's an axiom," says Harry. "You blackmail somebody, especially if they see no way out, no end in sight, there's a fair chance they will try to kill you. Either that or commit suicide."

"Variation on the theme," I tell him. "What Graves said. The Hoover Effect, remember? J. Edgar and his card catalogue of dirt. The dark secrets of the rich and powerful. As the story goes, Hoover used the information to advance the bureau and to protect himself. Stayed in office for forty years.

"Let's say someone in one of the government agencies found out that a few members of Congress were on the take. They had undisclosed offshore accounts. Let's say they were taking money overseas because it was easier and safer there than here. There're fewer FBI agents in Portugal than Poughkeepsie. Uncle Sam's reach may be long, but his resources aren't unlimited. Who knows that better than members of Congress who control the budget? They would even know the best places to do this. Let's say some of them have a field day. They start racking up money in foreign accounts. But someone finds out. Now the offenders are susceptible to extortion. They become PEPs. Whoever's doing it starts squeezing them for votes on bills, maybe information if they're on sensitive committees that meet behind closed doors.

"But then this person sees the possibilities. Why have just a few members in your pocket when you can have many? And why wait for them to be seduced by random events when you can orchestrate the seduction? Let's say they take the venture private, leave government, and turn political corruption into a growth industry. Now they've really got something.

"They also have an investment to protect. If you have some dirty politician by the collar, you don't want him taken out in the next election by some reform candidate. Let's assume somebody starts poking around, a nosy reporter, for example."

"Alex," says Harry.

"And Graves. Or worse, some competitor who finds out about some of the sins of one of your wayward members and tries to horn in on your action. What do you do? Unless you want to sit around and wait hoping they get struck by lightning, you go into the accident formation business."

"You think Serna was trying to squeeze somebody in Congress?"

"She was a lobbyist and the soul of ambition. If the opportunity availed itself, why not? Let's say she found some dirt, decided to put it to use, only to find herself standing in line behind some really nasty people. She turns up dead in a burned-out car."

"And Ives?"

"Why waste a good accident? Whoever's pulling Grimes's strings is probably an environmentalist. If they could, they would probably have put the whole lot of us on a bus and run it in front of a train. Save energy.

"Grimes could have gotten any lawyer she wanted to represent Betz if all they wanted was to spring him so they could kill him. But no, she wants me to do it. Why? Probably so they can line me up behind Betz and do us both with the same bullet."

"So what are you gonna do?"

"I'm gonna go meet Mr. Betz. The man is still breathing because he's smart."

"He's alive because he has insurance," says Harry.

"And if we want to stay alive we better get a piece of his policy."

Ana was trying to read his lips. She could only see one of them, Madriani. Something about members in your pocket . . . seduced by random events. She had him in her field glasses sitting in her car across the street from his house. She would have killed to know what they were talking about. For a moment she actually thought about the possibility in order to extract whatever they knew. Some clue, perhaps, as to who had the equipment. She didn't consider it hers any longer, because she no longer had a use for it.

Ana had lost the contract on the corporate executive in Europe, and with it a very large commission. It was too late. They had hired someone else. She was too busy trying to protect herself, due to her connection with the French electronics, that she couldn't take care of business. This hurt her reputation, and that made her angry.

The people who had the equipment were the ones using the lawyers, and they were being used; they were being followed. Ana knew this because of the Dumpster diver and the man she killed in Switzerland.

On her return from Europe Ana decided it was time for some technical assistance. She was alone, she was tired, and she needed sleep. At the same time she wanted to keep half an eye on the lawyers and where they went. She purchased four small devices known as Spark Nanos. Each about the size of a small cell phone, these were GPS trackers designed to allow parents to keep track of their children. What made the devices unusual was their battery life. The rechargeable lithium batteries could last for hundreds of hours on a single charge, depending on how the tracker was set.

Ana attached powerful magnets to the back of two of the devices. While the lawyers were inside the house talking, she slipped one of the trackers under the fender of each of their cars.

Using her laptop and linking her phone she had already set up geo fences. These are circular perimeters drawn on the Spark Nano's GPS maps. She put fences around their law office, Madriani's home, Hinds's apartment, and a few other strategic areas, including the airport.

Whenever either of the vehicles crossed one of the fences Ana would get a signal on her cell phone. By setting the device to search every five minutes she gained two hundred hours of battery life. Whenever they moved she would know it. She could then track their movement on the GPS. In a week she could swap out the devices with fresh recharged ones and still have spare time on the batteries.

She couldn't see Madriani's partner in the house across the street. He was down low in the room somewhere below the opening, the pass-through to the kitchen. If she didn't get a break soon, her hand would be forced. She would have to move on one or both of the lawyers.

The good news was she had picked up a client, a referral from some mutual acquaintances, a job in the area. At least her travel and her time would be paid for. The bad news was they were pressing her to get the job done. So far she had stalled them. But she knew she couldn't delay much longer. She didn't want to lose another job.

The problem was, if she used the same method to fulfill the new contract, having used an arrow in the San Diego area once already, authorities would connect the medical forensics in the two cases. A single arrow wound and one victim, a pathologist might classify merely as sharp force trauma. But a second victim with the same kind of wound in the same county crime lab, they would begin to see a pattern. With that they would start asking questions. It wouldn't take them long to realize they were dealing with a bow and broad-head arrows.

Ana would have to dump all of her weapons, the compound takedown bow, the smaller crossbow, and all of the supplies for assembling arrows and bolts. She certainly couldn't take the chance of carrying them through the airport. And keeping them in her possession was a risk if for any reason she was stopped and the police searched her car.

She would be bare, alone, and in a foreign country. She wanted to put some distance between herself and San Diego the minute she completed the new contract, so that by the time authorities went looking for sharp pointy objects she would be long gone. By then the alias she was traveling under would be smoke.

She had taken a room at the Del Coronado in order to be close to the law office. She would put this on the tab of her new employer. For now she would go back and get some sleep, and let her cell phone and the little Spark Nanos do the watching.

Forty-Eight

The US Federal Penitentiary, Maximum Administrative Facility (ADX), goes by several names: Florence ADMAX, Supermax, and the Alcatraz of the Rockies.

It's actually situated to the east of the Rocky Mountains on the downward slope in a ragged area leading to the Great Plains, dry and desolate, middle of nowhere.

It is there for a reason. It houses the most dangerous inmates in the federal prison system, people notorious for violence. Its occupants include members of the Mexican drug cartels, Islamic terrorists, and inmates who habitually cause problems in other institutions. Some of them are notorious escape artists.

Tonight I am doing research, working from home, looking for anything I can find on the Florence,

Colorado, facility. I am also searching for background on Betz and his case. Harry has pulled everything he can find on the trial and is trying to locate a copy of the transcript.

Fremont County, where the town of Florence is situated, sits about one hundred miles from Denver and about forty miles south of Colorado Springs and the US Air Force Academy. Mostly rural, sparse grasslands, rolling hills and desert, it has a population of a little over forty-seven thousand people.

But in the fifteen hundred square miles that comprise the county there are thirteen prisons, including state, local, and federal correctional facilities. These house almost nine thousand inmates.

The people at ADX, the federal Supermax, are a veritable rogue's gallery. Ted Kaczynski, the Unabomber, is there, as is Richard Reid, the Shoe Bomber. Terry Nichols, who was convicted in the Oklahoma City bombing, is also incarcerated there. Ramzi Yousef, who was involved in the first World Trade Center bombing, and Robert Hanssen, the FBI agent turned Russian spy, are doing fifteen consecutive life sentences at Florence. In all, there is room for 490 prisoners. Nowhere on the Internet is the name Rubin Betz listed. He languishes below the radar, perhaps by government design.

On first blush I would say that housing Betz at Supermax is itself an act of cruel and unusual punishment. You would think it is also highly dangerous, given the informational powder keg he is sitting on.

According to what I'm reading, inmates at Florence generally serve solitary time, one man to a cell. They spend twenty-three hours a day locked up. They are allowed out for five hours every week for private recreational activity.

Each cell boasts poured concrete amenities: a fixed bed, a fixed concrete stool in front of a fixed concrete desk. The commode includes a basin and drinking fountain all built into one, and there is a built-in concrete shower. All of the water to the cells is on a timer so that inmates can't flood the cubicles. A tiny opening the size of an arrow slit is the only window.

For entertainment they have a small black-and-white television that shows only educational and religious programs. According to one article, inmates do not know the location of their cell with reference to other parts of the institution. I can only assume this means that perhaps they are hooded and disoriented when they are being moved. They are also ankle and waist chained when on the move.

For the hard-core inmates, those who haven't earned other privileges, all recreation occurs in a subterranean

496 • STEVE MARTINI

concrete-sided pit similar to a swimming pool to maintain the sense of disorientation to prevent escape attempts.

The minimum term for a stay at Supermax is generally twenty-five years, though there are exceptions. For those who have earned benefits, there is limited interaction with other inmates.

In Betz's case, I'm assuming, except for a few guards and other prison staff, he is alone twenty-four hours a day. They wouldn't dare expose him to any of the other inmates, not in this place. They may as well shoot him.

I have been in contact with Proffit's office, which is acting as the intermediary between Grimes and me. For some reason the senator wants no direct contact. You would think I had the plague.

At one point they offered to transport Betz to California, to MCC, the Metropolitan Correctional Center in San Diego, as a "convenience" to me. This tells me precisely what kind of a threat he is. MCC is a twenty-three-story tower downtown where they house defendants pending trial. At one time inmates were punching holes in the concrete walls and letting themselves down on bedsheets to the sidewalks outside.

I told them no. If I was going to represent Betz I wanted to see him in his surroundings, where he's incarcerated. They haggled over this, as if perhaps they weren't anxious to have me view this. I can't imagine why. I told them it was that or nothing. I figured I might as well test them early and see what their reactions were. They caved.

Then, to my surprise, they offered a government jet to fly me there. I had been joking when I quipped about this with Harry. They are not. I'm only hoping it's round trip.

It goes without saying that I will not be allowed to take any of the usual electronics inside—no computer or cell phone, camera, or recording devices.

But there are certain things I will insist on which are nonnegotiable. I have no intention of telling them what these are in advance or asking permission. Otherwise they will deploy countermeasures to defeat them. Either these will be accepted or the entire exercise ends there. Unless they use force, I will leave.

I'm sure I will get the usual search, and probably more, along with the requirement that I sign a waiver of liability in the event that I'm taken hostage, wounded, or killed while inside.

Even thinking about this under the circumstances sends a chill up my spine.

The phone on my desk rings. I look at the clock. It's nearly midnight. It must be Harry. I pick it up.

"Hello."

"Hey! Finally caught you at home." It's Herman. "Where the hell have you guys been?"

"Long story. Where are you? No, on second thought, don't tell me. Are you guys OK?"

"For now," he says.

"How are you making this call?"

"SIM card," he says. "Not to worry. Got an endless supply. Soon as we're done, I'll toss this one, open another."

"Still, there's the tower." I'm concerned that perhaps they can track his location.

"Not to worry," says Herman. "Got it covered, but let's keep it short."

"Things look as if they may be coming to a head. You're gonna want to keep in touch. Can you check in, maybe every other day?"

"Can do," says Herman.

"Good. How's your charge?" I'm talking about Alex.

"He's OK, but like me, he wants to get home."

"Anything you need?"

"What's the sense of telling you?" he says. "You wouldn't be able to get it to us if I did."

He's right. "The messenger service was a problem, I take it?"

"Big-time. Very messy. You might check the local news there, couple of online sites. They reported it, but were a little wide of the mark on the details. You wanna read between the lines."

"Listen, we want to get you guys out of there."

"Couldn't be soon enough for me," says Herman. "Where and when?"

"Remember the place you used before?"

Herman thinks for a second, then realizes I'm talking about the place where they dropped in. The dirt strip thirty miles east of Ixtapa. "Oh, that one?" he says.

"That's the one. Can you get there?"

"No problem."

"How much lead time you need?"

"Minimal," says Herman.

I'm not sure what this means, but one thing's for certain, unless they have a rocket ship they're nowhere near Tampico, over on the Gulf Coast. "We'll make the arrangements at this end, let you know when," I tell him.

"How you gonna do that?"

"You call me?" I say.

"Better idea," says Herman. "There's an online message board." He gives me the name. It's in Tampico. I'm assuming Herman is doing this to throw anybody listening in off his track. He could collect the message from anywhere in the world. "Should have thought of this earlier," he says. "You know my handle. One I used to use for Telex."

"I do."

He uses the name Diggsme along with a traveling e-mail address.

"One message," he says. "Keep it cryptic and don't use it again. Just give us the time and the day."

"You're sure the location is OK?"

"It's good," he says.

"Give us a few days. Watch the board."

"I'll do it. Gotta go now."

"Take care of yourself."

"You too," he says, and he hangs up.

Forty-Nine

Three days later, early morning, they pick me up outside my house, a military staff car from Miramar, the Marine Air Station in San Diego. Harry is there to see me off.

"You know what to do if for some reason I don't come back?"

Harry nods. We have made contingency plans. I have called Sarah, my daughter, and Joselyn, my lover, who is still in Europe on a project, and told them both in general terms what is happening. I take my bag from Harry and step into the backseat of the blue sedan, and we're off.

The trip is comfortable and swift. The sleek blue and white military jet streaks northeast over the California desert, nips the northern edge of Arizona, and flies almost directly over Four Corners, where the borders of Arizona, Nevada, New Mexico, and Colorado meet. On a straight shot it heads over the shoulder of the southern Rockies and down their eastern flank. In just under two hours we land at the small airfield just outside Florence.

As I had requested, a gentleman from the Federal Bureau of Prisons, one of their executives from Washington, is waiting for me at the airport with a government car. He is personable, highly professional, and best of all, somebody I already know. I met Daniel Wells on a case years earlier when he was working for the Bureau of Prisons in San Diego.

From time to time we've kept in touch. We had children the same age and Dan was like me, single. He was divorced. I was widowed. But we haven't seen each other in almost fifteen years, so that when I step off the plane he has to look twice to be sure it's me.

"Dan, how are you?"

"Long time," he says. "But you're looking good."

"More wrinkles and gray than I would like."

"Yeah, but at least you still have some."

Dan has gone completely bald. I suspect he shaves what little he has left.

"It's good of you to meet me here. I appreciate it."

"Not at all. I'm happy to get out of Washington. I've got the car over here. Want me to take the bag?"

"No, I've got it. Traveling light." We head for the car.

On the way to Supermax we talk about the kids. He asks me if I've ever been out here before. I tell him no. If Dan has done any background on Betz, and I suspect he has, he doesn't say so. I fill him in on the reason for my request that he accompany me, the fact that I am carrying a single electronic device that I want to take with me inside the prison.

He listens politely and then says, "I don't know. They don't generally allow it."

"It's not a camera. It's not a recorder or a communication device. And," I tell him, "unless I can take it inside and use it, we can't go forward. We may as well not even go inside."

He turns his eyes from the road for a second and looks at me. "You're sure about this? You mean that?"

"I do. Betz does not know me. Unless I can give him absolute assurance that what he's telling me is confidential, that it can't be overheard or recorded by anyone else, I cannot in good conscience even talk to the man. I can't share the details, but I can tell you that his life hangs in the balance. And he may not be the only one."

"Sounds serious."

"It is."

"Well, we'll see what we can do."

More than twenty years ago when I was a young man, married with a daughter about eighteen months of age,

I had my first experience with white noise. Sarah was going through one of those brief periods when babies seem to cry incessantly. She was miserable and slowly driving us crazy. One day as I was getting ready to clean my study, she was screaming in the other room with her mother. I turned on the vacuum and suddenly she stopped. When I turned it off she started crying again. I turned it on and she quit.

Her mother, with Sarah in her arms, came into the room. We looked at each other and suddenly realized that we had discovered magic. There was something about the sound of the vacuum. We made a tape recording, played it in the car on trips, and sang its praises. It was white noise.

It is a range of audible wavelengths, constant in their tone, the most effective being low frequency, which tend to swallow up and mask other sounds, in our case the disturbing and uneven sounds that tend to make a baby irritable.

Today the same technique is used in manufactured devices called "white noise generators" as a sleep aid. Better than a pill, they work like the wheels of a train to send you to sand land.

They also have other purposes. One of them is as a countermeasure, to defeat listening devices such as parabolic and laser microphones that can tune in on a conversation some distance away. In the case of parabolic mics, this can include distances of up to fifty yards, depending on the size of the dish used to capture the sound waves. Laser mics, which are far more expensive but are known to be used by government agencies, have a range of about half a mile and are exceedingly sensitive.

It is what I'm carrying in my pocket, a small noise generator about the size of a cell phone. It is part of the reason I want Dan with me when I get to the prison. Without him, everything would come to a halt. Security would stop me at the door, take all of the electronics including the noise generator, and I would be playing on their turf.

They would, of course, give me the privacy of a clinical cement visiting cubical, Betz on one side of the glass, me on the other. They would no doubt promise to honor the attorney-client privilege. And then they would listen to everything we had to say. The stakes are too high in this case not to.

At reception, at Supermax, everything happens as expected. The guards just in front of the gated magnetometer ask for all of our electronics. Dan and I empty our pockets, take off our watches, and surrender our cell phones. He shows them his Bureau credentials and I show them the small white noise generator. They tell me it has to go in the basket and be held at the front desk to be reclaimed when I leave. It cannot go inside.

Dan explains to them and a few moments later one of the supervisors comes out. It seems he already has my name on a list. He shakes my hand. He and Dan exchange pleasantries. He looks at the device and asks me if I mind their examining it. I tell him no, as long as they do it in my presence. My concern is that if they take it in another room to look at it, when it comes back it may not work anymore. Harry and I tested it thoroughly with one of the technicians at the shop where we purchased it. It worked perfectly.

They do it at the counter while I watch. They turn it on, turn it off, take out the batteries. One of them unscrews the back of the case with a mini screwdriver, looks inside and then seals it back up. When I turn it on, the red light comes up. It's still working.

The supervisor tells me there is no need for it. They have a private conference area already set up. I tell him that we'll have to talk about that when I get inside.

He looks at the two guards, nods, and Dan and I go through the metal detector. The guard isn't happy about it, but he hands me the noise generator on the other side and we head to the sealed door beyond.

Fifty

Her name is Hannah Parish. She's an assistant US attorney. She introduces herself along with her boss, a senior supervising deputy attorney general, Fenton Yasuda, with the Criminal Division. It seems we all have our own surprises today. Parish and Yasuda are from the Department of Justice headquarters in Washington. No one told me they would be here.

"Why don't we go ahead and sit down," she says.

We are in a small conference room at the end of a long hall. We start to take chairs around the table. She looks at Dan and says, "I don't think there's any need for Mr. Wells to stay, do you?"

"I don't have anything to hide. And besides, he came all this way," I tell her.

She looks at me, smiles pleasantly, and tells me there may be some confidential matters that require discussion.

"Not as far as I'm concerned," I say. "Until I talk to my client, the only thing I'm prepared to talk about are the ground rules, in particular where he and I can meet and where we can have absolute confidence that what we say to each other is confidential."

Parish and her boss probably see this as an opportunity to take my deposition, to find out whatever they can about what I know.

"I understand you brought some kind of a noise generator with you."

"I did."

"Why would you do that?" she asks.

"For the same reason you use parabolic mics or worse, their laser cousins. You want to listen in and I don't want you to."

"I'm an attorney," she says. "I understand the sanctity of the attorney-client privilege."

"In that case, I'm sure you can understand the practical need to protect it, particularly when we consider the stakes involved in this case."

She looks at me, little slits for eyes. "So what do you propose?" she says.

"I'd like to talk to my client outside under the open sky. I assume he has seen daylight recently?"

"He gets exercise four times a week, outside in the recreation area," says the supervisor.

"Would that be the concrete pit?" I say.

He just looks at me.

"Then I assume it is. Let's hope the sunlight doesn't blind him. I believe you have an outdoor exercise track, surrounding a field." I know they do because I have seen it from the satellite photo on Google Earth. "I want to meet him there. Alone. No guards. No mics, just him and me."

"This is a maximum security prison," says the supervisor. "The people in this institution are highly dangerous."

"I don't doubt it for a minute. But if you're talking about Mr. Betz, I'll take my chances. You know as well as I do he represents no danger at all, at least not to me."

Parish, Yasuda, and the supervisor huddle at the other side of the table with their backs to me. When they turn around, Parish tells me they want to go in the other room and talk. What they want to do is stall for time until they can come up with some method to give me what I want and still listen in.

"Take it or leave it," I tell them. "I either talk to him now or else I walk. If I do, you can tell Senator Grimes for me that all bets are off."

"What do you mean?" says Parish.

"Just tell her, she'll know."

They look at each other. The supervisor shrugs, nods. "All right," she says. "It'll take us a few minutes to move him."

"Please don't take too long. I'd rather not have to leave."

"Give us ten minutes," says the supervisor.

I'm standing alone on the grass infield in the center of the fading green oval, some of it dirt, surrounded by the dusty track when I see him. He is hooded in black and manacled, wearing an orange prison jumpsuit. His hands are held to his side by a waist chain. For some reason they haven't bothered to put the ankle chains on. Probably because they know that Betz is going nowhere.

He is accompanied by three guards who shuttle him along like a blind man. With the hood over his head, he is exactly that. They shuffle along slowly, covering the seventy-five yards or so to where I'm standing.

Betz appears to be very slight of build. It's hard to tell in the jumpsuit. But he's not very tall, maybe five foot seven. Walking, he looks a little knock-kneed as if perhaps they're holding him up.

When they reach me I hear him breathing heavily through the hood. One of the guards tells Betz he may want to close his eyes for the sunlight. It is one of those brilliant Colorado days, blue skies and not a cloud overhead.

"Do you mind if he borrows one of your hats?" I ask them.

"Sure," says one of the guards. "He can use mine." He asks Betz if he's OK.

"Is that you, Walter?"

"It is."

"I'm all right."

"You might want to close your eyes. We're gonna take the hood off."

"OK."

They pull the hood from his head. His hands in pure reflex try to come up to shade his eyes, but the waist chain won't allow it. Betz squints, closes his eyes, and tries to look down toward the ground.

The guard puts the baseball cap on Betz's head and pulls the visor down low on his forehead to shade his eyes. "You OK?"

"Good. I'm fine. Thanks for the hat," he says.

"It's OK." The guard looks at me. "He's all yours. Do yourself a favor. Don't wander too far. Guards up in the towers." He gestures toward one of them with his head. "They will use deadly force if you get anywhere near the fence."

"Thanks for the warning."

The guards leave us.

I reach into my pocket, take out the white noise generator, and turn it on. It emits a low audible hum.

"What is that?" says Betz.

I explain it to him. He looks at the device, then back at me. I'm not sure he believes me.

"Sorry we had to meet out here under these circumstances. But I needed to get you away from the buildings where we could talk in private. You are Rubin Betz?"

"Last time I looked," he says. "Course that was a while ago." His face is gaunt, pale, lines etched under his eyes. For a man who is supposed to be forty-six, Betz could pass for sixty.

"My name is Paul Madriani. I'm a lawyer. I was sent here to represent you. Did anyone tell you I was coming?"

"Yeah, they told me. Who hired you?" he says.

"To tell you the truth, I'm not even sure myself. I'm not going to lie to you. For all I know, it may be the same people who put you in this place."

"Then why should I trust you?" he says.

"You don't have to. Just hear me out. I think I know what's happening. You've been in here now for what, almost two years?"

He nods.

"Things have happened that you may not know about. Do you ever get any visitors?"

He shakes his head. His eyes never leave me.

"So in that time you've had no visitors at all?"

"My lawyer," he says. "But he's dead. They told me he died in an accident. That was right after they put me in here. You tend to lose track of time."

"Then Olinda Serna never came to visit you?"

He looks at me but doesn't say anything.

"Did you know she was dead?"

By the expression on his face, the look in his eyes, I can tell that he didn't. "According to the police report it was an accident. But it wasn't. She was murdered."

"I need to sit down," he says.

Whatever little energy he had seems to abandon him with this news. There're a couple of benches out near the edge of the track. We move toward one of them and sit.

"How did she die?"

"Automobile collision and fire. It was all very carefully staged."

"When?"

"About two months ago, not too far from San Diego, in California."

He starts to cough, turns his head away from me, and for a moment seems to collect himself. When he looks back at me he has teared up.

"I take it you knew her pretty well?"

"We were lovers. We had been living together for quite a while. We kept it quiet, mostly for her career."

"Why didn't she come to visit you here?"

"She couldn't."

"Because of her career?"

"That and the fact that it was dangerous. Though staying away didn't save her, as you can see. She wanted to come visit. I told her not to. I'm sure people around her thought she was nothing but a flaming ball of ambition. That she just used people and moved on. But she didn't. She wasn't that way at all. She had a chip on her shoulder—Olinda against the world. She had a hard outer veneer, but once you cracked through it there was a big-hearted, generous person inside. To those in need. The kind of person who would take in stray dogs and cats, if you know what I mean. I know because I was one of them. When I got bounced from a job all my friends dropped me like I had leprosy. But not Olinda. She kept me going. Used her connections to give me a new start. You never know who your real friends are until you're down, when you need them. We had some good times," he says. "Is that what you came here to tell me? That she's dead?"

"No. I came here to try and get you out, if I can."

He shoots me a look as if trying to read my mind. "Why would you do that?"

I turn to look at him. "Do you want to stay here?"

"What, do you think I'm crazy? I don't have a choice. I leave here and the same people who got to her are gonna kill me. Who are you anyway?"

"I told you. My name is Paul Madriani. I'm a law—"

"No. I mean how did you get involved?"

"A long story." I tell him about the case, Alex and the collision in the desert. The fact that Ives was unconscious, an intended victim who escaped. I explain about the *Washington Gravesite*, the story they were working on, the PEPs, the politically exposed deposit holders at Gruber Bank. Then the name of the old Swiss banker, Simon Korff, and the fact that he was killed as well.

"Korff saw you, Serna, and Senator Maya Grimes at Gruber Bank. He told me that you and Serna acted as financial go-betweens for some powerful people in Washington. He told me there were boatloads of cash. Now the people who killed Serna and the banker are tidying up the remaining loose ends. Because of what I know, I am on their clean-up list along with a few of my close friends and associates with whom I've shared the news."

"I can't help you." He starts to get up from the bench.

"We can help each other."

"You're wondering how I stayed alive all this time," he says.

"You're holding something they want," I tell him.

"If you think I'm gonna tell you where it is, you're wrong."

"I don't want to know where it is."

This gets his attention. "Then what do you want?"

"I want to stay alive. In order to do that I've gotta get you out of here."

"How's that gonna help you?"

"You have information. They don't know where it is. That's why you're still alive. If I can get you out of here, tuck you away where you're safe and comfortable," I tell him, "and I'm the only one who knows where, then I'll have a piece of your protection. Unless you think you're better off here?"

He studies me for a moment, a hard direct stare, then says, "Why is it all of a sudden everybody wants me out?"

"Who else?"

"Two days ago they came to me with an offer."

"Who?"

"A lawyer from the Justice Department. Woman by the name of Parish."

"Go on."

"She's the one told me you were coming. She told me you were going to represent me—that is, if I agreed. She turned off the mic on my side of the glass, told me not to say anything, just listen. She said they were prepared to pay me a lot of money, and let me go."

"Who was prepared to pay?"

"The government. I'm just telling you what she told me. All they wanted in return was what I'm holding."

"Bank records?"

He looks at me and winks.

"If you do that and they release you, you'll be dead in a week," I tell him.

"Well, at least we agree on that."

"You don't have to say anything, but I'm assuming that whatever you have has some kind of a hair trigger on it. Anything happens to you, it goes public?"

"WikiLeaks on steroids," says Betz. "Their knowledge of that is what keeps me alive. But I'm running out of time."

"What do you mean?"

"How do I know I can trust you?"

"You don't. But then who else do you have? Is there another lawyer you'd like me to contact?"

He shakes his head. "I'm tired and I don't have much time. I'm gonna have to trust somebody." Resignation written all over his face. "May as well be you. Besides, what more can they do to me? The fact is," he says, "I'm dying. They don't know it yet, but I'm living on borrowed time."

Fifty-One

I am guessing that he has kept this secret, the fact that he is dying, to himself for so long that when he is finally able to share it with someone, the dam cracks, and he can't stop talking.

He tells me that his doctor diagnosed cancer in his pancreas just before sentencing, a short time before he arrived here. There was little they could do to treat it because it had already spread. They told him he had perhaps twelve to eighteen months. He is past that now. Betz has been living in hell. He couldn't tell authorities for fear that they would make his dying days even more miserable trying to extract the information from him, find out where the banking records were. He refused to give it up because he was bitter and angry. Perhaps that's the only thing keeping him alive.

"They cheated me out of the money," he says. "And now they're getting desperate. I wanted it for my daughter."

"What money? I don't understand."

"The Whistleblower Fund," he says. "I die in here, my daughter will never see a dime. It's what the lawyer offered me when she told me you were coming. But they're lying. I know they are. The minute they get what they want, they'll leave me here to rot."

"How much are we talking about?"

"A hundred and ten million dollars. They owe it to me."

As he says it I nearly fall off the bench.

"You're telling me that's what she offered you?"

He nods. "I turned state's evidence against the Swiss bank I used to work for. The information I gave them resulted in almost five thousand offshore numbered accounts being identified. It's why they put me in here. They knew if they put me anywhere else where I couldn't be protected, I'd be labeled as a snitch. I'd be dead in twenty-four hours. The taxes and penalties on the hidden accounts were substantial."

The Internal Revenue Service pays a reward for information based on a percentage of what they recover in revenue. This is embedded in federal law.

"But that's only part of it," says Betz. "The bulk of it is owing from the fines against the bank itself. The bank agreed to pay more than eight hundred million dollars in fines to the US Treasury in order to keep their executives out of prison on charges they conspired with the taxpayers to commit tax evasion. They owe me ten percent of what they recovered."

By the time he finishes my head is swimming—eighty million dollars from the bank alone.

"It's not the money. They don't care about the money. What they want are the records. If I hadn't told them about the PEPs, the politicians, they would have never charged me. It was my mistake," says Betz. "I thought they would be pleased. But they weren't. It was right after that someone tried to kill me. I realized then I had to do something to protect myself. Now it doesn't matter anymore. All that matters is my daughter. With her mother dead she'll be alone."

"What happened to her mother?"

He looks at me as if he's surprised I should ask the question. "You told me she was murdered."

"You mean Serna?"

"Olinda was her mother," he says.

I sit there with my jaw on the bench. The circle is now complete.

"No one knew," he says. "She told no one at the firm. She had the child before she went to work there. Years ago. But I figured you knew, since you knew everything else."

"How old is she?"

"Fourteen," he says. "And beautiful. She sure was the last time I saw her."

"Where is she now?"

"I can't tell you that," he says. "If they found out where she was and they got to her . . ."

"I understand. You don't have to say another word."

"Tell them I will turn everything over to them if they pay the money," says Betz. "If they release me now, immediately," he continues. "I just want to have some time to be with my daughter. I'll have to take my chances."

"No!" I think for a moment. "I don't think you'll have to do that."

"Why? What are you gonna do?"

"Don't tell anyone else about your condition. If they find out you're sick you'll never get out of here."

"I understand."

"Don't tell anyone else what we talked about. Is that clear?"

"Who the hell would I talk to in here?" he says.

"Don't even talk in your sleep. This is what we're going to do. . . ."

By the time I laid the small noise generator back down on the table in the conference room, the two government lawyers were already sitting across the table. They were waiting anxiously to hear what I had to say.

Grimes had made a fundamental mistake bringing me into the case. The problem for her was that I already knew too much. I knew that Betz was holding a hammer over their heads, and I knew its size and weight as well as the damage it would inflict if he dropped it. I didn't need to know where he was hiding it to be able to use its leverage. All that was required was the government's ignorance as to what Betz and I had discussed, the fact that I actually had no access to Thor's hammer. If the little white noise maker has worked, they won't know this.

Parish advises me that Dan Wells has decided to wait for me out in front in the reception area. He probably got tired of being slapped around by her.

"I understand you talked with my client before I had an opportunity to confer with him," I tell her.

She leans forward, begins to open her mouth.

"But we'll let that slide for the moment. The issue here is very clear. It appears that the government has overcharged Mr. Betz on successive criminal counts . . ."

"He was convicted by a jury," she says.

"On charges that would never have been brought by your department against a cooperating witness turning state's evidence in thousands of cases involving tax evasion, including evidence against his own employer, a foreign bank from which you extracted more than eight hundred million dollars in fines."

"The fact remains he was convicted."

"And why didn't you extend to him the courtesy, the consideration you would have extended to any other cooperating witness in a similar case? I'll tell you why . . ."

"Because he refused to fully cooperate," she says. "He has records . . ."

"I know what he has. And he offered them to you. But when you found out what they were, the political dynamite that was in them, you weren't interested."

"You mean he told you what was in them?" Parish has just told me what I needed to know. White noise still works.

"And I'll tell you why you weren't interested. Because you intended to bury them. When someone tried to kill him, Betz was forced to take precautions. He hid them."

"Do you know where they are?" she says.

"Why don't you just go and shoot him," I tell her. "Oh, that's right, you can't, because if you do, your world will come crashing down around your ears. You couldn't be sure whether the man who was trying to cooperate with you might have another copy, or whether after you buried the case, Mr. Betz would keep his mouth shut. So in order to coerce him you drummed up a case and tossed him in here."

"How many times do I have to say it? He was convicted by a jury of his peers."

"Say it as many times as you like," I tell her, "it doesn't change the facts of what you did."

"We offered him a fair deal," she says.

"Did you? Did you really?"

"Didn't he tell you? His freedom, immediately," she says, "plus one hundred and ten million dollars. All he has to do is tell us where those records are and sign a confidentiality agreement. As soon as we've secured them he can walk out of here a free man. If you want, you can wait and take him with you."

"Let me get this straight. You're offering him ten percent of the revenues recovered in this case, a case you would not have made without the evidence that he supplied."

"That's correct. And it's a lot of money," she says.

"The fact is, it's light. Perhaps you'd like to get the code and the regulations out and check it. Anything over two million dollars in revenue recovered is entitled to a whistleblower's award of between fifteen and thirty percent of the revenues recovered. I know because I had a case earlier this year. What was the total amount recovered here?"

"I'm not sure," she says. "I'd have to check." She looks at Yasuda, who is sitting next to her. He shrugs a shoulder. "We'd have to look," he says. "But I'm sure that if a mistake has been made, we'll be happy to correct it."

"Maybe someone can find a way to give him the two years of his life back while you're at it. Tell you what, we'll come back to that later, after our accountants have had a chance to sharpen their pencils. Let's get to the nub. After talking to Mr. Betz, this is what we've decided to do. Copies of the bank records. Those from Gruber Bank, S.A., in Lucerne. I think that's correct, isn't it?"

"Yes, that's the one," says Parish.

"Copies will be prepared. A copy will be delivered overnight to your offices in Washington, at the same time that we dispatch copies to the wire services, the networks, the cable stations, the *New York Times*, the *LA Times*, the *Wall Street Journal* . . ."

"You can't do that," she says.

"Why not?"

"Those are confidential tax records."

"No, they're not. They're records of a foreign bank. In fact, they're not even that. They're personal accountings made by Mr. Betz in the ordinary course of his employment. But I'm sure when people start checking, they'll find out pretty fast that the account numbers and the names on those accounts—some pretty prominent people, I might add—match up very neatly with the amounts on deposit at Gruber Bank. Some of them are whoppers," I tell her.

"You're bluffing," she says. "You don't have anything."

"Want to try me?"

Yasuda puts his hand out and lays it on her forearm. "Hannah."

She looks at him, retracts her fangs, and settles back into her chair.

"What is it exactly that you want, Mr. Madriani?" says Yasuda.

"First, I want my client released into my custody and I want it done before I leave here today. Apparently from what Hannah just said you've already cut the paperwork on this. Second, I will prepare the final written settlement agreement as regards the sum owing to Mr. Betz under the IRS Whistleblower Act. Your accountants can talk with our accountants as to the precise amount owed."

"What about the records?" says Yasuda.

"What assurance do we have that your office will pursue them? Investigate and prosecute?" I ask.

"None," he says. "That's a matter of prosecutorial discretion."

"In which case you already have my terms on that issue. We're prepared to release them to you simultaneously with a release to the media."

"That's unacceptable," says Yasuda.

"Fine. Then we can sort out the claim on the Whistleblower Fund by filing suit in the tax court. We will lodge an appeal in the Ninth Circuit regarding the manner in which you charged and thereafter incarcerated my client. I'm sure the court will be very interested in learning why you charged him in the manner you did, particularly given the evidence at trial regarding his extraordinary efforts of cooperation that you spurned. But before I do any of this, I will gather up the records of Mr. Betz, make a sufficient number of copies, and send them to every media outlet I can find."

"That would be highly irresponsible," says Yasuda. "Give us a moment."

"Take all the time you need."

He and Parish turn their backs and huddle at the table. I'm wondering if I should turn on the white noise for them.

Finally they turn around. "Let me lay it all on the table for you," he says. "If we release Mr. Betz, what assurances can you give us that he'll be safe? You know the risks."

"I do."

"Why don't you let us put him in witness protection?" says Yasuda.

"Of course, the final decision on that belongs to Mr. Betz. But I suspect he's had about enough protection from the federal government for the time being. If you're asking if I can give a guarantee as to his safety, the answer's no. But perhaps with a little assistance on your part we can afford him a reasonable amount of security until we can make other arrangements."

It is not Betz's security that is their primary concern. It is the security of the documents that they want.

"Good," says Yasuda. "Then we're agreed as to that issue. As for the money, we have no problems. We are more than willing to negotiate a corrected amount, consistent with the code and the regulations regarding the whistleblower award.

"It's the last item that's the problem," says Yasuda. "What will you do with the records if we do nothing more here today?"

"We will hold them for the time being," I tell him. "In point of fact, you're aware, as I am, that as long as these remain hidden with the risk that they will be delivered to the media if anything happens to Mr. Betz, they provide some added measure of security."

"Then can we agree to discuss this at a later date?"

"It's fine by me, but I wouldn't wait too long."

"Good." Yasuda looks at the supervisor sitting at the end of the table. "Please make the arrangements for Mr. Betz's release immediately. Get him some street clothes and some cash, a generous amount. We will treat it as an advance on the award." He looks at me. "You and I need to discuss security arrangements."

Yasuda doesn't know the half of it.

Fifty-Two

The day after arriving home from the ordeal at Supermax, I dispatched Harry to meet with Alex Ives's father. At Ives's office at the airport, the two of them made all the necessary arrangements. The small air cargo jet would return to Mexico, pick up Alex and Herman, and bring them back, at least partway.

I've been pushing everything else off my desk to deal with all of this, and I have a growing stack of mail and telephone messages screaming at me. One of them is from the judge's clerk downtown as we edge toward the meeting I'm trying to avoid, and another from the guy out in Del Mar, Becket.

As soon as Harry returned to the office he gave me the details, time and date for the pickup at the dirt strip east of Ixtapa. I sent a message to Herman on the

Internet bulletin board in Tampico, Mexico: "It is time to come home."

In cryptic terms I spelled out the details. He already knew the location. I let him know that I would watch the board for any message coming the other way in the event that they couldn't make it.

Because Alex lacks a passport we cannot fly him back the way he went out, directly across the border on the jet. Landing at a US airport, TSA, which does air cargo security, and ICE, Immigration and Customs, would nail him. They would probably see to it that the company transporting him lost their license, too. Alex would end up back in the pokey for violating the terms of his bail, and Harry and I would be sitting on a hot seat in front of some judge downtown.

With all of the stories about people walking across the southern border, the fact is, it isn't that easy.

So the jet, loaded with a light cargo of consumer electronics, will fly south to Mexico City and drop off part of its load. It will then make a quick detour west, taking less than an hour to the dirt strip, pick up Alex and Herman, and then head north. It will land again at Tijuana to deposit the rest of its cargo. Because the connecting flights, the two cargo drops, are within the country, Mexican authorities at Tijuana are not likely to take a hard look at the plane.

Herman and Alex will be picked up by a car near the cargo terminal at Tijuana. Alex's father has made arrangements for this. They will be driven to the fishing port at Ensenada, and from there, they will board a fast forty-two-foot sport fishing boat owned by an American buddy of Ives. He will transport them well out to sea, then north, up the coast, where they will land at Mission Bay, the boat's home port.

On board will be three American sport fishermen with bad sunburns, along with a couple of large yellowtail tuna that the skipper will buy off the docks in Ensenada.

If all goes well, Alex and Herman should be back in San Diego within two days. The question of where to hide Alex has also been solved, at least for the time being. I will hide him with Betz. Alex has always wanted to meet the whistleblower. Here is his chance.

Before I left the Supermax facility in Colorado, I made a phone call to another acquaintance in Washington, D.C. His name is Zeb Thorpe. Harry and I call him "Jug-Head." A former marine, Thorpe is actually the executive director for the National Security Branch of the FBI. At one time he held my life, along with Harry's and Herman's, in his hands. To the extent that you can trust anybody in circumstances like these, I trust Thorpe.

I asked him if he knew Fenton Yasuda. He did. According to Thorpe, Yasuda is a straight arrow, a career prosecutor who has worked his way up within the Department of Justice. Although the position he currently holds is an exempt appointment, he is no political hack. Thorpe says he is someone I can trust. So I do. Thorpe also gave me some other advice and said he would make a few phone calls.

With that, Yasuda and I, out of the presence of everyone else, made a deal. As agreed, the government transported Betz and me back to Miramar, the Marine Air Station near San Diego, where they will temporarily house Betz until other arrangements can be made. It was Thorpe who called ahead of me to the station and cleared the way.

The fact is, we have no other choice. I can't take Betz to my office or to my house. Neither place would be safe. The minute they knew he was there, they would descend on both of us.

I am hoping that Betz will be at Miramar no more than a few days, a week at most. US Marshals will provide security inside the compound. Marine guards at the gate filter everyone coming and going. If it is carefully worked out, arrangements might be made for his daughter to visit him there.

On the plane back Betz and I set up a code. He is to call me three times each day using the back line at the office and my home phone at night. I will not pick up, as I will not recognize the incoming phone number. He is to leave a message on voice mail that my laundry is ready to be picked up. If I don't get the message, I will call the marshals and start to worry.

My fear is not that someone will kill Betz, at least not immediately. The concern is that they may try to kidnap him in order to squeeze him for information as to the location of the Swiss bank records. Once they have those, none of us will be safe.

With everything that has happened, the strange thing is that we still have no clue as to who is behind all of the bloodletting. Is it being driven from within the government or from the outside? There is no question that Grimes is caught up in the middle of it. Other members of Congress as well. But I doubt that they are the ones perpetrating the violence. I could understand an individual member under pressure, being blackmailed, desperate enough to kill the person threatening them. But this, a highly organized series of assassinations, carefully planned and executed—it doesn't fit.

Instead, it is far more likely that the members, some whose names were given to Harry and me by the banker, Korff, are the commodities that are being protected. Someone invested in their corruption is shielding his capital outlay.

If Harry and I had anything solid, documents or a witness pointing us in the right direction, it would be something we could give to the D.A. or to the cops. Anything to get them off our backs on the case against Alex.

It's what I was hoping for in the declaration from Ben, her statement under penalty of perjury naming the man who hired her to lure Alex to the party, the man with the silver bird-headed cane. But I don't have it, and she's dead.

I could produce Betz. He could testify to the fact that others had a motive to kill Serna, but without something more it would be meaningless. The prosecution would claim that it was nothing but a desperate attempt to shower blame on a phantom conspiracy. They would demand to see the evidence, the mysterious bank records. The feds would be on us in a minute, US attorneys up to our hips, demanding that everything be sealed, motions to remove the entire matter to the federal courts. And while we were arguing, someone would stick a knife in my back. Betz would end up with another lawyer, someone looking to get a good grip on his throat to find out where the bank records are kept.

Bizarre as it is, we are still saddled with the vehicular homicide case and a meeting in front of a judge in his chambers the day after tomorrow. I am hoping that Alex will be back in time.

Fifty-Three

This morning Harry and I are closeted in the library at the office, busily working up notes with our accountant. We're going over the terms of the agreement, how to handle the money, the settlement between Betz and the government.

We have already hammered out the terms of his release. They are trying to sweeten the pot by dangling a full pardon. I doubt that it matters to Betz as long as he can see his daughter. Their first visit was this morning, and from the tone of his voice he was floating on air. She is the only thing that matters to him in life.

Our CPA, Bruce, is spread out at the table, becoming giddy as he crunches the numbers. He huddles over his computer, punching in figures. All that is missing from this picture is a green visor on his head and a handle he can pull periodically like a slot machine.

"We don't have all the numbers yet," he says. "We have the eight hundred million in fines from the bank, and some of the fines and penalties along with back taxes collected from the five thousand some odd individuals he turned over."

These are the US taxpayers with hidden accounts identified by Betz at his company's bank, his old Swiss employer.

"But we don't have them all as yet. And you say there could be more?"

He means the PEPs who were moved to Gruber Bank, though he doesn't know the terms or any of the details because we haven't given him any of it. None of us know the fate on those as yet.

"If they go public and end up in the tally," says Harry, "it's gonna be like finding the *Atocha*." Harry is talking about the Spanish treasure galleon that went down in the Caribbean back in the 1600s.

"Who are they?" says Bruce.

"Never mind." I look at Harry.

"Sorry," he says.

It is an irony that after all this time Harry and I, as a consequence of taking Alex Ives's drunk driving case, and in the process netting Betz as a client, stand to receive what may be a very large payday, though neither of us understand the full dimensions of it yet.

Rubin Betz is insisting that we take, at a minimum, ten percent of everything over one hundred and ten million, the original offer made to him by the government. He says that without me he would have never seen a dime over that amount and would probably still be sitting in his cell at Supermax. More important, because he is free, he has regular contact with his daughter.

The question, I wonder, is whether Grimes knew about this, and figured that maybe she was buying me off? During the phone call Proffit told me that I would be well compensated. But I never had a clue as to the amount. My guess is neither did he; otherwise he would have shouldered me aside and tried to grab it for himself. I suspect this is what happens when you rub up against the rich and powerful in D.C.: flecks of gold wrapped in bouquets of garbage rain down.

"I expect what they're going to want to do is go back to square one and start their calculations all over again," says Bruce. "They'll probably argue that the fine paid by the bank subject to the settlement is not 'revenue' within the meaning of the law. Therefore you get no part of it under the whistleblower program. The fact is, it's money paid to the US Treasury, they would have never gotten it without the information given to them by your client, and they clearly used it to calculate their original offer to him. They've dug themselves a hole," he says.

"Beyond that, you're going to want to leave the agreement open-ended in order to capture any future claims. It's gonna be a moving target by all appearances, developing as you go. The other three thousand taxpayers they're still working on."

"Can we do that?" I ask. "I was assuming they'd want a final figure."

"You can do whatever you want as long as the government agrees to it. If they refuse, I would file a claim in the tax court. Ordinarily my advice," he says, "is to take whatever they offer you and go. You can die of old age fighting with the government. But in this case, given the amounts, the fact that you've got a minor on the receiving end, you'd be a fool not to press it." Bruce used to work for the IRS. He knows the game, but he tells us we are plowing new ground here. "This is without question the biggest claim the Whistleblower Fund has ever seen," he says.

I make a note to keep the agreement open-ended to capture future claims.

"There may be more, but for the moment let's keep it conservative," I tell them. "Run the numbers on what we know, the figures we have right now. I'll draft the agreement to capture whatever might be owing from the rest of the five thousand we already know about. Anything else, we'll have to see."

"You and I'll have to talk about that." Harry wants a pound of flesh from the politicians.

The accountant starts punching numbers. "OK, so we start with what we know. The government claims revenue of one point one billion dollars, of which eight hundred million comes from fines paid by the bank. The balance comes from about two thousand of the five thousand hiding funds offshore. Working backwards at ten percent, that gets you to the hundred and ten million dollars they originally offered him.

"However, as we know, the statute and the regs call for a sliding scale of between fifteen and thirty percent of the amount recovered by the government. Let's start at the low end," says Bruce. He's working the keyboard. "Fifteen percent of one point one billion is one hundred and sixty-five million dollars. That's your client's payday, bottom line, minimum amount under the statute and the regs. That's as low as it's going to get for them."

"You mean . . ." says Harry.

"I mean unless there's some extraordinary reason that none of us know about, either they pay that or they'll be forced to pay by the tax court. They can delay, drag their feet, but ultimately you'll collect."

"That's fifty-five million dollars more than they offered him," says Harry. "That means . . . that means five and a half million dollars." Harry looks at him.

"Your fee, that's correct," says Bruce.

Harry is stunned.

"So that's where they'll start negotiating," says Bruce.

"What do you mean start?" says Harry.

"That will be their opener, lowball offer," says Bruce. "You on the other hand start at thirty percent. Make your best case. Without the assistance and the information from your client, what was the likely return and revenue to the government? Zero. You haggle. Where are you gonna end up? Somewhere in the middle," he says. "Let's just take a ballpark, split the difference, say around twenty-two and a half percent, give or take." He punches some more numbers, moves the mouse, does it again, then says, "Let's see, that's two hundred and forty-seven million, five hundred thousand dollars. Not to put too fine a point on it."

Harry, sitting across the table from me, has just turned white.

"Your fee," says Bruce. He does a few more calculations. "If I figure correctly, should be somewhere in the neighborhood of thirteen million, seven hundred and fifty thousand dollars. Now that's the stuff we know about, current claim," he says. "That doesn't include the other three thousand taxpayers they know about but are still working to tally up. If you extrapolate knowing what we know from the first two thousand," he says. "Figure another four hundred million in revenue to the government, at twenty-two and a half percent that's another ninety million for your client, nine million to you. So the total ballpark figure is, say . . . let's round it off, say three hundred and thirty-seven million dollars. That's your client's take. Your fee, thirty-three million, seven." He looks up at us. "Now that's the most you're going to get. You can make it easy on yourself by getting in their faces and then backing off a little, take a little less. At some point they'll cave and say 'good.' "

"Did you just say thirty-three million, seven hundred thousand dollars?" says Harry.

"That's what I said. And the good thing about all of this," says Bruce, "is that the money to pay the back taxes and penalties is already in the bank. There's no need for the IRS to discount any of it. So don't let them tell you they did. Everybody's getting a windfall here. You, them. This is money the government didn't know existed. Everybody but the taxpayer."

We sit there for a moment and catch our breath. "Bruce, I want to thank you for coming by."

"You guys don't look happy," he says.

"We're OK, I think it comes as a bit of a shock. I'll have to talk to Betz, make sure he understands what he's giving up. Check the statutes, make sure were not running afoul of anything. Assuming it's OK, it's gonna take a while to get used to the concept."

"What concept is that?" says Bruce.

"Having money." When it happens this suddenly it's hard to get your head around it. Like winning the lottery.

He starts to collect his stuff, puts the computer in his bag, and gathers his papers.

"I'll call you in a few days, as soon as we pull together a draft of the agreement. There's a lot to think about."

Bruce gets up, shakes my hand.

"Good to see you again." Bruce looks at Harry, who is just sitting at the table, stunned.

"Yeah. Good to see you." It's the first time I have ever seen him speechless. He blinks a couple of times before finally collecting himself enough to turn and look at Bruce, who is almost out the door.

"Are you sure about this?" says Harry. "To me, I don't know, but it sounds like a Ponzi scheme."

"It depends how hard you want to push them," says Bruce. "I wouldn't get too hard-core unless you want to fend off audits for the rest of your life. On the other hand, you will have the money to pay me if that happens." He smiles at us. "All I can say is, that's the ballpark you're playing in."

"Somebody gimme some Cracker Jacks," says Harry. Not even the slightest grin on his face. My partner, the ultimate contrarian, pessimist even among the doomsayers, may have just won the lottery. He has yet to see a dime, but the thought alone shatters everything he knows about the world and human nature.

Bruce laughs, heads out the door, and closes it behind him.

"Cheer up," I tell Harry. "That's the bad news. The good news is we probably won't live long enough to see any of it."

Fifty-Four

I'm hammering away on the computer in my office, working on the draft agreement for Betz, when Sally, our receptionist, raps on my door and opens it.

"What is it?"

"Package for you," she says. "Courier service just delivered it."

Out of the corner of my eye I see the FedEx letter pack.

"I would have given it to Mr. Hinds, but he's gone."

"Harry had to take care of something up near Mission Bay." In point of fact, he is picking up Alex and Herman. He will deliver Ives to the Marine Station at Miramar and introduce him to Betz, then take Herman home, where he can get some sleep.

"What's in the package?"

"I don't know. Do you want me to open it?"

"Please, if you don't mind." I'm in the middle of a thought on the agreement. I don't want to lose the threads.

She pulls the perforated tab on the letter pack and opens it. "Looks like some kind of a list. 'Defense Contractors Gala.' There's a note. 'Dear Mr. Madriani. Sorry to be so tardy on this, but I called your office and left a message and no one called back.'"

"Who's it from?"

"Let me see. A Mr. Rufus A. Becket."

I stop typing, turn in my chair, and say, "Let me see it."

She hands me the letter pack and the sheaf of papers with it. I drop the envelope on the desk. The note is neatly typed on stiff heavy stock stationery embossed at the top with the letters "RAB." Behind the single page note is the guest list from the party at Becket's house, the list I had asked for nearly a month ago when I first visited Becket at his house.

I read the note. He apologizes for being so late. The fact is, I never expected him to give me the list. But as I read the note I discover the reason why he did. His assistant, whose name is George, returned from vacation earlier in the week. George, it seems, remembers the events the night Alex passed out at the party.

I scan Becket's note. "At the bottom of the list you will see several names penned in ink. Among them are three individuals who were not originally invited to the event. However, because some of the other guests knew them, we included them and invited them to join us at the last minute. According to George it was one of these gentlemen and his two friends who took charge of the young man you were talking about when he fell ill. The man's name who took charge was Joseph Ying."

I set the note aside and flip to the last page of the guest list. There, written in ink, longhand, are eight or ten names. One of them at the top, in a fine measured cursive script, is the name Joseph Ying with an address listed in Hong Kong.

I turn back to the note. "If you require further assistance you may wish to talk to George personally. The number where he may be reached is . . ."

I pick up the phone and dial the number. On the second ring it's answered. "Hello, this is George Connor, how can I help you?"

"Mr. Connor. You don't know me but I'm acquainted with your employer, Mr. Becket. My name is Paul Madriani. I'm an attorney. . . ."

"Ah, yes," he says. "Mr. Becket informed me that you might be calling. It's about the party that night."

"That's correct. Mr. Becket sent me the guest list with a note. He says you had some involvement with a young man who got sick at the party who may have passed out."

"I did indeed," he says. "That young man was in very bad shape. In fact, by the time they got him to the car I would say he was unconscious."

"Who is 'they'?" I ask.

"The three gentlemen who helped him. They were late to the party. In fact, at the time I thought perhaps that the four of them were together, the young man and the other three. But Mr. Becket advises me that this may not have been the case. Perhaps because of what you told him."

"Would you recognize the young man again if you saw him or if I were to produce a photograph?"

"I believe so. But I doubt that that would be necessary."

"Why do you say that?"

"Because I got his name from his driver's license. When someone is that intoxicated at a private gathering you'd be remiss if you didn't get his name. If for no other reason than liability," says the man.

"You wrote it down?"

"It's on the guest list," he says. "The list you have is a copy of my working list, the one I used that night.

All the add-ons were penned on my list. It was with my papers, so you see, when you approached Mr. Becket he didn't have access to it because I was on vacation."

I flip to the back of the list again. Sure enough, there, buried among the other names in ink, is the name Alex Ives, address San Diego.

"This is your handwriting, then?"

"Correct. The gentleman in question was in no condition to write anything," he says. "In fact, they had to practically carry him to his car. By the time they got him there he seemed completely unconscious. I remember because I advised them to take him to the hospital. I was quite concerned. As I recall, Mr. Ying drove the young man's car when they left. The other two followed in another vehicle."

"You saw all of this?"

"I did. I walked them to the car because I wanted to make sure the young man got home safely."

"Can you give me an approximate time as to when this happened?"

"Let me think. Dinner had already been served—at least the main course, because I recall asking them if their friend had had anything to eat. They said they weren't sure. Ah, I remember. It would have been just a few minutes before nine. I remember because the sprinklers went on in one of the flowerbeds out in

550 · STEVE MARTINI

the front area. I got my shoes wet on the way back in. Those sprinklers are set to go on at nine."

"Can you describe the other men? The ones who helped Mr. Ives to his car? Would you recognize them if you saw them again?"

"I believe so. I would certainly recognize Mr. Ying. He did not appear to be Asian. But then who knows? If I had to guess, I would say he was Caucasian. He was older, about six feet in height, gray hair, very pale blue eyes, quite distinctive. I remember that about him. He was well dressed, though he was not wearing formal attire that evening, I know that. And the event was formal. Tuxedoes for men, evening gowns for women. They stood out because they weren't formally dressed, the four of them, including your friend. Oh, and Mr. Ying appeared to have a slight disability."

"In what way?"

"He carried a cane, a walking stick. It had a unique handle, almost black. It appeared to be tarnished silver."

"A bird's head?"

"How did you know?"

It was the cane Ben told me about. The one carried by the man who hired her to lure Alex to the party. His name is Joseph Ying.

"Listen, I wonder if you would mind signing a declaration for me, simply reciting the facts as you've told them to me here on the phone today. I have a court appearance tomorrow and a declaration from you as to these facts would be exceedingly helpful."

"No problem," he says. "I'd be happy to."

"I can dictate it and have my secretary type it up. Then I'll read it to you over the phone, make sure you have no problems with any of it. Once it's finalized I can deliver it out there myself, say in about ninety minutes."

"That would be fine."

"I assume you're at work, at Mr. Becket's house?"

"I am."

"I'll call you back in just a few minutes with the declaration."

"I'll be waiting."

We hang up.

I slump in my chair. Wait 'til I tell Harry. We finally have a witness, one we can use, one who's still breathing.

Fifty-Five

When I call him back and read the draft of the declaration over the phone, Becket's assistant, George, listens carefully. He makes a few minor corrections and then blesses the document.

I hang up and have my secretary make the amendments. She prints out the necessary copies and puts them in a file folder. The second she delivers this to my office, I'm out from behind the desk. "I should be back by three," I tell her. Then I grab the file and race out the door.

I cross the bridge, then keep the pedal close to the floor with one eye on the rearview mirror for the Highway Patrol as I head up I-5. The last thing I need is a ticket or worse, a safety inspection of the old Jeep. A delay like that and Becket's assistant will be gone before I can get there.

THE ENEMY INSIDE • 553

The declaration from George Connor should at least put to rest for the moment any hasty talk of a plea by the state. It is something I can present to the court in the morning. The fact that Connor saw Alex unconscious and totally incapacitated at nine P.M. that evening, two hours before the accident, raises serious problems for the state's case.

It would take more than an hour, probably close to ninety minutes, to drive the distance from Becket's house in Del Mar to the site of the accident east of town. To believe that Mr. Ying and his companions deposited Alex at his apartment, and that Ives recovered sufficiently to drive himself out to the accident site in the time allowed would be highly unlikely and close to impossible. That means that the only way Alex could have gotten there was if Ying or someone else drove him. And if that's the case, what was the purpose?

After I get Connor's signature on the declaration I will talk to him about testifying. If he's willing I will also have him meet with a graphic artist to work up a composite picture of the man named Ying.

Thirty minutes later I pull up under the spreading branches of the giant live oak out in front of Becket's house. I slam the door to my old Jeep, not bothering to lock it. The singed ragtop from the blast that killed

Ben is still there. I haven't had time to even think about getting it replaced.

I cross the street under the oak and head up the long circular drive to the front of the house. The walk hasn't gotten any shorter since the last time I was here. Finally I climb the white brick steps leading to the front door and ring the bell. A few seconds later the door opens. A tall man with dark hair and black horn-rimmed glasses is standing in front of me. "Can I help you?"

"I'm looking for Mr. Connor."

"Ah, you must be Mr. Madriani." He runs the fingers of his right hand through his forelock, brushing a few stray hairs from the rim of his spectacles. "I'm George Connor."

He offers his hand. We shake.

"Nice to meet you. I hope I didn't keep you waiting."

"Not at all." He welcomes me into the house and closes the heavy oak door behind me.

"I assume you had no trouble finding the place, being as you've been here once before?"

"No problem at all. I don't want to take up too much of your time. I have the declaration here." I start to open the file. "I brought a copy for you and one for Mr. Becket. I thought that since the party was at his house he might want one for his files."

"Good of you to think of it. I'm sure he would."

I start to pull out the documents.

"Why don't we go into the study? Mr. Becket's not here at the moment. I can read it and sign there if you don't mind."

"Whatever."

"Can I offer you something to drink?"

"No, I'm fine."

I follow him across the palatial oval entry. A checkerboard pattern of large black-and-white tiles covers the floor. There is the strong scent of lemon in the air, a smell as if someone has just polished the furniture. It's difficult to say if anyone else is here, a huge house, but it appears to be empty.

He leads me to the study, opens the door and we go inside. The walls of leather-bound volumes are as I remember, two stories high and looking like Dolittle's study. He closes the door behind us.

"Why don't you go ahead and take a seat over there by the desk," he says. "I'll be with you in just a moment."

The large partner's desk is still there with just enough minuscule grooves and gouges in its heavily waxed surface to certify its antiquity. I see one new item in the room, and like a discordant note on a sheet of music it is out of place. A large metal rolling box, the size of a large suitcase, with what looks like a checkered finish, either aluminum or stainless steel, is standing next to the desk. There is some kind of a design etched into the metal, perhaps the logo of the manufacturer. The case wasn't here the last time I visited Becket.

The French doors off to the left side of the desk lead out to the acres of manicured lawn and gardens behind the house.

The only thing on top of the desk is the antique brass desk lamp and the matching business cardholder from which Becket handed me one of his cards on my last visit.

When I turn to look behind me, I notice that Connor has disappeared. One of the bookshelves on the far back wall is swung open. The leather book spines are real, but they conceal a false-fronted door. I've seen these in movies. I'm tempted to go and take a closer look, to see where he went. What money can buy. It's a good thing I don't have a study like this. I'd never get anything done, playing with the toys.

I settle into one of the client chairs on this side of the desk and take out my pen when I notice a dark stain on my fingers along with a smudged dark streak on the palm of my right hand. It looks like the grime from motor oil after I've worked on my car. Whatever it is, it's penetrated deep into the skin of my hand.

When I look down I notice that I have tracked this onto the outside cover of the file folder. "Damn!" I open the folder with my left hand. There are black fingerprints on two copies of the declaration. "What the hell?" I am wondering if my pen has leaked. I examine it. It's fine.

I cast about looking for some Kleenex, anything to wipe off my hands. There is nothing. If I can get to a restroom I can at least wash my hands. I stand, turn, and look behind me. The concealed door is still ajar and there is no sign of Connor.

Where the hell did he go? "Hello!"

There is no answer.

As I turn back I end up dragging the file folder over the corner of the desk. It sweeps the brass cardholder and business cards onto the floor. The brass clatters as it hits the hard Spanish tile, business cards all over the place.

This is not my day. All I want to do is get Connor's signature and get the hell out of here, back to the office.

I bend down, grab the cardholder, and go after the cards on the slick hard tile. This is like trying to grasp a razor blade from the smooth glass surface of a mirror. My fingernails aren't sharp enough. I wrinkle a couple of the stiff cards as I grasp them, leaving a smudged black fingerprint on a third card. I start to stack them back into the holder. Not paying attention at first, finally my eyes focus on one of the cards in my hand. The name printed on it is not Rufus Becket. It's upside down. I turn it over.

As I stare at it the hairs on the back of my neck stand up as if suddenly freeze-dried. The name on the card is Joseph Ying.

What in the hell? I stand there for several seconds trying to process it. A voice behind me shatters the silence.

"I guess you're wondering what Ying's business cards are doing on Becket's desk."

I snap around to look at him. Connor is standing there ten feet away.

"What do you mean?" I shake my head as if I don't understand. I could tell him I didn't see anything, but I'm holding the evidence in my hand. My brain is racing, trying to figure some way to get out of the room, out of the house, and back to my car.

"Foolish mistake on my part," said Connor.

"I don't understand. I'm sorry. I knocked the cards onto the floor. Here, let me get them." I start to go down onto one knee.

"I wouldn't do that."

When I look up at him again he is pointing a pistol at me, something big and black, semiautomatic, with a bore the size of a railroad tunnel.

"I mean, here I go to all the trouble, dye my hair, and what do I do? I end up leaving Ying's business cards right there in plain view on the corner of the desk. I'm getting as bad as some of my help. Or maybe I'm just getting too old. That's the problem when you have too many names," he says. "It's hard to keep them straight."

"Who are you?"

"Pick a name," he says.

I could throw the brass cardholder at him and run, but he'd put a hole in me before I got three feet. So instead I stand there like a statue and ask another stupid question. "Where's Mr. Becket?"

"Who? Ah, you mean the short fat guy? The one you met the last time you were here?"

I nod.

"That was Nick, my gardener. Man's a frustrated actor. He does some summer stock at the community theater. But still, he did a pretty good job on short notice, don't you think?"

"Fooled me."

"You want to know the truth? You scared the crap out of us that day. Showing up at the door like that unannounced. You should have seen us scrambling. By the way, how do you like the hair?" he says. "Since I did it for you I'd like to know what you think." He absently runs the fingers of his left hand through the dark locks while he holds the pistol trained on me in his right.

"It's OK, except I wouldn't go swimming." I show him my dirty right palm.

He checks his left hand. There is nothing. Then he shifts the gun and checks the other one. "You're right."

From where I'm standing I can see a stain like motor oil on his fingers and the heel of his right palm as he looks at it. "You transferred it when we shook hands."

"OK, so I've made a few mistakes today. I'll have to read the directions on the bottle next time. See how long it takes to dry. I wasn't sure how detailed the description was you got from the girl. I didn't want you to turn and run the minute I opened the front door. As it turns out, I should have saved myself the trouble and dropped you out on the front stoop the second you rang the bell."

"I'm glad you didn't."

"Don't go all giddy on me," he says. "It's not gonna change the outcome. I hope you like fish, cuz you're gonna be sleeping with them tonight." He takes the horn-rimmed spectacles off as he continues to point the pistol at me. He folds them up one-handed against his chest and slips them into his pocket. "Just window-pane. I don't wear glasses. Don't need 'em."

"Bully for you," I tell him.

"Tell me, was she good?"

"Who?"

"The girl. You know. Ben? Did you get any?"

"You're sick."

"Yeah, but I can still get it up. I figure you and your Afro friend were in there for a while. You must have gotten something?"

"She was there with her boyfriend."

"I figured he probably watched."

"We were looking for information."

"Well, excuse me. What did she do, tell you to take a cold shower?"

I don't answer him.

"So you were looking for information. How much did she remember? About her meeting with me?"

"She remembered the name Becket."

"Yeah, I knew that was gonna be a problem. For a woman who was so gifted in the area of female charms, she had a quick mind to go with that great body, and educated too. All in all, a dangerous package, if you know what I mean. Here I go looking for some bubble brain in a brothel. Somebody who won't remember their own name next morning, and what do I draw? The bride of Einstein. The minute I gave her the name Becket, she says, 'Oh, that's easy to remember. Just like the Archbishop of Canterbury.' If the club hadn't been so crowded that night, I'd have shot her on the spot. I knew she'd remember it. And to make matters worse, Becket is the name on the title to the house here, so it couldn't be changed. That was my fault. But then how was I supposed to know anybody would ever find her? By the way, how did you do that?"

"Name association, a lot of shoe leather, and a tattoo."

"I suppose you could tell me all about it, if we had the time. But we don't."

"You know we gave everything to the police," I lie. "And my office knows I'm here."

"Don't screw with me," he says. "It's only gonna make it worse. No one knows where you are right now. Your partner is off somewhere up by Mission Bay. We can go watch him on television if you like. Your secretary believes you're going to be back by three, but you didn't tell her where you were going. Not according to the transcript I saw. And even if you did tell her it wouldn't matter, because you never arrived here. That's my story and I'm sticking to it."

"You bugged our office?"

"Seven ways from Sunday," he says.

"We had it swept."

"They have these little devices now with switches so you can turn 'em off when the man with the R.F.

detector comes around. Turn them back on again when he leaves. You can do it remotely. They don't find a thing. You gotta get with the times if you're going to do this shit. If I were you, I'd ask for my money back from the company that swept the place."

"Why don't I go do that?" I shift my eyes and shoot a quick glance at the door.

"I'd feel more comfortable if you sat down," he says. "Put the cardholder on the desk, along with the file folder."

I do it.

"Now you can turn that chair around to face me."

I do what he says.

"Take your coat off and drop it on the floor."

"I don't have any weapons."

"Do it!"

I take the coat off and drop it on the floor next to the chair.

Then he motions me into the chair with the muzzle of the pistol.

I sit.

"Eyes down," he says.

I look at the floor. A few seconds later I feel a hot burning sensation in the center of my chest as if a snake has sunk its fangs into me. When I look up I can trace two wires running from my upper torso to a bright

564 · STEVE MARTINI

yellow pistol-like device in his hand. Ten feet of hot conductor wire connect from the darts in my chest to the Taser gun in his hand. The darts are held in place by sharp jagged barbs.

"We're gonna be here just a few minutes while you answer some questions. How painful it gets is up to you," he says. "So why don't we just make it quick and easy?"

Fifty-Six

Three days earlier, just after five in the morning, Ana had been roused from a deep sleep by a signal from her cell phone. One of the lawyers, Hinds, was on the move. It woke her and caught her attention because it was so early.

She waited for him to break the geo fence surrounding the law office, but this didn't happen. Instead he crossed the other fence, the one surrounding Madriani's house. The two of them were meeting. They were headed somewhere.

Ana threw on her clothes and ran for the car. In less than seven minutes she was parked down the street from Madriani's house. She was just in time to watch as an official-looking dark blue sedan pulled into the lawyer's driveway.

Through the field glasses she tried to read what was printed on the driver's door. All she could read, in small white letters, was GOVERNMENT VEHICLE, OFFICIAL USE ONLY.

The two lawyers gave each other a quick hug. Madriani got in the backseat of the car and a second later it backed out of the driveway and drove in the other direction. Ana waited for Hinds to turn and walk toward the house before she pulled from the curb and followed the car.

Forty minutes later she watched as it disappeared down the same rabbit hole used by the Dumpster diver and his driver a month earlier—the guardhouse at the entrance to the Marine Corps Air Station at Miramar.

She couldn't follow him, but it set off alarm bells. The instant she got back to her hotel she set another geo fence around the Miramar Air Station. It wouldn't do any good in terms of tracking Madriani because he was in another car. But it would give her a signal if either of the lawyers went out there again in their own vehicles.

It made Ana wonder what was going on at Miramar. Maybe the lawyer was into this thing deeper than she thought. Was it possible? Could the lawyers be in collusion with the people who had the French auto-nav system? It didn't seem to make sense, since their own client was involved in the accident. But then who knows. Maybe they were on the take.

The next day and a half Ana spent scoping out the location of her new client's contracted hit, the job she had been delaying. She had been watching the place on and off over the last several days. She wanted to be able to move the instant she recovered the equipment. That is, if she could find it. She was prepared to wait two days, no more. If by then she didn't have it, she would grab one of the lawyers, probably Madriani, and subject him to enough pain that he would tell her everything he knew.

If after that she still couldn't find it, Ana would have no other choice. She would have to perform the new contract and disappear back to Europe and home.

She could pray that no one would find the navigational computer, trace it back to its French designers and from them to her. But Ana didn't like to leave such matters to fate. If they did find it and made the connection, everything in her life would unravel. Authorities would start linking passport pictures and fingerprints, aliases, and travel records to jobs she had performed on two continents over nearly a decade.

Interpol, the FBI, and every state intelligence service in the Western world would descend on the picturesque

568 • STEVE MARTINI

villa in southern France. They would find her grandmother and her aunt and destroy their refuge from the
world.

This morning she was back, tracking after the lawyers. She was getting ready to snag one of them. At
the moment it looked like it might be the older one,
Hinds.

He was driving north on I-5 when he took the
interchange at I-8. He went a few miles and got off
on Mission Bay Drive. Ana was just about to take the
off-ramp when the signal on her cell phone told her
that Madriani was now also on the move. His car had
broken the geo fence around the law office.

Ana let Hinds go. She shot past the off-ramp and
drove west toward the ocean. She turned off on Nimitz
Boulevard and pulled into a parking lot in front of a
motel to check her phone.

The tracker on the little Spark Nano under the
fender of Madriani's Jeep was set to report its location
at intervals of five minutes. It took three intervals, a full
fifteen minutes, before she could confirm that he was
headed north on I-5 and had passed the interchange at
I-8. He was driving fast, approaching the 805, running
north, out of the area.

Ana tossed her cell phone on the passenger seat,
started the engine, and took up the chase. Every few

minutes she glanced over at the phone to see if the GPS had updated his position. She was afraid he might turn off the highway at some point and she would fly past him.

When she looked over to check the phone, she realized it had timed itself out and gone dark.

"Damn." She kept her eyes on the road, reached over, and picked up the phone. It took a few seconds looking back and forth between the highway and the phone to key in the four-digit code to unlock it.

Seconds later the GPS showed Madriani moving west toward the ocean on what appeared to be a major thoroughfare off the highway. From the small map on the cell Ana couldn't identify the turnoff. She wanted to look more closely in order to study the phone, but she didn't dare. Traffic was moving too fast. If she took her eyes off the road to look at the small screen, she could end up like the charred occupants of the car at the gas station.

Ahead she saw a sign, a broad overpass with a long straight exit on her side of the divided freeway. There was a large curving cloverleaf on the other side. Whatever road it was it ran east and west, a major thoroughfare. She decided to take it.

At the top of the overpass Ana stopped at the signal and checked the phone once more. Distance was hard to calibrate on the small map.

She saw the flashing marker on the map noting Madriani's last position. He'd obviously moved on since then. She wouldn't get another GPS reading on him until the next timed interval.

She pinched the screen in an effort to zoom in, trying to read the street names on the map. Ana had no clue as to where she was or whether she and Madriani had even taken the same exit from the freeway.

If she could identify the street where the GPS marker was located she could look for signs along the way to see if they were on the same road.

The light turned green and traffic started to move. Ana laid the phone back down on the seat and took a left. She went west over the top of the freeway toward the ocean.

The road was good, two lanes in each direction and few stops. The traffic moved quickly, no congestion. She glanced down at the phone and noticed that the marker had moved.

She touched the screen quickly in order to keep it alive. Madriani was now moving on some side street off to her right, assuming he had used the same road she was on.

From the rapid glimpse she got at the small screen, the narrow thread he was traveling on looked like it snaked its way through a canyon. It was either that or the top of a ridge. She couldn't tell which. It was almost impossible to make out any details squinting at the small display from four feet away.

Ana almost reached over to touch the screen one more time and instead closed the leather cover and gave up on it. She decided she would move toward the ocean, stop, and park somewhere until she could check the map thoroughly and get her bearings.

By then Madriani would be farther along. But she could still find him, thanks to the GPS.

She passed through a residential area, large houses with late model luxury cars parked out front. There was a traffic signal ahead. It looked like a major intersection.

She touched the brake just as the GPS signal toned on her phone and began to play. Hinds was back home. He had tripped one of the geo fences, either at his apartment, Madriani's house, or the office. Ana was beginning to feel comfortable with the system. She wished she had gotten it earlier.

Before she could come to a complete stop, the light changed. She drove through the intersection, pulled to the right, and parked at the curb. She left the motor running, air conditioner humming, as she checked her phone.

Ana lifted the flip leather cover and punched in the

code. The map came up along with the circled geo fence. As Ana looked at it she realized that the signal wasn't coming from the law office, Hinds's apartment, or Madriani's house, the three areas she had fenced off. Instead the signal being emitted by the sensor on Madriani's car was coming from somewhere else.

As she looked at it she realized what it was. It was the electronic fence she had set up the day before. The one she put near the large oak tree in front of the gauche American knockoff of a French provincial estate house in the hills above Del Mar. The house was owned by the pigeon, her next victim, the new contract Ana was being paid to pluck by some high-ranking Chinese general.

Fifty-Seven

It's been said that a person who acquires the grace to die well has learned much. If that's the gold standard, I'm an idiot. If I have to die now, I am going out of this world kicking and screaming.

The man of a thousand names has me attached to two electrodes fired like bullets through the fabric of my shirt and planted into the flesh of my chest like industrial staples. I am seated facing him, my hands gripping the wooden arms of the heavy antique chair. With the massive partner's desk at my back, wired to the Taser and my assailant between me and the door, I have limited options for escape.

I could make a dash for the French doors that lead out into the garden. They are off to my right behind me, about eight feet away. I don't know if the twin doors are locked or bolted shut, or whether I could bust through them if I launched my body through the small glass panes. But tethered to the Taser I don't dare try. Any attempt to rise from the chair and he would drop me like a beached flounder and watch me flop around as he sent bolts through me like Zeus.

So far he has hit me with the Taser twice just to let me know how it works, enough voltage to send every muscle in my body into spasms. According to the cops, the official line for those who use them is that Tasers cause little or no pain. Feeling the continued burning sensation from the darts in my chest and the agony of muscle cramps caused by the little devils, I beg to differ. Catch one of the darts in the eye and you will lose your sight.

I settle into the chair and look for opportunities.

"Why don't you just tell me where he is and we can end this? Or better yet, tell me who has the information on the accounts, the bank records. You'd be saving yourself a lot of pain. If you tell me now, I'll let you go."

This is the first time he's tried that one. He must be getting desperate to think I'd believe it.

We have been over this four or five times already, the whereabouts of Betz and his cache of records. It always ends the same way, with me telling him I don't know, which in turn is met by a cascade of lethal threats followed by a Taser show as he lights me up. It's not that I don't believe him. I'm sure that given half a reason, he would disembowel me on the spot. It's just that I don't know what to tell him that will keep me alive. The instant he thinks he's gotten everything I have, he'll put a bullet in my head.

He knows that Betz is out, no longer caged at Supermax. I'm guessing he has a source inside. Probably one of the guards. Betz was wise to take out the insurance. He was not untouchable, even there.

Every so often the man of a thousand names waves the muzzle of the large pistol lazily in my direction just to remind me that he has it. When he does this the large bore down the barrel looks like the inky darkness of a deep well. It is old and vintage. It looks like a government-issue, forty-five auto. Something from a past war.

He paces back and forth, as if he were slow-mo moonwalking with the hand cannon in one hand and the Taser in the other. But he keeps a fair distance, about twelve feet between us, so that if I tried to charge him, I doubt if I would get halfway.

He's in no hurry. He's feeling safe, as if he has all the time in the world. It makes me think that he's alone in the house or whoever else is here won't be troubled if he kills me, hirelings who might well come in and help him or dispose of my body.

In the distance I can hear the sound of a gas-pow-ered garden tool of some kind. It's not a mower, either a Weedwacker or a leaf blower. A high whine. I can't tell if the sound of the motor is coming from this prop-erty or that of a neighbor.

"Why don't you tell me now? You know you will before we're done."

"Mind if I ask you a question?"

"Sure. I'll answer yours, you answer mine."

"What's your name?" I say.

"Why? You think we're gonna become friends?"

"No, it's just if somebody's gonna kill me, I'd like to know who they are."

"It's a fair question. You can call me Ishmael," he says.

"And I'm the white whale."

"You asked me. I told you. My turn."

"How did you get into this line of work?" I cut him off. His questions are beginning to bore me. They're always the same.

"You mean killing people like you? That comes easy," he says. "In fact, you keep running your mouth, it's gonna be a labor of love. And for the record, this isn't my line of work. It so happens I'm a petroleum engineer."

"You're kidding."

"Why? Don't I look smart enough?"

"Where did you go to school?"

"Why don't I just give you my Social Security card and a photograph, we can ten-print my fingers when we have coffee later. Why would you care? You're not going anywhere."

"You just said you'd let me go if I told you what you wanted to know."

"Yeah, but you haven't told me, have you?"

"I'm guessing that at some point you worked for the government. Which agency?"

"You're just burning up with questions, aren't you? Well, if you really want to know, I'll tell you. I worked for the government, sure. Long time ago. I worked for an office, I won't tell you where, but our job was to explore for oil overseas, in remote areas. This was before the age of green zealotry," he says. "You know the ones, subscribe to global warming or they'll cut your head off. That crowd.

"One day I came to work and found my desk cleaned out. The division I worked for was gone. They told us we were victims of the peace dividend. Us, along with half of the military and a fair piece of the country's intelligence apparatus.

"The leaders had all found religion. The concept of war was outdated. The green dogma that passes for

578 · STEVE MARTINI

enlightenment was sweeping the world. Guns were out and butter was in, enough to grease the welfare skids and keep the entitlement programs humming.

"The lesson I learned was that America had no leaders. What passed for leaders were herd animals. They were out front only because they wanted to be seen. They kept running into trees and off cliffs because they spent all their time looking back trying to figure out where the herd was going next so they could get back out in front."

"Take it you don't like politicians."

"I hate 'em. They come in handy from time to time, if you can pack them in your pocket. Otherwise they're worthless. They stripped the country bare. Laid waste its intelligence agencies and staked out the position that the United States was invulnerable. Anybody who attacked would have to be out of their minds.

"It took ten years before they discovered half the world was crazy and some of the people in the asylum were fashioning nuclear weapons. As for me, I didn't care. The experience had opened my eyes to opportunity. I found my niche."

"Murder Incorporated?"

"You keep running your mouth, I'm going to put a bullet in you. That's a hobby. I'm talking business.

The same people who told us we didn't need oil were the ones who'd stripped the country and told us there'd never be another war. But when winter rolled in and people started growing frost on their upper lips, they expected the bunker oilman to deliver. I had all those nice detailed maps prepared for the government. Why lock 'em away in some dusty file? So I went into business. Became an entrepreneur."

"Is that what you call it?"

"Say what you want. In the last twenty years I've made more money than God. I bought up the offshore oil resources, developed the oil, and sold it on the spot market. It ends up back here at three times the cost of the domestic supply that Washington won't let anybody drill. The politicians can claim they're protecting the environment and the taxpaying chumps pay the premium at the pump. It's a great system," he says. "Designed for the dull-witted by the corrupt. They say sheep are stupid. They've got nothing on the American voter. And they wonder where all their jobs have gone. Maybe they should take a closer look at the people they elect."

"Maybe they would if they knew you owned them."

He gives me another look at the business end of the pistol and then pushes the button on the Taser. The voltage hits me like a freight train. In an instant I am stiff as a board, every muscle in my body convulsing, along with a dry metallic taste in my mouth. I rattle around in the chair, banging up against the desk behind me. Visions of shock therapy. There is the taste of blood in my mouth. Suddenly it stops.

I slump over in the chair, breathless, as blood drips from my lip onto the front of my shirt. Somehow I bit my tongue. I think about the cops who use these things for recreation following an arrest. This gives me a whole new perspective.

"How'd that work for you? I can do it again if you'd like. What was it we were talking about? Oh yeah, politicians. I don't own all of them. There's always room for growth," he says.

I look up at him, anger fixed in my eyes. "For a man who seems so bitter, it sounds like you've done pretty well."

"I'm not bitter. I like my work."

He probably does, but he's twisted. I would say it out loud, but I don't want another taste of the Taser from Vlad the Impaler, his own form of aversion therapy. He wants me to talk, but he's conditioning me to keep my thoughts to myself.

"Of course, I'm not sitting where you are right now. Shall we start again?"

"Do we have to?"

"I'm only gonna ask you one more time. I'm wasting electricity. Guess I'm gonna have to put a bullet in you. Where is Betz, and where are the bank records?" He stands there looking at me, waiting for my answer.

When I don't say anything he moves a few steps closer. "Listen. I don't want to have to hurt you anymore." He lowers the muzzle of the gun half an inch, a measure of his sincerity. "You tell me what I want to know and I'll make certain there's no pain. You have my word. I promise."

"Tell you what. You give me the gun, I'll give you the same deal. And I won't even ask you any questions."

He cocks his head, looks at me. There is something predatory in his eyes.

The flash preceded by a nanosecond the impact of the bullet. It grazed the fabric at my knee and shattered the right front leg of the chair.

I land sprawled on the floor, my head slamming into the desk. The explosion of the round is still vibrating in my ears as the spent metal cartridge bounces and spins like a top on the tile floor ten feet away.

For a moment I'm dazed. A fine dusting of smoke, along with the sweet smell of nitrates from the gunpowder, permeates the air. I look at the shattered leg of the chair, wondering why it isn't me, if I'm just lucky or if he's that good.

Slowly I search with my hand along the inside seam of my right pant leg, hoping I won't feel the wet warmth of blood spreading through the worsted wool.

"Would you like another?" He holds both of the weapons up and says: "Pick your poison."

"You're gonna wreck your furniture," I tell him.

"No, this time I'll go for the kneecap."

"I don't know where the records are," I tell him.

"But you know where he is."

I shrug my head, a grudging concession.

"I'm done talking," he says.

"The government has him!"

"Where?"

"On a military base."

"Which one?"

"I don't know. But I can find out."

"How?"

"He checks in. He calls me three times a day, my office and my house. He leaves a coded message. If I need to talk to him I pick up, at which point we'd make arrangements to meet."

He offers a big sigh. "Now that wasn't so hard, was it?"

The fact is, I'm buying time. If I told him that Betz was at Miramar, there's a chance he'd kill me and try to figure some way to get onto the base himself. The man has connections. That's clear. This way he needs me to answer the telephone.

"One thing I do know."

"What's that?" he says.

"If you kill him, everything he has, all the information, will be released. I don't know the details. But it's set up for the broadest possible dissemination. He told me that much. If anything happens to him, the world is gonna know names, dates, deposits, amounts on hand, everything."

"You're sure he didn't tell you where it was?"

"No. He knows if he gives it up, if he loses that, he's dead."

I assume the Impaler already knew this, but it sets him to thinking. "Do you know what kind of arrangements they have for security? The military base. How many guards?"

"US Marshals. I don't know how many. And probably a regiment of military police."

"What time does Betz call?"

"Ten in the morning and three in the afternoon at the office. Eight o'clock at night at my house."

"Get up. Get on your feet," he says. He waves the gun at me, checks his watch. "There's too many people at your office. Anybody at the house?"

I shake my head.

"Then it looks like you're going home. We'll be going as soon as I can get some backup."

My head is spinning, as I am still on the floor. It takes a second before I process his words. He wants backup. Does that mean he is alone in the house? I can't be sure. If he is, he won't be for long. Once he has help, I am dead.

Fifty-Eight

S he had cased the house and its surroundings for the better part of two days, so that by the time Ana arrived at the mansion and saw Madriani's Jeep parked across the street, she already knew the layout.

She was also familiar with the household schedule. During the period that she had watched the place only three people came and went, a housekeeper who doubled as a cook, a groundskeeper, and the man himself. She recognized him from the picture sent to her by the Asian agents who hired her.

His name was Ying. Though he didn't look Asian, the contacts told her not to be confused. He was the one.

The housekeeper, a woman who appeared to be in her sixties, lived in. She had a room at the back of the house off the laundry. She went shopping each morning about eleven for food—probably perishables, fresh fruit, and vegetables. The one item Ana could confirm was the fresh baguette of French bread sticking out of the top of the bag each day. She never returned before one. She drove her own car that she parked at the side of the house. This afternoon the car was already gone. There was only the owner's Bentley parked in the circular drive.

The groundskeeper she could hear, well off in the distance. He was over the rise in the deepest part of the yard. From where she sat in the car he was at least a hundred and fifty meters away. He did not live in the house. He came each morning about seven and left around five.

As she peered from inside the car Ana could make out the man's head and part of his shoulders through the field glasses every so often when he straightened up. He was wearing a face mesh shield and hearing protectors as he whacked weeds with a gas-powered cutter.

Ana stepped out of the car and moved quickly to the trunk. She popped the lid with the car key and grabbed her bag. It was a fair-sized black tactical duffel with a strong wide strap made of webbing. Inside was the compound bow already strung and five laser-tipped broad-head arrows. She slung the strap over her shoulder, closed the car's trunk, and checked her watch. The hands were just touching noon.

She stopped for a moment, thought about what she was doing, and then headed across the street, under the massive oak tree. She kept her ear tuned for any change in noise coming from the Weedwacker. When she reached the edge of the circular drive where it curved toward the front door, she stepped up over the curb and onto the grass.

From here Ana moved quickly just outside the edge of a flowerbed that flanked the side of the house. She was careful to keep her feet out of the soft planting soil. Instead she stayed on the tough Bermuda grass where she knew she would leave no shoe prints.

When she reached the back of the house she checked one more time, glancing in the direction of the noise, which was now much louder. The groundskeeper was perhaps fifty meters away.

She had seen him through the glasses when staking out the house. He looked to be about fifty, short and squat; he didn't appear to represent dangerous brawn. Of course, if he was armed, that would be a different matter.

She laid the duffel on the ground, zipped it open, and uncased the bow with its mounted quiver of five arrows. She was going to hate to lose this equipment. But she would replace it when she got home. The fact that she was going to use the bow and arrows on one more job in the same area dictated that she dispose of it all where no one would find it before she headed for the airport and home. She would not take the chance that a medical examiner might connect the two cases and start looking for records of anyone traveling with such equipment. It was how you stayed alive in her line of work.

She donned the shooting gloves that covered the tips of her fingers. Then she unclipped one of the arrows and carefully laid the shaft on the bow's arrow rest while fitting the taut bowstring into the grooved nock of the fletched end of the arrow.

Ana was not surprised that for a large, expensive residence, there appeared to be no surveillance cameras or other security detection devices. She had seen this before on regular occasion, usually when the targets were underworld figures, drug dealers, and worse. They wanted no record of their own movements or activities on a memory bank somewhere. Especially if this was being piped to some outside security company. If you weren't careful you could end up exhibit number one on your own incriminating video.

She grabbed the duffel and slung it over her back. With the arrow threaded on the bow, she moved quickly along the back of the house. She passed under the kitchen windows and carefully skirted the covered patio with its hooded fire pit and chimney.

Here the lawn ended and changed to a concrete walkway. She stayed close to the house to avoid being seen from the second-story windows above. Other than the fact that they were inside Ana couldn't be sure where the lawyer and the man named Ying were situated.

The midday sun bore down. She could feel it on the back of her neck. Her dark clothing absorbed the heat and made her sweat as her mind chewed on all the various possibilities. What troubled her was how everything had suddenly converged. How did they know each other? What did the California lawyer have to do with the man a Chinese general wanted dead? She would be sure to ask him the instant she had him cornered under the point of an arrow.

Ana walked quickly, in a combat crouch, one hand on the bow, the other fingering the fletch end of the arrow. She was poised to pull and release on reflex, if she had to. She glanced down and saw her moving shadow etched by the noonday sun on the cement beneath her feet. This was a novelty she didn't like. With dark clothes you could disappear into the inky blackness of the night. But not here.

Ahead she could see a high-latticed fence harboring an esplanade of interwoven flowering vines. It separated the garden from the large oval swimming pool on the other side.

Five feet from the fence a sudden loud report froze Ana's feet to the concrete. It might have been a bowling ball dropped from a great height onto hardwood, except there was no bounce. She knew what it was. It came from somewhere inside the house, muffled by the interior walls. She had been around enough pistol ranges to recognize the stifled, flat report of indoor gunfire.

She turned and looked in the direction of the noisy Weedwacker. She couldn't see him, but she could hear the continuing ragged whine of his machine. Between the noise of the gas engine and the earmuffs, the gardener hadn't heard the shot.

Ana turned back to the mansion. The sound of the shot was close and directly in front of her. Her gaze settled on the area just beyond the latticed fence, a shaded alcove at the side of the house and a set of French doors just beyond.

For a moment she thought about retreating, going back to the car, leaving and returning later when it was dark. That was her plan. The matchup between Madriani and Ying had changed it. Now she wondered if one of them was dead. The possibility, however remote, that it might be Ying forced her to find out.

She had already lost one contract. She couldn't afford to lose another.

She steeled herself and moved forward, but the sound of the shot set her on edge. The bow was no match for a handgun. If she somehow lost the element of surprise, Ana would suddenly find herself on a suicide mission.

The instant she approached the arbor opening in the fence she knew she had a problem. The bright sunlight overhead and the shaded interior of the house made it impossible for Ana to see anything through the glass doors. Until she reached the shade of the alcove all she'd see was her own reflection in the glass. By then anyone inside with a gun could empty a clip into her head.

She looked to the exterior wall of the house and noticed that the lattice fence was freestanding. There was a narrow gap between the post at the end of the fence and the side of the house. She moved quickly.

The gap was narrow, little more than a foot. But Ana was slight. She passed the bow through the opening, then the bag. She squeezed through, reassembled everything on the other side and moved toward the alcove. She clung to the outer edge of the house for cover.

When she reached the corner of the alcove she peeked around into the shade. Over the distant whine of the Weedwacker she could hear voices inside. There was a wall of books, shelves, an empty chair behind a desk, and something else that caught her eye. She pulled back around the corner, laid the empty bag on the ground, and took a deep breath. Then she slipped around the corner into the shade of the alcove, the bow gripped in her hand, the nock on the end of the arrow held snug against the string.

She hugged the inside wall of the recessed area until she reached the corner, the edge of the glass, where the frame of the door and about six inches of wall gave her some cover. Now she could hear louder voices. They were talking. One of them was threatening the other.

Ana eased one eye over the edge of the wood to the glass pane. Madriani was on the floor in front of the desk. She could see his lower body. She couldn't tell if he was wounded. But he was moving. She could see his legs. The other man was Ying. She recognized him from the digital photographs sent to her by the Chinese agents. She had seen him through the field glasses while scouting the house. He had the gun, a semiautomatic pistol. She couldn't tell the caliber, but whatever it was, in terms of lethality, it outclassed the bow.

She pulled her head back. Ana knew she would get only one shot. She glanced at the handle of the door. It was probably locked, and even if it wasn't, the second she touched it he would hear her.

The problem was the glass. An arrow requires distance to build momentum. She would need at least a few feet to stretch out the bow and give the arrow some flight before the tip hit the smooth hard surface. Even then, it was a risk. If the arrow tip skidded before it punched through the glass it would deflect the flight of the arrow.

Fifty-Nine

"Sit in the other chair," he says. He points at it lazily with the pistol as if he might shoot this one next.

I roll to my side and struggle to get up on one knee. He has half an eye on me. Time is running out.

He transfers the pistol to his left hand while he works the cell phone with his right. He's laid the Taser on a small table near the spiral staircase a few feet away. Struggling with his thumb to punch numbers on the phone, calling somewhere for backup.

He is distracted. I shield what I am about to do with my body, my back to him as I struggle to my feet. It's now or never. In the time that he looks away, I reach out and grab the solid piece of oak, the hunk of wood with its shattered end that had been the leg of the chair.

It's about eight inches long and heavy. If I could close the distance on him I might have a chance.

With my other hand I grab the two wires and yank. The pain is excruciating, but the darts come loose. I leave the Taser wires and the two darts on the floor near the broken chair hoping he won't notice that I'm no longer wired at least long enough for me to make a move. His attention at the moment is directed at the phone.

He is talking on the phone when something dances off the edge of the desk over the back of my hand and across the floor. Like a fast red moth it covers the distance between us and climbs his leg in less than a second.

He sees it the same time I do, his back half turned, out of the corner of his eye. He stands. I am on one knee still getting up. We see the same thing, the solid red beam of light streaming across the room. Suddenly his eyes open wide. He spins around looking at the glass doors, the garden outside.

I turn my head to look. The blinding beam of red light refracted in the glass of the door scatters and then comes back together. A woman, thin as a wisp, outside, Diana the archer.

I turn back to look at him just as he aligns the pistol left-handed, getting a bead on her. I raise myself up and throw the heavy piece of oak with everything I've got. It misses the gun, grazes his hand, and hits him in the head just as he squeezes off the round.

The sound of the shot shatters the silence. I hear the tinkle of broken glass as it hits the tile behind me, but I don't turn to look. Instead I launch myself from one knee to my feet and charge him.

He sees me, drops the phone, and transfers the pistol to his right hand as he moves the muzzle down on me.

I'm looking up, staring straight down the barrel wondering if he's true to his word, whether I'll feel pain as the copper-coated lead enters my brain.

The bullet went wide. It shattered the glass and snapped past her ear. The vacant pane opened the avenue of flight as Ana pointed the laser at his chest and let the arrow fly. Just as she did, she saw the back of the lawyer rising up. There was nothing she could do but watch the red flare of the arrow.

Lunging forward, waiting for death, I feel something slice my ear as the red light tracking something yellow lodged itself in the center of his chest. He jerks as he pulls the trigger.

I hear the bullet slam into something behind me. The fleeting look on his face, something quizzical.

THE ENEMY INSIDE · 597

His knees buckle before I can reach him. He dissolves to the floor as I sail over the top and land on the tiles behind him. When I roll and look, I see his hand with the pistol still twitching.

Before I can get to my feet I hear another pane of glass being broken in the door. As I stand up I see the mystery lady drop a rock onto the cement outside. She slips her hand through the open pane and unlocks the door.

When I look down his hand is still moving. I step over him to try and pry the gun from his hand.

"Leave it!"

When I look up she has another arrow in the bow. This one is pointed at me. There's a large black duffel bag at her feet.

"I don't know who you are," I say. "I don't particularly care. But you saved my life. And I thank you." But I don't pick up the gun.

"I could say the same of you," she says. "What was it you threw at him?"

"A broken leg from the chair."

"Under the circumstances I really don't want to have to do this. But you saw me kill him. You're a witness. That is something I cannot afford to leave behind. I'm sorry," and she starts to flex the bow.

This is my first hint that she is not some Good Samaritan who simply happened by. "Hold on!"

But she doesn't. She has the bow fully extended, bringing it down on me. "Before I do, I need to know what your connection is. How do you know this man?"

"I don't. Give me a minute and I'll tell you what I know." My mind is racing, my heart pounding. I am exhausted, the adrenaline drained from my body. If I'm going to survive the next two minutes I am going to have to give her some reason.

She looks down at the dying form on the floor. His hand has stopped moving, but it's still holding the pistol, now in a death grip.

"First of all, you didn't commit a crime," I tell her. Thinking like a lawyer. I do what comes naturally, appeal to reason. Something in her demeanor tells me she is not going to be susceptible to emotion. Otherwise I'd be crying.

"In this state, defense of other, like self-defense, absolves all criminal intent in a homicide. So there's no need to worry about what I saw. You have an absolute defense. He was going to kill me and you prevented it. I will testify to that in any court."

She backs off a few steps as she relaxes the tension on the bow. Still, she doesn't seem convinced.

I take a deep breath, though the arrow is still pointed at me.

She's smiling.

"What's so funny?"

"The irony of it. The concept of legal absolution and getting paid for the deed at the same time."

"I didn't need to hear that. I'm not sure I did. And if I did, I already forgot it. If anyone ever needed killing, you're looking at him right there. If it were up to me I'd give you a medal."

I spend the next several minutes bringing her current on how I got involved, along with an abbreviated version of the events of the last two months. I skirt the edges on some of the facts, the details concerning Betz and some of the names of the people involved.

By the time I'm done, the arrow is at least pointed down, somewhere near my knees. I take this as a sign that maybe I'll live. But I'm still not sure.

"That's all fine," she says. "But if you're still around, what are you going to tell the authorities?"

Lady of few words, she arrives at the pivotal question. It is upon this that I will live or die. "Leave that to me. I'm not going to tell them about you."

"Then who killed him?"

"Who knows? He was a bad man. I'm sure he had his share of enemies."

"He had at least one that I know of."

"All I know is, I came out to get a signature on a document from someone who wasn't here, found the door open and a dead body inside. I don't even know who he is. Never saw the man before. And that's the truth. The man I met the last time I was here, the one who said he was Mr. Becket, was someone else. Seems you can't trust anybody anymore.

"The white lies I am prepared to tell the cops really don't matter, at least they don't to me, not under these circumstances. You may have been hired to come here to commit a criminal homicide, but that's not what you did. There was an intervening force, his attempt on my life. That absolves you of the act. If you hadn't shown up at the door I would be dead. We have a bond on this."

I suspect that some wily prosecutor probably could work up a case against her of conspiracy to commit, but I really don't care. And I keep the thought to myself. No sense giving her something to worry about.

She considers it for a few moments. "How do I know I can trust you?"

"What would I have to gain by telling the cops?"

"I don't know. You tell me."

"Nothing. I don't even know your name. I don't want to know."

Slowly she lowers the bow, unstrings the arrow with my name on it, and drops them both into the bag at her feet. She leans over the body and starts to unscrew the tip of the arrow that is protruding from his back.

"What are you doing?"

"I never leave anything behind."

"Forget I asked."

She kicks the body over and from the front she pulls the arrow out. She snaps the shaft in half and drops all of the parts, including the tip, in a plastic bag, then deposits this in the duffel as well. "Do you want me to take the gun from his hand?" she says.

"Leave it. It might be better that way. Someone killed him, but at least he put up a fight."

She picks up her bag and turns to go out the way she came.

"Why don't we use the front door," I tell her.

"I have to get my stuff," she says. She walks around the broken chair to the side of the partner's desk and grabs the handle on the large metal rolling case, the one I noticed when I first came in.

"That belongs to you?"

"Yeah, it's mine. He stole it from me and used it twice." She starts to roll it away when something catches her eye. She stops, looks down, and runs her finger along the side of the case. "Damn it!" she says.

"What's wrong?" My heart skips a beat.

"He put a hole in it. A small fortune in cutting-edge auto-electronics, and that ungodly sack of shit goes and shoots it!" She starts cursing in some language I don't understand, hands in the air, stamping her feet.

I don't know where she's from. I don't want to know. But if pressed to the wall, I'd have to say she has a Latin temper.

"After all of this." She leans over and examines the bullet hole. It is dead center in the middle of the box. "And he turns it into junk."

"What's in the box?"

"Trust me, you don't want to know." She gives me a look to kill.

"Let's pretend I never asked."

As we head for the front door I have visions of *Casablanca*, Bogart and Rains on a fog-shrouded runway. "Round up the usual suspects, Louis, I think this is the beginning of a beautiful friendship."

Epilogue

If I had to guess, I would say that whatever was in the large metal box that the lady archer rolled out of Becket's office that afternoon had something to do with the two fatal auto accidents. It was her use of the words "auto-electronics" to describe what was inside, and the fact that she said he had stolen it and used it twice. This and the research I had done leads me to conclude that whatever was in that box, it was used to kill Serna, Ben, and her boyfriend.

The panicked expression on the girl's face, the woman I knew as Ben, and the frantic and futile efforts of her boyfriend to control their car on its way to a fiery hell are engraved in my mind.

The woman with the arrows disappeared like a wisp in the wind two minutes after we left the house.

I waited a respectful period for her to get out of the area. This gave me time to clean up before I called the cops. In the bathroom I washed my face and got rid of the blood. I didn't use any towels. I used toilet tissues and flushed so there would be no trace of blood in the drain.

I grabbed my suit coat from the floor in the study to cover my soiled shirt, buttoned it up, straightened my tie, ran a comb through my hair, and called the cops. I told them the same story I'd given to her. The one where I came to the house with documents to be signed and found the dead body.

The Eagle is dead, but so is Rubin Betz. Fifty-seven days after I walked out of the house in Del Mar, the one I thought was owned by a man named Rufus Becket, who appears not to have existed, Betz finally lost his battle with pancreatic cancer. When he died, I felt as if I had lost a friend. For all of the mystery surrounding the whistleblower in the end, his motives for much of what he had done were simple and to the point. He was protecting his daughter, and to this I can relate. Call it the fraternity of fatherhood.

In the meantime the world has exploded. Whoever had the documents, wherever they were, they began to surface after Betz died, just as he said they would. Within little more than a week the details of political corruption saturated the media of the world. Heads began to roll.

In less than forty-five days, indictments were announced. Maya Grimes was charged, along with eight other members of Congress. And these were just the openers. Other names began to surface. It is likely that indictments will continue for at least another year, perhaps longer.

Many have proclaimed their innocence and vowed to fight, insisting that in the end they will be vindicated. Much of this is disintegrating under their feet even as they and their lawyers dodge the microphones and cameras. New details of foreign money and what it bought seem to surface each day. For some of them, the drip of information is becoming death by a thousand cuts.

As for Grimes, she and her attorneys are already huddled with federal prosecutors hunting for a deal. Rumor is she has offered to pay more than a billion dollars in fines on her offshore holdings, along with a promise to resign from the Senate. This for some short-term sentence, a rap on the knuckles.

She would be wise to move quickly before the Senate Ethics Committee and the entire chamber expel her. The rats are not only leaving the ship but are eating their own on the way. The media is asking serious questions as to the source of some of the money and what was sold, talk of possible capital punishment for acts of treason in which lives may have been lost.

It seems that perhaps what was once called the press, a fourth estate of dogged pursuers, is not in fact dead. It was merely paralyzed by partisan fervor. The news outlets finally found their bearings, remembered first principles, and followed the money. Maybe there is hope after all.

As for Betz and his estate, there was never any question that the government owed him the money, the massive whistleblower award. That they ever tried to link it to his continued silence is now being denied at the highest levels within the Justice Department. It wouldn't have mattered, for in the end they were forced to swallow a survivor's clause that I slipped into the settlement agreement that freed Betz. Under no circumstances may the government reclaim the money that has now flowed to his daughter within terms of the agreement.

We had one final conversation just before he died. Rubin realized the only way any of us would have peace was to allow the information to go public. Once all the tainted members were exposed and whoever owned them was out of business, the danger would evaporate.

What they say about sunlight is true. It is often the best disinfectant.

As for the gardener, the man I first thought was Rufus Becket, it turned out that he became my lodestone. Police detained him at the house and questioned him. With his employer dead on the floor, the gardener led them to a storehouse of documents, including transcripts of telephone conversations. Several of these documents established beyond any question why Olinda Serna was murdered and who did it. Alex Ives is free. The duce, an ancient term of California legal art dating from the time that drunk driving was charged under Vehicle Code Section 502, the case that Harry and I inherited as a favor to my daughter, Sarah, is over. But its legacy lives on.

Harry and I have disclaimed any of the mounting and additional fees now being netted from the politicians who have been caught, and who are now showering the Treasury with cash in bids to stay free. For us, this latter money is tainted. The fact that we counseled Betz in his ultimate decision to allow his hidden bank documents to be exposed, the act that caused the money to pile up, meant that we had a conflict. To take the additional funds would have lined our own pockets and might have muddied the water regarding his daughter's ability to receive her share of the added portion. A guardian has been appointed and other lawyers are now on the scene to assure that this happens.

Harry and I face an uncertain future. The thirty-five million dollars, the original fees awarded us by Betz for my work at Supermax, is now in process of being paid. This is like the serendipity of winning a lottery. The fact that it flowed from a dog of a case that neither of us wanted to take speaks to the mystery and caprice of wealth—the imponderable puzzle of who gets it and why.

How this will affect our lives in the future is anyone's guess.

Acknowledgments

Many people provided encouragement and support in the writing of this book, including family and friends.

Most of all, I wish to thank my assistant, Marianne Dargitz, who, for more than two decades, has provided not only her energy and unflagging support but also encouragement, which has guided me through difficult periods. Without her constant efforts and attention to detail, none of this would have been possible.

Among others, I wish to thank my publisher, William Morrow, and all the people at HarperCollins without whose unstinting care and love of the written word and book publishing as we know it, none of this would have happened. Most of all, I thank my editor, David Highfill, whose friendship over many years has been a constant source of encouragement and pleasure. I thank his editorial assistant, Chloe Moffett, and associate editor, Jessica Williams, who over the course of this work fielded my phone calls and handled many technical aspects during the transition from paper to digital editing.

I thank my agent, Esther Newberg of International Creative Management, and my New York lawyers, Mike Rudell and Eric Brown of Franklin, Weinrib, Rudell & Vassallo, for their constant attention and guidance to the business aspects of my publishing career.

For their caring interest, love, and constant encouragement I thank Al and Laura Parmisano, who have always been there for me during good times and bad. Last but not least, for her constant and unconditional love, I thank my daughter, Megan Martini, who makes all things possible for me.

HARPER LUXE

THE NEW LUXURY IN READING

We hope you enjoyed reading
our new, comfortable print size and found it
an experience you would like to repeat.

Well – you're in luck!

HarperLuxe offers the finest in fiction and
nonfiction books in this same larger print size and
paperback format. Light and easy to read, HarperLuxe
paperbacks are for book lovers who want to see
what they are reading without the strain.

For a full listing of titles and
new releases to come, please visit our website:

www.HarperLuxe.com

SEEING IS BELIEVING!

1272

F
MAR

Martini, Steve.

The enemy inside